ARTHUR A. LEVINE BOOKS | An Imprint of Scholastic Inc.

THE SUMMER PRINCE

ALAYA DAWN JOHNSON

Library of Congress Cataloging-in-Publication Data

Johnson, Alaya Dawn, 1982–
    The summer prince / Alaya Dawn Johnson. — 1st ed.
      p. cm.
    Summary: In a Brazil of the distant future, June Costa falls in love with Enki, a fellow artist and rebel against the strict limits of the legendary pyramid city of Palmares Três' matriarchal government, knowing that, like all Summer Kings before him, Enki is destined to die.
    ISBN 978-0-545-41779-2 (jacketed hardcover : alk. paper) [1. Kings, queens, rulers, etc. — Fiction. 2. Artists — Fiction. 3. Government, Resistance to — Fiction. 4. Love — Fiction. 5. Brazil — Fiction.] I. Title.
    PZ7.J6267Sum 2013
    [Fic] — dc23

                                                                                                  2012022236

10 9 8 7 6 5 4 3 2 1   13 14 15 16 17

First edition, March 2013

Printed in the U.S.A.   23

Book design by Phil Falco

For Lauren and Alexis, my Johnson sisters
and ultimate travel partners. Let's discover the
world together, balneários and all.

The lights are out in Palmares Três.
Why did they go out?
Because I told them to.

The lights are out in Palmares Três.
Why are you alone?
Because I left you.

The lights are out in Palmares Três.
How do I know?
Because I am dead.

SPRING

W hen I was eight, my papai took me to the park to watch a king die.

At first, all I saw were adults clad in bright blues and greens and reds, in feathers and sequins, in cloth glittering with gold and jewels. Carnival clothes for carnival day, but covered in the early-morning chill with darker coats and shawls. I looked up at this mass of grandes like I had stumbled into a gathering of orixás. I couldn't see their faces, but I could see their hands, the way they twisted them around each other, or clicked through a string of rosary beads. Some held candles, some held flowers. They were dressed for carnival, but they were quieter than I remembered from other years. The legs and torsos swayed and jostled, but no one danced. A few of the men cried. For the first time in my life, I knew a carnival without music.

I held my papai's hand. He did not look at me. A strange sigh swept over the crowd, like the wind howling past the cliffside during a winter storm. A woman's voice boomed through the park, but I was too young, too close to the ground to understand.

"I can't see," I said, tugging at my papai's hand.

With some difficulty — our neighbors had pressed forward, packing around us so tightly he hardly had room to turn around — he knelt.

"This is how the world works, June," he said to me. "Are you sure?"

I didn't understand his downcast mouth, the crying from the crowd, the austere finality of the woman's voice on our city's speakers. Carnival was supposed to be fun and beautiful. But I knew, because my papai never asked me idle questions, that I was to consider my answer. That if I said no, he would leave me on the ground where I could see nothing I didn't understand, and understand nothing of what I heard. And if I said yes, the answer would change my life.

I nodded. He lifted me, though I was heavy for my age, and perched me on his shoulders. If I blocked anyone's view, no one complained.

There was a holo in the sky. It projected a few meters above the heads of the people in the park, near the falls where I would play with Mamãe in the summer. Queen Serafina stood in a stark room of wood and stone — the high shrine. I liked her because her skin was dark and glossy and her hair silk-smooth. I had even gotten a Queen Serafina doll for my birthday last June. But today her face was fierce and still; today she held a blade in her hand.

Beside me, a man shook his head and murmured a prayer. I thought it sounded nice and wished I could join him. Mamãe didn't like the city shrines, so I'd never learned any prayers.

The holo angle widened, showing an altar with a miniature projection of our city glowing at the far end. A man had been bound with ropes beneath it, so the great hollow pyramid of Palmares Três looked like a crown. An appropriate symbol for our latest king, elected exactly one year ago.

"Why is Summer King Fidel tied down?" I asked Papai.

He squeezed my hand and shushed me gently. "Watch, June," he said.

"I honor our ancestors who were slaves, and their legacy for which we have named our city," Serafina said, icy and calm in her white ceremonial turban and white shift.

From the altar, Fidel responded in a steady voice, but his shoulders trembled and his eyes had dilated a permanent, unnatural black. "I honor the dead who have fallen like sugarcane before a scythe. I honor the men who lie beneath us and the women whose strength and wisdom have saved us."

"Heir of Zumbi, great king, you are infected," the Queen said, words almost familiar and ultimately incomprehensible. "Will you give this great city the gift of your sacrifice? In the name of Yemanjá, in the name of Oxalá, also called Christ, will you offer your soul to the orixás, and your choice to Palmares Três?"

Fidel nodded slowly, as though he was already swimming in Yemanjá's ocean. His too-black eyes stared wide, and I shivered. We were safe in the park on Tier Eight, while he was tied to the altar on Tier Ten, but still I felt as though he watched me. "I will," he said, and fell back, prone on the stone altar.

Now the man beside me wept openly, and even Papai wiped his eyes.

I was eight, and no one had told me what happened to the kings at the end of winter. In the end, no one needed to.

Serafina mounted the stairs to the altar. She touched Fidel's shoulder with her left hand; her right fingers tightened around the blade.

"You will mark your choice of the woman to be Queen," Serafina said. "In gesture or blood."

He nodded. A few seconds passed. She swept the knife across his throat, clean and irrevocable and deep. His mouth opened and closed like a fish in fresh air. His blood pulsed in spurts over her hands and dress and altar.

I cried, but I didn't want to stop seeing. "He must point!" I said, my stomach so tight I thought I might vomit.

The crying man beside me nodded. "It will be okay if he doesn't, filha," he said. "It's a moon year. Serafina is the only one in the room for him to pick."

I don't know that I understood him then. The five-year cycle, the elections, the Queens and their kings, the moon years and sun years — they govern our lives, but are not easily parsed. Especially not by an eight-year-old, shocked to tears by the sight of a young king killed by a beloved Queen.

And then Fidel managed. A bloody hand raised, trembling and final. He smacked it on Serafina's belly with enough force that its wet impact echoed over the tinkling of the falls. A bloody handprint marked her stomach, final and sure.

The holo focused on Fidel's body. In death, his eyes stayed wide open and impossibly black.

Papai took me home. Mamãe was in one of her rages, berating him for letting such a violent ceremony mar my carnival day.

"You'll let her have the celebration without showing her why?" he said.

"She's too young," said Mamãe.

I took a deep breath. "Did he want to die?" I asked Papai.

He regarded me very seriously. "I believe so, June. His sacrifice helps our city."

"Then it's okay," I said. "I'm old enough."

We call him the summer king, even though we choose him in the spring.

It is early September. Gil and I dance through a screaming throng of wakas, hoping to trick our way into the roped-off section in the front of the stadium. In a few minutes, all three young finalists for this year's summer king election will appear onstage, and we need to be as near to them as possible. I've never seen Enki up close before — holos don't count — and my excitement makes me feel like I'm vibrating. Gil turns, sees my eyes scanning the stage for any sign of them, and laughs.

"We have at least five minutes, June," he says, taking my hand to pull me forward.

"What if we miss him? What if the cameras don't see us?"

Gil shrugs; he respects my craving for fame and recognition, but he doesn't share it. One of the hundred things I love about him.

"It doesn't matter if they see," he says, pointing to the cloud of thumb-sized camera bots buzzing on and around the stage. "It matters if *he* does."

He. Enki. I take a deep breath and feel my pocket again for the reassuring weight of the portable holo we've smuggled inside. Just a week ago, Gil and I got around security bots in Gria Plaza to paint graffiti stencils on the side of an office building, but we've never attempted anything as daring as this. I've never invited exposure before. Oh, there was always a *chance* that some security bot would dart me and I'd wake up unmasked in a holding cell on Tier Two, but I'm not stupid. I may not be quite as good at running around the city as a grafiteiro from the verde, but I'm tiers above the other wakas in my school.

But today I'm dressed as myself, with a ticket bought in my own name, with my own money. Today we're planning to get caught. Mother and Auntie Yaha won't be pleased, but they never are. I think of it as a coming-out party — if this works, the whole city will see my art for the first time.

The stadium is the pride of the bottom tiers — built inside one of the dozens of spherical nodes that help give our hollow pyramid city its internal structure. The clear dome soars above us, high enough that on some days wispy clouds can form, obscuring from sight the pulsing, glowing city rising into the distance above. From this angle, transport pods shuttle through a glittering lattice of tubes like silver blood through luminous triangular arteries. Megatrusses lined with gardens and shops and houses stretch to our left and right. I'm caught off guard by the spectacle, one somehow more familiar to me from dramas than personal experience. Even though I've lived here all my life, I don't spend much time on the lower tiers during the day. Growing up on Tier Eight, I'm used to seeing the glowing pyramid lattice of Palmares Três from a loftier position.

Two guards stand in front of the velvet curtain separating the special seats from the general rabble. My stepmother is an Auntie, a rising star in our government. I could have asked her for help getting in here, but then she would have known that Gil and I were skipping

school to see the show. I couldn't bear the thought of another intermi-
nable argument with Mother, Auntie Yaha acting as frustrated
peacekeeper. I can't bear very much about either of them.

So Gil and I will have to improvise. I grin and my worries flow out
of me in the tense, gritty joy of danger and release. The guards check
tickets with a bulky security fono. Only wakas are allowed in this special section, since we're the ones the Aunties want to show asking
questions in a moon year election. Some grandes fill the stadium seats,
but most of this crowd is under thirty and respected for it — a rarity in
a city run mostly by women past their first century.

Gil squeezes my hand and approaches one of the guards. He casually hands over his flash — an identity chip embedded in the same
worn pyramid charm he's used since I've known him. The guard
swipes it over her fono, then frowns.

"You don't have a pass," she says.

Gil's bottom lip trembles and his eyes widen. "But I won the essay
contest for my school! My teacher told me everything was settled."

The woman sighs. The other guard, accepting latecomer flashes a
few meters away, raises her eyebrows in inquiry.

"Everything okay there?" she asks.

"He says he won a contest."

The second guard looks nervously back at the stage, then walks
over. "What's this about . . ." she says, but I don't have time to hear the
rest. In full sight of the five wakas still waiting to get in, I dash past
the guards distracted by Gil's beautiful pouting face and hurry for two
empty seats on the opposite side of the enclosure. I sit like I'm supposed to be there, and no one pays me much attention. Everyone stares
at the stage. I hope most of them support Enki. He's the surprise
favorite this election, the beautiful boy from the verde no one expected
to make it to the finals. He will win — he has to — but just to make
sure, I convinced Gil to help me with an art project.

A very public art project.

The glass dome turns smoky gray, gradually darkening the stadium until I can only see the lights on the stage and the smaller lights on the floor, leading to the exits. A moment later, Gil slips into the seat beside me. He bites his lip and squeezes my knee.

"I can't believe they let you in!" I whisper.

He rests his head against mine and breathes deep. "You know me, menina," he says. "All I ever have to do is smile."

I jab him with my elbow. My best friend in the whole world is vain as a peacock, but that's all right. He's pretty enough to justify it.

Auntie Isa, the highest-ranking member of the government aside from Queen Oreste, walks onstage in a careful spotlight. Cheers and chants sweep over the stadium audience until my ears ring with the combined jubilation of ten thousand people. Gil yells Enki's name in unison with a hundred or so others nearby, while different factions for Pasqual and Octavio chant their support. I would join Gil, but I can hardly breathe. I've been planning this for weeks, ever since I first saw Enki at the start of the contests.

Auntie Isa has round cheeks and full lips, skin about as light as mine and smooth, thin eyebrows that seem faded somehow — the only part of her that looks old. Beneath her iconic red turban, her face is ageless and familiar. She's been sub-queen for more than fifty years — five Queens have reigned with her by their side, but she's never put herself forward for the royal position.

"My children," she says once the noise has quieted. "I welcome you to King Alonso Stadium. In a week, the whole city will once again vote for our next king. I have gathered the finalists here this afternoon so that you might ask questions of these fine young men who have put themselves forward this moon year."

Our cacophonous cheers might be deafening to some grande, but I don't notice. I've found my voice, and I'm screaming with the rest. Even if something goes wrong with my small project, it won't matter. I'm overwhelmed with the sense of being part of history.

*   *   *

The first thing you should know about Enki is that he's dark. Darker than the coffee my mother and Auntie Yaha drink every morning, darker than the sky on a moonless night, not so dark as my pupils gone wide with pleasure, not so dark as ink. I have never seen anyone half so dark as him, though Auntie Yaha says she has. She travels to the flat cities sometimes, since she's an ambassador of Palmares Três. She's even been to Salvador — what's left of it. Most people don't have the tech to maintain appearance standards, she says.

"Though they wouldn't, even if they could," she always says, and flicks her wrist in her way that always means contemptuous dismissal. "We don't wallow in our differences the way flatlanders do."

I never understood what that meant until Enki. His mother lived in Salvador, they say, though I can't believe it, because I've seen the pictures and I don't understand how *anyone* could live there. She was six months pregnant with him when the Aunties granted her a rare amnesty pass. She was too late for all but the most basic gene mods. There was no time to conform to our appearance regulations, and all the better for him. Enki was born dark as molasses, not so dark as tar. Enki was born beautiful, and when he smiles, you can see he knows it. Perhaps he isn't so sure of its importance, but how he delights in our admiration.

The second thing you should know about Enki is that he grew up in the verde. At the top of our pyramid a great white light shines above the bay. The Queen lives there, way up on the hallowed Tier Ten, with a few of the highest-ranking Aunties. Tiers Eight and Nine are for less important Aunties and their functionaries. And so on until you reach the bottom. Until you find the verde.

Algae vats line the fortified concrete of the pyramid base like a string of giant fake emeralds — glass baubles filled with hints of brown and roiling green. When the waves hit them, they shake and bob. I've been out in the bay a few times, just to see what we look like from the outside (it's so easy to forget, sometimes, that there *is* an outside, and we should never forget). Tour boats are popular in the evening, so everyone can goggle at the flaming red sunset as it sparks off the metal and glass trusses. They say if you catch it at the right moment, the sun looks like a ruby placed by an orixá in the top of the pyramid.

I didn't think so. Mother took me out in celebration when she married Auntie Yaha. I didn't see a crown jewel, though. I saw blood. It drenched the great hollow pyramid of our city in the bay, spilling down the sides, over the megatrusses and transport pods and round plazas. I didn't look at the sun — even the protective glasses they gave us lay forgotten in my hand. I looked at the base, where the waves crash and the algae vats bobble. On the terraces between the vats, a few dozen people, comically tiny at such a distance, stared at us. None waved.

We call it the catinga, the stink, but they call it the verde. Green.

I'd never thought to ask why, before that moment. *How can they stand the smell?* is the standard question. The kind of idle discussion second only to the weather. But the base of our pyramid is beautiful. Amid all that blood of the dying sun, the verde was still alive.

The blue of the bay, the green of the verde. A rich girl on a boat, wary of a new mother and still grieving for her lost father.

And a boy? Is he among the inscrutable figures watching me watch them? Darker than the rest, but with the bright white of his smile, the light brown of his eyes and the skin of his palms? Does he laugh at us with his friends, or does he stare and wonder who I am?

Enki is from the verde, which means he grew up poor. It means he grew up with the ever-present stink of hydrogen-producing algae. It means that in the winter, when the cyclones roll in off the coast, he's stayed up nights listening to the thunderous crashing. It means that if he came up from the verde, unless he was very careful, he would carry its smell with him, its look and its poverty, and he would be judged for it.

The third thing you should know about Enki is that he wants to die.

He doesn't seem like that kind of boy, I know. They almost never do. But he wants to be a summer king, and so he wants to die.

Gil and I don't talk about it much. What's the point? That's what it means to be summer king. Their choice of the Queen wouldn't matter if they didn't die to make it.

But I can't help but think about that day on the boat, and the silent, almost motionless figures suspended in the lurid green.

What is it like, to grow up beautiful in the verde?

Three finalists, and one will be king. They're seated on three chairs, facing the crowd like degree candidates at university. Pasqual to the left, his eyes lowered, perhaps out of humility, but more likely because he knows how the wakas swoon over his lashes. Pasqual is tall; he looks like a dandelion — a weed with a wild thatch of unusually red-tinged hair that seems to draw the cameras to him like flies to a picnic. He arranges angelic orchestrations of classical music and could solve quadratic equations when he was three. When he smiles, even I have to catch my breath.

Octavio sits to Pasqual's left, and he stares straight out at the anonymous mass of us. He's the least affected of the three, as though he's indifferent to his presence on the stage. I'm surprised he's advanced this far, but then, the summer king contest is never predictable. Octavio is smaller, but not small. He rarely smiles and speaks only when the contest demands it. He isn't particularly beautiful, though I wouldn't call him plain. He writes, which is an unusual skill for a moon prince. Normally, they do something flash, like rivet surfing or capoeira or even just singing. He writes love poems to someone who even now remains anonymous, despite the efforts of a hundred thousand desperate girls and boys. Octavio's poems make my heart feel small in my chest. They make me want to cry and rage at the same time.

These two are brilliant; they are the sort of boys any waka would die to spend an evening with.

I hate them both.

Gil and I don't care that it's a moon year and none of these boys will have any real power. Let the king five years from now, the next sun year, pick a new Queen. We just want our beautiful boy, our true moon prince. We want Enki more than we've wanted anything before.

Enki leans back in his chair with a bright smile, like he's almost as giddy as the rest of us to see him onstage. Auntie Isa orates about the historic nature of our city and our unique system of king elections. Gil and I don't pay much attention. He's pulled out his holo projector and mine is on my lap. I've decided to turn them on close to the end of the event, when Enki is speaking. That way my stunt should get the most attention.

But then Auntie Isa says a name far more interesting than the endless nattering about first King Alonso and his original selection of first Queen Odete. "The distinguished ambassador from Tokyo 10, Ueda-sama, will have the honor of asking our three finalists the first question."

This prompts a strange mixture of nervous laughter and frenetic clapping. I remember Auntie Yaha talking about how some people see the ambassador's visit to the city as a sign that the Aunties might ease our restrictions on new tech. Tokyo 10 is famous for their nanotech and a new breakthrough for turning living humans into immortal data streams. I've read the reports, but the descriptions of Tokyo 10 might as well be a pre-dislocation fantasy for all I understand them. I flirt with our regulations for the sake of my projects, but I've never seen anything even approaching the technology that must seem normal to the ambassador.

But the man who shakes Auntie Isa's hand with a deferential smile looks strangely normal. No body-mod appendages like wings or webbed hands or antennae or the dozens of other things I've seen in pictures. His face has the smooth agelessness of Auntie Isa's, which makes me think he must be very old. His voice is soft but steady, with barely a trace of an accent.

"My thanks, Auntie Isa. It is an honor to be allowed to celebrate such an important cultural moment with all of you. My question for these three young men is simple. What plans do you have if you don't win?"

Gil and I glance at each other, surprised and intrigued. No one has ever asked a question like that before, not even Sebastião, our top gossip caster. It's rude in a way I can't quite articulate — only an outsider like Ueda-sama could get away with asking it.

Pasqual answers first. "I want to be king," he says. "This city is my city, and you are my people. I can think of no greater honor than to be your sacrifice."

Gil claps; I roll my eyes. Pasqual is such a grandstander, with this booming, theatrical voice that would make a statue shiver. He wields his charisma like a bludgeon, so it doesn't even matter that he didn't answer the ambassador's real question.

Octavio stays seated, a line between his eyebrows while he answers slowly and with great care.

"I have thought about it, of course I have, though my chief desire is the same as Pasqual's. But were I to lose, I certainly wouldn't regret living out my life — though with far fewer people watching on, I'm sure." His small, self-deprecating smile makes me warm to him despite myself. I don't want Octavio to be king, but I imagine he would be a good friend.

Enki stands for his response. He opens his mouth, but then closes it without speaking and walks with abrupt grace over to where Ueda-sama waits on the side of the stage.

"We haven't met formally," Enki says, extending his hand. Ueda-sama accepts the gesture smoothly, which reminds me of Auntie Yaha. The skills of career diplomats. "It's a good question," Enki says, his eyes dancing, "but didn't anyone tell you not to take us seriously?"

I giggle — high and tight and brief, more to release tension than express mirth. As usual, Enki walks so close to the edge of acceptable behavior that his feet bleed. Sometimes I wonder if he could make the Aunties angry enough to disqualify him from the contest. It hasn't happened yet, but flirting with the ambassador of the most preeminent tech city in the world might just cross that line.

But Ueda-sama answers him before Auntie Isa can intervene. "I think," says the ambassador from a city of immortals, "that a man proposing to die deserves the respect of that choice."

Enki nods. "By reminding us of the lives we will abandon?"

Even Ueda-sama winces at the heart of his question, stripped raw beneath the bemused lash of Enki's tongue. "You need a reminder?" he says.

Gil squeezes my hand hard enough to hurt, and I squeeze back.

The smile leaves Enki's eyes, but it finds his mouth. He buries the long fingers of his left hand deep into dreadlocked hair. "No," he says. "Sometimes I think about it. I would play peteca, because I'm not very good right now. I'd dance, of course." He flashes a smile at the mostly bewildered wakas in the audience, which provokes relieved laughter. "Nothing special."

"So you've decided it doesn't matter if you lose that life?"

"Saying good-bye to it was the hardest thing I've ever done," Enki says. They are standing very close together. "But I still chose this city," he says, addressing the darkened mass of us, instead of the ambassador. "And I hope she will choose me."

The cheers and stomping feet shake the floor of the stadium. Gil turns to me. I can't hear him over the din, but I can read his lips. "Now?" he asks.

It's earlier than I planned, but I nod impulsively. "Three, two, one," I say, tapping his arm to the count. On *one*, we both switch on our projectors and hold them high above our heads.

I had to use two projectors to program the image because one wouldn't have been enough to attract attention in such a large space. But the split image means Gil and I need to hold them at exactly the right height and distance from each other. From below I can't tell if we've managed it. My shoulders ache; sweat traces an itchy line down my temple, but it seems that no one has noticed us at all.

Enki basks in the rapture of his chosen audience. My grimace turns half smile. But as the noise subsides, Auntie Isa thanks the ambassador for his question with the barest hint of annoyance. Enki bows slightly from his hips and walks back to the other finalists.

I bite my lip to distract myself from the fierce burn in my biceps and shoulder blades.

"Damn it!" I say, loud enough in the quieting stadium for my neighbors to glare at me. I imagined turning on the holo-sign to shocked attention and general approbation. I hadn't prepared for this — what good is public art if no one even *notices*? Gil glances at me, probably waiting for a sign that I've had enough.

But then Enki pauses, turns his head, and squints. "Is that . . ." he says, peering out at us like he's caught sight of Venus on a clear night.

He's seen it. The familiar floating hologram of our pyramid city, but with a ghostly, dark handprint at its heart — a clear echo of Fidel, our last moon year king, who marked Serafina with his bloody hand. At the top rotate the words *The wakas of Palmares Três want Enki*. The bottom of the pyramid glows green with miniature algae vats. Beneath that, the words *This year, our light comes up from the verde*.

He laughs and claps his hands. "I hope so," he says, and sits back down. Auntie Isa ignores us entirely, focused as she is on restoring order and control to the event. But why should I care — the only one who matters laughed at my sign and now everyone must be staring at it, wondering who had the audacity to do such a thing. I imagine I can hear a few of the camera bots buzz a little closer overhead. If I'm lucky, this will rate a second- or third-tier gossip cast.

Gil and I grin at each other in a moment of pure triumph. But I don't want to overstay my welcome, so we shut off the projectors just as the two security guards finally get around to asking us to leave.

Sometimes I imagine the end of the world.

Not this end of the world. The other one, four hundred years ago.

You know those pictures they show us on Memorial Day? The thousands upon thousands of tiny white crosses sticking out of the dirt like daisies. The char pits after the bodies piled too high to bury, belching clouds of black smoke that spread like oil above Rio and São Paulo. It's strange for a boy to look at that, no matter how long ago, and not imagine how it must have been. It must have looked like Armageddon when the cold came, when the dirty bombs devastated Pernambuco. Hundreds of millions more died in the nuclear wars and the freezing and the southern migrations.

I know all that, but it's not what I imagine.

I imagine I'm a Queen. Odete, sitting in a bomb shelter somewhere on the coast of Bahia, in a country that had once been Brazil, and trying to force a new world from the screaming mouth of the old one. What wouldn't I do? What wouldn't I create? Who wouldn't I sacrifice, if it would keep the world from ever dying again?

So I take my lover, my king, and I put him on a pedestal and I cut him down. A man, like the ones who ruined the world.

I take from the world I know: Candomblé, which always respected a woman's power. Catholicism, which always understood the transformation of sacrifice. And Palmares, that legendary self-made city the slaves carved themselves in the jungle, proof that a better world can be built from a bad one.

And so, Palmares Três. Odete's utopia was even more improbable than my birth, and yet here we both are. Don't you ever wonder how we came to such a strange place from the way the world was before?

When the world is destroyed, someone must remake the world. I think you'd call that art.

All of Palmares Três will vote for our next summer king in less than five hours, so of course our social studies teacher picked today to give us an exam. Even Bebel begged him not to, and I swear she thinks exams are only marginally less enjoyable than parties. And so my classmates and I find ourselves hunched over lesson arrays in one of the exam rooms, high cubicle partitions blocking me from seeing anything but the tops of their heads. I tried to study, despite the extreme temptation to do nothing but stare at gossip feeds all day. My holo-sign didn't make a huge sensation, but a few casters mentioned it. Not the great triumph made lurid in my fantasies, but I don't mind. Just that taste of performance makes me realize how small and confining my art has grown lately. Even Gil and my occasional excursions with a can of grafiteiro spray seem tame compared with this glimpse of what I could do.

But back in the real world, I'm a student, not a famous artist. I shake my head and start to write.

Bebel finishes early. Since we aren't allowed to leave before the period ends, my most competitive classmate leans back conspicuously in her chair and lets out a long, satisfied sigh.

"Were you coming or taking a test?" I mutter, just loud enough for Paul and Gil to strangle their laughter. The teacher looks up sharply from the front of the room but doesn't say anything.

The ordeal is over soon enough. I'm grateful because he gave us one softball: *Explain the evolution of the moon and sun year traditions of the summer king ceremony. Why do moon year kings only have a symbolic role in reaffirming the current Queen, rather than choosing a new one?*

Given all the history lessons even the low-brow gossip casters have been giving us for the past month, the answer is almost fun to write. Maybe that's why Bebel sounded so satisfied? But no, I refuse to give her even that much credit.

I run through the standard answer — two hundred years ago, the king Luiz was the youngest king ever elected and the most popular in a very long time. In his honor, that Queen legislated that all moon kings should be wakas, or under thirty, and that sun year kings, elected when the Queens have reached their two-term limit, should all be respected adults. So they stopped the original practice of only allowing a selection "in gesture or blood," and waited until after the sun year king spoke his choice to cut his throat. Only during the suddenly symbolic moon year did they keep with tradition; with just the current

Queen allowed in the room, her selection for the next term is an inevitable formality. I add to this some of my own speculation: that Luiz's election coincided with the first major life-extension technologies. With grandes suddenly living fifty, a hundred years longer than they had before, wakas had even less of a voice in politics. What better time to make sure that they always had a waka king? Cynical, maybe, but it still works. I haven't paid this much attention to politics in my life. Our last sun year, the contest was dignified and reserved — and I hardly remember any of it.

I finish barely a minute before the timer shuts off our arrays. I stretch and stand up, looking around for Gil. We have plans for this evening.

"Excited about the election?"

It's Bebel, sounding entirely too pleased with herself. She's a huge Pasqual fan, of course, because Bebel could only like someone as self-consciously perfect as herself.

"Enki will win if this city has any sense at all," I say, just to annoy her.

I succeed admirably; her thick eyebrows flash upward and her shoulders rise defensively. "I think they're all very good," she says with her trademark touch of holier-than-thou superiority.

"Maybe Octavio will get through," says Paul, blithely coming between us. "He ran circles around Pasqual in that debate."

Bebel blows back an errant puff of hair, raises her flawless voice. "Pasqual is a composer, not a politician!"

Not too many people can stand up to Bebel in a passion. "Pasqual is great," Paul says, holding up his hands. "I just think Octavio did better in the debate."

"A summer king," says another girl in our class, "should be good at politics *and* art."

"Even in the moon year?" Bebel asks.

"Especially then."

"Maybe," Gil says, "he should respect art and understand politics."

"Maybe," I say, grinning, "it helps when you win the debates *and* dance like a god."

Bebel sighs. "Yes, June, we all know you love Enki."

"Anyone with a soul loves Enki," I say.

Paul nods slowly. "I think they're all great, and if Enki invited me back to his house, you know I wouldn't complain, but . . . I would never declare. I couldn't."

"I wanted to declare," says another boy, drawn into our conversation. "But my papai begged me not to. He said he'd miss me if I were gone. But I thought . . . well, I could have been a *king*, you know? It seems worth it."

Paul shudders. "Not to me. You couldn't pay me. I want to die old, two hundred and fifty at least."

Bebel gives him a derisive smile. "Well, aren't you the world's oldest waka, Paul."

"I'm just trying to be sensible," he says, but he looks away. He knows everyone is laughing at him. No wonder he doesn't like Enki. My favorite candidate might be brilliant and wild and creative, but no one could accuse him of being sensible.

Beside me, Gil has gone unusually still. I tap his shoulder, a question. "I thought about it," he says softly, though we can all hear.

I feel something drop in my stomach — shock or fear or anger, how could I know which? He hasn't told me this before, but maybe I should have known.

"My mamãe never said anything," he says. "She knew what I was thinking and she never tried to stop me."

"She didn't care?" Bebel asks, stupid even by her own standards. Gil's mother is young, almost a waka, and he's put up with more than his share of derision because of it.

"She cared more than anything. She loved me enough to let me go and I loved her enough to stay."

Bebel nods slowly. The conversation continues, thoughtful and excited at once, but I don't really hear it. A familiar sensation grips me: I'm getting an idea.

I think about Gil and his mother, about Queen Odete and Queen Oreste, about Enki. I think about the millions in our city all waiting to hear who will be king. I think about the mystifying, endless chain of events that brought us here. Four hundred years ago, there was no Palmares Três, no Aunties, no summer kings, no elections. Four hundred years ago, there was just plague and war and destruction. Four hundred years ago, the boys that I love would probably be dead, because at its peak, the Y Plague wiped out 70 percent of all males. They're fine now, of course. Palmares Três is proud of its perfectly even gender demographics. But still, it's as though I can feel the strength of all our ancestors bearing us up. They are the heavy trunk and thick boughs of a tree on which I am only the tiniest budding leaf.

I'm dimly aware of Gil steering me toward my bag and out of the exam room. But the world has fallen away. My thoughts race too far and too fast. Trees, I'm thinking, and life and ancestors written in me and across me, *yes* that's it, *across me*, and now the way forward clears like a window wiped of frost.

I've discovered my next art project. Its immediate grip eases, and I realize that we're outside. I stop in my tracks and turn to him.

"I need to get into your mamãe's cosmetic stash," I say.

This is a new request, and a little daring, since his mother has a cosmetic and costumer license that allows her to get regulated tech. But Gil just shrugs. "Anything for a new idea," he says. "What is it this time?"

"She won't miss it too much, I promise," I say, and kiss him on his cheek.

For a moment, I wonder if his eyes are a little too distant. Did some part of that conversation back in school disturb him? Stupid Bebel implying that his mamãe was too young to care about him properly?

But then he shakes his head and does a little shuffle-dance and looks so much like the carefree, gentle Gil I love that I stop worrying.

"What's the project?" he asks, like he always does.

I hold his hand and tell him about my tree.

Five hours later, I am watching a light sink into my skin. The knot of tiny crystalline tubes has submerged halfway, but I need more skin implant gel to finish the job. I want to implant two branches' worth of lights today, from my collarbone to my elbow on my left side. Today's final one glitters in the crook of my elbow. I almost like how it looks, with my hyper-permeable skin lufting gently at its edges. My skin is usually too dark to see the veins underneath, but the gel reveals their intricate tracery. Still, my skin is getting more opaque by the minute. I click my tongue and look at the door hopefully, as though that will make Gil hurry. I misjudged the amount of gel I needed, which posed a problem, given that we'd used the last from Gil's mamãe's supply closet. But you need a cosmetics license to buy even the most low-level body-modding tech, and they don't give those to wakas. Gil left half an hour ago, promising to find some. I hope he doesn't get caught. But I feel safe enough; he never does.

And perhaps my thoughts summon him, because the door slides open a moment later, and he dashes in with a flushed smile and a clear tube in his hand.

"Have they finished counting the votes yet?" he asks, tossing it to me.

I pop open the tube and smear on just a little. My skin tingles but it doesn't hurt. "Since five seconds ago when you checked your fono? How did you get this?"

"A vendor I know in Gria Plaza," he says. "I was afraid I'd miss the announcement."

"But you still went?" I say as the light finally stops sinking just below my top layer of skin.

He shakes his head and turns up the volume on Sebastião. It won't be much longer now. "I couldn't leave you like that, June," he says.

Gil rubs my upper arm; my lights flash in his wake. I'm impressed with even this minor realization of my great idea. The colored lights came from Gil's mamãe as well, though I was sure they'd never been intended for skin implanting. My latest art project is a body tree, all done in colored skin lights. When I'm done, the branches and leaves should travel all the way down my torso and up my neck. The tips of the branches will brush against my unadorned cheeks. It should be very dramatic, but at the moment, I look a little strange.

On the left-hand holo, they're showing a recap of the final competition. Octavio's poem is first, and if he spoke it to me just then, I might be tempted to forget even Enki. The poem speaks of longing and love — and I have to wonder if the one he loves is dead, because how else could they resist him? And how else could he leave them?

Pasqual is next, and the plaintive string section playing the melody of "Manhã de Carnaval" gives me shivers. He plays the guitar from the front of the stage.

"I'd forgotten how pretty that song can be," Gil says a little wistfully, into the silence that follows his last note.

"Traitor," I say again, without much conviction.

And then it's Enki's turn. We've already seen this once, but Gil and I reach for each other at the exact same moment. His pulse thrums beneath my fingertips and my own lights flash like falling stars. The wakas in the audience stop their screaming. They're like us: breathless and silent, waiting for their beautiful boy.

Here's how Enki becomes the summer king:

He walks into the spotlight dressed like a slave in old-Brazil: off-white burlap sackcloth trousers, ragged at the hem, short-sleeved shirt with a jagged gash of a collar. His ear-length dreadlocks are loose and lighter colored than I've seen them. Later, we will learn that he has snuck out of the city to literally rub road dust into his hair.

His feet are bare, like the poorest refugee from the flat cities. Like someone unaware of even the most basic courtesy due the Queen of the most powerful city in South America.

There's a gasp when he first lifts his right leg. The skin on the soles of his feet is even lighter than mine, and I'm as light-skinned as anyone is allowed to be in Palmares Três.

He puts his foot down. Pauses. Lifts up the other.

Still balanced on one leg, he spins. We're so tense, so worried and exhilarated, that laughter pops like a bubble. It's gentle, barely there, but Enki smiles. He puts his foot down and now, again, he's barefoot on the stage.

His rudeness of going barefoot would be bad enough in the presence of the Aunties.

But he's facing Queen Oreste.

We wonder what will happen. Our worries change from *Maybe he won't win* to *Maybe the Queen will turn him out of the city.*

"My Queen," says Enki. His voice isn't very low, but it's smooth as a guitar.

He doesn't bow, though he's a boy, because only the summer king doesn't bow to the Queen.

For a very long time, she is still. She doesn't seem to breathe, and neither do we. Her eyebrows are drawn together — her only sign of emotion.

"What is this, Enki?" says the Queen. "Do you not honor me?"

Enki's smile is wide and bright. "I give you the greatest honor," he says.

"You are dressed in the manner of a slave," says she, "in a city where there are none."

"There aren't," he agrees, though now his smile seems too sharp for his words. "But there is the verde."

"And what of it?"

"I am dressed in the manner of my people."

"Are we not your people?" And we see that the Queen is torn between amusement and anger. Enki is leading her in a dance, but has not tapped out its rhythm.

"You are everything to me."

"And yet you come before us hardly as a king."

"I come before you," says Enki, "as a simple verde boy."

He takes a quick step back, almost skipping, and his dust-lightened hair bobs around his ears.

"I will leave you as a king."

And when the drums start, that's how he dances: as a king.

Gil's mother is a tailor, so she always has piles of cloth she doesn't know what to do with. Gil says he's sick of clothes, he doesn't know why I like them so much, and I say that I'm an artist, and an artist who neglects personal adornment is like a singer who can't keep a tune.

Anyway, Gil is full of shit, because when I take the time to make him beautiful, he's happy as a cock. He's just too lazy to think about it, and he knows he'd be gorgeous in sackcloth. I love Gil's mother because she doesn't care what we do. With so many orders for the celebration of a new summer king, she can hardly see past silk and sequins, so when we come racing into her studio practically screaming with joy, she tosses some fabric at us and mutters something about a new turban for one of the Aunties.

"There's tape in the basket," she calls, "but stitch what you can — I still need some!"

"No worries," I say, sifting through the swatches of fabric with steady hands. "I know how to use a needle."

She grins at me. "Just 'cause I taught you, filha. Now go on, and take care of my boy."

This doesn't even get a rise out of Gil. He just laughs and waves her on. "June's Auntie Yaha got us tickets to the reception tonight. We're about to meet the summer king himself, Mamãe," he says. "I'm burning so bright, you could as well take care of a meteor."

Gil's mother laughs, but her eyes are frowning. "That Enki," she says, "*he* may be a meteor, but you're just a boy, Gil. He'll burn you up."

Gil puts a mocking hand on his heart, though he knows his mother is serious. "Oh, but to burn up in that comet's tail," he says, and then I'm laughing, I can't help myself.

"It's all right," I say before she can start again. "Enki won't notice us anyway. He'll have the Queen to worry about, remember?" The king isn't the Queen's consort in any technical sense, but he'll be expected to stay close to her during his first public appearance after the election.

She still seems hesitant, as though there's something she's forgotten to say and she can't remember if it's important. "Oh, Oreste. I thought she would eat him alive on that stage! I remember how it was with Fidel . . ." She would have been the same age as Fidel back then, I realize. Gil's mamãe is so mature it's easy to forget that she's nearly as young as us. She laughs wistfully. "We were mad that year, I swear. I don't know how any of us survived it."

I remember seeing Enki's name flash across the holo; the screaming of the crowd as they showered him with feathers and flowers and love notes. I remember how happily he smiled and how carefully he walked in his bare feet to accept the circlet of cacao from the Queen.

"We'll survive it," I say, while I remember that our kings never will.

We walk into the ballroom at the top of Royal Tower precisely one hour late. Auntie Yaha is there with Mother. Auntie Yaha smiles when she sees the two of us and she waves, though she doesn't break away from Mother and another man I eventually recognize as the ambassador Ueda-sama. The views from up here are majestic and nearly panoramic. A corner of the ballroom floor is a giant glass bubble that projects out into the city from a precise angle, such that you can see all the way down through the hollow body of Palmares Três and into the bright green-blue waters of the bay. Tonight, a web of lights glitters all the way down to the water. To mark Enki's election, the legendary lights of our pyramid city have turned celebratory. They flash and sparkle like the implants in my skin, and I'm grateful that I took the time to place a few more before we arrived here. Now, if you squint, it looks like it might be a branch of a tree. At least that's what Gil swore, and he knows I'd kill him if he lied. This party is more than exclusive; no more than five hundred people have been allowed into this special room. Five hundred well-connected, influential people, and even Auntie Yaha must have had to call in a favor to get Gil and me inside. Camera bots buzz overhead, broadcasting us to the rest of the city on this celebratory, festive night.

The lights of Palmares Três are white, so we "sparkle on the bay" as the song says, though if you ask me they could use some color. I press my nose into the smudge-proof glass and make out the greening hump of A Castanha, one of the four volcanic islands that dot the bay like petrified gods. Up here, suspended above the water, I feel as though I can do anything.

Enki hasn't arrived yet. The dozen wakas in the room have been eyeing Gil since we entered. I outdid myself this time, putting him in black, which he likes, but with every element subtly asymmetric — not so much lopsided as rakish. Myself I clothed as simply as possible: a strapless wrap of blue secured with a blue flower, and a matching one in my ear.

One does not, as Gil's mother would tell me, upstage glowing skin.

"Would you dance?" Gil asks, extending his one gloved hand toward me in a gesture so formal I nearly laugh. But it also feels right in this enclave of the Aunties — and now of our very own summer king. I take Gil's hand.

"My pleasure," I tell him, just as formally.

No one else is dancing, which is exactly why he asked me.

The music is classical: so familiar I could sing the bass line in my sleep, but it's still insistent for all that. That's the thing about samba.

Four hundred years and the famous standards still don't sound old so much as familiar. Gil and I have joked that if we hear "Eu Vim da Bahia" one more time, we might throw ourselves into the bay, but then I'm caught off guard by João Gilberto's deceptively difficult rhythmic patterns, his gentle voice, and I think, okay, there's worse music to be forced to listen to.

The song changes to something faster, good for dancing. I'm not a great dancer, but I know how to follow. Gil is the best sort of partner: one who makes you look more skilled than you are.

I feel when Mother notices us. In the corner of my eye, I can see her go still and turn away from the ambassador, who seems confused. Auntie Yaha purses her lips and I smile. Gil's in another world, of course. I'll tell him what a scene we made when we're done and he's had time to come back down. Gil dances like an orixá, and he knows it. He's charming and smart and gorgeous and all the wakas we know are crazy for him. I'm lucky he's my best friend.

We're moving fast, I have to pay attention if I don't want to make an ass of myself. But even so, I'm getting lost in the rhythm. The *one-two-three* that my feet know better than my brain. The way my hips shake and the feel of the polymer silk sliding over my breasts. Gil spins me one way and then the other. I laugh and he dips me. I kick up one leg, not caring that anyone can see up my dress or that I'm in danger of losing my shoe. Gil smiles that secretive, crooked smile. He pulls me up and then his arms are on my hips and I'm flying above his head as the samba pulses around us and I see the city glittering beneath me.

This is the best moment of my life.

And then I see him.

He's on the edge of the glass floor, alone, though a crowd surrounds him like a horseshoe. He's looking at us with those bright eyes. Maybe Gil can tell that something has happened because he puts me down gently and turns around.

Even I can see the spark when Gil meets Enki's eyes. The air leaves the room. Or maybe that's just me, wondering if my heart might fall out of my chest when I lose the comforting warmth of Gil's hands. He heads toward Enki, still dancing, though I don't think he realizes it.

Enki is dressed simply, though he no longer wears the "verde boy" clothes from his final performance. Leather sandals, white pants, and a loose blue shirt. He looks like he might be selling cupuaçu in Gria Plaza, and he's captured the attention of every person in the room.

But Enki only has eyes for Gil.

Should I have known this would happen? I feel my disappointment like some foreign object lodged in my chest. Completely irrational.

It's like what Gil's mamãe told me, when Mother first got engaged to Auntie Yaha five months after my papai died. *Love is complicated*, she said, *and it never works the way you think it should.*

Gil and Enki don't speak. Or maybe they do, but none of us can hear it. Maybe in the way Gil touches Enki's palms, the way Enki's feet start that shuffle-shuffle, there's a conversation. *I've loved you for so long* and *You're beautiful, won't you dance?* I didn't bring a fono with me, but there's a holo array on the far wall, behind the band, and I can see them reflected in it from different angles. Gil and I have been in the background of a dozen gossip items — inevitable, when your step-mother is an Auntie — but this is the first time anyone will remember our names.

Gil, the one who caught the eye of the new summer king.

June, the one left behind.

Above me, the buzzing camera bots let me know I'm in their eyes, a lone figure suspended over the city. I wonder how my skin lights will look on the holos. Can they see the swirls? The colors? Can they see how frantically they pulse when I look at the two of them, together?

I can't tell if Gil is leading, or Enki. They move slowly — the song has switched to "Velha Infância" and though I know they both could be flashy, they instead make a dance of their intimacy. Enki pauses, still and watchful as a deer. His hand is raised. Fingertips hardly touching, Gil moves in a circle around him — a satellite orbiting our newly chosen moon. Enki smiles at him, full and uninhibited, and my hands cover my mouth, my lights strobe helplessly.

Gil closes his eyes for a moment. He stops moving. Slowly, he sinks to his knees like he's falling through water. The singer falters and then it's just the violin and the guitar and the drums, insistent as a heartbeat.

Gil kneels there, head bent, penitent and worshipful before our new summer king. Alone on the dance floor, I am the only one facing Enki. I'm the only one who can see his surprise, the slight bob in his throat as he regards the top of my best friend's head. I expect Enki to touch his shoulder, like the Queen would a petitioner. I expect him to say something that acknowledges Gil's gesture without exposing too much of himself.

But this is Enki, and I should know better.

"Coração," Enki whispers. I have never heard his voice in person before. It is the same, but it makes me shiver — a ghost from my dreams has entered my waking life. Gil's shoulders begin to tremble. I think he is crying. I want to go to him, and I know I have no place in this.

Enki squats, bending so his head is below Gil's. He puts one hand under Gil's chin and lifts.

"Thank you," Enki mouths.

And then they kiss.

Have I stumbled? Or just lost the feeling in my feet? Because I feel the smooth glass of the floor through the thin fabric of my dress and I think I've fallen. I wonder if I've stopped breathing. Suddenly, Auntie Yaha is beside me.

"June, June," she says, so insistently I wonder how long she's tried to get my attention. I look up at her, expecting disapproval, and getting something that confuses me. Her lips frown, but her eyes are sad. It's her eyes that make me take her hand.

"Come," she says, "filha, come. Your mother and I will take you home."

*　　*　　*

I spend the night alone and shivering, my cheek pressed against the window and my body covered in a nest of blankets. I tried sleeping, but all I could think of were the lights of the city and the ruffle of wind on the bay. The worst is this feeling that I've lost them *both*. The Enki of my foolish dreams and Gil, my best friend. He put me down on the glass and never once thought of me after. I'm afraid it will never be the same between us, and I'm furious for being afraid. How can I begrudge Gil that wide-eyed, worshipful happiness? How can I be jealous of him for the dance? But this ache that I know shouldn't be there slides through every part of me.

I don't actually know Enki. I'm not stupid. I'm aware this attachment I feel is the product of emotional investment in the largely stage-managed and manufactured spectacle of the royal election. I know that a thousand wakas are probably crying themselves to sleep tonight, just like me.

I'm an artist, after all, and I live for spectacle, for the construction of emotional states and the evocation of suppressed feelings. I can appreciate what Enki has done with his election — the way he subverted it while simultaneously triumphing within its rules. I don't envy Queen Oreste in her efforts to manage him during this year. The summer kings of moon years might not have any political clout, but I think grandes underestimate the power of desire.

But Enki is also himself. He is the boy who turned a dance before the Queen into a political statement, the boy who came up from the verde to steal our hearts, and is it so silly, so unbelievable that I'd allowed myself to fantasize? To think that he might look at me in the way he looked at Gil tonight, that it might have been my lips he kissed, my cheek he caressed?

I squeeze my hand into a fist. *No.* That's a story a little girl tells herself to fall asleep at night, and I am done with fairy tales. I want art, pure and clean and uncompromising. I want Gil to be happy and I want to be happy for him. I can love Enki as the summer king without dreaming of his kisses.

On the horizon, I see a pale glow, the barest hint of dawn. The waves get higher and choppier. The wind whistles past the trusses. I know the signs; there's a storm coming.

Down in the verde, they will be sealing their windows, huddling in spaces away from the waves. Even so, every year a few unlucky people are washed out. Last sun year, there was a big political debate over what the next Queen should do to help the plight of the catinga, but as far as I can tell, Oreste has done nothing but make a brief visit during her first coronation tour.

Before I know it, I scramble out from under the covers. I'm practically naked, but I've stopped shivering.

It's almost dawn. Auntie Yaha and Mother snore in the other room. They won't notice when I leave. They never do. I pull on my black overalls and high-necked jacket. My shoes and gloves are black too, with special grippy bottoms that are technically illegal without a license, though Gil's mother didn't say anything when I asked for them.

Hunting outfits, Gil calls them, and my smile when I find my grafiteiro spray can is perhaps a little fierce, and very hungry.

You ask me why I want to die, like you have no idea, like you haven't known all this time exactly what I want to do. It hurts to know that you don't understand this part of me, though together we've made so much more of it than I could have ever dreamed on my own.

Samba is dance, it is spirit, it is the space between the world and nothing, between the orixás of my grandmothers and the Jesus of my grandfathers. It is a rhythm so fast you can hardly think it. It is a dance so subtle that when your feet move, you had better let yourself follow them. Samba is life.

In the pop-rattle-pop of the pandeiro and the whoop-whoo of the cuíca and the strum-pause-strum of the guitar, I am open, I am divine, my entrails are on the floor and anyone can read them.

Why do I want to die?
Why do you?

I jump a ride to the verde in four different pods, going all the way up to Gria Plaza with an Auntie's secretary in a pale gray suit before I find a night janitor finally on her way back home. I make up some story about how I accidentally dropped my flash in the bay. I don't sound like I'm from the verde, but I make sure I don't sound like I'm from Tier Eight either, and anyway, she's too tired to do much but shrug and let me sit across from her.

It's hard to take the public lines this late, and if I used my flash, Auntie Yaha would know where I've gone. Gil and I learned this early: Cover your tracks and use the city. Pods will take you anywhere you want to go, but the city knows who calls them. For a moment, I feel as if Gil is beside me, but then I turn and realize his space is empty. Will it always be like that now?

"Up early for a student," the woman says. Her skin is light, like mine. Usually that means you're poor, but sometimes it just means you have a strange papai.

"I work some nights," I say.

"Doing what?"

"Spiders," I say. "Basic maintenance, you know."

"You're an engineer," she says, and I smile because I know she doesn't believe it.

"Good with my hands," I say. She clicks her tongue and shakes her head. I look out the window, through the maze of trusses that extends as far as I can see this deep in the pyramid. Our pod shakes when it passes close to one of the giant spider bots as it ejects nanotubes from its thorax to repair one of the transport megatrusses. Our little pod is barely larger than one of its knee joints. The bots are at least two hundred years old by now, but the city keeps them running because they do their job and I suppose the Aunties don't want to invite any new tech into the city. Spider bots live in a concrete warehouse at the center of the base, a place so damp and dangerous only the gangs from the verde venture inside, and they never stay for long.

This one has dents like butterfly wings on its left side, and one of its legs is made of a darker metal than the others. A lot of the spider bots have gone into retirement these days, and only the engineers know for sure which ones still work.

"Did you catch the feeds tonight?" the woman asks. I turn around, forcing my expression into something neutral and curious.

"Did something happen?" I say, and my voice cracks on the last syllable. I cough.

She chuckles a little, and I wonder if that's a blush I see creeping up her cheeks. "That Enki, crazy boy. He's already lighting a fire under the Aunties."

Gil, kneeling before our beautiful boy. Gil, his seat empty beside me. "What . . . what did he do?"

"You really didn't hear? Picked his first consort already, right under Oreste's nose. Ay, you should have seen that samba, I thought my tabletop would catch fire." She giggles. To my surprise, I join her, and if my laughter is a little hysterical, at least it's genuine.

Oh, if Gil were going to abandon me, he could hardly have done it better.

"What did Oreste say?" I ask.

The woman leans back in her seat, relaxing into the gossip in that intimate way I remember from my papai when he was alive. "Oh, the Queen didn't *say* anything. She just *looked*. I tell you, I don't envy our boy this morning."

I like that *our boy*. It means that she believes I belong in the verde. And maybe in some ways I do.

"But he's the summer king now," I say, watching the glow of the dawn sun behind purple-black thunderclouds. This will be a big one, and I'm heading *into* the verde. I bite my lip in anticipation.

"You're young. I've seen, oh, four moon years in my time. Enki is wilder than any of them, and he's just begun. The Aunties, they like you wakas to have an outlet. Someone they're not afraid of for you to obsess over. But if he has too much of his own mind?"

"You can't think they'll do anything. Everyone would see."

The woman shrugs. "The Aunties have their ways. We could watch the whole time and not see anything at all."

I smell the verde before I see it. The pod jerks as it aligns with a different tube and then we're hurtling toward the green. The waves break higher and higher even as I watch.

The woman sees it too, and her eyebrows pull together. "Get home quick, filha," she says. "This will be a bad one."

"Sure," I say. I can feel my lights hot against my shirt. Auntie Yaha would faint if she knew what I was about to do. I can barely breathe through my joy.

The pod lets us out a few terraces beneath Carioca Plaza — the hub of the verde that on good days has the most vibrant street fair in the city, though now it's mostly deserted.

The wind starts in earnest as we walk out of the pod, and I grip the woman's arm to keep her from falling.

"You have a place to go?" she yells, fighting with the wind.

I just nod, try to look reassuring. She opens her mouth to say something and then shrugs and hurries off. I watch her until she disappears into the warren of passages within the concrete. The waves aren't too high yet. I hope she'll be safe.

As if in warning, the wind punches past me and I hit the railing hard enough to knock my breath away. I gasp for a frightening moment before my lungs start to work again. I curse and pull on my gloves with shaking hands. The stickiness of the nanohooks steadies me. I don't activate them in my shoes just yet — you can walk with them on, but it's exhausting, and I don't think the weather's turned bad enough.

The sun must have risen by now, but you'd hardly know it. It's so dark I almost wish I'd brought a light. But lights make it easier for other people to see you too. People like the Palmares guards. There aren't normally many officers or bots down in the verde (battles with local gangs are bad for publicity), but I know that there will be more than usual in anticipation of Enki's coronation tour. Another thing I know: Cameras like the verde hasn't seen in a hundred years will be gathering in Carioca Plaza this evening, where the Queen's own pod will deign to travel, if it can brave the stink. And she and Enki will process to the outside, to the terraces lined with the algae vats and that breathtaking view of the bay. And to get a better picture, the cameras will of course flit over the water to capture the Queen and her new summer king, overlooking the waters of their great city.

The cameras will expect to capture the startlingly beautiful effect of the setting sun lighting up the algae vats like jewels. After all, you can't smell the catinga on a holo. They will expect Enki to smile and play nice to make up for his gross breach of etiquette at the coronation party.

They will not get what they expect.

Between the waves and the rain, I'm soaked by the time I make it to the northern bayside of the terraces. The wind is stronger here and the sky has lost even a hint of the sun. On balance, I'm glad — no one will be out here this morning. They'd be crazy to brave it.

I've given up and turned on the nanohooks in my shoes. Each step requires a laborious yank in precisely the right direction before they'll let go, but it's better than letting a wave carry me into the bay.

I feel for my spray paint beneath my vest, reassure myself that it's secure, and then pull on my face mask. In case there are cameras flitting around that haven't drowned yet, I don't want them able to identify me. Better to be another masked grafiteiro, probably from one of the gangs, than recognized as June Costa, stepdaughter of an Auntie.

I might live for the moments when I can frustrate and annoy Auntie Yaha, but even I don't know what she would do if I pushed her that far. Better to be anonymous. Given what happened at the coronation party, I'm not in the mood for public performance.

"Here goes," I mutter after checking for the fifth time that the nanohooks in my gloves are working. I wait for a lull in the waves, climb to the top of the railing, and launch myself as high as I can jump.

I swing my knees to my chest so I'm bent double, hanging by my hands and one foot from an algae vat. Inside, the microscopic, living bits of green swish around, releasing a stink I can smell despite the wind. I press my other foot into the side and wait for that reassuring, subtle snap as the nanohooks engage. And then I release my hands and hang, wild and free by my feet while wave after wave chokes me and I have only instinct to guide me higher up the smooth glass curve of the algae vat. I plant my hands, shake the water out of my eyes, and let out a whoop of sheer terror, sheer joy.

And for the next half hour, that's my life. Plant my hands, release one foot, then the other. Creep like an inchworm across the deceptively large bulk of the vats. I would be sweating if I weren't so wet, but at least I'm not cold. I keep moving. This is higher up than I've ever gone with Gil. Higher than we've ever dared. I've long since cleared the terraces. Only repair bots and technicians venture as high along the base pyramids as I'm going. It's exhilarating and it's exhausting. I wonder how I'll get down, but then I put the thought out of my head, think of Enki dancing before the Queen, think of Gil dancing before Enki, and keep going.

I'm trembling by the time I clear the last row of vats. Up here, I'm protected from the weather a bit by the overhang of the giant bubble of Carioca Plaza. I let myself relax, lean into the grip of the nanohooks, and take a deep breath.

It isn't the wind or the waves that get me, but a skittering mushi bot that for some reason hasn't retreated to its storage hole to wait out the weather. Its six sparkling mechanical legs slice through the fabric on my right arm as it crawls over me, on its way to repair a fissure in the concrete. I shriek and flinch at the sharp sting of salt water in the cut. The mushi bot pauses and turns its metallic head. It concludes that I am a foreign object invading its territory.

If I were an engineer, I'd have special clothing and a flash that would disarm the bot's defense mechanisms.

If I were an engineer, I wouldn't be here in the first place.

The mushi bot runs toward me, the sharp fringes in its legs alert and buzzing. I know I'll get sliced to ribbons if I let it run over me so I start to dash, crab-like, over the concrete slope. But my human hands and nanohooks are no match for the mushi bot's specially engineered legs, and I yelp as it slices into my hip.

I curse, and then again, because I don't know how I'm supposed to get out of this one now. If only Gil were here!

I look down, back at the smooth glass of the algae vats, and get an idea.

Quickly, knowing that if I wait much longer the other mushi bots might wake up to see what the fuss is about, I scramble back down, slipping down the concrete in my haste. I don't land so much as bump onto the hard surface of the first vat, slick with rain. I start to slide down and only at the last minute manage to get one hand to stick.

The mushi bot doesn't manage even that much. Its sharp-cutting legs and concrete saliva, perfectly engineered for the top half of the concrete pyramid, are useless just a few feet away, on the glass of the algae vats. It tries to stay upright, but the surface is too slick and the wind is too strong. I watch as it plummets over the side. Suspended in the air, legs flailing uselessly and metallic antennae swatting the air in robotic panic. I wonder how it came so close to beating me. It looks almost comical before a gust of wind pushes it out over the bay and it disappears from view.

Laboriously, almost numb from exhaustion and the giddy aftermath of terror, I climb back up the vat. There are no more mushi bots on the concrete, but I look around carefully before I reach into my vest and pull out my paint can. There's usually enough pigment packed into each of these for a mural.

Which is what I came here for.

"My name is June," I say, like I say every time, "and I'm the best artist in Palmares Três."

You're the best artist here, Gil said to me when we were thirteen, the day we first loved each other. *The best artist in Palmares Três.* Even then, I knew it wasn't true, but I knew why he said it: because I had to believe that one day it could be.

His mamãe was the best artist at that show, the disaster that became the yardstick by which I measured all others. Her series of child-sized mannequins depicting the stages of life of a waka in Palmares Três made me bite back tears. She dressed a child in a smock made lovely by a border of hand-stitched coffee beans and sugarcane. The older ones wore a shimmering aquamarine dress with a wistful bow gathered like flowers beneath her chin; a soccer jersey for a team that didn't exist and shockingly orange cleats; and the last mannequin came of age in a simple wide skirt and blouse in blushing pink and a turban the color of dried blood.

I had known Gil before the show, but he was new to our school and new to our tier — a strange, awkward boy with more angles than sides and eyes as large as oranges. We smiled at each other during lunch and talked a few times, but whispers always seemed to follow the new boy wherever he went. I couldn't understand what they meant and I didn't know if I dared let the whispers follow me too.

But then he attended the art show when I hadn't expected to see him, and he introduced me to his mamãe. I thought at first that she was his sister. She looked so *young* beside him, her face fresh in a way that antiaging treatments could never replicate.

"June, this is my mamãe. She's also in the show. Entry thirty-seven."

No one exhibiting in this contest could be older than thirty — it was a special, unusual opportunity for artists normally overlooked. I wondered about what that meant, and what the gossip I hadn't understood must have pricked and torn apart. Gil held his angles at a firm hundred and eighty degrees, staring at me with monstrous eyes at once hurt and proud and so watchfully angry.

And then I remembered. "Entry thirty-seven? The clothes?" The theme of the contest was "Graceful Beginnings," and I didn't think anyone had captured its spirit better.

"Oh, yes," she said, and grinned at me, less self-conscious than poor Gil. "Did you like it?"

"It's amazing!" I said. "My favorite in the whole show. If I could wear that dress with the bow, I'd die happy."

His mamãe and I talked for another ten minutes before one of the judges called her away. I started to say something to Gil, because he was staring at me again, and I knew already that I would hate to hurt him. But before I could get a word out, he draped his long arms and scrawny chest over my blossoming one. I hugged him back. In a city that thought wakas were useless, having a baby at sixteen would be as tough for the kid as the mother.

"Your mamãe is great," I said. "I wish mine were half so interesting."

He beamed at me, and I beamed back, bubbly with the joy of our discovery.

Then a judge asked me over to explain my entry, and suddenly, my parents were there just as they'd promised. The four of us walked over to my installation. I was the second-youngest person selected to exhibit for the Tier Eight contest, which filled me with a pride that barely matched my terror. I'd used every skill I possessed to create something that I felt sure my musician papai would be able to appreciate.

I nervously explained the piece, an overwrought exploration of the life of seminal pre-dislocation musician Maria Bethânia, complete with twenty-eight paintings of her early life and a life-sized ancient tombstone scrawled with graffiti. I meant this to convey how endings give rise to new beginnings, but mostly it conveyed that I wasn't very good at graffiti. Mamãe pasted on her best university-president smile and hugged me. The judge nodded thoughtfully. And Papai shook his head sadly and said, "It's nice, June, but where's her music?"

In its own way, that was worse than what happened after. To Papai, music was the highest form of art. Nothing I did could come close.

When they gave out the awards, it surprised no one that Gil's mamãe won the first prize. But more than a few heads turned when the last judge called out my name for third place. I was nearly at the podium when she nervously explained that my name had been read in error, could I please take my seat. I turned, numb with horror, but not before I glanced at the judge's fono array, listing the exhibitors. She had accidentally arranged it in reverse order — I wasn't third from the top, but third from the bottom. Forty-seventh out of fifty. I ran out of the auditorium; at least now I wouldn't have to sit beside my papai's quiet disappointment.

I didn't go far, just up the stairs to the roof of the exhibition hall. Gil found me a few minutes later, a gesture so unexpectedly generous that my tears dried on my cheeks.

"I was terrible," I said. "At least you admit it."

Gil smiled. "Nothing about June Costa is terrible." I liked the way my name tasted on his lips, as if I were a sweet and juicy fruit, rarely in season.

"But I wasn't any good. Not like your mamãe."

He stepped closer to me, and across a bridge of centimeters, I noted how his angles were already rounding, his muscles filling to match his height, the awkwardly broad planes of his forehead and cheeks subtly transforming into something that would be beautiful. But he was already the most beautiful person in the world to me just then.

"I think you're good. I mean, that gravestone was a little . . ."

I gave a shaky laugh. "Too much? Sometimes I *wish* I could make music like my papai. Real art."

Gil caught my hand and twirled me left, then right, then caught me against his chest. We laughed in tandem.

"What you do is real art."

"He doesn't think so. He loves Maria Bethânia. I thought he'd appreciate . . ."

"He will, June. He loves you."

For a moment, I believed him. If I tried hard enough, if I made myself good enough, if one day I won the prize instead of running out of the auditorium . . .

"The best artist in Palmares Três," I repeated for him, loving the peppery audacity of the words. Believing them just enough to make anything possible.

I never told you this, but I can feel my death. I've felt it since that first night, when they knelt me before the altar and I drank the wine, ate the sacred wafer, the body and blood of Jesus and Yemanjá, marrow and gristle and bone and nanobots. The Holy Communion roared behind my eyes, and the doctor said I wouldn't feel a thing (the only place in the body with no nerve endings: the brain), but I did. The bots spoke to me then like the city speaks to me now. They said move, move, move, which meant die. Did I know that then? I'm not sure.

The knowledge that I would die was like açaí, rich and bitter, and all I could think was that I wanted more.

Mother is waiting for me when I stumble back home. My clothes are wet and my hair is like a nest of seaweed, and I'm almost sad that Auntie Yaha isn't there with her, since it makes her crazy when I don't "look my best."

Mother has crossed her arms and legs. Her lips are pursed and I think about how Mother is always like that now, careful to not open any part of herself. Papai hated that side of her. And I will never be like her, no matter what.

"It's almost two in the afternoon," she says.

I shrug, standing awkwardly in the vestibule, dripping on the tiles. I want to take off my clothes, but I don't dare in case Mother notices the smeared paint and guesses at what I've spent this day doing.

"And there was a storm," she says. "But then, I see you already knew that."

"I took a walk," I say finally, because there's no getting away if I don't pretend to have this conversation.

"You missed school."

"It's the day after the election. Enki's going to the verde with the Queen in a few hours. Do you think *anyone's* in school?"

"The responsible wakas are. I'm sure Bebel —"

"I'm sure Bebel is perfect as ever. Unfortunately, you have me."

Mother's lips are squeezed so tight, it's a wonder they don't turn to diamonds. "She has scored above you on every exam this year, June," she says, as if I didn't even speak. "You know as well as I do there are only so many slots open in the university programs. Do you want to have to go to Tier Eight Community?"

I grimace. "I'm an artist."

"And you don't want to go to the University of Palmares? Train in their art program with Juliana Consecu? Exhibit in their gallery? You don't want that kind of pedigree?"

Of course I do, which is why Mother has to bring it up. She's always been the one interested in my art — as though she could use it to win me from Papai, as though I wasn't good enough to prove myself to him on my own. And even with him dead, she can't shake the habit.

"An artist can create anywhere," I say.

Her lips unbend slightly. I wouldn't dare call it a smile, but it's a little looser than her habitual expression. I guard myself against it. "And an artist can only support herself with proper connections."

"Well," I say, "wouldn't you know all about that."

She doesn't even flinch. She just narrows her eyes, closing even more of herself. That's Mother all over — these days I can't even *hurt* her.

I sigh. "Where's Auntie Yaha, anyway?"

"Damage control with that ambassador from Tokyo 10. Your Gil put on quite a show."

I giggle without meaning to. I don't understand how that was just last night, and this is only this afternoon, and so much has happened I feel as if I could squeeze a whole lifetime inside.

My mother is halfway to her room, but she pauses in a strangely tentative way and turns back around.

"June," she says, "are you . . . what happened with Gil, last night, you looked . . ."

She literally can't force it out. My laughter gets louder, harder.

"Don't strain yourself, Mother," I say. "I'm fine."

And, just then, it's nothing but the truth.

These days Mother is mostly a housewife, but she used to be one of the most important grandes in Palmares Três. She was the president of the University of Palmares, one of our three big schools. Not quite the best, though you never said that in her hearing. When he was alive, Papai was a music professor there. He taught modern trends in interpretations of twentieth-century classical music. They met when she first started in administration, and he'd already been teaching for years. He'd been married once, when he was a waka, but it ended badly and he'd never tried again until Mother.

I think they loved each other. At least, I can remember the way Papai would sometimes sing to Mother when she'd had a bad day at work. I remember the trip through the flat cities that she'd arranged for their fortieth anniversary. Papai had never seen Salvador, and I remembered how excited he was to visit the famed ruins of Rio de Janeiro. He must have taken a hundred holos on the glass beach at Ipanema, smiling like a child from inside his decontamination suit, and I looked dutifully at each one when he came back.

That was a year before he died, my papai.

I've never looked at that footage since.

I didn't know it then, but that trip was how Mother met Auntie Yaha, who was Auntie Yaha even then, and the newly appointed flatling ambassador of Palmares Três. She was young for an Auntie, much younger than my mother, but still about fifty, definitely no waka.

We had a fight the morning of their wedding. I asked her if she'd slept with Auntie Yaha when Papai was still alive. If while Papai was destroying bandwidth taking every possible angle of the Ipanema glass, wondering if it would be here or here that Tom Jobim had seen that most famous schoolgirl walking to the beach every morning, she had snuck out of her hotel room and betrayed him with the woman who was now supposed to be my new mother.

"You know *nothing*," Mother had said. "Your papai is gone. He left me and I'm still here. What would you have me do, become a nun?"

"It hasn't even been a year!" I screamed. "If you're so desperate, why not just pay for it?"

"You stupid waka," she said, leaning forward. She was in her wedding dress — bright red — and seated before the changing mirror. "What do you know of love?"

"Papai loved you," I said, because I believed it.

Mother scrunched her face, like she'd accidentally caught a whiff of the verde. "Your papai is dead."

"Stop saying that!"

She gave me a pitying look. She raised her hands like she might embrace me, but I flinched and she rested them again in her lap. "Oh, filha," she said. "Won't you let it go? Your mamãe is about to be married."

"Papai was right," I said, standing. "Better to die than get old like this."

I used to love my mother, you understand.

Some days, I'm almost sure she used to love me.

The revelation of my second piece of public art happens far more successfully than my first.

Just like I guessed, Queen Oreste escorts an even-more-dazzling Enki through the streets of the verde. Enki is smiling and silent, as though he knows that after his face and his words and his kiss have been on the holos nonstop for the last day all he really needs to do is let us look at him. On the tiny holo in my room (I couldn't bear to watch this with Mother), I wonder if his eyes look even brighter, his lips even redder. I wonder which mods he's picked already, and which he'll choose as his year goes on. It's one of the chief benefits of being summer king — a license to receive the rare and expensive self-modification technology that even the Aunties don't have much access to. He could make his skin glow like a lantern, he could access holos and feeds with his contracting pupils, he could even use a simple twitch of his fingers to steer his own pod through the tunnels of the city. Those are all the mods I've heard of the summer kings using, but watching Enki now I wonder if he will bother with any of them. From the beginning, Enki has lived to surprise us. To pull on the turbans of the Aunties and laughingly subvert their every desire. How would his mods be any different? For the first time, I wonder how many mods exist in the cities that don't have laws against them like Palmares Três. What could Enki turn himself into, given the opportunity?

But for now he walks through his old neighborhood, smiling as though he doesn't notice the catinga that the Queen guards against with a scented handkerchief. Tens of thousands line the streets, cheering as he walks past. A lot of wakas, of course, but even more grandes, and I'm surprised at how much they all seem to love him. I've seen the footage of other moon years, and now I'm sure of it — Enki is our most popular summer king in even grande memory, let alone waka. I don't see Gil, but then I didn't expect to. None of my pings are from him either, though I've got about twenty from what seems like my entire class. Including Bebel. She could hardly help but gloat over my holo debut last night. Every time a caster starts to show the footage, I switch. I know what I must have looked like, standing alone while watching the two of them. More important, I know what I felt like, and I don't need to feel that ever again, let alone thirty times an hour.

I wish Gil were with me, but prior experience tells me he's probably sleeping it off. And when he wakes up? Will he move on from Enki, like he does most everyone else, or will their relationship turn into something deeper?

But, no, I won't anticipate anything until it happens — everyone knows that summer kings screw like mayflies.

I turn back to my holo, make the volume amphitheater loud, and wait for what only I know is about to happen.

Enki pauses a moment before stepping out onto the terraces. I could swear he's waiting for the flitting cameras to have time to zoom over the water and stabilize themselves in the still-gusting wind before he steps out. Enki always did love an entrance.

When he steps out, his loose embroidered shirt billows behind him. To his left, Queen Oreste keeps a hand on her crimson turban, which is threatening to blow away. Some angles pull back to capture the breathtaking backdrop of the algae vats reflecting the lingering wisps of storm clouds. Framed by the terraced vats, Enki and the Queen stand like statues.

And then, the first camera notices. The chatter on my feeds gets cacophonous as the vidders and casters try to figure out what they're seeing. I turn down the volume.

A second later, what had been a strange, unexpected splash of color at the corner of a hundred angles resolves itself into something recognizable.

Into a mural.

"It looks like a picture of Enki kissing someone," Sebastião says on my main feed. He pauses. "Goodness, he's kissing that waka from last night. Someone in the verde wants to cause trouble — if Oreste wasn't happy about Enki's behavior last night, I can only imagine how she'll feel now. We'll hold for Oreste's reaction." Sebastião waves his hand a little helplessly. "It's nice, though, isn't it?"

I grin and fall back on my bed with stifled joy. Gil was harder for me to draw, though I've known him for years. But a painting like this is so necessarily reductive, and I know far too much of Gil to ever capture his essence in paint. In some ways, I feel like that about Enki, though we've never even met.

I flip through the other feeds and they're all discussing my art — who painted it, what it means, how Oreste and the Aunties will react to yet another affront by the wakas against the dignity of the office. They're sure that it's wakas, though it seems to me that it could just as easily have been a grande from the verde.

Oreste and Enki can't see the mural, though it's clear from their expressions they know something has happened. Enki starts to laugh and dashes to the railing of the terrace. He cranes his neck, but can't see it from that vantage. So he walks over to some waka at the front of the crowd — a girl so overcome by his presence I wonder if she might faint — and borrows her fono.

He looks at it for a moment and though the feeds are chattering — *How will he react? Where is Gil and has he seen this? What will the Aunties do?* — I hear them like a buzz in my ears.

"I am June," I whisper into my sleeve, and hope I won't vomit.

Enki silently hands the fono to the Queen. It's an old model, nearly as big as his palm, and it doesn't project very well, but she can get the gist. In a fit of highly uncharacteristic emotion, Oreste hurls the fono over the railing and into the bay. Enki looks back at the waka, who stands there with her face pale and mouth open. He shakes his head and turns out to the water, facing the buzzing cloud of cameras.

And he salutes them.

"From one artist to another," he says, to me, *to me*, and then I'm muffling my screams with my pillow and Gil finally pings me.

I'm barely in school for ten minutes before Principal Ieyascu pings me to say that she wants me in her office. Being the kind of girl who has attempted to keep illicit pop-art activities on the deep down low, I'm a little worried.

"What could it be?" I ask Gil, who sits beside me though every waka in the school has been falling over him since he walked in. We're supposed to be studying, but even the teachers don't bother to keep us quiet.

He looks around and then leans close to my ear. "You were careful, right?"

"Unlike you, I tried to keep my face *out* of the holos."

Gil laughs and flashes that superstar smile that hasn't worked on me since we were fourteen. "Oh, but you're missing out, June. I have an interview tonight with Sebastião; you want to come along?"

He tosses this out as casually as an invitation to his house for dinner, but even I gasp a little. Sebastião is our top gossip caster, the kind of feed-hound who is a celebrity in his own right.

"Gil . . ."

His smile falls away. "June, sometimes you have to step out."

"I don't want to be . . . not that girl."

Not the one left behind on the dance floor. The one whose stupid, half-formed dreams of the summer king broke in full view of a million people. Gil can see what I mean, and he still hasn't really explained what happened that night, so we leave it. He's happy and high as a comet. I won't be the one to bring him down.

"I'll just have to see what the giant wants. If I'm not back in an hour, look for my body."

Gil bites his lip a little — a disarming gesture from before he became Tier Eight's resident sex god. I smile at him, run my fingers through his thick, kinky hair, and leave before I can do anything stupid like cry or beg him to come with me.

Even if she somehow knows everything, I don't care. The mural that the mushi bots have by now succeeded in scrubbing out of existence was one of the triumphs of my admittedly short career. Enki saluted me on camera. Gil could barely speak when we first saw each other.

My lights are warm and I watch their faint glow reflected along the opaque glass walls of Principal Ieyascu's waiting room.

"Will you *please* turn those down, June?"

I whirl around and look up, surprised to see Principal Ieyascu with her arms crossed and her expression — as usual — forbidding. She's a grande's grande, and has been principal at this school long enough to know Auntie Yaha from her waka days. She's also giant, nearly seven feet tall, and hates sitting down.

"Turn . . . what?" I say, suddenly too nervous to do more than gape.

She rolls her eyes and takes a few clicking steps toward me. "Those body modifications under your skin, June. The ones that are certainly against school policy and quite possibly violate the Queen's edicts against technological self-modification, should I choose to press the issue."

I swallow and take a deep breath, which brings the lights down to a subtle glow. I should be able to control the brightness at will, but I haven't practiced enough to be good at it.

"It will have to do," Principal Ieyascu says. "Now, shall we go inside my office?"

She presses a hand to the dark glass wall, which pulls apart smoothly at her touch. Her actual office is only slightly less chilly. There's a single glass table, clear of everything except a twenty-first-century fountain pen I know must be worth at least a million reals. The chair behind the desk I think might be made of actual dead-cow-skin leather. For her guests, there are two seats of molded glass. They look uncomfortable, and there's only one free.

The other girl has a thick puff of dark honey hair she swears is natural but we all know must be modded. She's fidgeting in the glass chair, but smiles at me when I sit next to her.

I force myself to smile back, since it wouldn't do for Principal Ieyascu to see me be petty. At least I know that if Bebel the Perfect is here, then my graffiti exploits are probably still a secret.

"So why are we here?" I ask, craning my head to look up at Ieyascu, who has of course chosen to pace before her glass wall instead of sitting down like a normal non-giant.

"If you don't rediscover your manners, June, you might find yourself back in class." She pauses and looks between the two of us. "And I think you would regret that very much."

Regret *not* being in the principal's office? That's strange, even for Ieyascu, so I bob my head and mutter a dutiful apology. Bebel dips her honey bush too, though we both know she didn't do anything to warrant an apology. I grit my teeth. That's Bebel all over — always careful to be considerate when someone important is watching.

"Well, good. As I'm sure you are wondering — even though you were far more discreet about it, Bebel — there is a reason why I've called you both here. I trust you have heard of the Queen's Award?"

This is like asking us if we'd heard of the summer king, and did we know one has just been elected? Bebel nods politely. Every moon and sun year (and sometimes other years, if she feels like it), the Queen sponsors one high school student, providing full tuition to any university program plus a showcase of her talent and stipend money as she starts her career. The list of past recipients could double as a guide to the most important people in Palmares Três. Queen Oreste herself won about a billion years ago when she was a waka. When I was younger, Mother would make a point of taking me to the exhibitions of the finalists, as though she really thought that one day I could join their ranks.

Bebel and I gape at Ieyascu.

"You have? Good. Then perhaps you will understand the honor bestowed upon you — the result of certain *connections* or not — when I inform you that you, June, and you, Bebel, have each been named one of the ten finalists."

I don't even register her jibe. I'm too busy trying to keep the room in the proper orientation. Bebel shrieks a little and then turns to me with a huge grin on her face.

"June!" she says.

"Bebel?"

"Good luck!"

"Uh . . . thanks. You too."

Ieyascu raps her desk and we turn back to face her, abruptly. "The final decision will be made in winter, at the end of the summer king's term. Until that point, you will do whatever you can to prove to the Queen that you have the talent to make yourself worthy of the honor. You submit nothing formally to her. Rest assured that having picked you out of the hundred thousand eligible wakas, she has her eye on your endeavors, and you should strive to make them as impressive as possible."

Bebel is glowing bright as her fake honey hair. She's a singer and a musician, which is why we're on the same art track. I can see her already confecting visions of being featured on all the feeds, of the rapturous audiences who will fall over themselves to compliment her talent.

She's Bebel the Perfect, and I know that whoever the other eight wakas are, she has a good chance of winning.

But I'm her competition, and that means she won't. I remember that other contest, that utter failure, and feel a gladness close to fury that I've been given this second chance. To prove myself to him, to do something with my art so great that no one can deny it.

Bebel leaves before me, dashing out the door with most un-Bebel-like haste, probably to gloat with her friends. Ieyascu's voice reels me back before I can escape as well.

"June," she says. Her voice is softer, almost weary. She's standing beside one of her glass walls, which she's turned into a window. For a moment, I swear she looks *old*, like in the video-holos of the twentieth century, all wrinkled and broken down. The effect passes and she straightens her shoulders.

"I hope, for Yaha's sake, that you rise to this occasion. We've all noticed how you've been slipping this past year. If you fall now — well, let's just say that Yaha will have a lot to answer for, Auntie or not."

I open my mouth to say something, but nothing comes out. Quick as that, my joy at this opportunity has turned cold and bitter.

Like everything Mother and Auntie Yaha touch these days.

"Thank you," I say, almost meaning it. "I'll do my best."

Auntie Yaha is with Ueda-sama when I find her in the hallway outside her office. The ambassador seems to recognize me from the coronation party, but he offers me his hand and his name. Auntie Yaha is wary, but she passes off my interruption as though she were expecting me.

"My stepdaughter, June," she says, her smile somehow conveying reassurance despite not being particularly genuine. "Ueda-sama is the chief ambassador of Tokyo 10."

"Enchanted," I say. "I hope you're having a nice time in our city. I believe I saw you the other night at the party?"

He nods vigorously. "Such interesting customs you have here, June. The trouble of translation . . . I'd been led to imagine your summer king was some sort of consort for your Queen. And I now see it's quite different."

"Consort?" I say, smiling. Auntie Yaha will kill me when this is over, and I don't care at all. "Well, there's some of that too, don't get me wrong. I don't see much hope for Enki and Oreste, but you're right, it wasn't very good manners for Enki to ignore her like that on his election day. Moon year kings don't have any power — I'm sure she thought he wouldn't dare."

Auntie Yaha discreetly attempts to steer Ueda-sama farther down the hall, but he pauses, forcing her to hover behind him like some lost camera bot. "No power? I had it explained to me rather differently."

Auntie Yaha's mask is slipping. "Power isn't that simple a matter, June."

"Funny," I say, "I've noticed that."

I think that's when she realizes what this is about. She nods her head slowly and then turns to Ueda-sama with a blinding smile and a reassuring pat on the back. Somehow, she convinces him to wait in her office while she marches me to the far end of the hallway. No need to worry about eavesdroppers so deep in Royal Tower, with its sound-proof walls and strict anti-bot policy.

"I thought you'd be happy," she says. Something I appreciate about Auntie Yaha: At least she can drop the act every once in a while. Unlike her wife. "This is what you wanted."

"Not because you bought it for me!"

"You're talented, June. You know that. I just made sure it came to the Queen's attention. I didn't need to do more. I know you've always wanted this."

I want to scream, but I have a feeling that it would draw undue attention even in this place. "And who did I push out, Yaha? What amazing waka's life have I ruined, and she doesn't even know it? All so you can go back home and tell Mother that you've bribed me a future?"

It's strange, Auntie Yaha has only known me for two years, but she's the one I can hurt. And so I always try to hurt her.

I know what that says about me.

"Your mother didn't ask me to do this."

My surprise feels a little like disappointment. Mother's interference has always been so reliable. Has she even given up on that?

"She'll still blame me if I make you lose your post."

Yaha puts that reassuring hand on my shoulder. "You'll do fine, June," she says.

I shake it off. I wish I could have gotten the nomination on my own, but it doesn't matter now. I've always had something to prove. "I'll *win*."

Gil sees Enki once more that week, though they're discreet enough to keep it off all but the most speculative gossip feeds. Gil isn't in school the next day and I finally find him that evening, half naked in his mother's garden, blasting the latest from King Zumbi, one of the verde's biggest blocos, and dancing with a sunflower.

"She any good?" I ask when I'm close enough to hear him over the music.

Gil plants a kiss in the middle of the sunflower's dark brown center and laughs. "She's beautiful," he says. He reaches for my hand and, despite myself, I dance with him for a little while. I can't refuse Gil when he's so present and happy. I force all thoughts about the last dance out of my mind; it's easier than I would have guessed.

Maybe my feelings weren't hurt as much as my pride, after all.

We dance until his sweat gleams in the sunlight and my shirt feels damp. I break it off, 'cause on his own Gil would dance until he passed out (he has, I've seen it), and dip my feet in the koi pond to cool off.

Gil does a back handspring and seems for a moment like he might keep moving. He still has it, I can see, that manic energy that sometimes nothing can dissipate. But I raise my eyebrows at him and he takes a deep breath and sits beside me.

"I've been nominated for the Queen's Award," I tell him in a rush. It was hard to hold it in this long, but it's no good talking when he needs to dance.

"June!" He hugs me and I let myself enjoy the thrill of his surprise and approval before I have to ruin it with the truth.

"Auntie Yaha pulled strings," I say. "I didn't really earn it. But I'll win anyway, no matter what I have to do. There won't be anything she can say to me if I win it."

Gil looks sad, as he always does when I talk about my family. "You mean your mamãe?"

"Papai too," I say softly. "He'd be proud, I'm sure of it. I'll make real art. Great art."

Gil's jittery, almost vibrating. I rub my hand up and down his sweat-slick back until he relaxes a little and leans into it. "Nice night?" I say.

"Dazzling," he says, like a sigh. "Enki is . . ."

I hold my breath.

"Just like he seems. Only, deeper."

"I'm so happy for you, Gil."

"Don't be. I think I'm drowning in him. And I'm hardly his only one."

"Well," I say, flicking my toes at a carp that gets too close. "He's hardly your only one either."

Gil and I solved our virginity problem together a few years ago, but unlike him, I haven't done much since.

"He could be. June, he could. Last night, he took me to the very top, to the light, and he pushed me back against that hot glass. I thought it would burn me, and we did it again and again."

I imagine it and feel myself flushing. "That doesn't sound very discreet."

Gil laughs. "I don't know, he said he talked to the bots and they promised to leave us alone."

"He *talked* . . . what does that even mean?"

"How should I know? Maybe it's a new mod?"

But I'm almost sure the Aunties don't have anything that would let a human chat with a bot. I wonder what Enki is doing. If he's getting himself into trouble, will he drag Gil into it also? Suddenly, I'm very glad that Enki picked Gil instead of me. If my dreamy love for him had turned this hard and real, I don't know how I'd be able to deal with it.

"Gil," I say, holding his hand until he looks at me. "Listen. You do what you want to do, that's the way it's always been, and I don't want to change that. But Enki is the summer king. The *summer king*, Gil. He stopped being a boy you could love the moment Oreste crowned him, and he will be dead this time next year. So you can't let yourself . . . I mean, I don't want you to . . . don't be hurt. That's all. I just don't want you to hurt."

I never thought he'd get mad at me, but I thought maybe he'd be dismissive and mocking. I thought maybe he'd tell me I couldn't understand because I'm so inexperienced. But he just starts to cry.

"He told me about the others," he says. I wrap my arms around his waist, hold him. "I asked. It shouldn't have meant anything. It did."

"Maybe that's what the moon year is for, querido. Make us love him and break our hearts."

"Enki is different."

He is. I think that's what makes this worse.

This is the story of a war between the wakas and the grandes.

You might think I'm speaking of something universal, of youth and age, because I've read the classics and the teachers would have us believe that's all we're seeing here, a repeat of that endless struggle between virility and senescence, between spontaneity and care, between creativity and knowledge.

You know, insert your bullshit here.

Here's the thing: There hasn't been "age" in that old-fashioned, *Dorian Gray* sense in about two hundred years. Ever since the Hoshigawa technique was perfected back when men were still only 30 percent of the world population. Death before a hundred and fifty has become optional. And these days, two hundred is pretty much guaranteed. Ms. Hoshigawa herself only died last year, the day after her two hundred and fifty-first birthday. Vertical cities around the world had a day of mourning. Gil and I celebrated the day on the rock of A Castanha in the bay, getting drunk on cachaça and chalking doodles on wet stone.

"Kill me if I ever get that old," Gil said.

"Hey, by the time we hit two hundred and fifty, there will probably be grandes twice our age."

He grimaced. "What's the point of *life*, June, if you don't live it?"

"Some do. Some grandes live."

"While they suffocate the rest of us."

I couldn't deny it. Just that morning, I'd gotten a polite rejection from yet another gallery, saying they only accepted work from "mature" artists. At this rate, I wouldn't get so much as a painting in a show before I turned forty.

"Your mamãe has lots of work, these days," I said, trying to make that doomed feeling in my stomach go away. "She's almost a waka, and designing dresses for Aunties."

Gil hurled our empty bottle off the cliff. It biodegraded as soon as it hit the water. "And when they realize how old she is, grandes still look at me like I must be half feral."

I bit my lip. I wondered when it would be okay for Gil and his mamãe; when her talent and maturity would matter more than her age, as though she could never be good enough with a son just sixteen years younger.

"Grandes can be assholes," I said finally.

Gil sighed and closed his eyes. We were silent for a long time, so long I got sleepy and rested my head on his shoulder. Through my lidded eyes, I could see water bluer than the sky, and the city like some clean and bright geometric heaven. Gil stroked my hair and I felt warm and happy as a lizard in the sun.

"Will you kiri, Gil?" It was my greatest fear, but at that moment the terror couldn't touch me. I felt as though I could see us both too clearly for fear.

"Maybe," he said. "Probably. Yes."

I knew. I don't know how, but I did. "Not too soon," I said.

"No, of course not. God, we're only sixteen."

My papai was a hundred and forty.

Had been a hundred and forty.

The first time the lights go out in Palmares Três, Gil and I are in the third row of the orchestra seats in City Hall, awaiting the summer king's first public address. The first two rows are filled with important people, mostly Aunties, but a few other dignitaries. I even see three Uncles — men who have entered politics, though they're not as influential as Aunties. Quite a few sun year summer kings have been Uncles.

It's been a week since Enki's election and I'm exhausted. I've spent the past two nights feverishly sketching, designing, and discarding one idea after another. I need to strike quickly and brilliantly if I want to prove myself to the Queen and the other finalists. It's an open secret that Auntie Yaha got me in — it probably would be even if it weren't true, and that makes me hate what she did even more.

Bebel is already planning a free concert in Gria Plaza. I wish I didn't know, because it's only making me crazier, but of course she had to *tell* me in that way of hers, like we're best friends and not implacable enemies. She even had the nerve to ask Gil to dance for her, but he refused.

I almost stayed at home. I have more important things to think about than even Enki, but Gil begged and so of course I agreed. You don't abandon a friend in love. And if my heart races at the thought of seeing him again, well, I'm a waka with a pulse. That doesn't mean I want him.

There are camera bots everywhere and occasionally they buzz near the two of us, but I stare straight ahead and pretend not to notice. Right now, I want to be invisible. I want to come up with an idea that will make Bebel look like she's leading a sing-along at a birthday party. And when it's ready, I want the world to know my name.

"I still think you should do the garden," Gil says. "Vines growing out of the trains? You'd definitely get attention."

"It's too derivative. Juliana Consecu did that installation with roses five years ago, remember? Everyone will think I'm just imitating her."

"And the graffiti? We both know you're great at that." He flashes me a smile and I catch myself wondering how much the bots can hear, and if anyone could possibly put together his cryptic statement with the painting that interrupted the royal tour six days ago.

"Not so great," I say way too casually, and then Gil finally realizes that maybe we should be more careful.

The truth is, I am good at graffiti, but I'm not sure I'm better than the big grafiteiros from the verde, and I don't know how the Queen feels about it as an art form. It's not technically illegal in public spaces, but the bots sure do get rid of it quickly.

"Oh, God," I say, burying my head in my hands, "I have no idea! I swear, I could kill Auntie Yaha."

"You'd rather not be a finalist?"

I glower at him, because he knows I wanted this more than anything. It's more than a second chance: It's the only chance.

Gil rubs my arm. "When they see what you can do, no one will care who your stepmother is."

A moment later, the lights dim to a cool twilight. Auntie Isa walks onto the stage, wearing her official red turban.

"Thank you, all," she says when she reaches the podium. "Tonight marks the beginning of a very special time for all citizens of our great city. We Aunties and the Queen are incredibly pleased by the election of Enki as our new summer king, and we have full confidence that he will fulfill the duties of the position as befits the royalty of Palmares Três."

She waits for dutiful applause, while Gil and I look at each other meaningfully. "Looks like Enki has already pissed off the Aunties," I say.

"I bet they're even sadder they didn't rig it for Pasqual."

"And now, I present to you our summer king!"

Auntie Isa steps to the side of the podium, clapping her gloved hands politely. Gil and I go crazy, along with about half the audience. Now that I'm here my heart pounds and my lights flash and all I can think is how much I want to see his face again. Gil is so lucky.

Enki walks out. He wears all black this time, and it reminds me of my hunting outfit. But who would he have to hide from, up on that stage?

He waits for the noise to subside, though it takes a while. In the meantime, he nods politely at a few familiar faces in the audience: Gil, a few of the Aunties, the ambassador from Tokyo 10. His eyes slide over me like water. I had wondered if he even saw me, suspended in the air above Gil. I suppose I have my answer.

Eventually we grow quiet and Enki smiles. Gil groans a little.

"Thank you," he says, as though he means it. "Here's something I thought you might like."

I have time to catch Auntie Maria glancing at the woman next to her, and then there's a noise like a rainstorm and the whole world disappears.

For a moment, I think I've gone blind. Then someone two rows away flashes a portable light and I realize what's happened.

The lights — the famous lights of Palmares Três — have gone out.

"June?"

That's Gil, groping for my hand. People are shouting. Nearby, someone prays.

And then, as abruptly as they went out, the lights come back on.

The room goes eerily silent. We look around. It's not hard to see what's changed.

There are about thirty wakas onstage instead of Enki. They're dressed in fraying sackcloth and their feet are bare. From the back of the audience, the drums start.

It's a mad rhythm, reminiscent of what Enki did for the Queen, but wilder. The wakas onstage move as if they might die if they sit still. Beside me, Gil is gaping. His hips twitch. A camera bot comes too close and bounces off my forehead. The audience seems torn between laughter and outrage. En masse, the Aunties leave their seats in the first two rows and head deep into Royal Tower for damage control.

It takes me a moment to recover from my surprise and understand what this means. The wakas are from the verde, the poorest part of our city, and their clothes recall the slavery of our ancestors. Their clothes, their dance, Enki's presence speak more eloquently than words: What does this distant Queen know of the verde? What has she done for it? The hypocrisy of Palmares Três dances on that stage, and though it shocks me, I can't help but want to join them.

Gil and I look at each other. Barefoot wakas are laughing and dancing.

"Shall we?" Gil says.

I nod, grip his hand, and we leap over the chairs to reach the aisle. The wakas onstage welcome us inside, and before we know it there are a dozen more, then the entire theater has filled with us dancing and clapping like it's carnival already, and all the grandes just stare and cluck their tongues.

And that's when I realize it.

From one artist to another, he said.

Enki is an artist — just like me.

*   *   *

I wear my hunting outfit, though I suppose regular clothes would do, because it feels like armor and I need every advantage I have to make it through this night.

I've decided on a project for the Queen's Award.

It turns out that all I needed was the right partner.

I go to Tier Ten, where only the Queen and the highest-ranking Aunties have their apartments. More like palaces, really, and so high up in the pyramid that the city regulates the oxygen content in the air. The pod takes me up but balks when I want to open the door.

A face I recognize, but can't quite place, hovers on the pod's tiny holo.

"Yaha?" she says. "What do you need so late?"

"Oh," I say, and it doesn't take much to induce a blush. "I'm so sorry. It's just . . ."

"Who are you?" says the woman. Her bobbing head gets larger — she's leaning in to look at me.

"Ah, I'm so sorry!" I say, sounding like a moron and grateful for it. "It's just that I'm so desperate to see Enki, so I took my stepmother's flash. . . ."

She sighs. "You're Yaha's stepdaughter? I'm afraid the summer king isn't taking visitors, dear."

"Oh, but can't you just ask him! Tell him I'd do anything —"

"I can pass a message, June, but it's not my place to interrupt the summer king for this sort of . . . well."

My smile feels as if it lights my face. *This will work.* "Oh, thank you! Tell him I'd like to see him, like one artist to another. Is that okay?"

The woman smiles. "It's lovely, dear. I hope you get what you want. Now, I'm telling your pod to take you back home, all right?"

I nod and her image flicks out. I'm very still on the ride home.

All I can do now is wait.

*   *   *

The ping the next day is anonymous, and has only two words: *spider-web midnight.*

I don't tell Gil. I'm not sure why, except if Enki refuses me, at least only the two of us will know I failed. And besides, Gil might make the same assumption as the Tier Ten gatekeeper. This isn't about sex. This isn't a love story. I'm not doing this so a king can choose me and make me special.

I'm doing this so two artists can create work together that they could never imagine alone.

So I'm on my own again, pod-hopping in my hunting outfit until I make it to the verde. It's even harder from there. I find one of the horizontal transport tunnels, the kind that delivers goods straight to the industrial heart of the city. There's no way to hop a pod through these. The only vehicles allowed to go through are used by the engineers, and they shut down except for emergencies at the end of the workday.

So I have to crawl.

As I'm creeping along the ceiling (the only place in these old tunnels safe from electrocution), I wonder how Enki will manage to get there. He's from the verde, so perhaps he knows the ways the gangs use. I've heard rumors of easier walking paths, but I don't know them. If everyone had to use nanohooks in the transport tunnels, trips to the heart would be pretty much limited to spoiled Tier Eight kids with access to technology of questionable legality.

But I know his choice of location is a test. If I can't get there on my own, then there's no way I could be the one who did that graffiti; then I really am the ditzy waka I seemed.

By the time I reach the internal node that marks the end of the first transport tunnel, my back is soaked with sweat. From here, the way is easier. The spider warehouse is down a short tunnel from the main node.

I don't have to worry about security bots or even a door blocking the way to the sleeping mechanical giants. Spider bots are so massive and old there's not much worth stealing. I climb down the ladder as silently as possible, but even my breath seems to echo off their giant silver bellies.

"Hello?" I whisper.

Nothing.

I check my fono for the time, which is a few minutes after midnight. Is he late? Did he leave when I didn't show up exactly on time? I shake my head and walk farther into the maze. No, not after going through all this trouble. He'd want to see who I am.

"Gil is my friend," I whisper, a little louder this time. "But the casters love him, and I don't want them to know about this."

I look around and see nothing but my face, reflected and distorted in a dozen giant silver thoraxes.

And then, something darker.

"You're the one from that first night, aren't you? The girl with the lights."

He leans against a spider to my right. His white shirt is unmistakable; I don't know how I missed him.

"I didn't think you saw me," I say, after a thick swallow. The force of his physical presence is stronger than I remembered. My eyes trace the lean muscles in his arms before I realize what I'm doing and focus firmly on his eyes.

"Did I?" he says nonsensically. "I must have. Gil was . . . memorable."

"He has that effect on people."

Enki smiles and steps closer to me. "So that explains the mural? I thought it was one of the grafiteiros from the verde, but of course not, it had to be someone who knew him."

Enki stops talking and walks around me, a man looking over an expensive bot he might just buy. I make myself still, though inside I am trembling and hot. I swore this wouldn't be a fairy tale, and now it isn't. But I'm afraid of what that makes it.

"What do you propose, June Costa?"

I move in front of him, deliberately cutting his circuit short. Before I can think, I reach out, touch his shoulder with my gloved hand, and feel the suck of the activating nanohooks. His eyes widen. I have bound us, and he knows it.

He is so beautiful, so warm and cruel and distant that I think, without the connection, I might just run away.

"You're an artist," I say. "And I don't think anyone but me truly understands what you mean by that. Not that you paint or you sculpt or you see the world in colors. You mean that you manipulate, that you express yourself on objects and use them to express you. You mean that when you chose to be the summer king, you chose to use your own body as a canvas that no one could ignore." I have to stop for a moment, catch my breath. If this works, not even Bebel can beat me for the Queen's Award.

"That's very interesting." But his pupils have dilated, turning his light eyes black. He is precisely my height, and our eyes are locked as firmly as my hand on his shoulder.

"And in exchange," I say, barely a whisper, "you die."

"It seemed a fair trade."

"Let me help you."

"Why should I?"

"My name is June," I say, "and I'm the best artist in Palmares Três."

It hurts, and I wondered for a while if the Aunties made it like that so we go quietly to the slaughter. But now I see that it has to be this way, that you cannot force the human body, the human mind in such unnatural directions without a payment. In the Tokyos, they have subverted this rule, continued their self-augmentation until the body itself became uninhabitable. They haven't transcended the body as they say. Of course they haven't. Who wouldn't rather be neurons and synapses and electrochemicals and sweet, sticky orgasms? They live in their data streams because their bodies won't have them.

My body won't have me.

Did you realize this, when we first made our pact in that mausoleum to ancient technology? You said my body was a canvas.

But a human canvas can't live. It can only flare and make a record of its dying.

This is a record of my dying.

SUMMER

On the twenty-fifth of December, Enki and I look over the bare cliff edge of O Quilombola, the easternmost island in the bay. We are arguing, because we always argue, and I'm thinking that I'm in no danger of falling in love with him, since right now I feel *in hate* with him, though that isn't really true either.

"Just blast it open, June," he says, and kicks a cascade of volcanic scree into the rippling waters a hundred meters below.

I gulp and remind myself that I'm wearing my nanohook boots. In the city, a monument to the comforts of technology, this is reassuring. Out here, in the raw embrace of nature, I've never felt more exposed.

"We'll destroy the cliff face. There'll be nothing left to plant the lights on. Plus, you know, the Aunties will kill you."

Enki turns to me, dreadlocks swinging, and smiles that slow, mad smile.

"I don't know if you heard this," he says, leaning out at a dangerous angle over the water, "but they're already planning to."

I grimace. "You know what I mean."

"Of course I do, bem-querer. You're saying that we shouldn't deface public property for art."

I open my mouth. Close it again. "That is not —"

"Exactly what you mean?"

"It's an *island*, Enki. It's been sitting in this bay, minding its business for the last ten thousand years. Can't we just . . . work with it?"

He leans out all the way. The nanohooks in his shoes catch him, of course, but I still shriek. Enki giggles and hangs, an upside-down crucifixion, Prometheus laughing on the rock. The sun brings out the blues in his skin and the fleeting glitter of some of the mods he won't explain.

"Work with it?" he repeats. But I don't say anything, because by now I recognize his *considering* voice. He detaches one foot and settles himself into an upside-down crouch.

"O Quilombola," he says, caressing the rock, "will you help us make you beautiful?"

I purse my lips, but they still turn up in a smile. "What does he say?"

"He says . . . he says there are crab holes."

This is strange, even for Enki. I kneel on the cliff edge, pray to Yemanjá, and lean as far out as I can, my nanohooks firmly planted on the rock.

"You okay down there?"

Enki clucks his tongue, but I can't see his face. He's looking at something beneath him. "Always worrying, always worrying."

"Someone has to be down here on the ground."

"And me in midair?"

My breath stutters in my chest. My blood rushes to my head. I should get up — Enki isn't going anywhere — but I can't. The song he's referencing is old-classical and rare, not even South American. "How do you know all this music, Enki?"

He's still looking at something in the rock. I don't know how he hasn't passed out yet, hanging upside down. He must have found some sort of crevice, because his right arm has disappeared to the elbow.

"How do you, June?"

"My papai," I say. "I asked first."

"My mamãe."

This renders me silent again. Suddenly, Enki laughs, and pulls out his arm. He holds a bright green crab still dripping with water.

"O Quilombola has an answer," he says. "Here," and without any further warning, hands me the crab. I grip it by its head, trying very hard not to shudder. I like crabs plenty when they're cooked, but right now its helplessly flailing legs remind me of a mushi bot.

"You want to make art with crabs?"

"That's one way of looking at it." He turns back around and sticks his hand in a different hole, a meter below the first.

"Why am I holding this?"

"Because it's wet."

"Genius, Enki."

"Oh, you can't figure it out, June?"

Against my better judgment, I carefully disengage my right boot, twist for a vertigo-inducing moment, and take a step farther down the rock. I do it one more time, so my head is finally level with Enki's.

"It's a crab," I say. "Why wouldn't it be wet?"

Enki pulls his hand out of the rock. He's holding another crab, smaller, but the same species.

"Also wet," he says. He lets the crab skitter up his arm before it hops onto the rock and disappears down another hole.

"You think the crabs are climbing from the ocean through the rock holes?"

"How else would they get up here?"

"Crawling?"

Enki detaches his left boot, so he's swinging wildly on the sheer cliff face. I watch him with what feels like a crab in my throat, knowing that at just the slightest wrong angle the nanohooks could give way. He's laughing, of course he is, swaying like a pendulum right by my face. Our noses brush and my breath comes out in a fierce exhale.

"A demonstration," he says.

"You know the water is twenty meters beneath us, right?"

He stops his wild swinging and reaches for my free hand. I'm terrified, but I relax a little when he twines his fingers in mine. This isn't the first time — sometimes Enki just likes to touch — but it never gets any easier. In my head, the two of us are all and only about art, but that doesn't stop my skin from tingling and my stomach from leaping into my throat. I've gotten good at ignoring it. With his other hand, he reaches for the crab, still struggling weakly.

"Now watch," he says, and puts the crab down on the cliff face.

It tries to scramble into a hole but Enki shoos it away. Enki *herds* it, until it goes farther down the cliff edge. And he follows.

Of course, he's still holding my hand and he won't let go. My arm stretches. I shriek, but he doesn't even look at me.

"You bastard!" I yell, but even then I'm detaching a boot, planting it on the rock, detaching the other —

— all so I can *walk* down a cliff face at the behest of the summer king.

"You are insane!" I say, and he just laughs.

I think he wants to run, but he can't with me along, and I don't know whether I should feel grateful that he won't leave me alone or terrified. The poor crab doesn't know what to do. Enki shoos it away from every hole, every other direction it might want to go except for down, down, down.

And then something very strange happens.

We hit a part of the cliff that's smooth and sheer, straight down to the water below. It's not any harder for our nanohook boots. Scared as I am, I don't even think about the sudden lack of pitted rock and protuberances. But the crab, that poor crab scuttles and slides, straight down the cliff face and into the water below.

Enki and I turn to each other at the same moment. "You knew that would happen?" I say.

He shrugs. "I just guessed."

I look back down. The crab was swimming a moment before, but now it's disappeared. "They climb up through the rock," I say.

"Which means it's probably honeycombed with passages."

"We can just thread the lights through it! Light it up from the inside!"

Enki closes his eyes for a moment. As if the world has turned too beautiful for him to even look at. My hand tightens around his, and I look for both of us.

"Should we jump?" he says.

His eyes have opened again.

"Enki . . ."

"Come on, June," he says. "Sometimes you have to step out."

That's what Gil says. I wonder if that's where he first heard it.

I know he's expecting me to plant my feet in the rock and refuse to do anything so dangerous. But he's right, and I've done so many crazy things these past few months I don't see how I can draw the line here.

"We won't cut ourselves on the rock?"

"Nah, see the dark blue? It's one of the deepest parts of the bay."

"All right."

Enki lets off a yell loud enough to send a few birds on the rock above screeching away.

"On three," he says. My thighs are burning from the effort of holding myself horizontal for so long. The sun is hot and sizzling on my exposed neck and arms. Enki's hand is as warm as a lamp beneath mine.

My heart feels like it might explode.

He counts steady and slow. I'm ready — if we don't do this at exactly the same moment, we'll need a medic to get us off the island.

I feel his *three* like a heartbeat.

For a moment I am empty. For a moment I am flying and I am flying and Enki is the other me at the end of my arm and the blue of the water above us is the same as the sky below.

Our shouts echo in tandem. A defiant scream at the Aunties and the Queen and every grande in Palmares Três.

We hit the water. We plunge deep inside, and I'm shocked at how icy it is despite the searing heat of the sun above. I open my eyes. Enki's hair billows around him like sea anemones. A few feet away from us, fish nibble on a bed of seaweed. And crabs — dozens and dozens of green crabs just like the one Enki chased down here — crawl in and out of the gaping holes in the rock.

Underwater, sound is strange. All I can hear is close and far away. My heartbeat and Enki's, pounding like ceremonial drums. A pod of dolphins calling to one another too far out to see. The sunlight filters down in streams so clear they look like bars of gold.

Enki runs his hand through the cloud of my hair. He smiles, because Enki thinks the world is beautiful.

I kick first and he follows me, up through this quiet, sun-streamed world and back into the air. I gasp when we break the surface, get a little of my breath back, all so I can laugh.

I rub the brackish bay water from my eyes. "That . . . was . . . amazing!"

Enki smiles. "Happy Christmas, June."

I'd forgotten. Most Palmarinas don't celebrate it, though I've heard that in Salvador there are traditional Catholics who celebrate it like carnival. Maybe that's why Enki gave me the present of this day: for the memory of his mother's home, in the summer of our own.

Gil comes over that evening for our monthly family dinner. Mother has insisted upon it since Papai's death, no matter how much I protest. I think at this point she does it to spite me. Gil comes when he can to help lessen the tension, but today I dread the upcoming two hours of stilted conversation and waylay him on the stairs to our house.

"What do you say we ditch and find a bloco party in Founders Park?"

He perches on the end of the railing and pretends to consider. "I don't think it's anyone good tonight."

"It could be a howler monkey, Gil, I'd still dance."

"Bad day?"

I think about Enki under the water, and my hair, which has dried into a saltwater Afro I refuse to comb out.

"It's been sort of perfect."

Gil tilts his head. He knows I've been out with Enki today, and the considering look in his eyes makes me say nervously, "Just our project. It's going to be amazing." I don't want him to think there's anything more than that between me and Enki.

He leaves it alone. "And what makes you think this will be any less?"

"Mother? Auntie Yaha? You've heard of them?"

"Could be worse. You get to spend an evening with three people who love you."

My expression could make one of his sunflowers turn away, but Gil just meets it, eyebrows raised higher than my own. "Well, at least I love you, menina, so it'll have to do."

"Oh," I say, "you're smoother than glass. Let's get this over with."

I don't tell him how happy his words make me. That's not how Gil and I work.

Besides, he knows anyway.

Mother is sitting at the table when we walk in, sipping red wine with her thick, loosely curled hair uncharacteristically down. Auntie Yaha lights actual wax-burning candles. Even I've noticed how hard she's been trying since I confronted her about the Queen's Award. I can't bring myself to appreciate it.

"Gil!" she says, and kisses him on both cheeks. "We're so glad you could come."

"Yes," says Mother. "You've been so busy lately."

I glare at Mother, noting the hint of disapproval in her tone, but Gil just smiles. "Never too busy for June."

Auntie Yaha gives one of her smoothing-over chuckles and then we all sit down. Gil could have a bright future as a diplomat if it weren't for the dancing.

Well, that and his flamboyant choice in sexual partners.

He and Enki have hardly been exclusive with each other in the last two months, but they remain the golden couple of all the gossip casters. I can always tell when Gil's been with Enki, because he moves like he might start dancing at any moment and he hardly hears a word I say to him.

Enki, on the other hand, is a cipher. The gossip casters say he's with someone nearly every night, but I wouldn't be able to tell from his demeanor with me. He almost never mentions Gil, and when he does, I can't tell how he feels about him. I can hardly tell how Enki feels about *me*. Not that I care, so long as we get to make our art together.

Gil asked me once if Enki loved him. I said that maybe summer kings don't feel things the way we do. Maybe with everything so compressed and escalated, he can't really love like a human with another two hundred years in front of her. That made Gil cry, so I stopped talking.

I can smell the food — hot peppers and coconut milk and stewed shrimp and that unmistakable musk of palm oil for deep-frying — but the table is bare. Instead, Mother holds out her hands to either side and after a shocked moment I realize that she means for us to join hands. All of us. Together.

Auntie Yaha leads by example and holds Mother's and Gil's hands. Gil gives me a little smile and I hold his and Mother's.

A circle, complete.

"I thought we'd give our thanks," Mother says.

We are hardly a religious family. The last time I've even seen the inside of a city shrine was a week after Papai died. When he was alive, sometimes Papai would lead us in a song, usually a Christian hymn or a song for Yemanjá, so we could "honor our ancestors." No one took it very seriously — Papai just loved music, and we'd humor him.

I want to refuse, but Mother looks deadly serious and I can't bear to make this go sour so early. So I duck my head.

"Yemanjá and Ogum, divine orixás who have blessed this city, may you also bless my daughter, and guide her through these pivotal moments, so that she might keep the gifts of her youth and gain the wisdom of her elders. May she not squander her great opportunities on pursuits she might later come to regret. May she reach her full flower as the composed, polished adult I know she can —"

"Mamãe!"

I rip my hand from her increasingly tight grip. Her head snaps up and we glare at each other — she wants to intimidate me, but I'm her daughter, and I learned how to match her years ago.

"It's a *blessing*, June."

"Sounded like a lecture to me."

"Well, how else can I make you listen?"

"I promise, I'm not listening."

"Your papai —"

I stand. The chair rocks on its legs, the only sound in the room. "You will not. Not him."

Auntie Yaha puts her hand on my shoulder. I shake it off. "June," she says, "honey, just sit down, okay? We don't have to talk about any of this if you don't want to."

I can't take my eyes off Mother. "*She's* the one who started it!"

"You're the one who was nominated for the most prestigious award in the city and won't lift a finger to win it! Do you know what your stepmother has been going through at work because of your neglect?"

"Valencia, don't —"

"Someone has to say it, Yaha. June has been squandering everyone's goodwill and all of her talent. She has us walking on eggshells around her because of her papai, and I'm done!"

"Stop talking about Papai!"

"Why, June? I lost him too."

The blood rushing past my ears sounds like the ocean, that noisy quiet with my heartbeat buried inside. I feel Gil's hands on my shoulders. He guides me away from the table. My feet follow.

I don't know where we're going. I can't think. It's been so long since I've seen my papai, sometimes his face blurs in my memory. I can't remember if he had a mole in front of his left ear or right, or how long his mustache was. But sometimes I hear his voice. He tells me not to care what others think. He says, "Find your own fulfillment, June," and usually this makes me happier, only now I can't stop shaking.

Gil has taken me outside, to our tiny garden that a woman from the verde comes to weed and water twice a week. It's not near as nice as Gil's, but anything is better than that dining table and its wax-burning candles.

Gil doesn't say anything. He just holds me as we look across the bay. The sun has mostly vanished, but in its lingering glow we can see the humps of the four siblings like sleeping gods. I imagine how they will look when Enki and I are done with them, and something in me manages to smile. They'll be worthy of Papai. *He* would be proud of me, I'm sure of it, the opposite of Mother and her endless opprobrium.

Gil looks at me. He pulls at the end of one of my curls and flicks off the crusted salt.

"Feel better?"

"I hate her."

"I know, menina."

"I told you they don't love me."

Gil just sighs, and I wonder why he's so sure they do.

"Have you thought of telling them why you're not doing anything for the Queen's Award?"

"Yaha is an *Auntie*. The whole point of this is to create the art before they can stop me, and then reveal everything in the fall." I plan to make a big splash in the middle of the year, and then build on it publicly until the end.

"I know. But if you ask her, I bet Auntie Yaha won't tell the others. And it would make your mother feel better."

I snort. "Because I really care about that."

Except, I do, sometimes. I remember the way that we used to be before Papai died. We were never as close as Papai and I, but we didn't hate each other. I didn't sometimes imagine what it would be like if she chose to kiri and feel this terrible satisfaction.

I don't want her to die, I'm almost sure I don't.

"It's okay to cry," he says.

"Gil, you know I hate it when you sound like an agony auntie."

He laughs. "Am I wrong?"

"It's fine for you to cry. You're a beautiful boy."

"So girls don't cry? June, I never knew you were so conventional."

I've cried in front of Gil before, but not since Papai died.

"You know," I say, "Mother taught me to paint? She's not that good, really, but she saw how I loved to smear my fingers in anything, so she bought me one of those child-safe kits and a big canvas. We painted food. Is that strange? I don't know, but I thought there wasn't anything more beautiful than the bright red of a shrimp in a vatapá stew. The green of that cilantro. I tried to paint the smells too. I'm sure it just looked like blobs of paint, but she swore she loved them. Papai was sad because he'd thought I might do music like him, but Mamãe . . ." Could it be that, once, her interest in my art wasn't about Papai? Only about helping me find myself?

The moment the sun completes its descent, the lights of Palmares Três switch on, bathing the bay in their gentle white glow.

Then they blur, and I'm not surprised or ashamed.

I'm called June because I was born on the first day of June, though that's not much of an explanation since I'm called June, not Júnia or something. English names aren't unheard of. There are still some English families in Palmares Três, ones who came here during the great migration after the plague and the bombs and the cold, gray fallout (we just ended up with something like seasons, but the poor North Americans! I know there are still some people who live in New York, but I'd die if I had to wear thermal underwear every day).

So the real reason is my mamãe. Mother.

Her grandfather was English, someplace way north. Toronto, I think, or Glasgow. One of those lost cities. He had a daughter from before he even met my great-grandmother, and her name was April.

He kept a few pictures of her and somehow they survived. They're flat, but otherwise bright and clear. April is about my age in them, and she's wearing weird clothes, a blue robe and a square hat with some sort of fringe. Mother says it's a graduation photo, and that's what they would wear centuries ago. April doesn't look a thing like me: She has straight blonde hair, her skin is milk pale like most North Americans, and her lips are thin, but in her eyes I think I can see a little of my mother. They are wide and stare straight ahead, like a sword that could pierce you. They're not eyes that make many friends, and they don't really care.

A few years after that photo was taken, my great-grandfather and April became refugees, escaping from the wars and the piles of corpses and the cold, which was worse back then. They hear about this city in what was Brazil, a new pyramid city, built from a Japanese design, called Palmares Três. Not too many people were escaping to Bahia back then, let alone white North Americans. But for some reason, April loved Brazil. That's the part of the story where Mother gets a little misty-eyed, don't ask me why. Mother and her immigrant stories. Apparently, April had been studying Portuguese in school, and she was obsessed with classical music, though I guess it wasn't classical back then. And she convinced her father that they should escape south. The other North Americans were heading to their west coast (just in time for an atomic bomb to hit San Francisco, naturally), and some of them even tried to go overseas to West Africa or East Asia. But April wanted samba, Mother says, she wanted a city of women, because men had done so much to destroy the world. So she and my great-grandfather went to Bahia.

It took them two years, mostly on foot, and a lot of the time there were wars and natural disasters they couldn't push their way through. But they came as some of the very first registered immigrants. The city wasn't even half built yet. But if I go to the public library, I can access their names on the registries. There's even a photo of the two of them, and April looks so different in that one it frightens me. Her skin is darker — still too pale for Palmares Três, but she doesn't look quite so strange. Her hair is short, almost not there at all, and so ragged I think she hacked it off with a machete. And her eyes, those stare-straight-ahead eyes, they are brittle as glass. They are a wall keeping back so much pain that I took one look at the photo and turned off the array.

I guess that's why Mother doesn't keep that one in the family album.

April and her father lived in what would be Palmares Três for about six months. Then boatloads of refugees from the wars in São Paulo and Rio came up the coast, and there was a debate about what to do with them. By this time everyone knew there wasn't a cure for the Y Plague, and Palmares Três hadn't had any big outbreaks. My great-grandfather wanted to stay in the city and keep it quarantined. April wanted to help the refugees. They had a huge argument, Mamãe says, and then April left to deliver food and supplies. The Aunties back then had decided to let the refugees stay out on the largest of the islands in the bay. I don't remember what they called it before, but now, of course, we call it A Quarentena. The quarantine.

She died out there. No one is really sure how. I didn't understand this for a long time, because she was treating people sick with the plague, what else could have happened? But once, Mamãe implied that she might have been murdered by some deranged refugee.

"Rape," she said, "it's a terrible thing. Terrible. We are so lucky here, June." But she was drunk so I just put her to bed while nodding my head reassuringly.

April died and my great-grandfather never got over it. Once, after Papai died, I tried to imagine how I'd feel if my last conversation with him had been an argument.

Let's just say I understand why he's never smiling in the family album. Eventually he met his second wife, a true Brasileira from Salvador, and they had a daughter. He didn't name her April — or June or August, for that matter. He gave her a good Bahian name, Folade.

And she had a daughter, who was my mother, Valencia. And when Valencia had her daughter, for some reason she thought about her grandfather, who had died when Valencia was a waka like me. April's story had always appealed to Mother, I guess it was because of those straight-ahead eyes. The kind of eyes that can abandon someone they love for the sake of plague-ridden refugees wasting away on a rock. Mother planned everything very carefully. She arranged for the daughter she would name April to be conceived in time for a guaranteed April birth. But the doctors said there was something wrong with Mother's first pregnancy and so she had to try again two months too late. And when I was born, my mother for once decided to work with what I had given her.

And so she called me June.

My mamãe died a few weeks before your papai, I don't know if you knew that. It wasn't a kiri, though she was only forty-five. It's not a secret how she died, but for some reason none of the gossip casters dredged it up from the municipal files, or maybe they did and figured it was too arbitrary, too sad to get views. They like me a lot, the gossip casters. I'm like a meteor before them, but they want me bright and young and don't like anything that might bring me down.

Before I have to be, anyway.

But my mamãe died in an accident. Ironic, given that she'd left Salvador just so she could feel safe. She would always tell me how she missed Salvador, but wouldn't go back to the city with its bombs and gang wars and poverty for all the money in Royal Tower.

But then a spider bot malfunctioned on her line to the verde late one night and her pod was caught in the slowly collapsing tube. She suffocated before any rescue crews could get to her. Probably she would have survived if she lived in one of the upper tiers, but it took the crews half an hour to bother with the verde.

You wonder how I speak to the city. You should wonder how I feel her. That corrosive pressure of an artery collapsing, the sudden weight of everything supported above, previously so secure, now in danger. Imagine her terror as the

humans and bots scurry to the scene, unsure of where she hurts, when it's obvi-
ous to her as a gaping wound?

You think the city doesn't feel this? You think it's a metaphor?

It is, it isn't. Sometimes metaphors are literal.

My mamãe loved Salvador, with its broken-down streets, its towering ruins
riddled with blast holes. Street vendors would sell acarajé and bolo de carimã
and bright orange Fanta tablets on the walls when the shooting died down. She
said nothing tasted as good as the crunch of an acarajé patty, deep-fried in
palm oil and dusted with a passing bullet.

But she came here to live in the verde, with its catinga and the milk that is
always a day past fresh. She came here so she could have me, and I am more of
this city than even you, with a family from the first wave of settlers.

I am this city because I chose her.

And now she has chosen me.

We are down in the verde, me in my hunting outfit, Enki in a pair of
cut-off jeans and a football jersey. I said that maybe he should wear
black, and he said his skin wasn't enough?

"It has to get on the Sé line five minutes before the opening speech,"
Enki says, not making much effort to keep quiet.

"You know I'm only going to be able to stash it on two trains . . .
three if I'm sprinting."

"Then sprint."

"And what if someone notices?"

"Say you're practicing."

"For what?"

"You're a waka. Let them think whatever they want."

He hasn't looked at me much tonight. I think something's happened, but it's not like Enki would ever tell me. His movements up the
side of the algae vat are jerky, restless, physically punishing. His muscles bulge like cords beneath his skin, but even he gasps with exertion
by the time he makes the final leap to the back of the vat.

There's a small gap for cabling between the outside of the vat and the crawl space that the bioengineers use to access the algae. Enki can't fit, but I'm just small enough.

"Well," Enki says when I finally catch up to him. "Go on."

I roll my eyes and stick my head in. Then I freeze. From farther down the crawl space, I hear a shuffle and a buzz. I pull my head out.

"There's something in there," I whisper, my lips brushing his ear. "We should hide."

Enki tilts his head, as though he's trying to catch a sound. I can barely breathe — I don't know what the Aunties would do to us if we got caught, but it wouldn't be good. Enki doesn't seem worried, though. He laughs a little, purses his lips, and whistles.

I nearly hit him.

"What the hell was that for?" I whisper.

"Just a little bot," he says, not very quietly. "I told her to go away."

"You . . . Enki, what kind of mods do you have?"

It's the first time I've asked him this question, though I've wondered plenty.

His eyes get a little wide and he reaches for my left hand with his right. The nanohooks in our gloves don't grip each other, but I still feel as if he's trapped me.

"Isn't it rude to ask your king about his personal adornments?"

"Not when he claims to do impossible things."

"Maybe there are no impossible things."

He says this last with his cheek against mine. I think my heart might run away inside my chest. I think he knows.

"You can't fly," I say. "You can't live forever. You can't read minds."

"I can read yours."

"Really."

Enki is grinning. I can feel his lips by my ear. "Sure. You think I'm crazy. You really want to sleep with me."

I flinch back, rip my hand from his. He isn't smiling now — he looks sort of curious.

"You verde rat!"

"Huh," he says. "I was just guessing with that last one."

I blush and Enki tactfully pokes his head through the opening to the crawl space.

I do not *want* to sleep with him. It would be like having sex with a thunderstorm. I *fantasize* about plenty of things I don't want. He's Gil's; I can't forget that.

"Little bot is gone," he says, "but something bigger might come along that might not want to listen to me. I still need practice."

"Enki . . ."

I don't know why — my tone, maybe, or just whatever has been bothering him all night — but he finally answers me.

"All of them."

"All?"

"Ones they don't even know about. Ones they've never even dreamed of."

"But how —"

His finger hovers over my lips. "Are you sure you want the answer?"

I'm not. I don't know where Enki might be getting these wild mods, this biotechnology so advanced even the Aunties don't have it, but I know Enki. I know how few inhibitions he has, how many limits he'll stretch and stretch just to see how they'll break. However he's getting these, it won't be legal. However he's changing himself, once I know, I'll never be able to see him the same way.

"Wait here," I say, and swing my legs inside the crawl space. I have to suck in my stomach and I think the squeeze might have bruised my breasts, but eventually I'm inside.

Enki tosses a mask and gloves in after me. I put them on and step closer to the hatch that opens onto the algae vat. About a dozen cables snake out from underneath. Each helps siphon the pure hydrogen gas to the fuel cells that power the city. The water by-product gets recycled into our sinks and fountains. Energy at no cost, some would say, but Enki and I know better. The cost is the verde, the catinga, the several hundred thousand souls who live at this literal bottom tier of society. On Tier Eight, we can forget this place even exists, except when someone like Enki forces us to remember.

Except when Enki and I force people to remember.

We're doing this as a trial run for our big project with the lights on the islands in the bay. We want to make sure we have everyone's attention first, before we put on the grandest art show I've ever heard of. Not that Mother or Auntie Yaha would consider what we're planning art. They'd call it a prank at best, petty vandalism at worst. I'd tell them that transgression is part of what makes art *work*, but I admit I'm a little afraid that the Aunties might agree with them.

I sparked our idea for the four siblings, but this part of our project is Enki's. I'm committed now, but I know I'm walking close to the edge. Studying past winners of the Queen's Award, it seems to me that they never pick someone too predictable. They appreciate irreverence and a certain iconoclasm. Still, I don't want to go too far.

The hatch operates with a simple gasket mechanism, but it still needs a flash to unlock. Enki's would probably work, but they'd know he was down here. So he convinced a bioengineer to let us borrow hers. Enki implied the involvement of sexual favors, but I didn't press for details.

"You ready?" Enki says as he pokes his head in.

I brush the side of the mask, activating a complete seal around my mouth and nose. The catinga, which is oppressive this close to the opening of the vats, recedes like the tide before a storm.

I nod and he hands me the flash: It's embedded in an old copper coin from the actual state of Brazil. A flash can be anywhere, of course — implanted in your iris or the spine of a paper book — but I guess Enki's engineer is a history buff. I wave it in front of the hatch and immediately hear the bolts snap back inside the metal door.

I signal to Enki to activate his mask — even though it's mostly siphoned, the pure hydrogen gas could be poisonous. Once the mask seals, I grip the gasket handles and twist. A grunt of effort, and it's free.

With the mask on, the algae of the verde doesn't smell like anything except plastic, but it looks like a witch's cauldron. A hundred thousand shades of green glint in the weak artificial light of the tunnel, belching and exhaling and plopping like sloppy wet kisses.

"No wonder it smells so bad," I say, but it's nearly inaudible behind the air seal of the mask. Enki gestures, reminding me that we shouldn't linger. I grab the bag and try not to think about what I'm about to do. Even with gloves on, that primordial soup looks like it might dissolve me alive.

I dunk the first container in the soup. There's a dried enzyme inside that will activate when I shake it to change the metabolic cycles of the algae. I'm unclear on the mechanics, but after five minutes the algae will produce carbon dioxide instead of hydrogen as a by-product. They'll smell just as bad, but they won't poison anyone.

Something scrapes the concrete at the far end of the tunnel. I turn to Enki, hoping it's just another cleaning bot, but his eyebrows have come together in that particular way I know means trouble. He doesn't bother to speak, just looks at me, and I hear him perfectly: *Move your ass.*

I dip the last container in the vat, seal it, and slam the hatch back down. It's too late to pretend that no one's been here. But if I hurry, hopefully they won't know *who*. The noise gets louder. I recognize the clanking footsteps as they hurry closer: a sentry bot, surely alerted by now that something is wrong.

Enki has ripped off his mask. He drops the three filled containers into his knapsack and yanks me with merciless strength through the gap in the wall.

Well, now I *definitely* have bruises on my breasts.

I still haven't removed my algae-vat gloves, so Enki holds me in his left arm while he crawls out of the line of sight of the bot. It will see us if it bothers to stick its head up, but we're counting on its lack of imagination.

It checks the locked vat and pauses, considering. But then it continues on at a more leisurely pace. One of Auntie Maria's minions will probably get an anomalous report in the morning, but with any luck, she won't think anything of it.

Enki lets out a breathy laugh and releases the seal on my mask.

"Jesus, June, you're heavy. Hook your feet at least."

I do, but he still holds on. I like the feel of his arm around me. This thing between us is intellect and art, not sex, but I'm realizing that doesn't make it less intense. I take my time with my gloves, and the whiff of catinga makes me remember my worries.

"Enki, what do you think Oreste will do?"

"Hate it. What else does she do?" He swings his head around and laughs. "Oh, but you're talking about the award."

"What if we're going too far?"

"Where else would we be going?"

"You don't understand, I *have* to win."

His arm around me tightens and he lifts me up so I am level with his eyes. "I understand, bem-querer," he says softly. "But how much of yourself will you give them in exchange? I'm not the best partner if you want to dance politics."

He means, do I want to leave our project, do I want to escape back into the safety of respectability, do I want to walk away from the heat in his hands and the shimmer beneath his skin? But I can't. I won't. Enki became king by reminding people that the verde exists; I'll get away with the same.

"This will work," I say.

He smiles. "Just remember to sprint."

At school the next day, I can't keep still. I itch, I ache, I have verde in my bag and art in my hands. Unfortunately, I have to be here. After this performance, the Aunties will know that Enki has an accomplice. And since they will probably try to stop her, it behooves me to make myself as inconspicuous as possible. The Aunties and Oreste might think I'm doing nothing for the Queen's Award now, but I can't wait to see their faces in the fall.

As soon as we break for lunch, I pull Gil aside and hand him my fono and flash.

He frowns as he takes them. "You're sure about this?" he asks. I've explained some of what Enki and I are planning, but Gil only seems to see the danger of it, not the potential.

I smile and go on my toes to kiss him on the forehead. "I'll be careful. It will be amazing, just watch."

Gil salutes me before I walk away. I only have half an hour to plant the first container. Without my fono, I'll need to check the public displays for the time. Enki thinks the grandes can trace us through our fonos and our flash, which is why I left them with Gil.

I've stashed my bag in one of the older practice rooms in the bottom of the school building. I figured that no one would be there to notice the slight odor even three layers of airtight bags can't hide.

But as soon as I open the door, her voice drowns me. God, I hate Bebel's voice. It's so broad and smooth and weirdly innocent even as it dominates a room. She's the only singer in our generation who will attempt "Zumbi Rei." Somehow, even though she is the ten thousandth vocalist to sing the part, she makes it new.

Did I say I hate her voice? I do. It's not my fault the she-devil can sing like an angel.

Right now she's singing "Roda Viva," because she wouldn't be Bebel without a nauseating command of the classical repertoire. She's accompanied by another waka on guitar while she makes a simple beat with a pandeiro. The guitarist turns his head and I realize it's Pasqual. I spent months staring at him for the summer king contest, but in real life he seems almost unassuming. Pasqual and Octavio are both finalists for the Queen's Award. Apparently it's a customary honor in a moon year, but I haven't met either of them in person yet. The top ten are supposed to meet Oreste herself soon, and I've been curious to see the rest of my competition.

Bebel *beams* at me when I walk in, while she and Pasqual finish their song. I meant to grab my bag and walk away, but my feet don't want to move. I said that art should be transgressive, and it should, but listening to two of the most gifted musicians of our generation, I realize that there can be transgression in beauty. Papai would love this.

For the first time, I start to seriously question whether I'll win the Queen's Award.

"June!" Bebel flutes as soon as she's done. "What are you doing here? What did you think? It's still a little rough."

Rough? I cough. "Beautiful, Bebel. Really."

She pauses, then smiles. "That means a lot from you, June. Thank you."

Pasqual puts down the guitar. "You're one of the other finalists, right? A visual artist?"

Four months ago, meeting Pasqual would have rendered me speechless. But I've spent the night crawling through the verde with the summer king, and very little fazes me these days.

"That's what I started in," I say. "But I'm branching out."

Even Bebel looks curious. That's my Bebel — deep down, she's just as competitive as I am, she just hides it better.

"Really?" Pasqual says. "Have I missed one of your projects?"

"No," I say, smiling. "When I have one, you won't miss it."

Bebel, of course, breaks through the tension like a battering ram. "That's very mysterious, June. And I *told* Ieyascu you must be plotting something."

"You did?"

"Sure. She was asking me if I thought you'd drop out. And I said she didn't know June if she thought that for a second."

"I'm . . ." *Appalled? Confused?* ". . . surprised."

"Don't be. A good rival is almost like a friend, isn't she? You make me try harder."

Something like a smile lifts the corners of her mouth, but her eyes stay serious.

Perhaps Bebel's always seen me far more clearly than I see her. All those times I thought she was faking or playing nice for the grandes or just trying to get under my skin, could she actually have been *supporting* me? Because she liked the competition?

"I have to go," I say. "See you around, Bebel. Pasqual."

I stumble backward, grab my bag from under the bench, and open the door. I can't have much time left. Enki is depending on me.

And Bebel needs a good rival.

Every five years, the summer king chairs special sessions of parliament and is meant to lead discussions of major reforms or new legislation. But in moon years, this position tends to be reduced to an opening convocation and listening to long, boring debates about transport-pod modification. The summer king is free to offer his opinion, and the Aunties are free to ignore him. All government sessions are publicly broadcast — since Enki became summer king, more wakas than usual have started watching parliament, hoping for a glimpse of him. That means everyone will see it. And another reason we know the gossip casters will be over it like stink on fish?

You can't ignore your nose.

Six minutes before parliament begins its afternoon session, I deposit the first canister in an empty public train waiting on the Sé line. It says "Not in Service" but the doors close as soon as I open my first little piece of the verde inside. Enki told me it would be waiting here. I asked how he knew, and he said the city told him. The stink is instant and overpowering. The car stops at the Gria transfer station just long enough to let me out. A few of the people on the platform stare at me with bored curiosity, but my hunting outfit looks a lot like the uniform of an engineer and they don't make much of it. If they catch a whiff of catinga, they don't take it as anything out of the ordinary. I gauge my time from the public holo in the center of the platform. Five minutes to go. Someone has switched one of the four feeds to the parliamentary session. I smile. I sprint.

Next is the Amarela line. At the end of the platform, my Not in Service train awaits. I get in, the doors shut, and it rockets forward, so quickly that I nearly fall on top of the canister. Close call. I don't think I'd ever get clean again if I got the stink on my skin. I stash it under a row of seats and wait for the car to stop. It does at Royal Plaza. This is the trickiest part of the plan: With parliament in session, Auntie Maria, our head of security, has officers all over the platform. The cars that take the Aunties to the parliament building aren't even open to normal citizens like me. But they do break down, and I walk as calmly as you please into the one that even I didn't believe would be waiting. I don't ride this one — it would be too dangerous — I just pretend to check something on the array by the door while I roll the canister ever so gently inside. I step back and the door closes just as the loosened lid slides off, releasing its odor.

I wait a few seconds to make sure that nothing's gone wrong. But though a few of the grandes on the platform give me hard looks, I can tell by now it's just general distaste at having a waka near their distinguished government proceedings. Sun goggles cover half my face and I've bound my hair in a scarf, but if someone gets a good look they'll probably still be able to identify me. I walk right past one of Auntie Maria's security agents, a woman with a white pyramid pinned to her lapel and a dazzle in her irises that indicates a certain kind of biomod.

"I hope you're not missing school, filha," she says.

I smile at her and pray I don't look memorable. "Just wanted to sit in the park for my lunch break."

She nods and turns away. A moment later, she frowns as though someone is speaking to her, and her mod-eyes glint. I hurry toward the park. It's small, but since the Aunties use it, there's a large holo right by the water lily pond.

I sit on a bench a few feet away, take a deep breath, and count to five.

"Summer King," says Auntie Isa from her place beside Oreste's empty chair. "Will you convene the session?"

Enki rises, nods graciously, and walks to the center podium.

The summer king customarily delivers a brief poem or statement before he convenes the special sessions. Enki gives them quite a bit more than that.

"In the verde," says Enki, as serious as I've ever seen him, "we love the storms. Sometimes, when we see one come in, the blocos will set up in the terraces and play until the rain drives us inside."

He pauses here, as though considering his next words, though I can tell he's just savoring the moment. My last present from the verde must have gone through. Everyone in the audience shuffles uncomfortably. Nostrils flair, discreet coughs echo through the chamber. Some look at Enki, others at one another or the doorways.

Enki takes a deep breath, as though he doesn't notice a thing. "We have a saying," he says as murmurs from his audience rise to a wave, "you can't smell the catinga until it comes back home."

In the background, I can just make out several guards hurrying through the doors. Enki surveys his work and smiles, a sun breaking through clouds.

"I hereby convene parliament."

As he saunters back to his seat, Auntie Isa rushes the podium with a handkerchief covering her nose and murder in her eyes. People stand up and hurry to the doors. They don't know the smell will be even worse in the hallway. Our transport pods are all connected to the ventilation system. It's meant to help refresh the air supply in the tunnels, but it can go the other direction. It can carry the fetid stink of the verde straight to the noses of people who pretend it doesn't exist.

In the park, the first of the escapees from parliament gather before the holo. The other feeds have all switched to the news: Gria Plaza in a panic, the shawls of well-to-do women fluttering as they race to open air. Office workers in Tier Eight crowd the walkways — the smell ought to have reached school, by now. When Auntie Yaha and Mother complain about the stink tonight, they'll have me to thank, though they won't know it.

Back in Parliament, Auntie Isa declares an emergency end to the session, due to "an unexpected problem with our air-filtration system."

The parliamentary feed cuts black, and we're left with the breathless casters, speculating about everything from a broken vat in the verde to a system-wide collapse of Palmares Três. I leave them to it.

It's a curious thing, this art that I don't sign my name to. I like anonymity more than I thought I would. For once, I don't consider how this will play with the Aunties or how it increases my chances of winning the Queen's Award. In this moment, I'm just June, the best artist in Palmares Três.

You always did love lights. You glowed on that dance floor when Gil held you in the air. I said I didn't notice, but I did. Your tree has grown since then. Once I said I could read your mind, but I can tell your mood without even glancing at your face. Anger, that's the easiest of all — a pulse and a flash, like a cracking whip. When you're excited, you show your brightest colors. There's a way the branches along your arm seem to sway in a lazy breeze when you've just had an idea for an art project.

When you saw the ocean for the first time, I thought I could see them flower.

To love light, you have to love dark. I'm not trying to be profound, I know you'll understand. I don't mean that you have to hate to love, or that you have to die to live.

I mean that sometimes, you turn out the lights just to turn them back on.

*   *   *

Bebel and Pasqual are very drunk, which perhaps explains why she hooks her arm on mine and says, none too quietly, "Do you think we'd get much attention for a threesome?" in the middle of our finalists' dinner. With camera bots buzzing everywhere, this particular tidbit will be all over the bottom feeds in, oh, *now*, along with my blush.

"Uh, Bebel, people are watching —"

She giggles. "The point, my June. Aren't you the one all about Spectacle and Art?"

She has me there. Across the room, Enki pretends he can't see me while Gil so casually fondles the back of his neck. Octavio sits in a corner, looking morose, and rebuffing any attempt by one of us to converse. A few Aunties mill about, but our Queen has yet to make an appearance. I've spent all day working on my light-tree — two nights ago, a cleaning bot climbed through our garden and handed me a bag filled with light implants. I don't know where Enki found them — they're naturalist-grade programmable, and they adjust their light to the hue of my skin. I couldn't thank him, but I gave the little bot a few flowers from our garden, in case she found her way back.

The tree unfurls, now. First its branches, then its light-leaves. The branches cover my breasts and collarbone. I haven't had a chance to do the trunk.

Not that Mother would let me out of the house wearing something that would show it, anyway.

Gil and Enki look the part of the city's wonder couple, dazzling in matching outfits Gil's mamãe designed. The Aunties are not pleased with their summer king. Security officers tail him the moment he leaves his apartments, according to Gil. Aside from the late-night delivery, I haven't heard a word from him since our perhaps-too-successful catinga project. Everyone knows Enki is responsible, but since he was very prominently giving a speech at the time, no one can quite figure out how. Current speculation is running high on Gil as his accomplice, which made the two of us laugh ourselves sore alone in his garden. Gil plays it up — he's an attention whore, and he knows it protects me. I worry about how they'll react when I reveal myself, but then I think about how wonderful the four siblings will look on their big night and I relax. It's too good not to win.

Pasqual wraps his arm around Bebel and hands her another flute of sparkling wine. I'm not so sure this is a good idea, but Bebel's too high to listen to me. Maybe I'm just inclined to be judgmental. I'm in a room with two of my favorite people in the world and I can't even speak to them. Technically I could talk to Gil, but he's glued like a limpet to Enki's side tonight, and I'm not sure I'd want to get in the middle of that even if it weren't for the Greatest Art Project in History. I've had a few flutes of that sparkling wine myself, and the memory of Bebel's heavenly voice singing "Roda Viva" keeps melding with Enki's as he says, *You really want to sleep with me*, and maybe I can't deny the way my stomach warms in his presence, but that doesn't mean I'll ever act on it. I didn't approach him because I wanted to be his lover, and besides, if Enki felt that way about me he would have done something by now. I gulp down my glass before I can register my sudden rush of disappointment.

I swear, I hate wine. It's such an Auntie drug, so old-world, and why they want to be old-world when they run a *city of women* is beyond me, but there you go, that's grandes in a nutshell: hypocrite central station.

My thoughts have turned so circular and maudlin that I'm grateful when someone taps me on the shoulder.

"You're the visual artist, right?" she says. It's one of the other finalists, the one from the verde.

"June," I say. "And you're . . ."

I can't remember for the life of me, so I shrug and she laughs. "That confident about the competition, huh? I'm Lucia, and I code."

"Code? Like, games?"

"Or like nanobots."

My eyes widen. Could *this* be where Enki is getting them? "Biomods?"

"I wish. In this city, you'd have better luck buying nuclear weapons. Mine are lower-level. Self-assembling machines. Lately, I've been working on replication."

"Wow. And the Aunties are okay with that?"

"Are the Aunties *okay* with anything? I don't think any of us are doing things they're completely comfortable with."

I look around the room and see exactly what she means. This is a brilliant, wild, and transgressive group of wakas. The Aunties should be screaming to see us all in a room together, exchanging ideas. And yet Auntie Maria smiles as she chats with Auntie Yaha. I see Auntie Nara who, as our head of culture, probably picked most of us. They don't look horrified, they look pleased. As though they can think of nothing better than the sight of this group, the future leaders of their city of lights.

"They picked us," I say.

Lucia smiles. "Strange, isn't it?"

The music dims and the doors to the dining room glide open soundlessly. Servers take our empty glasses of wine.

"Welcome," says Queen Oreste from the head of the table. "It would be my honor to have you join me for dinner."

I sit between Bebel and Pasqual, across from Gil and Enki. I try not to look at either of them, but Gil catches my eye and smiles in a way that makes something unwind, deep in my belly.

The food is very refined — we start with a single scoop of sorbet of açaí and banana, and follow that with prawns stewed in coconut milk and chiles. No one but the Aunties eats much. Now that I can feel the pressure of their judgment, even the smell of the chiles can't entice me.

"Nazare," Oreste says, and the head of a boy at the other end of the table snaps up with a crack. "The Aunties and I have been very impressed with your level of playing recently. Have you set up any demonstration events, perhaps? I'm sure Faro would love to test his skills against yours."

Nazare's spoon starts to clank against his bowl and he puts it down hastily. He's tall, angular, with long wiry arms that are likely to make him the best peteca player in Palmares Três in a few years. Unfortunately, skill on the court doesn't make him particularly adept in social situations, and it's clear that he's overwhelmed by the Queen's attention.

"I . . . ah . . . *Faro?*" His voice cracks, and Pasqual is drunk enough to giggle. I glare at him.

Oreste smiles and softens her voice. "Yes, dear. I have it on very good authority that Faro has been particularly impressed with your skills. I think a friendly demonstration match would be just what the city would like to see from one of its finest wakas."

Nazare stammers out something that might be agreement, but Oreste doesn't wait, she's already training that deceptively welcoming gaze on another finalist, questioning her about her skills. As she goes around the table, I realize that every other finalist has either done something publicly or is planning a demonstration. As she circles around to me, the tension in the room quietly rises — it seems that everyone has heard that I've done nothing since my nomination. Even Gil can't stop looking at me, but Enki is cool as he pleases, and I think that his crown of cacao has never looked more appropriate. Pasqual smoothly informs her of his work with Bebel as well as a new theorem he's close to completing (I'd forgotten how infuriating his grande-pleasing insouciance can be). Oreste gives him a smile I'd almost call flirtatious, and then she turns to me.

"June," she says, "my blazing light. I hear you're working on something special?"

She has? Then I remember Bebel and Ieyascu. "You could say that."

Her smile gets a little harder. It's strange, but in her presence I can understand why she's our Queen. She's brilliant, manipulative, and beautiful. It's no surprise she convinced the summer king four years ago to name her Queen before his death.

"So secretive, June! But you're among friends here."

My lights pulse with my sudden agitation. I know I have to tread carefully, but I'm an artist, not a politician. I don't know what to say.

Then Enki starts to laugh, and I don't have to say anything. The sound is carefree, debatably inebriated. It dispels the charged atmosphere of Oreste's questioning like a grounding wire.

"Something is funny, King?" she says, an attempt at polite curiosity that barely hides her annoyance.

"Her face, Oreste! How can you stand it?"

"Stand *what*, Enki?"

"Pushing them into these corners and smiling at them. You're like a cat playing with a mouse, I swear."

"I am *not* a mouse," I say before I can stop myself.

Enki flashes that smile at me, and for the barest moment I can see his joy like a nod in my direction. He walks a tightrope, knowing the slightest misstep will reveal our secret to Oreste, and utterly convinced he won't fall.

"You're being rude, Enki," says our Queen. She's not hiding anything now.

"You're being cruel. So the girl hasn't done anything yet. You picked her, didn't you? Maybe you should wait and see what she can offer instead of grooming her like a prize turkey."

Silence. It stretches for five, maybe six seconds. I'm not sure anyone even breathes. Enki catches my eye, like he's saying, "Well, I tried," and then, clear as the bay in a calm, I know what I have to do.

I laugh.

"Well," snaps Oreste, "I'm glad you two find this funny."

I meant it as a distraction, but the mirth turns genuine and almost uncontrollable as soon as it leaves my belly.

Bebel touches my arm, genuinely concerned.

"Summer King," I say between the fountaining laughter.

"June?"

"I'm not a turkey either."

The city sounds different in the verde. She speaks to us with the same voice, but in a different tone. She apologizes so much we sometimes call her the Sorry Lady and we all learn very early not to rely on her for much of anything. In the verde, we flash a transport pod and sometimes she'll say "I'm sorry, I can't send you one right now." We ask her for the weather cliffside on Tier Seven and she'll say, "I'm sorry, I can't access my sensors right now. Would you like to try again later?"

You're surprised. That's never happened to you on Tier Eight.

So we jack our standard-issue fonos. We mod them so when we ask where the security bots are, the city will treat us like we've never smelled the catinga. A tech-head in the verde is one step below an orixá.

I grew up desperate to speak to the city. I would look at the office workers in Gria Plaza and wonder what secrets she had told them. When I asked my mamãe, she would laugh and say the city didn't tell anyone secrets, she just used more resources for the top tiers to answer questions.

"The city isn't really a person," she told me. "She can't tell you anything important."

But she was wrong, my mamãe.

The tech-heads think they're speaking to the city, but they're wrong too.

The city has a voice, but I had to become a king to hear her.

Sunday morning. Auntie Yaha goes to services, but Mother stays home with me. At first I'm worried that she wants to talk, but she seems content enough to sit in her chair that overlooks the garden and read. I force myself to do some schoolwork, as I cannot bear to let Bebel get so far ahead of me. I don't feel so annoyed anymore when I think of her. She's right, isn't she? A good rival is almost like a good friend.

Almost.

God, I miss Gil. I ping him again, not that I expect an answer. He's out with Enki, as all the world knows.

"June?"

Mother speaks so softly I can hardly hear her over the morning birdcall.

"I'm working, you know."

"I just need a moment."

Her tone is so uncharacteristically diffident that I lever myself off the cushions. She's turned on the garden holo, and I hear him laughing and saying "querida" before I see his head bobbing over the hydrangeas. There's a little hand, then a little body, and it's me, and my papai is teaching me to dance. In the distance, the ghost of my mother says, "Careful, João, I think she's getting better than you!"

I just stand a foot beside Mother's chair and watch. In two years, I've never looked at a holo. I haven't heard his voice or even the music he loved to teach. In two years, I haven't gone a day without thinking of my papai, but somehow I still forgot who he was.

"Try again, June," he says. The music in the background gets louder, but I would recognize this in my sleep. He sings "Send in the Clowns" and I clap and stutter along with him.

"João," says Mamãe, "she's too young for English. We should teach her some good classical music. Make her smart."

The music changes. *"Baiana que entra no samba,"* Mamãe sings. I laugh. The holo stops; the ghosts disappear.

"Ma — Mother . . ."

She doesn't even glance up at me. "It's his birthday tomorrow."

"I know."

"Sometimes I forget," she says. "How nice it was with the three of us."

"I . . ." I think I have too, and it shames me to admit it.

"June, do you think the three of us, with Auntie Yaha, do you think we could ever —"

"No," I say, harsh and unthinking and immediate.

Now she turns to me. I expect her anger, but I'm shocked to see something like grief in the set of her shoulders. "Your papai would never have wanted —"

"Stop."

"You can't do this, June! It's been two years. You can't claim the only right to think about him, talk about him, *miss* him —"

"He was *my* papai."

"He was my husband."

"And you're the reason he's dead!"

The birds are so loud I want to shoot them. Mother's straight-ahead April eyes glitter, but they don't even blink.

"You really believe that."

I can't speak. I don't know what I believe, I only know that I want it to be true, I want it to be all her fault, because otherwise I can hardly bear to think about that man with his slow smile and long mustache and musician's calluses. Sometimes I wake up in the middle of the night, convinced that he isn't really gone, that I just dreamed it all, thank God, and then I hear Mother and Auntie Yaha in the next room and I hate her all over again. He knew I loved art, but he will never know June, the best artist in Palmares Três.

My fono chirps. It's Gil, saving me.

"I have to go," I say. I don't wait for a response. But she's subsided, a straight-backed figure alone in the solitude of a garden, and when I think, *I miss you*, I don't only mean my papai.

Gil is playing football by the falls in Gria Park. It's not a game yet, just a few wakas kicking a ball around on the grass. Gil passes it to me and I kick it back so hard it sails past him.

"My team?" he says after he's got it back again.

I grin. "Of course."

The other wakas on the green divide themselves more or less evenly, and we start. Gil plays forward and I keep up with him, though I'm usually more comfortable as a defender. I'm in a mood to hit things, and no one seems inclined to stop me.

Gil scores our first goal, and the cheering is louder than I'd expect for some weekend pickup game. We've developed quite the audience. I hear the growing swarm of camera bots and realize: It's Gil. With all the bot restrictions in school, it's easy to forget that he's become a minor celebrity. I jog with him on our way back to center field. "I thought you were with Enki?"

"He wanted to be alone." He shrugs and slows down. "June, you know, if you and he are, I mean . . ."

"No!" I say, far too forcefully. Gil gives me a look that makes me swallow the rest of my denials.

"You know I wouldn't mind it, right? If you did."

"I don't. We haven't."

The ball is back in play. Gil chases the opposing team's forward hard down the field. I don't try to keep up, just wait, open and forgotten until he passes me the ball between the legs of another player. I sprint back down the field, heart pumping madly. I trip in a tangle of legs, and when I look up, the goalie's caught the ball.

Gil helps me up. "I think he's working on your project."

I had wondered what he would do now that the Aunties are keeping such a close watch, but I knew that he wouldn't give up on it. I grin. "Mother will die when she realizes what I've been doing for the Queen's Award."

Gil glances at me. It isn't hard to read his disapproval. "June . . . why won't you just *tell her*?"

I sigh. "She might stop me."

"You know she won't."

"Gil, come on!" one of the other players shouts. Gil shrugs and jogs away. We win, three to two, but not much thanks to me. I'm too confused, too unreasonably angry about Gil's defense of my family to focus.

Gil and I walk under the falls with the other players when we're done, hot and tired. None of the camera bots venture very close to the mist and noise. It's as private as we're going to get, out here in the park.

"Gil, if you want to say something, then out with it." He tilts his head up to the pouring water, which courses down his naked back. If there are a few wakas ogling him from the side of the falls, I don't really blame them.

Gil purses his lips, not like he's angry, like he's frustrated. "It's been more than two years," he says. "Have you and your mamãe even talked about him since?"

"Well, it's her fault —"

"No! It isn't, and I'll scream if you say it one more time. Your papai is dead because he chose it, June. You can't blame your mamãe, you can't blame Auntie Yaha. You can't blame yourself. He's dead because he felt it was his time and there's *nothing any of you could do about it.*"

I might be shaking. I don't know, but it feels good and tangible and safe when he puts his hands on my shoulders. "She loves you. Trust her."

But I can never trust her again.

I wrench myself away from Gil. "If you think that, you don't know me at all."

Gil flexes his hands. "June . . . we're . . . there's no one I know better."

"Then you should be on my side! Why do you always defend my mamãe when she . . . when you know . . ."

"You think I like seeing you like this? Tearing yourself apart, finding anyone else to blame when, really, a decision like your papai's —"

"Gil."

He stops. The water beads on my forehead and slides down my hairline. My breathing is fast and harsh. My chest hurts, I hurt, and more than anything I never want to cry again. He takes my hand. I let him.

I don't know what the cameras or the casters make of the way he leads me off the field and out of the park. I feel like I might shatter, like my love for Gil is all that keeps the fissures from spreading.

My papai was João, from a long line of Joãos, and when I was younger I thought that meant Gilberto himself. When he was a waka, he dropped out of school and joined a shipping crew to Eurasia. He saw the great cube cities of Lisbon and Rome. He saw the ruins of London and the great string of Tokyos spilling into the Pacific Ocean like giant triangular dice. He learned guitar on that ship, and then cavaquinho and the laughing beat of the cuíca. Halfway around the world, my papai discovered his truest love was the music of old-Brazil, and so he came back home.

Until his anniversary trip, he never left. He just learned and played and taught, all in his own unassuming way. At the memorial, everyone described him as quiet, dependable, pleasant. Only I remembered him as passionate, occasionally joyous.

But a year before he died, he stopped playing guitar. The samba of my youth fell silent in the background, but I suppose I never noticed. I was too busy sneaking away with Gil to dance in the park and see the hottest new bloco. My father still taught, my mother still ran from university fund-raisers to board meetings, and as far as I knew, that's the way it would be forever.

But there's no such thing as forever. There's only fifteen years and thirty-three days and a distracted kiss on your forehead before he walks away.

I've forgotten the music, his only explanation. I was never good enough to give it back to him.

In the back of the practice room, I listen to Bebel and Pasqual rehearse with their band, and hardly think of anything at all. I can feel competitive later. Right now it's too petty an emotion to sustain. In the middle of the song, Bebel curses and waves her arms. The band stops. They look about as confused as I feel: The music felt good to me, but she's not satisfied.

"You're coming in too slow," she says to the flautist. "You're the third voice in the round. You have to play like a *voice*, not a flute."

The flautist mumbles something like an apology. I smile; Bebel isn't so sweet when she's intent on perfection. Pasqual gives her such a passionate look that I'm pretty sure Bebel's offer of a threesome has turned to a duet.

They start again, a few measures before the carefully arranged vocal harmonies that make the increasingly frantic and enveloping final thirty seconds of "Roda Viva." And as I listen to the flute merging with Bebel's voice, I have an idea.

A wheel of life. The love that twines through our hearts and spins our worlds and ties us all together. The green of the verde, the lights of Palmares Três, the voices we hear and the ones we don't.

What binds this city more than its music? More than the shuffling pandeiro we all learn to play before we can walk? More than the songs we know like prayers? And yet I've forgotten all about it, despite all the times Papai tried to tell me.

The song ends. I amble over to Bebel, who is still flushed from music and working and being perfect. I gesture and she walks off with me to the far corner of the room. Perhaps it's reckless to trust even Bebel this far, but I don't want the others to hear me.

"If I ask you to sing that in a month, would you?" I say.

She tilts her head. "But we're planning to debut later."

"I heard a rumor of something big. It's happening soon. If you do this, no one will forget."

Bebel knows I wouldn't say something like this lightly. She leans in. "Where?"

"Anywhere. Here."

"What should I tell the others?"

"Say someone passed you the information. But don't mention me."

Bebel touches my palm. "June, is *this* it? Your big secret project?"

"No," I lie. "Just something I heard from some wakas in the verde."

She nods slowly — not quite believing me, but willing to pretend. "All right," she says. "I'll do it. Will you tell them?"

"They'll probably contact you. If you get any anonymous pings, that's it."

Pasqual walks over to the two of us. I'm struck again by how strange my life has become these last few months — it's like all the boys I know are beautiful.

"Still working on that secret project, June?"

"I want to make it perfect," I say.

"Well, don't make it so perfect you forget to finish it in time."

I match his patronizing smile with my own. "No," I say. "I'll just make it perfect enough to win."

Bebel's eyes crinkle in a smile that's surprisingly genuine. "Believe her, Pasqual. Remember, June, that time in first year when you painted all the tables to look like a banquet?"

"And all the chairs were giant fruit! I'd forgotten about that."

"Ieyascu was our teacher that year, remember? She sent you home and I swear I thought you were the coolest girl in the school."

I stare at her. "I just thought you were competitive."

"I learned from the best."

I let out a surprised giggle. Bebel starts to laugh too, and I wonder how I never *noticed* her in all this time I struggled so hard to beat her.

Pasqual looks between the two of us. But the corners of his mouth turn up, as though anything that makes Bebel happy is good enough for him.

"We should get back," he says gently. "I think we might need to slow down the intro a bit."

Bebel lets her fingers stray into his thick, curly hair. "Of course, meu bombril," she says.

Pasqual nods at me. "Good luck with the project, June."

Bebel squeezes my hand and goes back to the waiting band with

Pasqual. I bite my lip and turn away before anyone can see my excitement.

The best art project ever? Just got a little bit better.

I decide to walk home instead of flashing a pod, because sometimes it's good to think, and nothing is prettier than Palmares Três in the summer. It used to be summer all the time in this part of old-Brazil, of course. I like to imagine that world, where the marmelo never died in the frost. Where liana flourished in the wild, and not just in the hothouses of Tier Six. Still, we do our best in the summer. The walking paths of Tier Eight are lined with flowering fruit trees. The smell is heavenly, and I can't help but think of the verde and the catinga that Enki and I so briefly delivered to the upper tiers. There are no banana trees in the verde. Nothing but concrete and algae. Here on Tier Eight, the walkways are either wood or mulch. They twine through the summer growth like paths in a forest. A strange kind of forest, a thousand feet above the water. The glass of the megatruss has been raised, letting in the warm breeze from the bay.

I go into one of my favorite places, a tiny grotto tucked at the end of a forgotten turn from the main path, hidden by the ferns and magnolia. It has a perfect view of the four siblings. I used to come here with Papai. After he died, I would return sometimes to think and sketch. Today, I turn to face the descending sun, its heat full on my face, my arms, my naked shoulders. I'm alone, and after a moment I untie the top of my halter-neck dress. I lean back in the grass, let the sun stream over my breasts. My nipples ease out in the lazy warmth. The red-gold light of the sun glints on the fine hair of my stomach, a shading of peach fuzz. The trunk of my tree still stops just below my heart, but the lights I have are muted in the presence of the sun. I can feel them pulse, but I can hardly see them. My ears fill with the basso drone of evening cicadas, the chirruping of plovers, and the soft mechanic whir of the pods rushing through the tunnels beneath me.

For once, even my thoughts fall silent. I watch. I breathe. My hand drifts to my stomach, then lower, beneath my folded-over dress and my underwear. I bite my lip, but there's no one here but me and the seabirds.

The sun makes me savor it. I'm slow and deliberate and not thinking of anyone much at all, which is strange of me. I think about art. I look out on the bay and imagine the four siblings gauded in their luminous finery. I imagine how it will seem from up here on Tier Eight, because I know I'll never get to see it. The shimmering array growing more and more frantic as the voices compound and coalesce. In the dark, it will look as though the four islands are dancing.

Like Gil and Enki, that night it all began.

At that bare thought of him, I gasp and shudder and fall back against the grass and packed dirt. A worm slides past my ear while I pant.

"Should I come back?"

I sit up so fast I feel dizzy. It's Enki, leaning against the guardrail. I can hardly see his face, the sun is so bright behind him.

"I didn't hear you," I say stupidly.

I think he smiles; at least, I can hear it in his voice. "You wouldn't have."

I'm embarrassed, not because of what he saw me do, but because of what I was thinking when I did it.

"How did you get away?" I ask. I yank up my dress.

"From the Aunties?" He steps away from the balcony, shattering my illusion of anonymity. He's my beautiful boy, reborn and so much more immediate than I remember. My breath comes short for a moment, as though my body anticipates a different sort of pleasure.

Which you are never going to get, June.

My fingers slip; the ties of the dress fall back over my shoulders. I try again.

"Gil said you had spies and minders."

Enki kneels in front of me. Gently, he takes the ends of the dress from my clumsy fingers and ties them together in a simple bow.

He smiles. "I could have gotten away from the Aunties anytime. But sometimes it's useful to make them think they can hold me, you know? And it's never any trouble with Gil."

No, it wouldn't be, would it? These days, if Enki's troublemaking began and ended with his less-than-diplomatic selection of Gil as his primary partner, the Aunties would probably dance in Royal Park.

"You want to go out to the islands?" I ask. "I haven't been able to get more lights yet."

He shakes his head, a strange smile playing on his lips. He looks like a mischievous god. Even when Enki is completely honest, I never know what he's thinking.

"Am I only art to you, June?"

No, I think. "Of course," I say.

He stands and offers me his hand. After a moment, I take it. "I thought I could show you something," he says. "Nothing to do with art."

"But everything has to do with art." .

Now Enki stares at me. His light brown eyes look like pieces of colored glass in the red light of sunset. He leans forward. I feel smooth and still, a fly drowning in amber. We stay like that for an endless moment, hung in time like the sun from the sky, waiting and watching each other. What will Gil think?

And then something loud and mechanical buzzes behind me.

I turn around, but Enki's already let go of my hand. He frowns. It's a camera bot, and I can't tell from this distance if it's a caster's or one of Auntie Maria's.

"I told them not to follow," he mutters. He draws his eyebrows even further together and his eyes *flash* somehow, though I can hardly believe it even as I watch. They turn yellow or green and then back again, and suddenly the camera bot is wobbling in the air like it's drunk. Enki snatches it and hurls it over the side of the balcony.

"I think we should hurry," he says.

"Was that . . ."

A mod? But I trail off. His gaze is steady. He has that look, like he might tell me if I ask.

Do you really want to know? I can hear him say.

I don't. Not now. Not when I felt . . . not when we almost . . .

Just this once, I want to forget that Enki is the summer king. Today I don't want to remember what that means.

I learned to fight like every kid in the verde, with fists and feet and an eye to avoiding them. I learned to jump higher than most, kick harder, to feel the rhythm of the roda so deep beneath my eyeballs that even when it was my blood on the concrete floors, the pain felt like just another beat. You love my skin (you will ask how I know that when you've never said it, but you might as well ask how I know that the wakas love me or the grandes envy me or that our city is the most beautiful in the world). On Tier Eight, a negro like me has the beauty of the exotic, the forbidden. You forget that the slaves were black too, and the morenas like you couldn't wait to become as white as our masters.

In the verde, they remember. In the verde, no one wants a negro baby — we're too close to what that used to represent.

There aren't any slaves in the verde, but in the roda, we still fight like master might catch us.

And they made me fight hardest of all.

We go to the spiderweb. I say I've already done this with him and he grins and says not like this you haven't. I laugh though I don't know what he's planning. But he's Enki, and that's enough.

The noise hits us before we even drop down through the garbage vent Enki uses to take us there. *Much* easier than crab-walking upside down through the transport tunnel. Good thing too, because I'm still wearing my dress and neither of us has our nanohooks.

The voices that reverberate through the cavernous room are raucous and wild. I recognize the sound of wakas before I see them. When I do, I'm surprised to find a few grandes here and there. They're probably not too old, but after thirty-five pretty much all grandes look the same. Boys and girls, most of them in the wide pants and colored shirts that proclaim their membership in one or another of the verde's gangs. These are all amarelo or vermelho, colors well known for their blocos and the occasional fight, though those aren't usually fatal.

Tonight everyone seems friendly enough. Near one fat-bellied spider so old its skin is rusting, two blocos prepare to make music. The verde blocos are the vanguard of the naturalist music trend. They make their own instruments or use broken-down antiques that they'll patch up in interesting ways. Most of them won't even use amps, performing instead in spaces with natural acoustics. The tech-heavy electronica of my mother's generation might as well be a declaration of war in the verde. And I'm not inclined to make it — I was raised with my father's classical music, but I grew up with the modern blocos. I'd heard of these impromptu music sessions in the verde, but I'd never thought I would be lucky enough to see one. The musicians for the amarelo and vermelho blocos shout good-natured insults at one another as they wet the skin of their cuíca drums, test the tension of their pandeiros, run practiced fingers over the single string of hand-made berimbaus.

"Oy, Felix!" a girl in a yellow shirt calls out. "Your cuíca sounds like a rusted spider!"

A boy in red gives his drum a squeeze and fills the room with its booming laughter. "You mean your papai? Or is that just how he sounds when your mamãe leaves the bed?"

There's laughter, a few groans. The amarela girl bites her tongue and starts a hard, challenging samba on her pandeiro. Someone nearby shouts and gives a running tumble, springing on his hands high into the air before landing upright. Everyone claps. I turn to Enki.

"Gil can't even do that."

"Then someone should teach him."

The rest of the bloco amarelo fall in with her lead. A whistle blows, shrill and high, and I feel something rising in my throat, like a shout and a laugh and a song all at once.

"Enki, what is this?"

We're still on the edge of the crowd, not quite hidden, but unnoticed in the shadows of the great machines. "It's a still night," he says.

"What?"

"When the winds don't blow, and the catinga gets worse, the blocos will come here sometimes."

"To dance?"

His eyes are still on the crowd, but I think his smile is meant for me. "And fight."

He walks into the crowd; I'm right behind him. The knowledge of his presence runs through like wind riffling the bay. They part for us, but they don't stop dancing. When we reach the blocos, the girl on pandeiro raises her arms and releases her rhythm in a shiver of tiny shaking cymbals. The rest of the bloco stops playing.

"The summer king!"

"Pia," Enki says, and they hug.

"Didn't think we'd see you again."

"How could I stay away on a still night?"

She looks thoughtful. "I wondered, you know. It's our first of the summer."

"Oy," Felix, the vermelho boy with the cuíca, calls. "Is this a contest or a reunion?"

"Don't you see we're in the presence of royalty?" someone calls from the crowd.

Felix spits. "Like I'll bow to some trumped-up verde negro. He's no better than any of us."

The nervous laughter covers an oppressive silence.

Enki sketches a mocking bow. "Don't worry," he says. "These things don't last."

"Isn't that right," Felix says. His smirk is too hard — he's uncomfortable, unsure of Enki's popularity here in his home.

"So prove it, vermelho," Enki says. His voice is very soft and low in a way I haven't heard before. I know it means something, but nothing in my life has prepared me for this scene. There are wakas in the crowd singing to the air, holding on to one another and rocking. I know they're tripping, and not on something as safe and familiar as wine or Auntie Yaha's weekend blues either. Others are tuning in to what look like foreign feeds on an ancient, bulky holo modded with wires and tape.

"Give us a dance," Enki says.

Felix's lips pull back in a snarl and he actually starts his band with the cuíca, which rarely happens. It's so insistent that it works, somehow. The vermelhos are mad, pounding and plucking and scraping so fast I'm sure they must be hopped on something illegal.

And the wakas dance. Some just sway, but others move so fast I'm sure their feet will be all blisters by morning. I expect Enki to dance with the rest of them — even I'm trying — but he just stands there and smiles.

Like he knows something else is coming.

Suddenly, in the middle of the beat, Felix curses and throws down his drum. The musicians take a few more bars to realize he's stopped.

"What, *my lord*," he says, getting into Enki's face like I wish he wouldn't. "The music isn't good enough for you? Three months out of the catinga, and he thinks his shit smells better than ours."

Enki doesn't move. Not even when some of Felix's spit gets on his face. "I'm just wondering if you fight with as little soul as you play."

To my right, the bloco amarelo laughs. One of them plucks the berimbau and they start in on a beat that's simpler, softer, and instantly recognizable as a challenge. It excites me, but it seems to set the crowd on fire. Before I know it, I'm herded with the rest, back and back until we form the ring, the roda viva of the song.

With Enki and Felix in the middle.

I'm not going to cling to Enki like some hapless girl in an old-Brazil drama, begging him to save himself. I remember the way he said *fight* before, and the effortlessly deliberate way he goaded Felix into this contest. He's a man and a king besides, and nothing I can say will sway him.

But I am worried, I will admit that, because I haven't seen capoeira fought like this outside of a holo — without pads, on a concrete floor, with a circle of chanting onlookers and a bloco for the drums.

They say things like this happen in the verde. But I'm a Tier Eight brat, and my stepmother is an Auntie.

No wonder Enki wanted to take me here.

The drums get louder. The berimbau twangs and booms, speaks of violence and grace. Enki moves like a tiger, Felix like a monkey. I have no doubt about who will win, but I wonder how hard it will be.

"Good luck, Enki," I say. It isn't a whisper, though it isn't very loud, certainly not over the drums and the chanting crowd, but Enki turns and winks at me. Just for a second, no one else notices, but my worry eases.

I watch.

They strip their shirts. Enki bounces on his toes, shakes out his hands. Felix shuffles around him, not caring much for the dance of capoeira. His eyes are nothing but violence. I think there must be something else between them, some injured past that brought them here. Then, faster than I can think, Enki flips into a sideways tumble, his left hand barely grazing the ground. Felix whirls, ducks instinctively, which is good because Enki's already kicking at the air where his head used to be.

Felix rolls away and Enki drops to a crouch. Felix is panting; Enki gleams like a god. Their smiles are eerily similar, feral and hungry.

"Forgotten how to play, Summer King?" Felix says.

"Forgotten how to dance, vermelhinho?"

Pia, the amarela girl, shouts and then trills, a sound from the deep of her throat that raises the hair on my arms. The drums get louder, but no one chants. You don't sing for this kind of fight.

Felix runs toward Enki headfirst. What he lacks in grace he makes up in raw power: His first blow to the head doesn't land, but his second to the ribs does. We all hear the smack, but Enki doesn't even seem to notice. He just springs into a forward flip, arcing over Felix's head like it's no more trouble than jumping a log. Felix doesn't even have time to turn. Enki's leg shoots out and hooks, sending the vermelho boy crashing to the concrete floor.

I hiss. It sounded painful, and when Felix surges to his feet, he's gripping his shoulder. Enki cocks his head, as if to say, *Had enough?* but of course vermelho boy hasn't. He can't just lose like this in front of his bloco and his gang. Enki knows it, he loves it, but that doesn't mean his offer wasn't sincere.

"Enough," Felix says, and that's when the play turns ugly.

Felix jumps into a flying kick that doesn't connect, but drops into a leg sweep that does. Enki catches himself fast, but not fast enough to block the hard, vicious connect Felix's shoes make with his hip. He winces this time, and I feel obscurely relieved at the reminder of his humanity. Sometimes, even to me, Enki seems like he's made of stone.

Enki springs from his half crouch into a scissor kick I'm pretty sure should be impossible. Felix hits the concrete face-first, temple bloody from the kick and his nose bloody from the fall. Enki waits for him to climb to his knees, then kicks him in the ribs. Around me, wakas laugh and clap. Enki's putting on a show, even if Felix doesn't seem to know it. Felix's body blurs as he starts a series of flips and leaps I can't keep track of. Enki goes still, watching and waiting, and when the blows finally come he evades them as easily as an overhanging branch. He laughs, and we all laugh with him. I think that every waka in this room — even the vermelhos — must have voted for him. Here, the summer king has his court. I only hope Felix realizes it soon enough to salvage some of his pride.

Or maybe he won't have to.

Above us, the massive gates that shield the spiderweb from the vortex of garbage chutes and information hubs start to rumble and groan. The eight triangular metal slabs slide back, letting in the brightness of the city's lights — and then a great black shadow.

"Spider!" Pia shouts. She and her bloco scramble to gather up their instruments. "Out! Hurry!"

Wakas run in every direction — shouting for friends, instruments, money. But I stand still. I look up.

The mechanical legs come into view first, carefully gripping the docking tube as it lowers itself into the web. They creak as they move, but not so much as I might have expected, given its size and weight. The bot is probably two hundred years old, with the dents and patches to prove it, but I'm overcome by the sight of it, by its sheer size and unexpected grace.

It keeps the city alive with a thorax full of nanotubes.

And if I stay here much longer, it might crush me when it docks.

Enki's hand grips my wrist, an anchor in the sea of fleeing people. "June?"

Funny, I think, he's asking if I'm all right. "Okay," I say, but I don't move.

And then something strange happens. The belly of the beast descends, reflecting our running shapes indistinctly. Its noise drowns even my heartbeat, even his voice. But I see his face when something intrudes, surprises him . . . hurts him? His mouth opens like he gasps. He stumbles a little and I steady him.

Then I feel the blood.

I move quickly, not so much thinking as *operating*. Some part of me must know what to do, even when most of me is going, *Why? How? Is he okay?* We stumble away, through the remaining crowd and then apart, because I'm afraid whatever hurt him might do it again. When we're at the terraces, alone by the still water and the concrete and the stink, I let him sink against the wall.

"Are you —"

"Fine. I think someone stabbed me."

"That's not . . ."

He shrugs. "Relatively speaking."

He lifts his hands. There's a deep cut high along his rib cage, like someone was aiming for his heart and missed. The free-flowing blood soaks his pants. He begins to shiver despite the warm, still air.

"That's a knife wound," I say, as though I hope he'll shake his head and say, *No, I just tripped.*

He raises his eyebrows. "Clever, for a Tier Eight brat."

"Was it Felix?"

"I doubt it. Vermelhinho was clear on the other side of the web."

I rip my dress and press the wadded-up fabric to the gushing hole in his side. My hands shake, but Enki is holding his own shit together and both of us pretend not to notice.

"Enki, who would want to kill you?"

His smile is sad, which scares me. "June, who wouldn't?"

When he convinces me he'll be okay, I let him call a pod. The Aunties will wonder how he hurt himself, but that's better than bleeding out in the verde. He's stopped shivering by the time it arrives, which I think might be a bad sign, but he's right, no one gets knife wounds on Tier Eight, and I just don't know.

"Should I go with you? Will you be okay?"

He leans against the open door, flushed and stoic and beautiful as always.

"Don't worry," he says, and fingers my hairline with the hand not holding in his blood. "The Aunties are saving me for themselves." He laughs, then stops with a wince. "I wanted you to have a verde night, but not quite like this."

"It was a wonderful night." It was. I'm jumping from a cliff every time I'm with him, but I love the fall too much to stop. He sighs, a sound with more fondness than it has any right to.

"Oh, June, it's always art with you."

*　　*　　*

I declared for summer king at the feet of Auntie Isa, alongside a hundred other boys. In the other cities, Ueda told me, they scoff at the barbarity of our system, at what they call senseless murder every five years. I told him that we all choose it, that for the three months of the contest no one who changes his mind is forced to stay, that the eventual king is so firmly set on his path that no one could sway him. He said, Why die?

Why trade your future, why give your life, why put your head on that altar and let them slice your throat like a sacred cow?

Isn't it obvious? I should have told him.

It's good to be a king.

The wind is high enough to form whitecaps on the normally calm waters of the bay, strong enough to blow sharp sprays of brackish water that drench us before we're even halfway home from O Quilombola. Less than an hour till our grand debut, I'm silent and focused. The tension whips through my light-tree like a storm. But Enki's even looser than normal. He leans back in our tiny boat, trails his hand in the water, and takes deep breaths of the wet air like he's saving some for later.

I've hooked the feed from Bebel's practice room into my fono, and I check it nervously every few seconds as I steer. We've tied so much of this into the music that now our success hinges on it. Well, that and the lights, and the recording of voices I've spliced from dozens of other feeds hidden throughout the city, and the blocks Enki has sworn will stop the Aunties from shutting down our performance early, and —

I stare at my fono. "The voice track is three seconds too long."

"I found something new last night. It's better now."

He raises his eyebrows a fraction. His smile frightens me and he knows it. I realize I've always been a little afraid of him, these past few months. I've just been too ashamed to admit it. Because I'm not afraid he's hurt our project — I trust his sensibility as much as my own. I'm afraid our *best* art might make me lose the Queen's Award.

I start to shiver. He takes my hand from the console and the boat stops, left to lurch on the choppy water. "The original track is still there," he says, surprisingly gentle. "You can change it back."

I could listen to it now. I could argue with him about whatever transgressive, dangerous bit he has inserted without my knowledge. I could let the best artist I know learn exactly how cowardly and self-serving my ambitions are. He's going to die at the end of winter, but I still want the approval of the Queen who will cut his throat.

I feel sick, but I tell myself it's the rocking of the boat. My finger hovers over the fono, a nervous jitter away from betraying everything I've ever believed about myself. Am I really so desperate for establishment approval? But then I think about Mother and Auntie Yaha, and how they'll look at me differently if I can pull this off. If this time I win. *How much of yourself will you give them in exchange?* Enki once asked me. I never answered.

My hand falls to my side. I want to win this award, but not at the expense of the most ambitious art project I've ever attempted. If he's gone too far, I just won't ever tell anyone of my involvement. I'll do Auntie-friendly art in the fall and winter and I'll take my chances. Even if I don't win, at least that way I won't hate myself.

"It's good?" I ask, just to see that smile.

"Oh, June," he says, and smiles, and puts his arms around me so I'm resting against his chest and warm, wet thighs. I feel strangely relaxed and yet hyperaware of every inch of our exposed, touching skin. I want to sit like this forever. "You hear that?" he says after a moment.

I listen, but there's just the hum of the city, the evening birds calling, the water smacking the boat. "What?"

"There's a storm coming."

I look around, panicked. "A storm? How soon? How can you tell?"

"An hour, maybe. The wind. It's whistling from the east."

I swear, Enki has the ears of a bat. Or he modded them that way, never mind how. "Do you think —"

"It will work, June. Or it won't. Nothing we can do about it now."

And this, for whatever reason, relaxes me. It's true. For the past month, we've spent late, grueling nights crawling the four siblings, installing lights and feeds and programming them to respond to remote stimuli.

To respond to the city herself.

I've coordinated with Bebel — in person and anonymously — so that she knows precisely when to start and how long to sing. I've skipped school to spend hours in the markets of the city, in its pods and its meeting halls and sometimes even its homes, to find the ones whose voices will bring this all together. And now summer is almost over. Its wet heat beads our skin, oppresses us because it knows the chill that rides behind it. In two weeks, parliament will start its special sessions again, and Enki will have so much to do that a project as intricate and grand and brash as this will be impossible.

I should probably start the boat up again, since we're drifting too far west of our mooring, but I just trace the muscles of Enki's left calf with a wet finger. We still have half an hour. We'll get back in plenty of time. On the water, maybe the rules don't apply. Maybe here I don't have to wonder what he feels for me, or what Gil will say. When I started this, I swore we would only be art. And maybe we are — good art has a habit of breaking boundaries.

The sun is setting behind the city, but with the clouds rolling in, all we can see is a gradual dimming of light and the occasional angry streak of red.

"There's a song," I say.

"There's always a song," he says.

"It's English. It's about a storm. Or it's about love."

Enki's hands play on my skin. "Same thing, my mamãe would say."

"My papai too. He taught me, do you know it? *Look for the silver lining whenever a cloud appears in the blue.*"

Enki laughs, but he joins me. *"Remember somewhere the sun is shining..."*

I break off. "Wait, what's next? English is so weird, I swear, it's like singing rocks."

"Well, in our mouths, anyway."

I giggle. It's true, Enki and I between us can just barely keep a tune. His voice is low and scratchy and skips through the notes. I have my mother's voice: thin as a reed and a great disappointment to my papai when he realized it would never get much better. But with Enki, my voice is a joy, not a lingering shame.

"I think," Enki says, *"And so the right thing to do is make it shine for you."*

We stumble through the next stanza, pausing every other line to argue over the tune or the words. Enki insists it's *An artful of joys the sadness*, which I point out isn't proper English, and doesn't make any sense besides, and he counters that since when did these weird old songs make any sense? After a protracted three minutes, we agree on *An artful joy fills with sadness*, which doesn't seem right either, but I privately admit that Enki is right, and there's nothing quite as nonsensical as an old English song lyric. We do, however, agree on a triumphant finish, belting *"Try to find the sunny side of life!"* as if the storm clouds might actually listen to us.

A particularly strong wave nearly knocks us out of the boat.

"Twenty minutes," Enki says, though he doesn't check his fono. "We should get back."

I swallow and nod. I lost my nerves in the song, but now, slipping from the warmth of his chest, his arms, his thighs, I feel I'm losing something else.

"Who was your mamãe to know all those songs, Enki?"

He looks away from me, and I think he'll ignore the question or deflect it, but instead he shakes his head, looks back up. He starts to cry, just a little. I don't know if I should comfort him or pretend I don't notice.

"A historian," he says. "She studied at the university in Salvador, before the Pernambuco guerrillas bombed it. She made two copies of everything she could recover from their classified servers, before the 'bucos took it over. She buried one in her garden in the body of an old rag doll, so no one would know what it was if they found it, and then she walked to Palmares Três."

"She *walked* . . ."

"It took her two months. She almost died a dozen times. And she had no idea if the Aunties would take her in. They refuse thousands each year, did you know that? They don't like contamination, our Aunties."

"So why . . ." I gasp. "The library?"

He smiles, and wipes his eyes. "A penniless Salvadorense six months pregnant with a negro bastard? It was her only chance."

I take his hand. "Do you hate us?"

"I used to."

This seems to still my heart. There's a distant bitterness in his voice, something almost nostalgic. "Used to?"

He turns to me. My other hand falls off the boat's console and now we're bobbing again, like my thoughts, tossed in a storm. "I always loved everything too much, even after she died. I would love the lights, the blocos, the spiderweb, the street fairs. I hated the catinga, who doesn't, but I know you've seen it, how beautiful those vats can look when the light hits them. I wasn't made for that kind of hate, but I felt it anyway."

"And now?"

He laughs. I want to hug him but I don't, I won't. "June, June," he says. "You say you don't want to know, you turn away at every chance, but then you ask and ask. Why not be like Gil, why not pretend I'm unknowable and perfect, like some orixá?"

My lights feel hot as the sun on my skin. If I look down, I'm sure they'll be visible beneath my wet shirt. But the rest of me is cold and afraid and ready to run.

Like I have all summer.

"I can't be like Gil," I say. "He thinks everyone deserves love. He thinks the people who should love us will. He thinks the people he loves will always return it. And they do, because he's Gil. But I'm not easy to love, I haven't trusted that since . . . sometimes I think I'm alone as you are, Enki."

"Then ask, June."

I can barely hear myself over the wind. "Why don't you hate anymore?"

"Because I've infected myself with bio-nanobots that stop it."

I love him. I shouldn't, I swore I wouldn't, but I have no more defenses. My next question is as inevitable as death.

"Do you love me?"

"I love the whole world."

And he kisses me.

My skin burns like fire, but this is what she sees, the city that he loves:

The four siblings glow like falling stars, transmuting and flowing into one another in a feedback loop I spent weeks perfecting. They kindle slowly, four smoldering lumps of coal floating in the bay. The lights of the city itself dim, allowing the crowds that rush to the glass and the parks and the walkways to witness our display more clearly.

The lights begin in a gentle, familiar white, but soon enough a hint of color appears. Green blooms first on O Quilombola, our crab island that glows with an intensity those watchers in the city can't quite describe, but will fascinate them. Then A Castanha, A Velha Preta, and finally the massive lump of A Quarentena (just on its city-facing side, because we would have needed a year to collect enough lights to cover the whole island). And then more colors — the orange of bougainvillea, the purple of açaí berries, the red of hibiscus — bursting and fading in the sea of limned verde.

This would have been enough. I realize that as I watch with Enki at the very base of the great pyramid, where gray and white barnacles cling to the pylons and night fish brush against our feet. If we had just lit the four siblings, we would have created an object worthy of our ambitions.

At least, everyone else would have seen it that way. Gil would still hug me and tell me I'm a genius, I would still impress Queen Oreste and the Aunties when I reveal my involvement in a week. They might even have remembered it for a while, at least until the next sun year, and the selection of a new Queen. I might mention it to my children as something fun I did one time.

And it would do nothing at all. It would change nothing at all. It would move no one at all, and so it wouldn't really be art, would it?

"Bebel," I say to my fono, almost a whisper though it doesn't need to be. "You ready?"

"They'll never forget this, will they?" she whispers back.

"Not even if they tried."

Where's her music? he had asked. *Here, Papai, here.*

I watch the seconds tick down. Over my shoulder, Enki smiles and I let him run his fingers through the interface. It pulses green: connection verified. Bebel and her musicians are now jacked into the city.

Bebel's voice slips over the speakers, low and gorgeous. For the first time, I think of how the opening lines of the song relate to my papai. She speaks of being alive and yet feeling like you're among the dead. I wonder if that's how he felt in those last bleak days when he seemed a stranger to me.

And maybe Bebel deserves the Queen's Award more than any of us — her voice treads that high wire of sorrow and joy so deftly you forget there's a drop on either side. At the sound, the lights on the islands explode. The initial burst is so fierce I need to squint, though Enki is wide-eyed and still.

Are there bio-nanobots for that too?

I've mapped each shade of color to a sound — orange for her round voice, brown for Pasqual's guitar, shades of red and green for the other instruments. I didn't know how well it would work until this moment.

It's chaotic and muddy and stark all at once. It's music imagined as light, and I can hardly bear to look away.

But there's one last thing to do.

In the middle of a verse, before the final, ever-faster, multi-harmonic ramp through the chorus that almost everyone knows, Bebel pauses. The city holds her breath, and so do I. What did he add? How much will I regret this in the morning? Enki touches my forehead, like he's blessing whatever choice I make.

I play his track.

"Pepi," a woman says, "I told you to eat it, you want to make your mamãe sad? I made it just for you."

And another voice.

"Come on, baby, menina, coração, it won't hurt, it's just — oh, shit, that *hurt*! What'd you do —"

And another.

"We're going to kick ass tonight, after what those vermelhos tried to pull last time —"

And more and more, all at once, overlapping one another and silencing and looping and feeding back into the lights of the four siblings, the city speaking and the city listening.

And then, quite clearly despite the layering voices, I hear one that surprises me. Oreste: "That boy will be the death of me, I swear, Maria. Why did we ever allow his election?"

"Because of the wakas, Queen. And the verde."

Oreste sighs. "Always the wakas and the verde."

All the voices cut. I'm trembling, staring at Enki and wondering how he ever managed to catch Oreste and Auntie Maria saying something so damning. I'll never be able to claim this project. Not if I want to win the Queen's Award. The knowledge is restful, in a way.

He was right. His version is better.

I try to catch his eyes, but he's gone rigid and distant, staring at the now-dormant lights of the four siblings. I wonder what's wrong, but not for long. A memory of his voice speaks into the silence:

"You can't smell the catinga," he says (he said), to a roomful of shocked Aunties covering their noses and rushing to the doors, "until it comes back home."

The harmonizing singers get louder, more insistent, striking their words off of one another like metal on metal, flashing sparks.

"June," Enki says as the crescendo is crashing over me, over the islands, over the city. He says it more than once, I think, before I finally hear him.

He's shaking. When I touch him, he flinches like it hurts.

The song ends.

And in the breath the city takes — that drawn-out, stunned silence that should be my moment of greatest satisfaction — I am terrified.

"The city," he says. "Something is collapsing in the city."

We run.

Up through long-disused emergency stairs, so dusty and caked with the droppings of a century of roosting seabirds that I sneeze uncontrollably. When I fall, Enki pulls me up, rough and hard, by the elbow. I take them two at a time, Enki does three. My thighs burn like the lights on O Quilombola and at first I think his energy must be a mod but then I realize it's just Enki.

When we reach the terraces, my shirt sticks to my skin and each gasping breath sears a little. Enki bends over with something more than just exhaustion. Even here, there's a crowd, though almost no one lives on the bottom terrace. At first, people only glance at us as we push them aside, racing for the one pod station on this level. But then someone points, and someone else laughs, and then the crowd turns into a swarm with us at the center.

"Enki! That was some trick —"

"Oreste will think twice next time —"

"Something to tell my grandkids —"

Enki stops running when the people get too close, hemming us in. His muscles tense, he looks around with sharp, darting motions, like a panicked bird. He's still shaking, and I know why.

Because he can feel the city. Because he can hear her.

Because he has infected himself with bio-nanobots that let him do that.

And I can see, clear as if I read the instruction manual that came with his mods, that if we don't hurry, if we don't get to where this collapse is going to happen and stop it, the pain of the city will be his own pain.

But Enki isn't a city, he's a human, and he might not survive that.

"Let us through!" I shout. "We have to find the Aunties."

The voices mingle, but not like the roda viva of the song. Like a faceless, screaming monster, demanding our attention and our love and our time when we have none to spare.

"Please clear the way for official security business."

The pleasantly officious female voice is so incongruous in this setting that Enki and I stare at each other.

"Security bots," he says after a second.

"Crap. Auntie Maria."

No, Auntie Maria wouldn't be very happy about what the city heard her say.

The leviathan crowd quiets. They hesitate — should they protect their boy hero, their summer prince? Or should they run, before one of them gets caught in Auntie Maria's notoriously sticky grip?

"Please clear the way for official security business."

The voice is closer now, but we still can't see the bots through the crowd.

"Go," Enki says suddenly. He puts his arms around my shoulders, angles himself so his back is to the bots and I'm shielded from their view.

"But . . ."

"What can they do to me, June? It's the fastest way to get their attention. I'll try to convince them. But if they catch you with me, they'll know who you are."

And they'll know I was involved in an art project that exposed the Queen and one of her trusted advisers to the entire city. He knew what it meant when I didn't listen to the file. He understood what I was sacrificing.

But if they catch me now, my chance of getting the Queen's Award goes very close to zero. It seems trivial, in the face of what might happen to the city, and yet Enki still considers it.

I love the whole world, he said. Not me in particular. It's my stupid lips and skin and pulse that make him seem to reciprocate. What meaning does love have when you're not capable of anything else?

The crowd shouts. I hear the crash of thrown objects.

"— official security business!"

"It's on the Sé line," he says. He closes his eyes, the shivering redoubles. "High up, between eight and nine on the western face. There should be a spider there, it's . . . oh, God."

Enki sinks to his knees so fast I nearly buckle with him. "What —"

He opens his eyes. "It's going to fall off. Something is wrong with its thorax. It's too old, the nanotubes aren't actually regenerating. Can't support its weight."

"So tell them, Enki!"

"They won't believe me."

I kneel, so my head is level with his. "You're the summer king," I say.

"With a dozen mods so illegal they don't even have names. Who just hijacked the city for an art show."

"What . . . what should I do?"

There's a blast, shrieks. The security bots must be firing air guns into the crowd. I wince — that always looked painful on the holos.

Enki laughs a little and rests his head in the hollow between my neck and shoulder. This close, I can sense his struggle to just keep himself conscious.

"Find Ueda. The ambassador from Tokyo 10. Tell him he has to speak with Auntie Maria immediately. Tell him to confess everything. That's the only way they'll believe me."

Confess everything? If I thought my heart stuttered earlier tonight, when Enki talked about bio-nanobots and loving the whole world, that's nothing compared to the slow-growing horror that roots itself there now.

"What did you do, Enki?"

"Sometimes I think you're lucky, June. That you can hate."

Take a deep breath. Save the city. Think later. "Why will he believe me?"

"Tell him . . . tell him I said the first night, he asked me to whip him before we —"

I let him go like he's caught fire. I think I might drown in my horror. Of all the people for him to sleep with, and of all the reasons for him to do it — Enki smiles like it's the last time he'll see me.

Everyone knows the summer kings screw like mayflies.

But not all of them screw foreign dignitaries for illegal biomods.

"Summer King, please come with us. We are on official security business."

Maybe Enki stands. Maybe they drag him away. I don't know; I'm already elbowing my way through the crowd, blinking back tears, hating Enki with all my heart.

Determined to save him.

I grab a pod by shoving the person who flashed it out the doors as they're closing. I tell it to go to Tier Eight, and pray these tunnels are still safe. As the pod rockets through the city, I jack into the operator and beg her to let me speak to Ueda-sama.

"I'm sorry, June," says the city, that same pleasant, reassuring voice I've heard all my life. "But Ueda-sama has not given you clearance.

Would you like to leave a message with the department of foreign affairs?"

"No, listen, it's an emergency. Believe me, he'll want to hear this. It's about Enki."

"I'm sorry, June, but the department cannot allow access to any level-ten personnel without clearance. Perhaps I could file your message with the department as urgent?"

"No!"

"There's no need to be agitated —"

"A spider bot is about to crash on Tier Nine!"

The voice pauses. "I have no information of that kind, June," she says. "None of our warning systems have triggered. Spider operation is perfectly normal."

"None?" I say.

"No, June. We are fully operational. Would you like to leave that message?"

"That's . . . no, never mind. Thank you."

"You're quite welcome, June."

The city jacks out. I'm left staring at the now-blank face of my fono, hurtling through the city in someone else's pod and wondering the kinds of things that would have been unthinkable even an hour ago.

None of our warning systems have triggered.

Why would Enki be able to feel something in the city that the city's own warning systems can't detect? This is Palmares Três, the jewel on the bay, and surely a structural failure of this magnitude would show up on multiple warning sensors.

But I remember Enki's face as he collapsed on the floor, looking as if he could literally feel the city's pain. He seemed so sure. He took for granted that I would believe him.

Now there's only one way for me to get through to Ueda-sama, and using it will mean ruining my plan to win the Queen's Award.

"Bebel will probably win," I mutter.

Is it worth it? How will I feel if it turns out that his mods have caused strange side effects, made Enki imagine things that aren't there? There's a reason the Aunties have made so many mods illegal, after all. If people in Tokyo 10 feel like destroying their bodies, that doesn't mean we have to do it here.

"How could he have done this to himself?"

I've been pacing as much as the pod will let me, but this thought makes me freeze. I look down at my hands, cut and raw from planting so many lights on hard rocks. I think about how to me, this is nothing, no price at all for the beauty of the art I created tonight.

I remember what I said to him when I convinced him to be my partner.

You chose to use your own body as a canvas that no one could ignore.

I understood that then. When all I'd seen was a laugh, a plunge of lights, music and wakas and dance. It was nothing, the grandes thought. Just a prank. But I heard that note and predicted the symphony. I didn't take it far enough, though, did I?

Enki will die at the end of winter. Why not do everything to his body that he possibly can? Why not experience every enhancement, every altered state, every different way of being that modern technology has to offer? And if Palmares Três has made itself too backward to have it, why not look elsewhere, to perhaps the most advanced city on the planet?

Enki will never be a grande. He'll never have children and teach them the lyrics to his mother's old songs, he'll never walk the paths of the verde and complain that it looked nicer fifty years ago, he'll never try to play football in the park and realize he's not as young as he used to be.

He has always known what that meant; he has always understood what his art demanded. And me?

I was just playing at being radical, trying on transgression like my skin lights, secure that I could cut it out and go right back to graduating and university just as soon as the year was over.

Just as soon as Enki *died*.

The pod shuffles to a stop at Tier Eight. The doors open. I blink at the jostling crowd on the platform, so unusual for this time of night.

"Destination?" the pod queries when I don't leave.

I let it read my own flash. "Royal Tower," I say.

And then I ping Auntie Yaha.

In the throne room, the Aunties yell at one another.

"The city has confirmed that all sectors are fully operational," says Auntie Serena, the municipal director. "For the fifth time."

"I don't know why we should believe the boy," says Auntie Isa. "He's just causing more trouble."

Ueda-sama, still disheveled from his rush to Royal Tower, coughs. "I'm afraid," he begins, then tries louder. "The biomodifications allow him to have a special rapport with AI interface. He has made connections your systems don't have. And your systems . . ." He coughs again. "They're rather out of date."

Auntie Serena bristles at this. "They've served us quite well for the last century, Ambassador Ueda. Palmares Três hasn't had a municipal disaster even close to the ones brought on by your city's addiction to biomodification —"

"Serena!" Auntie Yaha says, and Auntie Serena stumbles to a stop. Apparently even disgraced foreign dignitaries can't have their city's ethics derided to their faces.

They go on like that, while I stand in the corner, wondering what I should do, wondering how much time we have left before the slow-moving bot loses its grip and crashes. How can they debate like this when there's even a chance that thousands of people might die? The megatrusses are strong, but a spider bot is big enough to damage them. I don't know where they've taken Enki, but Auntie Maria is conspicuously absent, and I suppose that whatever he told them was unconvincing.

"Has anyone actually checked on the bot?" Queen Oreste says from her chair at the head of the conference table. The room quiets.

"It's moving slowly," Auntie Serena says, "but you know those old clankers. There's no indication anything is abnormal."

"We should order it back down to the storage pod as a precautionary measure."

Auntie Serena looks suddenly uncomfortable. "I have, Queen."

"And?"

"It's slow."

"Perhaps," Auntie Yaha says, and I can feel her discomfort, her fury even from my shadowed space ten meters behind her. "Perhaps we should evacuate the west side of tiers Eight and Seven, just in case."

"Just because a spider bot is *slow*?" says Auntie Isa.

"The modifications —" Ueda-sama begins, but Queen Oreste waves her hand in distaste.

"There is a reason we don't allow such things in our city, Ambassador. Inhuman abilities don't mesh well with human brains. Auntie Maria tells me that Enki is nearly insensible because of the effects of these modifications. I don't think it's wise to trust him on this."

Nearly insensible? It must be close, then. I ache for what I imagine he's feeling. And I'm furious, because a disaster is about to fall on our city, and they will do nothing about it.

"You have to evacuate," I say.

They ignore me.

"It's going to happen soon," I say, even louder. "If he's in that much pain, the city knows it's going to happen soon."

Auntie Yaha turns to me, red with fury. "June," she bites out, "will you please shut up?"

The other Aunties shuffle uncomfortably, but none so much as look at me. Not even Queen Oreste.

What will happen to Enki when that spider drops?

What will happen to the city?

I know what I have to do. I want the Queen's Award so badly I could get on my knees and beg, but I don't hesitate.

A brush of my fingers, and I see the familiar array of my fono. I jack into the city.

"Yes, June?" she whispers, low in my ear.

"I need you to send a message," I say.

"To whom, June?"

"Enki."

"You don't have clearance for the summer king, June."

I smile. "That's okay. I just want you to know, City, I want *you* to know that I need cameras. Lots of cameras in the throne room, in about thirty seconds."

"I don't know what to do with this information, June," she says.

"Could you tell all the parts of yourself? Even the small ones?"

"I can do that," she says. "I still don't . . . I see now. He says, *Does forty work?*"

I lean back against the wall and close my eyes. "Yeah. Forty works."

They arrive like a plague of locusts, streaming through the open windows and doors and even cracks in the wall. Some of them wobble and die after hitting the anti-camera technology, but the throne room is one of the few areas of Royal Tower open to certain kinds of camera bots. These are plenty enough eyes to see exactly what I'm going to do.

"What is going on?" Queen Oreste says, rising from her seat.

I don't give them time to wonder. I stride to the front of the room and stop right beside her.

"There's a malfunctioning spider bot on the second megatruss, west side, Tier Nine," I say, clearly as I can to the expectant horde. "The summer king has acquired bio-nanomods that allow him to interface with the city in a way no one has ever done before. I think we all know how old and outdated the spider bots are. The city's systems are malfunctioning, but the bot is going to collapse, and any residents of tiers Seven and Eight on the west side are in severe danger. You should all get out now, if you can. And if any engineers can do something to stop it from falling, now is the time to try."

I stop, take a deep breath. There. That should do it.

"June."

It's the Queen. I turn to her, slowly. "How do you know?" she says. "Why are you so sure about him?"

"I've seen him do it," I say quietly. "Dozens of times before, I've seen him do things that are impossible unless he's talking to the city."

"But *why you?*" says the Queen, insistent.

I sigh and face the cameras.

"I'm his collaborator."

FALL

I won't call what I did with Ueda a mistake, though I know 'I should. *Remember how Sebastião justified it? He said that summer kings were above morality, and he was right, and he was wrong.*

Gods are what people worship. Men are what die.

The trouble, the truth that I realized only after I saw you facing those cameras, was that I love Gil. And now you will say that I love everyone, and I do, but not all in the same way. You're the other reason he didn't declare, I don't know that he told you. Even before we met I owed you his life. Maybe he could have beat me, but then, maybe not. If he were the summer king, if I were the boy dancing on glass, would we have come together? Would he still love me?

Would I still hurt him?

I won't call it a mistake — though it was a mistake.

The summer kings are gods, and we are finally, in the end, just men.

Gil peels the shells from shrimp as if he's undressing them for the evening. Beside him, shoulders touching, Enki dices cilantro with surprising care. I offered to help, but they both insisted I rest on the hammock Enki has strung across his living room. In a large frying pan, coconut milk stews with palm oil and chiles and a dozen other spices. I've been watching them cook for the past half hour. Gil got his mamãe to write down the family recipe for him, which as far as I'm concerned warrants all the time in the world. A vatapá stew is not something anyone should rush, and from the smells drifting over my lazy, swinging perch, this promises to be delicious.

From behind, Enki and Gil could easily pose for a holo feature on the summer king's contented domesticity, but I can see the cracks. Enki's movements are uncharacteristically slow and deliberate to control the jittery aftereffects of some unnamed mod. Gil asks him perfectly pleasantly to check on the stewing chiles, but there's more pain than warmth behind the words.

Enki could have banged half of Tier Eight without hurting Gil as much as a few sessions with Ueda-sama. A broken spider bot rusts in the bay, a fallen mechanical giant, a monument to the consequences of our city's enforced technological backwardness. Not even the Aunties can ignore it — not when the only thing that saved Tier Seven was the quick work of several technicians who made an impromptu chute of mushi bots and another nearby spider bot. If not for my desperate message — which the whole city knows the Aunties tried to prevent me from sending — a few thousand people would probably be dead right now. Which made Enki's indiscretions with the ambassador from Tokyo 10 barely rate a few hours of shocked consternation. They care about the exotic, illegal biomods that Ueda-sama gave Enki, not what he got in exchange. There are more important struggles: Fault lines between technophiles and tech isolationists have erupted into an ideological war, its battleground the streets and transport hubs and parliamentary hearings.

But in this room, the real conflict threads through our spoken words, in the way Gil stiffens when Enki touches his ear, in the way Enki glances at me as if he wishes I could do something to help.

I was angry with Enki at first, but mostly because I wanted his kiss on the water to mean something. Gil hates what Enki's done because he doesn't believe Enki could ever love someone like Ueda. He thinks Enki is losing his soul, sleeping with people for nothing but material goods. But he doesn't understand that Enki loves the whole world. Why *shouldn't* he love Ueda-sama? Why *shouldn't* he love me? I want to talk to him about it, but he avoids any conversation about Enki's mods, and I've been too afraid to tell him about our kiss. Too afraid that he'll hate me for it.

So instead I watch holos, seeing how the casters react to my sudden, dramatic involvement in the life of their summer king. Most assume we're romantically as well as artistically involved, though I've denied it in my few interviews. A kiss is nothing, and it's none of their business besides. Some are even sympathetic about my probation for the Queen's Award. Auntie Isa says none of my collaborations with Enki will be eligible for consideration, and that if we do it again, I'll be disqualified entirely. I've decided that this means I still have a slight chance. If I didn't, why bother with probation? Enki looks baffled and a little pitying when I mention it, but I don't care. I still want the Queen's Award, and I'll do as much as I can with any chance they give me.

"That finalist from the verde has been on all the news feeds," I say when the silence stretches too thin.

Gil's shoulders sag in relief. "You're right, I saw her on Ricarda yesterday. What's her name?"

"Lucia," Enki says. He's perfectly still; even his mouth barely moves. Some sort of mod effect, I've learned, and when it starts, he often loses touch with reality for hours at a time.

"Do you know her?" I ask. Now that technology is suddenly the most important issue in the city, Lucia's projects have reached municipal prominence overnight.

He moves his head very slowly toward me, like he's pulling it away from a wall coated in sticky glue. Sweat beads on his forehead. Gil frowns and takes his hand.

"Heard of her," Enki says. "She was getting to be the biggest techhead in the verde. She could jack all sorts of things to do what they weren't supposed to. Fonos that could pick up banned feeds from Salvador, Lisbon, even a few of the Tokyos." His shoulders jerk and his movements regain their normal grace, the spell over with an abruptness

I've grown used to. Gil moves away from him to turn down the heat on the stove. I start to get up, but the hammock seems to encase my limbs; it's too awkward to move, and I give up too easily.

"Tech-head?" Gil says.

Enki laughs and plants a kiss at the base of Gil's neck. "How many times have you been to the verde, menino? You never saw the bootleggers in Carioca Plaza?"

Gil freezes, then relaxes into Enki's arms. He's taller than Enki, and more obviously muscular, and yet Enki dominates him so carelessly. Enki is trying to apologize in his own emotionally blunt way; he's trying to say that it doesn't matter what he does with other people, as long as he and Gil are together.

Maybe that will persuade Gil eventually. Now, Gil just closes his eyes. "The ones selling those cobbled-together fonos?"

"The best in the city," Enki says. "Tech-heads rewire the basic models."

Now this makes me sit up in my hammock, nearly tumble to Enki's bamboo floor. "I thought they did that because they couldn't afford real ones."

Enki snorts and looks at me over his shoulder. "What we can't afford, June, is to accept the little they give us. Standard-issue fonos? We have just as much of a right to speak to the city as any Tier Eight brat."

This stings, though I wonder if Enki meant it to. I walk over. Enki watches me carefully. "So what do the jacked fonos do?" I ask him.

"Show nearby security bots so the grafiteiros can avoid them. Access the up-tier city voice."

"The city's voice is different in the verde?" This shocks me. I've heard her all my life, answering simple questions and directing me when I'm lost.

Enki shrugs; he can't even bother to respond to such privileged ignorance.

I try again. These days, I feel as if I'm nothing but one prolonged attempt. "They jack the fonos to speak to the city?"

For a moment, Enki's eyes turn as reflective as a cat's. "They try," he says.

On the night of his eighteenth birthday, Enki sits on a throne of shells and shale and fallen blooms; Gil and I sprawl at his feet. The rock of A Quarentena pulses like a beast beneath us — the insistent boom of bloco amarelo blasting up through the island itself — and dancing on it are the hundred luckiest wakas in the city. Enki is on a trip, riding some wave of his mods. Occasionally, he reaches down to touch Gil, who is too still beneath him. City lights bathe us. Near the pylons, a muddy rainbow shoots from the colored array grafiteiros have hacked onto the fallen body of the spider that nearly hit the city.

Camera bots flit everywhere, but none get too close to us. We invited Sebastião and a few other casters to the birthday party, since these days there's no avoiding them, and there's something flash about letting them bask in the glow of our fame.

I finished my tree last night, and I take a hollow delight in the knowledge of what Mother will think when she sees the dress I'm wearing to show it off. Gil's mamãe helped me make it, though she made me swear not to tell. She worries about Gil, his mamãe, and she's not the only one. His introspective, quiet listlessness hasn't improved in the week since our dinner at Enki's house. In the two weeks since I outed myself in the throne room, I don't think I've seen him dance once. I want to hate Enki for him, but I think Enki might have infected me with his biomods, because these days I find it harder and harder to hate anyone.

Especially the ones I love.

"Gil," I say, rolling closer to him on our pile of beautiful detritus (because Enki and I haven't given up on art, how could we, though I hope the Aunties won't have enough imagination to notice). "Could I wear your coat?"

Gil opens his eyes. He seems confused for a moment; his pupils are dilated a near-black that perhaps the low light could excuse, but I suspect shouldn't.

"Your tree," he says, so softly I know his words by the shape of his lips.

"It's cold," I say, though it isn't, not really.

He puts it around my shoulders; I'm glad, because it means that whatever he took, it wasn't enough for a trip.

"Dance with me?" I say.

Gil closes his eyes as if he wants to say no, but he nods.

For the first time all night, I feel something like happiness. It's been a hard few weeks for all of us — even Enki, though the way mods grip him sometimes, it can be hard to credit him with any human emotion.

I slide off the throne, Gil's long spangled coat flapping behind me. Gil even smiles when he helps me up. As soon as we step outside the invisible bubble surrounding Enki's makeshift throne, the cameras swarm close. I swat a few away and they back off. The same can't be said of the wakas, unfortunately.

Two weeks ago, no one had heard of June Costa, but now I'm as regular an item on caster feeds as Gil. Plenty of wakas hate me, but the ones we invited to this party don't — or at least they'd never admit it.

"June!" a girl calls, so young I wonder how she snagged an invite. She points to her arms, where she's implanted a crude version of my skin lights. The design is pretty, though, and I smile at her.

It isn't as grand as shutting down the city with a light and sound installation, but there are worse things than being admired and influential. I wonder if the Aunties are watching me; I wonder if Mother is. What would she think of my light-tree if Papai were still alive? I imagine her commenting on the richness of the colors, or the intricacy of the leaves. If I had the Queen's Award, could she finally see me again? Could she forgive every poisoned thing between us?

Gil just stands in the gyrating crowd as though he's heard of dancing but can't quite remember what it is. I take his hand and hold it over my heart.

"You're warm," he says.

I shake my hips in answer and tip back my head, so Palmares Três hangs upside down from a purple sky. A moment later, Gil pulls me closer. He laughs. It's harsh and sharp, but it's laughter and it's dancing, and I hope that maybe Gil has gotten over the worst of his sadness.

The moon sets, and we're still dancing, wet with sweat and drunk on movement. A few cameras still hover nearby, but not so many as before. Even the gossip casters get tired eventually, and it's Enki they're really after, not Gil or me.

I wrap my arms around Gil's slick neck and rest my head against his collarbone. "He's sorry, you know."

"I know. But he'd do it again."

"That's Enki, isn't it? The other side of what we love."

"That he doesn't care how he hurts other people?"

"No, no," I say, aching and wondering how Gil can't see what's so clear to me. "That he knows exactly how he hurts people, and he cares, and he does it anyway."

Gil stops dancing with the abruptness of a slap. He starts to walk — away from Enki, away from the dancers and the cameras, though a few try to follow us. I glance at Enki and they drop, lifeless, to the rock. My sandals slip as I chase after him. I balance myself with outflung arms and keep running.

Gil finally stops close to the edge. He stares at the waves crashing against the worn rock. He won't look at me even when I touch his hip.

"Why Ueda?" he says. "He's a king, there's no guarantees of anything, I understand that, June, I swear I do, but why some grande he cares nothing for? Why whore himself like he doesn't even matter?"

"But," I say, "he whored himself for the most important thing in the world."

Now Gil turns to me; I almost wish he hadn't. He's screaming and furious. "For mind-twisting biomods he can hardly control?"

"Art."

Gil wipes his eyes and laughs. "You two are insane, you know that? The way you privilege art —"

"We kissed."

I say it fast, so I don't lose my nerve. Gil stares at me. This is it. This is how I'll lose my best friend in the whole world. If he was upset about *Ueda* . . .

"When?"

A sob catches in my throat, but I answer him. "Right before our show. On the water. Gil, I'm sorry, I didn't mean —"

"So he *hasn't* forgotten how."

I'm braced for a storm of betrayed fury. Not his gentle, relieved smile or the softness in his eyes. "Gil?"

He takes my hands. "I told you before, you know, that I wouldn't mind. I don't. If he has to be with someone else . . . oh, June, as long as he isn't destroying himself with people like Ueda-sama . . ."

He's *relieved*. He hugs me, so fiercely that for a moment I can't breathe.

"I love you both more than anyone but my mamãe," he whispers. "I think you can reach that part of him . . . the one that scares me. You can keep him safe."

I don't think anyone can keep our summer king safe, but I don't say so. Gil has offered me absolution, however undeserved. I am greedy enough to take it.

"He asked for her to come," Auntie Yaha says.

She and Mother sit beside each other at the table, though they don't touch. Across from them, I pick at an acarajé patty that has gone cold while they argue.

"I don't see why June should meet with some disgraced foreign dignitary. What if he tries to get her to trade sex for city secrets?"

"I don't have any city secrets, Mother. And I promise, I'm in no danger of sleeping with him."

Mother rolls her eyes. "It's all you wakas do these days, isn't it? I watch the holos, since you won't tell me anything anymore. I see how you are around that negro prince —"

"You mean the *summer king* —"

"I mean the one who has turned himself into an international incident! Gil is one thing, that waka mother of his couldn't raise a cat, but *you*, June —"

"Valencia! June!" Auntie Yaha reaches across the table, touching my hand and quieting me before I start to scream something Mother really won't forgive.

"Enki is the summer king, like him or not," she says. "But, June, it would be nice if you could tell your mother and me more about what you do, so we don't have to worry so much."

I roll my eyes. "If by 'worry' you mean 'scream at me,' then no thanks."

"Maybe we wouldn't have to scream if you weren't neglecting any hope of your future to participate in this waka orgy."

"Who I have sex with is none of your business, Mother."

"So you are sleeping with him!"

"What were you, a nun at seventeen?"

"I wasn't an attention whore, throwing myself at celebrities every night."

"You're jealous that I'm famous."

"I'm embarrassed that my daughter doesn't know how to comport herself in public."

I'm suddenly so tired of this. I don't even know how to speak to her without yelling anymore. So I stand. "I'll be happy to go to dinner with you, Auntie Yaha," I say.

"June," she says, a note in her voice closer to pleading than I've ever heard. "Sit down. You and your mother —"

"Are never going to work it out. You should really stop trying."

I leave, and Auntie Yaha doesn't call me back. Mother doesn't even look at me.

She is my mother and I hate her. But I wish that I didn't.

I want to go to the park, or my grotto in the walkway, or even school to talk to Bebel, but I just can't bear the feeling of a city's eyes on me right now, so I hide in my room.

I ping Gil a few times, but he doesn't respond. I flip on my holo and see why: at least four feeds of him and Enki sharing an afternoon picnic in Royal Park. Sebastião has a clip on repeat of Enki reaching into the white pulpy flesh of a durian fruit and Gil licking it off his fingers. My heart starts to race just looking, so I shut everything off and wonder if I might scream. I dreamed of fame, back when Gil and I were just two anonymous wakas. I imagined caster interviews and winning the Queen's Award, choking up when I thanked my papai during the acceptance speech. And though this reality feels stickier than my daydreams, I can't bring myself to regret it.

Enki says that Oreste hates me now, but she gave Auntie Yaha the chair of an important committee. I still might win the Queen's Award if I play this properly. I'm certainly the most notorious of the finalists. The number of technophiles grows by the day, and they all appreciate what I did to save the city. It's like with Enki: Love is its own kind of power.

That's what sticks in my thoughts when I take out my long-buried sheets of drawing paper and start to sketch. I've spent so much time constructing high-concept art that I'd nearly forgotten the simpler sensation of a pencil scratch on wood-pulp paper. It's all obscenely expensive, but Mother insisted I learn proper art, and she's made sure I've had a steady supply all my life.

Even the last two years.

I sketch my tree and then I put Gil and Enki in its branches. The image makes me feel warm. My tension holds in my fingers, but it leaves that space behind my eyes. Soon enough, that one is as finished as I can make it. Instead of taking a breath, stretching my cramping hand, admiring my work, I reach for another sheet of paper and start again. This time I'm surprised to find myself sketching Auntie Yaha at the wedding, in her simple turban of patterned linen and a wide blue skirt. She smiles off frame, a new bride. As I sketch, I realize that I found her beautiful. Was it possible that for a moment I hoped my mother could find some happiness with her new wife? That maybe this would ease the distance between us? I must have, because that hope permeates the sketch itself, a message across time.

"Oh."

I drop the paper, whirl around. Auntie Yaha is standing in the open door. Her turban is red, her clothes far from plain, and she's still beautiful, though I have hardly seen her genuine smile in a year.

"I . . . do you want it?" I ask.

She stares at me for a long time without answering. I wonder if something in the sketch offends her, but it isn't that kind of stillness. Finally, she just shakes her head and looks away. Yaha is an Auntie, no matter how much she looks like a waka in my drawing, and so I stay quiet while she composes herself.

"We should leave soon," she says, clipped and brusque. "The reservation is at seven."

"We're doing this in public?"

"Best for the city to see our good relations. You're not bad at politics for a waka, June, but you should leave this to me."

I want to snap that she has my political skills to thank for her new committee chair. But instead I say, "I'll be ready in five minutes." I'm tired of hurting people just because I can. I don't know why I ever enjoyed it.

I wear pants and a simple high-neck tunic — the lines are nice and a bit of webbing at the neck lets my lights peek through, but it's surprisingly conservative given my outfits of late. Auntie Yaha nods in satisfaction when I step into the hall. Mother peers at me from her chair by the garden, but she doesn't say anything and I pretend I don't see her.

Auntie Yaha has a government pod take us directly to Xique, the node on Tier Six known for its chic restaurants and wild clubs. Gil and I don't bother with it much, since the music's better in Founders Park or the verde, and there are too many grandes around for our tastes. Still, it feels very sophisticated to alight from the sliding pod door with Auntie Yaha. Heads swivel as we step out, at first because anyone who can get permission for private transport into Xique in the evening has to be important, and then because they recognize me. Cameras swarm, but I barely notice them. You can get used to almost anything.

Ueda-sama steps from his own personal transport a moment later. "June," he says, and bends slightly at the hips. After a moment, I return the greeting. Auntie Yaha touches us both on our shoulders, exuding the professional friendliness that I'm sure is the real reason for her new promotion.

"I'm so glad that we can finally talk," the ambassador of Tokyo 10 says.

I smile, emulating Auntie Yaha for the sake of the cameras. "These are certainly better circumstances," I say, and he shakes his head, a single rueful gesture that surprises me because it feels honest.

"Shall we?" Auntie Yaha says, indicating the crowded walkway that leads into the heart of the node. Lucky for us, the restaurant is close to the platform. Any longer of a walk, and we would have needed a few of Auntie Maria's security bots just to push through the crowd. Auntie Yaha and Ueda-sama make small talk while I try to seem serene and unruffled. Mostly I agreed to this because I knew it would help Enki. He might not care what Oreste thinks of him, but she is Queen, and she's spent the past month stymieing him at every opportunity.

But I'm curious too. Ueda-sama is a grande's grande — a hundred if he's a day. He and Enki don't seem to even be from the same planet, but they had an affair for months. Ueda-sama is smooth and pleasant like a still pool: so reflective it's impossible to see beneath his surface. Did Enki see? Did he even bother to try? Maybe he kept their relations strictly transactional, like the whore Gil accused him of being.

I don't wonder what Ueda-sama saw in Enki. He's the summer king, and even outside Palmares Três, he can have almost anyone he wants.

The restaurant is expensive and trendy, one of the new kind that re-creates ancient culinary styles. This one emulates old-Japan, which I gather Auntie Yaha selected in deference to Ueda-sama. He wears a curious expression when we remove our shoes and step inside. It's as if someone has jostled the reflecting pool. For a moment, I can discern the miles beneath the surface but none of the detail. I only know that he seems sad and happy and nostalgic and in physical pain all at once. There's a word for that, as Enki would say.

"Do you have *saudade* in Japanese?" I ask.

Ueda-sama freezes like a figure in a holo, halfway to kneeling at the table. He blinks, and the ripples get wider. "*Natsukashii* comes closest," he says. "But no, not really. There's a good reason you use it in so many of your songs."

I squat on my ankles and wonder how long it will take before my feet completely fall asleep. If they really used to eat like this in old-Japan, I don't know how anyone ever walked.

Auntie Yaha, her expression bland enough to match Ueda-sama's reflecting pool, just laughs and turns the conversation deftly to the differences between old and new Portuguese. I tune her out. Ueda-sama is interesting, I decide. And not unattractive, for all that he's ancient. From a certain angle, he looks like someone with special knowledge. Someone you want to befriend because of the off chance of hearing his stories. He's not the first person I've met from another city, but he's the first from so far away. He's the first who knows what happens to human societies when they don't put limits on technology.

The first course arrives, carried in by a quiet woman in a silk robe. The tiny ceramic plates are arrayed with delicate strips of fish.

Ueda-sama tastes his first. He closes his eyes with the first bite. He groans, though so softly only Auntie Yaha and I can hear it.

He opens his eyes as if startled to find us still there. He clears his throat. "My apologies. I forgot myself. It's been much too long since I've been able to enjoy such food."

I put a piece in my mouth. The raw fish tastes good, though I'm not sure why it made Ueda-sama groan as if he'd asked Enki to whip him.

"You don't have old-Japan food in Tokyo 10?" Auntie Yaha asks, and I think she must truly be surprised, because she almost never admits lacking any cultural knowledge.

Ueda-sama smiles, smooth and reflective once more. "We used to. Not very much need of it, these days, given all the changes. The ones like me — grandes, if you will, June — are not so many to warrant it."

His *given all the changes* feels charged, at once glib and all-encompassing, the same way Principal Ieyascu talks about the nuclear cold or first-wave immigration. I glance at Auntie Yaha, but she just nods in sympathy. I put down my chopsticks and struggle to remember all I ever learned about Tokyo 10 and their notorious mods. I'm once again struck by how strange it is for the ambassador from such an infamous place to look so . . . normal. Completely human. Even Enki has more mods.

"Why are you here?" I ask, suddenly.

Auntie Yaha gives my thigh a warning squeeze. "June . . ."

"I wanted to meet you. To apologize, frankly, for my role in that spectacle last month."

I wave them both away. "No, I don't mean that. There's nothing you could have done about that. I mean why are *you* here, in Palmares Três? In a, well, a real human body. Why can't you connect to the city with your brain or see a holo in your retinas or just download yourself?"

Auntie Yaha sighs and lifts another piece of the fish to her mouth. Ueda-sama gets that look again, that saudade.

"Because I can't."

"You can't?"

He shrugs. "There are some people whose bodies can't take the mods, for whatever reason. In my case, I'm simply too old. To someone like me, Tokyo 10 can feel like a ghost city. Millions and millions of people live as data streams in the cloud, but barely a hundred thousand of us have kept our bodies. We're the only ones who can travel to see the rest of the world, though. We're the only ones who can taste perfectly prepared sashimi and shake hands and . . ."

I remember what Enki said: *The first night, he asked me to whip him.* And I understand, more completely than I like, how one can crave sensation itself, no matter how unpleasant. I wonder how he feels about having his unusual preferences exposed to public scrutiny.

"So you became an ambassador," I say.

"It seemed preferable to *hara-kiri*, at the time."

I recognize the foreign word, though it takes me a moment to realize why. We have it too, in a shortened form: *kiri.* We must have taken it from the Japanese-Brazilian immigrants who first came here from São Paulo.

"How old are you, Ueda-sama?"

"Three hundred and four, at the end of winter."

I feel my eyes widen. They must have found a new treatment in Tokyo 10, because I've never heard of even the oldest grande making it past two hundred and fifty.

"Does Enki know?"

He laughs. "Do you know what he said to me, right after we first met? 'You can't recapture your youth, but would you like to screw it?'"

Auntie Yaha chokes on her fish. I thump her back and smile, because I love how Enki looks when he says things he knows are outrageous. I'm frightened of the way he dares the world, but I love it too. Maybe that's what Gil meant when he said I could keep him safe? In deference to Auntie Yaha's stricken sensibilities (and the server coming within easy earshot), we return the conversation to the banal for the rest of the night. The food is light, but there's enough of it that I feel satisfied in the end.

We walk back to the platform in relative silence, but it's companionable, not tense. I like Ueda-sama, a connection that surprises me. And between him and Enki, I'm beginning to think the Aunties might have a point about the dangers of too much tech.

"A pleasure," he says, bowing to me again when his pod arrives. He nods at Auntie Yaha. "I owe you a debt for arranging this," he says.

Auntie Yaha, who has clearly had more than enough unexpected social breaches in one night, does not even bother with a polite denial. They exchange smiles, each other's perfect mirror.

"Ueda," I say just as he steps into his pod. He pauses and turns around.

"Yes?"

"You and Enki understand each other, don't you?"

This time, at least, his smile is certainly genuine. "I think so, June."

The first thing I remember is a song. It vibrates, deep and wide, in my mamãe's chest. I am on her back, half asleep. The song is familiar, a popular street tune from Salvador that bloco amarelo turned into a summer hit five or six years ago. I danced to it then, when everyone but me had forgotten where it came from.

I liked it that way.

My mamãe wasn't singing to me. In the memory, I somehow know this. She thinks I'm asleep. She thinks I'm too young to understand. She's singing for herself. For her memories of her own mamãe, and the world they lived in before militias tore it apart. She's singing for her future, and maybe for the lover who fathered me, though I heard no more than three words about him growing up ("Better off gone," and I always wondered if she meant for him, or for us). But the song is filled with love, and I know it holds me tight as the linen cloth pressing me to her spine. The noises of Palmares Três wash over me as they always have: the waves pounding against the pylons, the susurrus of pods shunting through transport tunnels above, the shrieking of children, the complaints of their parents, the creak of algae vats rocking in the breeze.

I am in love. With my mamãe, who doesn't think of me. With the city, who will hate me.

With my life, which one day I will choose to end.

The stencils start going up a week after the party on A Quarentena. Or maybe they started earlier, everything's a rumor, but I first notice it painted on a window on the eastern side of our school building. It's Enki and it's me in silhouette, our hair tangling and merging in the middle. My hand is raised, shooting out light. Enki's mouth is open; he's sucking in the world around him, while his own hands fade into a pixelated glow. There aren't any words.

We all know what it means anyway.

Everyone whispers in school. Bebel makes a point of putting her arm around me at lunch, and I don't understand why until I overhear the tail end of the conversation she's trying to distract me from.

"Why is she even here? Why doesn't she download herself already —"

"You know I heard Enki gave her mods? I swear I saw her eyes glowing earlier today. And I voted for him too."

"Pasqual was so much better."

Bebel's hands are warm on my cheeks; she makes me look at her. "They don't know you," she says. "I don't care what side you're on; you're still my friend."

What side I'm on? Friend? I don't understand anything, but I find myself nodding anyway. "You too," I say, and then I feel better.

Here's the trouble: The spider bot rotting in the bay has made it impossible for the Aunties to ignore the issue of outside technology any longer. And you'd think that wakas would be all for awesome new mods, but it turns out almost everyone from the high tiers is wary of the extreme technology pioneered in Tokyo 10. The verde, on the other hand, is a technophile stronghold, though I doubt I would have understood why before Enki.

Ueda-sama has kept conspicuously silent on the subject of trade between our cities, though he's been hounded by the top-tier news casters about it. I haven't said a word. I didn't think anyone would care what I thought, but it turns out that someone does. I think back to that simple, brilliant image stenciled on the side of the school building. I've become an icon, like it or not. Not for the isolationists, where my sympathies mostly lie. For the technophiles.

Gil skipped school, but he comes in time for the evening bell to catch me before I leave. We both like school these days, since it's the one place we can be sure we won't be caught by cameras.

"They're everywhere," he says, pulling me into an empty meeting room. I don't see him until he grabs my hand, but I'm not afraid. I recognize Gil just by the feel of his skin.

I'm confused, though. "Camera bots? Of course they are, Gil."

He shakes his head. "The graffiti. The stencils. There's one on the side of the school building, didn't you see it?"

"The thing with me and Enki?"

"It's *everywhere*. They're saying you designed it. They're saying that you're the new icon of the technophiles. Is it . . ."

After a moment, I understand. "You believe them?"

"How would I know, June? You've done crazier things without asking my permission."

This makes me want to cry, but I laugh instead. "I'd tell you if I were planning anything like this. You know that, right?"

"I know that," he says, but it's almost a question.

"And I didn't design that stencil."

"Don't know why I thought you had," he says. His fingers trace my lights. "It's too good for you not to brag about."

I hit him lightly on the arm. "I never brag. I only accept fully justified praise."

"Well, in that case."

We're silent for a while, sitting side by side on the floor. Eventually Gil rests his head on my shoulder, I wrap my arms around his waist.

"The mods, and Ueda-sama and, you know, all of that stuff about the city's systems failing, June, it's okay if you think . . . I mean, about the tech . . ."

He trails off, eyes closed, but his throat works as if he hopes I might take the words from him. And I do.

"I see what they're doing to him as well as you do, Gil. I don't want us to turn into Tokyo 10."

Gil's shoulders sag in relief. I can't think of anyone less suited for mods than Gil. He's so very physical and human — I try to imagine him in a data stream, without the slick of his sweat after a dance, that pungent musk of earth and youth. A disembodied collection of data can dance forever, but how much would that be worth without the tension of pushing up against the limits of a body?

And yet.

"But the Aunties are wrong to close us off so much," I find myself saying. "We're still using technology that's more than a century old to run the city. It's dangerous."

"That's very pragmatic," Gil says after a moment. He opens his eyes. "Much too levelheaded for a waka."

"You know," I say, "sometimes I don't feel very much like a waka these days."

Sebastião is short, with snow-white hair, though he's only sixty, and a smile that always makes you feel like you're in on a joke. He's notorious for his ability to elicit confessions in interviews and yet generally remain well-liked among the crowd that cares about these sorts of things. He's a gossip caster, not really into news, but what with Enki's role in parliament and the escalating tensions between isolationists and technophiles, the line between gossip and news has become a matter of attitude.

Which I suppose is why he's asking me for my opinion on the recently proposed bill that would allow limited access to new technology from foreign cities.

"Too little, too late?" says Sebastião, leaning forward, smiling as though he finds the whole situation slightly ridiculous and knows I do too. "After all," he continues, "the bill gives the Queen complete discretion over what technology is actually allowed in. And there's as yet no clause about how the new technology will make the city herself safer."

This isn't my first interview, but it feels like it. "Well, Enki has a connection with the city —"

Sebastião waves his hand. "That works until September, but what then?"

I think I'm going to choke, right here on a live feed with the one gossip caster even the Aunties care about, with half the city overanalyzing my every public move and the other half hating me on principle. My hands curl into fists. My lights are strobing like some ancient call for help. It's the fall already, and there's so much we still haven't done together, and I don't want to think about this, I don't want to remember what it is to be a summer king, what it means to be left behind. I don't understand how Sebastião — who is so unapologetic about his love for Enki — can speak of it so casually.

But then, he's a grande, and Enki is only his latest in a long line of dead boys.

"I . . ."

He waits expectantly. I force air into my lungs. If Enki can do what he does, I can certainly manage an interview.

"I think we can learn from what he's done with the city's natural AI. Some part of the city knew it was in danger from the spider bot. If technology from other cities can help us integrate her consciousness in a better way, then I don't see how that's a problem."

Sebastião nods thoughtfully. My hands unclench. "So, we hear there's trouble in paradise."

"What?"

He chuckles and shakes his head, as though he's caught me doing something naughty. "Poor Gil is an isolationist to his core. That can't be easy for Enki. And now you coming between them — maybe a daring young artist like you can understand our prince better than the beautiful Gil?"

I try not to look as dowdy as I feel, when he puts it like that. Of course I could never compete with Gil for looks, but it's never occurred to me that I have to. "I'm not coming between anyone," I say as calmly as I can. "Enki and I don't have that kind of relationship."

I'm not lying, though part of me wishes I were. He hasn't touched me since our kiss on the water. And I haven't dared touch him.

"So you always say." Sebastião's smile makes me wonder just how much my expression revealed. "Well, then, at least tell us which side you come down on? Technophiles or isolationists? Enki or Gil?"

And I don't know. I want to be like I was with Gil: pragmatic, seeing the points on both sides. But I know that this debate will never work like that. The Aunties have been so hard-line on technology because they knew they could never stop a trickle from becoming a flood. Sure, I can say that some of it's good, some of it's bad, but no one wants to hear that, and mostly they're right.

Eventually you have to make a decision. Eventually you need to pick a side.

Enki or Gil.

"You can't samba in a data stream," I hear myself saying, and remember that Enki loves to dance too.

Enki pokes his head over my garden wall, and I shriek before I recognize him. He's wearing his nanohook gloves and boots, and he grins like a trickster god.

"You couldn't have pinged me?" I say, heart racing.

He drops into my mother's gardenias, crushing a few before sprawling into the carefully demarcated path. "This seemed like more fun," he says, and his voice sounds lucid and mod-free for the first time in days, a river bursting through a dam.

I put down my latest sheets of drawing paper and crawl over to where he lies. His eyes scan some point between the fall clouds and their reflected image on the glass. I touch his hand.

"Aren't you cold?" The last traces of summer have surrendered to early-evening chills and gray rains, but Enki still wears short pants and a sleeveless shirt with a hole by the collar, as if it's January in the verde.

He giggles and pushes his fingers between mine, hard against the soft webbing. I bite my cheek.

"Warm, right?" he says, and it takes me minutes, years to decipher syllables to speech to meaning. But he's right, his skin is so hot it would be uncomfortable if I hadn't already been shivering with autumn chill.

I let our hands rest on his chest and lie down beside him. Water from the dirt path seeps into my clothes; I don't care.

"Which one?" I say.

He turns so his nose is less than an inch from mine. "Technophile or isolationist?" he says, and I snort with involuntary laughter.

"The mods. Which one heats you up?"

He lets his free hand tangle in my bombril hair. "Which one? All of them? None?"

"Enki, do you always have to be so —"

"It's a side effect," he says, and there's not much laughter anymore. "Like the trips. Or the pain. Just something the mods do because they have to work in my brain, and they haven't had a hundred million years of evolution to balance things out."

"Oh."

"June."

"Yes?"

"Do you know how sick I am of talking about these goddamned mods?"

When I break, I feel it like a physical snap, a sharp flare of pain running between my chest and my groin as I kiss him.

My tongue slides along his teeth, the inside of his lips. His hand tightens around mine until it ought to hurt, but all I can feel is the pressure and the heat and the wet/rough of our tongues hitting, searching, finding each other again. He tastes like a summer rain on packed earth, like the wind that clears the verde for those few precious hours before the catinga comes home.

It ends, because he ends it. I don't know how long after.

"Is it Gil?" I whisper when I can. I take my hand from his.

I can't read him, but then I never could. His eyes are black like he's high, but I know he isn't. Enki never takes anything.

"No," he says. He sits up, looks around the garden as if he's never seen it before. My lips don't tingle, they vibrate like a plucked string. My heart beats faster than a pandeiro.

Enki isn't even breathing hard.

It was different, the first time. Gentle and a little confused, like he hadn't realized he meant to kiss me until he did. A sweet press of lips on lips that demanded nothing but the acknowledgment of shared joy.

Now I am nothing but demands and frustrations and denial. I am that kiss, and I am unfulfilled. I watch him; what else can I do?

He stands and walks over to my discarded papers. For a long time, he studies them, detached and frighteningly remote. I can't even remember what I was drawing. I'm consumed with simple, stupid things: the line of his corded bicep, the white of his teeth, the skin taut over his collarbone, the light brown tips of the dreadlocks that fall onto his forehead.

"I look like that to you?" he says.

For a moment, I think his mods have reached into my brain, seen through my fevered eyes. "Like what?"

"Like I'm dead already."

He shows me the drawing. Gil and Enki looking at each other, only Gil's legs are twisting like a banyan trunk, and Enki's fingers have turned into feathers.

"You're not dead," I say.

"Flying away. That's the same thing, to you."

"It isn't." It is.

He smiles, sinks back to the ground, and I wonder if maybe his body does tremble, just a little. Has he finally felt the cold?

"You'll still have Gil," he says.

"Do we have to talk about this?"

"You love him."

"Of course I do."

"Gil's easy to love, isn't he?"

I relax suddenly. The tension that I had thought would crack me in two turns to something softer in the warmth of Enki's rueful smile.

"Unlike the two of us," I say.

"I love you, June."

I dismiss this, because his mods make him love everyone. "So why won't you . . ."

He pushes the drawing toward me, far enough back that there's no chance we can touch.

"Because of this," he says, and it means nothing, and it means everything.

You're probably wondering why this is for you and not Gil.

So I'll tell you a story.

Once upon a time, there lived a young spirit of a lagoon so deep in the rain forest that even now only monkeys live there. He called himself Ikne, and all the world loved him. The nearby trees grew their greenest leaves, flowers unfurled their brightest petals and exhaled their sharpest scents. If a fish was lucky enough to live in the lagoon, it grew sleek and fat and happy, and spent every day singing of Ikne to his less fortunate fishy friends. If Ikne wasn't always happy, he was more often than most. His life was good. Bright. He could live a long time like this, become an ancient spirit like the ones of caves and mountains, live to complain about kids these days and play arthritic peteca on the municipal courts.

And so Ikne walked away from his idyll and got a job sharpshooting for the Pernambuco guerrillas in Salvador. It wasn't an easy life, and one day he got shot in the stomach by a lead bullet. The bullet fell in love with him, of course, but she couldn't stop the slow bleed of his gastric cavity into his pancreas, and she felt terrible, which was too bad, since he'd known all along what would happen.

He died; he always said he would.

Someone had to take out the bullet.

Demonstrators catch Ueda-sama on his way to a private meeting with Queen Oreste. I don't see right when it happens. I'm busy with another one of my drawings, at least the tenth this week. I've been wondering if they're too simple for the Queen's Award, but after the spectacle of this summer, maybe simplicity is my best chance.

When Mother calls me to the veranda, for once in my life I don't argue.

"What is that?" Mother asks, pointing at something on the edge of the holo. All I can see is the crowd, thousands and thousands of tiny people milling around our floor like toy soldiers. After a moment, I recognize the location from my own exploits: the transport platform in Royal Plaza. The crowd surges toward something, but I can't see what. They just chant and sing and stomp the ground as if they can shake the earth.

"Find some more angles," I say.

Mother flips and flips, but all the cameras must be hovering in the same small area. Parts of the holo start to flicker, which means the feeds can't get enough data for a full three-dimensional projection.

"Why don't the cameras move?" she mutters.

I sit down next to her and hold her hand.

Even without the text overlay, I would know these protesters are technophiles. Plenty of Palmarinas have been trying to break us open to technology for a very long time. With more popular support than they've had in decades, the technophiles have been staging bigger and bigger protests for the last few weeks. Most have been in the verde, until now.

"Is that Ueda-sama?" Mother asks.

One man seems to float on top of the crowd, like a piece of seaweed atop a wave. When Mother zooms, I can see the individuals in the crowd lifting him above their heads and passing him around. Ueda-sama yells for help, but at least he doesn't seem hurt. The air above him shimmers and darts, as if it's filled with a thousand camera bots. Only, with the feed shorting out, there can't possibly be so many cameras.

"What kind of bots are those?" I ask. Mother's breath hitches. She puts her hand to her mouth.

"Oh," she says.

"You've seen them before?"

She turns to me, something in her face that makes my breath stick in my throat, my heart pound.

"Find the boy," she says, so softly her voice is barely audible over the chants of the holo-crowd.

"The boy?"

"Those bots are guarding the protesters. They might not let the ambassador go."

"Guarding?" I ask, and then I understand what she means. That glinting swarm of metal is some kind of illegal-tech *weapon,* and it's keeping away most of the cameras as well as any security bots.

"They wouldn't hurt him!"

"I don't know, June. Maybe they only want to talk to him. But maybe they don't."

With a ferocity that surprises me, Mother waves her hand and the miniature crowd vanishes. The absence of their noise doesn't sound so much like silence as pressure, a held breath.

She takes my hands. Hers are cold, as they always are, and I remember a time when I would complain about it, when I was little and she would pull my hair into tight braids, and I would feel her long, cool fingers trace the parts along my scalp.

"Mamãe?"

"Get him," she says. "Go find your summer prince and stop this." The Aunties have taken to calling Enki that — as though to call him *prince* instead of *king* takes away some of his power. But in Mother's voice, that *prince* carries all the power in the world. It carries hope.

I nod, kiss her forehead, and run for the door.

A swarm of disaffected camera bots awaits me alongside a few human casters.

I start to push my way past them, then pause. Maybe I'm going about this the wrong way. I persist in thinking of my newfound notoriety as a problem, but perhaps if I'm clever, I can turn it to my advantage.

I give a little smile my mother might see if she watches the feeds. I hope that she trusts me.

"Enki and Gil and I are going to speak to the protesters in Royal Plaza," I say.

"Do you think you can stop them?" It's one of the casters, someone I don't recognize, probably third or fourth tier.

"From doing what?" I ask. "Hurting Ueda-sama? I hope they weren't going to do that, anyway. From wanting access to the world's tech? I don't think anyone can stop that, do you?"

"So it's true you side with the technophiles?"

"Did you design the graffiti?"

"Are you sleeping with Enki?"

I can't answer these questions; I wouldn't even if I had the time. So I just shake my head and run the rest of the way through them, laughing a little like I'm chasing a football in the park after school. If they follow me, I don't really mind. Gil and Enki will find me at Royal Plaza and we'll save Ueda-sama from those strange bots that worried my mamãe so much. I haven't felt this in control — this *sure* — in months, at least since Enki and I made our roda viva for the city. For once, the sensation of a million eyes judging my every breath and thought and gesture is a pleasure, not a burden. I want to jump and flip and cartwheel from the exhilaration of it, from the power and the privilege.

And I realize that I now understand Enki a little better than I did before.

Someone offers me her pod on the local platform, so I don't have to wait to call one. I hardly see her, though I hope I remember to say thank you. A few of the casters try to ride with me, but I only allow the woman who asked me the first question.

"Did you recognize those bots swarming above the crowd?" I ask her. "They didn't look like cameras."

The caster's back goes rigid and she glances at the half-dozen bots that flew in with us. Maybe a few are hers, but who knows. I start to doubt she'll answer me, but then she shrugs and leans back against the curved chrome wall of the pod.

"Weapons," she says. "A defensive nanotech cloud developed by the Pernambuco militia in Salvador. At least that's everyone's best guess. Your side is in some deep trouble, June."

"They're not my side," I say reflexively. "And Salvador? How could they ever get through our security?"

I remember Enki's story of how his mamãe had to bribe the Aunties to live here. If a pregnant, destitute refugee could hardly make it, how could lethal weapons?

"They could if someone let them in," the caster says. "Probably someone high in Royal Tower, with ties to Salvador."

She leans in as she says this, as if she's expecting some sort of reaction. It's that, more than her actual words, that makes me understand her implication.

But it's so absurd that all I can do is laugh. "Enki?" I say. "Enki is the most nonviolent person in this city. He loves Palmares Três."

"His mother —"

"Loved it too."

The pod glides to a stop. The doors open on to a press of people so dense I wonder how I'll find Enki and Gil, let alone get through to Ueda-sama. The caster and I share a worried look, but the crowd doesn't seem particularly violent. In fact, aside from the people closest to the pod, they aren't paying any attention to us at all. I start to push my way through them. I look back for the caster, but she's pressed against the back wall of the pod, crossing her arms over her chest. Her chin juts out with a mixture of stubbornness and fear.

"Not coming?" I say.

She shrugs in a fair approximation of nonchalance. "Looks dangerous."

"Could make your career," I say.

"Not everyone has to be famous, June."

I wince. "Of course not." My rush of delight in my newfound power fades, leaving behind a more familiar weariness.

Just beyond the pod doors, people start yelling for the summer king. "Is that him?" someone says. "And his lover?"

I look over my shoulder. "Last chance." But I know what her answer will be.

She just smiles. "I think their pod must be on the other side of the platform. Be careful."

I nod and elbow my way through the crowd. I don't attempt to cover my face but no one pays me much attention. They're all too busy surging to the far end of the platform. The private pod bay isn't very large in Royal Plaza, so I don't have to go far to see what has so captured everyone's attention.

Enki and Gil stand on top of a pod. Enki holds Gil tight around the waist and whispers something in his ear. Gil looks scared and Enki looks like even he might be getting close. I struggle through the crowd, but the nearer I get to Enki's makeshift podium, the more people push back. Everyone wants to see.

Enki straightens and faces the people shouting his name. He raises his hand. The roar of voices quiets to a river of whispers. I lean forward and wait with the rest.

And then something curious happens: He opens his mouth, but his voice comes out of the city's emergency speakers.

"Palmarinas," his voice says, though his lips hardly move. "I can't know what you think of me. I can't know if you're technophile or isolationist. At the moment, I think it doesn't matter. The ambassador from Tokyo 10 has nothing to do with this. I'd like to save him, but I can only do that if you let me through."

The speakers cough out an abrupt burst of sound and Enki wobbles, just slightly. I shout his name and try to shove my way closer. They'll never see me.

"Please let the summer king through," says the city's more familiar voice, over her emergency speakers. She has somehow matched his inflections, conveyed the warmth and the abstraction and the imperiousness. How have I never noticed the way the city and Enki resemble each other? Or perhaps they've grown together over the months, like a young vine curling up the trunk of an ancient tree. Enki climbs down from the pod, agile as ever, but maybe only I see the careful way Gil watches him, makes sure he doesn't fall.

As one, the oddly silent crowd surges back far enough to clear a path for Enki and Gil. The crowd's momentum nearly crushes me as I try to push against them. When I'm almost at the front, someone blocks my way. He turns to yell at me, pauses, and then smiles.

"Hello, June," says this complete stranger, this grande in engineer's clothes.

"Hello?" I say.

"Summer King," he hollers when Enki passes close by. They both turn — Enki with relaxed curiosity, Gil like he's ready to hit someone.

"Found something for you," the man says. He lets me through.

"We thought you got stuck somewhere," Gil says, hugging me.

"I nearly did." I turn to Enki. He's walking fast; I have to jog to keep up. Ahead of us the crowd parts like the old biblical sea. The gap points us to Ueda-sama like an arrow.

I'm so happy to see them both I could dance. Everything that felt overwhelming and frightening on the pod feels manageable, maybe even exciting. Together, the three of us are invincible, maybe the strongest weapon this city has ever had.

"What are we going to do?" I say.

"I thought we'd try to talk," Enki says. "Whoever wants to speak for them, can."

"And what should we say?" I ask. "Please be nice and give Ueda back, he can't do anything? He can do *everything*, and they know it."

"He doesn't deserve to die," says Gil.

"They're not going to kill him!" I say, shocked. "They wouldn't. He's too valuable as a hostage."

Enki shrugs. "For the leaders. But the mob might hurt him anyway."

I want to argue with him. Instead, I say, "Have you talked with Oreste?"

He shakes his head. "There's some sort of dampening field over most of Royal Tower. The city feels it like a cold spot. It's new defensive tech."

"Like the cloud?"

He just nods. Gil takes a few steps away from me and curses. "Who would do that, Enki? Who could have smuggled this tech into the city?"

Enki raises an eyebrow. "Someone who stands to benefit? An Auntie, or someone close enough to negotiate a deal."

This surprises even Gil. "An *Auntie*?"

Enki laughs and caresses the edge of his lover's ear. "We'll know soon enough, meu bombril," he says, softly enough that it feels wrong I can hear him. "I know how much she means to you."

He means the city, threatened by a mob and weaponized nanotech. No mention of poor Ueda-sama, caught in the middle of this conflict so far away from anyone he loves. Even Enki, with all his mods, probably feels less for Ueda than he does the plants in my mother's garden.

The crowd thins as we move away from the transportation hub and toward the main square of Royal Plaza. A combination of security bots and human officers have cleared away most of the people not actively protesting. This makes it easy for us to see what has changed since the last chance I had to look at a holo feed: a cage, suspended above the crowd, topped by something giant, metallic, and spiky. It looks the way I imagined stars when I was a child, but more dangerous.

"Is that the cloud?" I whisper.

"Where did they get a cage?" Gil asks. "Is Ueda-sama inside it?"

Enki rests his hand briefly on the back of my neck. "They're both the cloud," he says. "They've told it to reshape itself."

I try to wrap my head around a bot that can turn itself into anything you ask of it, that can be a cage or a star with just a bit of programming.

"This is what the technophiles want?" I ask.

Gil purses his lips, disdain masking terror. "Of course," he says.

Enki doesn't look at either of us. "Or what someone wants for the technophiles."

The crowd has gotten smaller, or perhaps just denser, a screaming mass of people corralled by the encircling security bots and what looks to be the entirety of our army — four hundred women, standing at attention with stun rifles. The defensive cloud has retreated with the mob, but a few silvery oblong protrusions are aimed with frightening deliberation at the soldiers. The non-protesters who had crowded the transport platform have scattered. Not many people are keen on witnessing history when they might get shot in the process.

Within the military barricade, the technophile protesters chant with red-faced ferocity. Things like "Tech will save us" and "Adapt or go extinct." At least Ueda looks unhurt in the silvery cage that sways slightly in the center of the crowd.

Enki strides forward, an unerring progression toward the line of human guards. As I hurry to catch him, I remember what he said about the tech: Someone had to have helped smuggle it in. Someone with clout and reach. Someone like an Auntie.

The security guards won't let us cross the line.

"I humbly apologize, Summer King," says an officer in the stifling black suit of a high-ranked guard. "We're under orders not to let anyone through."

Enki cocks his head, like a bird. "Could I order you to let me through?"

She dares a look at him, then averts her gaze. "No."

A moment later, the bars of the cage start to ripple and pulse. Even the chanting falters as the closest protesters fall back in surprise. With the abruptness of a flock of birds lofting into air, the substance of the bars of the cage breaks apart and coalesces into a different form entirely.

Into a picture.

I don't recognize it at first, even though I've seen that iconic stencil of Enki and me all week. It's Gil who understands exactly what this means.

"They want to speak to *Enki*," he says. "Not Oreste."

It seems so inevitable, once I see that unnaturally flowering invitation. He's the summer king, and because of his extreme self-modding, he has become the symbol for a legion of frustrated technophiles in Palmares Três.

Above us, the shadows move. Behind us, a few more people have dared to creep closer to the soldiers' line, despite shouts to clear the area.

There is a moment; it is sweet and slow and quiet as a summer afternoon. I look up. The misshapen star above us has realigned its firm, metallic points so they all face in our direction. Its skin wavers like a heat sheen.

Enki turns and shouts something to the people behind us. I can't hear him; there's too much thunder in the plaza and I wonder why, because I hadn't seen a storm coming. Something hits me. From the ground, I see Enki's silhouette on the side of an impossible prison, and a huddled shape just beyond it.

Gil lies on top of me. We are covered in blood. Enki has fallen a few feet away from us. The blood on his hands stains the yellow shirt of the girl gasping in his lap.

"Oh, God," I say. I can barely hear my own voice past the hollow drone in my skull. Guards swarm around us. Gil closes his eyes, averts his face from something I understand a moment too late. A boy, a waka, lying right beside me on the flagstones with a hole in his head.

I have his blood in my hair. I crawl over to Enki, shake off restraining hands as if they are gnats. Sound returns gradually: screams, mostly, peppered with shouts and sobs. The girl in his lap has stopped moving.

"She's dead," I say.

He looks up at me and keeps her in his lap.

From beyond the barricade, people start to chant his name. *Enki. Enki. Enki.* I wish the thunder would rain on *them.* I wish I couldn't smell another waka's blood.

"Are you what they think you are?" I ask.

Enki gives me a look that isn't long, but drags at me. A *What am I to you?* and an *Are you ready?* and *love* and *love* and *love.* He puts the girl down. His eyes roll white; Gil catches him before he falls. A second later, through the holo and the emergency speakers, I hear the city.

"Hello, technophile protesters," she says, smooth and pleasant as always. "The summer king requests that you release your hostage, the foreign dignitary Ueda Toshio, immediately. The king will be happy to hear your grievances at such time."

The city's voice falls like a blanket on the protesters. Their angry buzzing turns fractured and bewildered. It's unfair, maybe, that Enki can use the city herself for his cause, as though he has reached into the memories of every Palmarina and sung to them their mothers' lullabies. But two people are dead and Ueda might follow them and I love her, my city, for all her flaws. At the moment, I don't care what Enki has to do to save her.

We three stand and wait. There are two dead wakas behind us, and the star overhead could thunder at any moment, but I try not to think. Not to hate.

The mob — suddenly quiet, as though they were equally shocked by the violence — parts to let people through: Ueda-sama, shackled at the wrists and ankles, with a much younger escort.

"That's Lucia," I say. The nanotech finalist for the Queen's Award. "I guess we know what side she came down on."

"Murderers?" Gil says.

I wrap my arm around his waist.

Lucia looks scared as she approaches us, like a kid forced to give a speech at a grande's party. But perhaps we just look bloody and implacable.

Ueda-sama is ten times the age of most of the protesters in Royal Plaza. When he smiles, suddenly he looks it. "Hello, Enki," he says. "Took you long enough."

Enki's eyes are still lidded. "Hello, Ueda," he says.

"We have demands," Lucia says in a decent attempt at bravado. She seems shocked, almost confused. Had she planned the attack or just lost control of her tech?

"Hostage takers usually do," says Gil.

Lucia ignores him. "The ambassador will be released when the Aunties agree to immediate unilateral trade agreements between

Palmares Três and Tokyo 10, with further technologically advanced cities to be added pending negotiations with their representatives. They want you to lead these efforts until your tenure . . ." Lucia breaks off and swallows.

Ueda-sama laughs as if he has a sea urchin in his throat. "Well?" he says. "They have your Queen and most of the Aunties trapped in the tower."

Enki is silent for a moment. "I'll help open the city," he says.

Ueda shakes his head. "They're barbarians," he says very undiplomatically. "You know they'll still let the Aunties kill you, even with new tech."

"*That* was always a mutual agreement, Ueda," Enki says, with more sadness than I'm used to. "We're all Palmarinas, technophile or not."

Their names were Wanadi and Regina. Both wakas, just nineteen, and now famous for the worst reason of all: dying young and violently. The funeral for the first Palmarinas ever killed by war nanotech is lavish and somber. Enki walks with Oreste and the parents at the front of the procession. I'm with Gil, toward the back of the first column of Aunties and Uncles and various secretaries. It doesn't escape my notice that the swarm of camera bots seems thicker toward our end, but I just squeeze Gil's hand and keep walking.

Everything is changing so fast I can't make out any pattern. I only see what I most fear: that my city is dying, that it's somehow my fault, that there's nothing anyone can do to stop it. Parliament starts an emergency session tomorrow morning, and all the news casters think the Aunties will be forced to grant technophile demands. Of course, most casters think that Enki is on the technophile side, and I know it's more complicated than that. But Enki is strange and unpredictable at the best of times, and no matter what he does, there might be no stopping what his first meeting with Ueda-sama set in motion. After the technophiles surrendered and the nanocloud dispersed, Lucia tried to escape with the rest of the mob, but Auntie Maria arrested her a day later. They granted the other protesters amnesty. But I've heard that no one can find the nanocloud. No one knows when the technophiles might call it back again, or why they shot indiscriminately into the crowd in the first place.

My eyes have been affixed to the moving holo at the front of the procession — footage of Wanadi and Regina, happy and alive. They look so familiar, so much like me and my friends that it makes me want to cry, though I never knew them. They weren't technophiles or isolationists, just wakas trying to make sense of their lives. Bad luck brought them to Royal Plaza that afternoon. Stuck in the tide of gawkers and counter-protesters, they'd been pushed to the front of the crowd, and ricocheting bullets had caught him in the head and her in the chest.

"They really think it's intimidating," Gil says softly, his lips brushing against my ear.

"What?" I say, shaking my head, turning to him.

He pushes his fingers through mine, in that way that means he's worried. I would try to reassure him, but he tilts his head. I follow the direction of his gaze.

Up ahead, rivets frame the famous tiered waterfall of Royal Park and the jewel of the bay behind it. Before the waterfall, a large, empty platform will eventually seat the Queen, Enki, and a few dozen high-ranking Aunties. Facing that are a hundred or so seats in a cordoned-off area, where Gil and I will watch. And beyond that, what must be every security bot in the city stands at attention, thousands and thousands of them in careful, silent, endless rows of impassive pewter faces and black armbands. They surround the crowd of at least ten thousand people who have come to witness what I suppose must be history.

And it's apropos, in a gut-wrenching way, that the method the Aunties have chosen to reassert their authority after the technophile riots suddenly appears so useless and backward and old-fashioned. After all, what can even three thousand security bots do against a metastasizing, ever-adapting nanocloud whose only purpose is escalating death?

"The Aunties have already lost, haven't they?" I whisper.

Gil's grip on my hand gets so tight it's painful. I don't try to stop him. "I think maybe they know it, June. But maybe even that kind of anachronism is preferable to . . ."

His shoulders shake very slightly. Gil watched those two wakas die. As much as anyone in the city, he knows that death cloud. He knows what the technophiles and their allies have unleashed. "The past stands in the path of the future, knowing it will be crushed," I say softly, but not so softly that the closest camera bots can't hear me. I don't care anymore.

Gil looks up again as we're walking past the gauntlet of rigid bots. "That's your kind of art, June."

And he's right; it is.

But Oreste didn't become Queen by relying on symbolic gestures.

Our Queen leaves the eulogies to parents and friends; she only gets up to speak at the end, and then only for less than a minute.

In her simple white skirt and turban, she looks implacable and powerful and icy in her fury. I'm close enough to not need the holos to see the thick arch of her brows, the lines around her eyes and mouth she has never erased. She regards us, this human sea drowning the park, for nearly a minute. Hardly a cough disturbs the absolute silence; only the rush of the waterfall behind her and the softer, more insistent crash of waves against pylons far, far below.

If I can hardly breathe, I know I'm not alone. Oreste is more ruthless than any Auntie because she is *the* Auntie.

"That this has happened in my city, during my reign, is my own sin and one that cannot be forgiven. Wanadi and Regina are dead. Nothing will bring them back. But they are dead because some in this city are convinced they will be happier or their lives will be better with the kind of destructive technology that has so ripped apart cities as separate as Tokyo 10 and Salvador. I know they still think so, despite these twin tragedies, and despite the absolute inevitability of many more. Some might say it is futile to fight against the tide of the future. I believe there are many futures. The one that I, and all of us here today, must work toward is one where Palmares Três remains the jewel on the bay. Where we retain our strength and our core and our *humanity* as we meet our destiny."

No one claps, but behind me someone trills, like a woman catching the spirit during a service, like a mother at her daughter's wedding. The sound is high. Oreste pauses, halfway to her seat. Suddenly, another woman trills, and then another, a growing sea of ululation, disconcerting me with its determination and pride. Maybe a few wakas join in, I don't know. But this is a grande sound for a grande love and I wonder what it says about me that I can feel it vibrating in my throat.

Regina had your lights on her arms; they turned green before she died. I know you think she died while I held her. I know you think there was nothing we could have done, but that isn't true either. I saw, because the city saw, and now there's not so much difference between us as there used to be.

Regina's lights turned green, like your display on O Quilombola, like the jewels of the verde. She died with a half-kilo of nano-produced shrapnel lodged in her spine, but her lights — the lights from the fad that you started — said that she struggled to live. If I had demanded medics instead of waiting on the protesters, could I have saved her life? Could I have kept the promise of that green flash?

Power has responsibility, that's what they tell me. They should say that power has guilt and guilt has grief and no mod but death can take that away.

"I love you, June," says the city as Enki turns a cartwheel past the mountain of cushions in the corner of his living room.

"Enki," I say, "why does the city love me?"

He balances on one leg, hand outstretched for another maneuver, but perfectly steady. "Why shouldn't she?"

He's speaking without using his mouth again; but it's the third time this week, and necessity has made me overcome my initial revulsion at the disconnect between his lips and the voice slipping from the speakers.

"She's not human?"

He starts up again, flipping and springing so fast and so high I'm sure it must be augmented by his mods. "So that's what matters?" the speakers say.

"She's a *city*!"

He runs, jumps high enough to touch the ceiling, and rolls when he hits the floor. He stays down there, sprawled on his back, a sheen of sweat catching on the lights suddenly flickering above us. He isn't breathing hard, but maybe the sweat reminds both of us what can be so easy to forget these days: He's human too.

"She's me," he says, and it's his own mouth, his own lungs, his own rough vocal cords. I find myself on my knees beside him. He stares unblinking at an empty ceiling. His fingertips graze my palm, and I am breathless and dumb. "We are bound up," he says. "I stitched her pieces together with myself as the thread. She doesn't always like it, you know. Sometimes she blames me."

"Then why do it?"

"Because she raised me. Because she's true. Because her sewage maintenance lines don't know what her fono network is doing."

I frown, though perhaps it's useless to try to make sense of him. "Do they need to?"

"The Aunties have forced her to be so unnaturally disconnected just so they can have more control."

"But I love you, June," says the city again, and she is subdued and resigned.

Shaking, I fall down beside Enki on the floor. It jars me, but I don't mind. "Why, City?" I ask.

She pauses. "Because Enki used the love of you to tie my external weather sensors to my municipal energy production unit."

Enki starts to laugh, both his own voice and over the speakers. The stereo makes me want to cover my ears. "What she means is that she loves you because I do."

I know he doesn't feel anything for me like what he does for Gil, but today I almost believe him. What if his love is something more than just his mods? Nothing would make me happier, and nothing would scare me more.

"That doesn't make any sense."

"You know these things never do."

He turns over and kisses me. I hold my breath and wait for it to end. I can't handle Enki like this, so himself and so alien and crystal clear. I want my beautiful boy back, the one who danced barefoot before Oreste, the one whose mind was a cipher and whose words I obsessively dowsed for meaning. Now it's fall, and it will soon be winter, and he is burning so bright I can hardly look at him. Especially not this close. Especially not with his tongue touching mine.

"I'm sorry," he says, breaking it off. Above us the lights flicker, one second on, one second off, like a message in ancient code.

When are you ever sorry? I tremble in relief. I wish he would do it again.

"You wanted to tell me something," I say, because it's the only thing left.

He waves his hand dismissively. "Oreste wants you to talk to Lucia. The nano girl. Convince her to help keep the war tech out of the city. And give the name of whatever Auntie betrayed us in the first place, of course."

"Me?"

"She says the girl respects you."

"Why should I agree?"

He smiles and touches my jaw. "You haven't said no to Oreste yet."

The Aunties have kept Lucia in a facility on Tier Two since the demonstration five days ago. Apparently, they've attempted to cut a deal with her this entire time, but since she's still sitting by the window in a small, self-contained, two-room apartment, I assume that she hasn't agreed.

And so Oreste sent me, inadvertent icon of the technophiles. It makes a certain kind of sense, but I don't think I'm going to have much luck. Lucia grimaces when I walk into the room. She doesn't do anything so childish as ignore me, but it couldn't be much clearer that she wishes I hadn't come.

"I'm here because Oreste asked," I say, instead of hello.

"You think that's going to help your case?" She has a piece of cloth in her hands, and she twists it back and forth with restless, relentless energy.

"Just thought I should be honest about it."

"Clever way to get back in her graces. You still want the award, don't you? Octavio said you were ruthless." I ignore this statement, because acknowledging it might make me run from the room. My desire for this award has started to feel very wrong if I think about it too much. She turns back to the window.

The cloth in her hands is red and ragged around the edges. She's too young to wear a red headscarf, so I wonder who it belongs to, why she grips it so tight her knuckles have turned pale.

Her hair is kinky and matted — she hasn't combed it in a few days at least. Her bloodshot eyes scan the view from her window, bleakly watching the pods shunting through transport tunnels and the water rippling by internal pylons down at the base. The view fascinates me for a moment — in my neighborhood, the only buildings with internal views are storage facilities. But I imagine that this look at the city's apparently endless heart is more familiar to Lucia.

"If you wanted," I say, "could you do something to disable the weapon tech? Could you make it so we don't have to be afraid of that silver cloud again?"

Lucia doesn't look at me, but she pulls the cloth, hard, between her knees. The edge of it starts to rip. "If I wanted," she says, almost mocking me. "This is ridiculous, you have to know that. They're *Aunties*. They own the whole world, and suddenly, I'm the only one who knows enough about nanotech to save them?"

"So you could?"

She pulls harder and the rip travels clear down its length. Lucia stares at the pieces for a moment, tosses them to the floor.

"My contact had to give me the schematics to set up the cloud. I modified them to work with the city. Not enough, I guess. I tried to make it shoot paper bullets."

After the protest, I'd gotten a clear look at what was left of Regina's body. Dozens and dozens of variously shaped chunks of metal had been hurled at her with such force they left scorch marks in the ground beneath. Some unlucky people near her had needed replacement limbs and reconstructive surgery.

"That was some goddamned paper," I say.

She squeezes her eyes shut for a moment, but when she opens them again, they're still wet. "I didn't mean for it to hurt anyone. It was supposed to intimidate you, not . . ." She swallows. "I *told* it."

"Maybe you can't tell war tech not to kill."

Her chin juts out a little. "You don't know anything. The principles of propagation are the same, no matter the nano system. They don't have an *essence*."

I shrug. "Maybe they do."

"If you know so much, why don't you disable the cloud for them?"

She's shaking, just a little. I wonder who recruited her. Which of the respected elders from the inner circle had told her she would be doing a good deed? Which of them has abandoned her now?

I step a little closer, remembering the look of that thing, the cool shadow of it above all of us, that sensation of it watching and waiting for violence without any particular emotion at all.

I might not like Oreste, I might not agree with how the Aunties have handled things so far, but I can't let anything like that in my city again. Not if there's something I can do to stop it.

"No one's seen the cloud since it dissipated."

"Maybe it's gone."

"Maybe it's growing flowers."

"Whatever. Doesn't matter. No one else can reaggregate it."

She's stopped looking at me again. I shrug and kneel down; the torn headscarf lies near my feet. When I pick it up, I can see the intricate paneling, the embroidered design along the edges. This isn't just a woman's red scarf, it's a matriarch's. I think about what it means that this technophile's prize possession is an ancient piece of cloth, probably hand sewn three generations before.

I finger the rip. It's along one of the seams, at least. None of the original design has been destroyed. "I know someone who can fix this," I say. "A whiz with a needle."

"I'll give it to a sewing nanopropagator," she says, "once I get out of here."

I finger the gold embroidery. I think about a bot that turns *paper* to *metal chunks*, but I just shrug. "Okay," I say.

I hold it out to her. She snatches it back. "What would *you* do, June? No one is stopping your art. But the thing I love? Everyone wants to hold it back, push it down, keep a leash on it. Even before they put me here, you had all the freedom."

I think that she's wrong, that Oreste has forbidden plenty already. But then, the cost of my defiance was never a detention facility or a trial. Lucia has risked a lot more than disqualification from the Queen's Award for her passion. If I squint, I can see how this must look to her. How insufferable my visit must seem.

I hold that in my head, like the background of a painting. Then I walk past it.

"I haven't killed anyone."

She gasps and then sucks in air with a noisy whistle, like I've hit her in the stomach. She swings her legs to the floor, but doesn't seem steady enough to stand up. "I didn't —"

"You did. You programmed the bot. Why do you think whoever asked you asked, Lucia? No one else in this city knows more than you about nanotech. You've even built your own machines. None of the plan would have worked if you hadn't agreed. And you *knew* where that tech came from."

"I told it not to! The Pernambuco guerrillas must have sent us faulty tech . . ."

"That killed people. Funny, Lucia, I'd say it did exactly what it was designed to do. And you know what else I think?"

"That you're an ignorant, stuck-up, Tier Eight brat who doesn't know shit?"

I smile. "That the Auntie who put you here knew it. Sure, no problem if you could change things, but then, if it fired real bullets, if it hurt real people, so much the better, right? The cloud disappears as soon as you break up, and now we all know the technophiles can access it anytime."

"I'm the only one."

I take a step until I'm a handsbreadth away from her. Even I'm shaking now, with the horror of what happened to Regina and Wanadi. With how much worse it can get unless I can convince this stupid, selfish, naive, *scared* waka to help.

"*You are not,*" I whisper as fiercely as I can. I imagine Gil behind me, his horror at what is happening to his city as fierce as my own. I imagine Enki, quietly aware of what he's helped to unleash. "They would be fools not to have watched your every move. Maybe you were the only one at first, but now you're disposable. It's been five days, Lucia. Has anyone come for you? Are any of your important friends helping you? Two wakas are dead because of what you did. You'll let them kill more? You'll let that cloud hang over Palmares Três forever?"

She opens her mouth, chokes, and presses a tight knuckle to her eyes. I wait and watch while she cries. I feel curious and empty and watchful. I pity her, but so distantly it feels frigid.

"And what will happen to me if I do? I get to go back to the verde. I've already lost the Queen's Award. If I give you our one government ally, I lose the nanotech too. I'll just be stupid Lucia Bolana, future vat custodian."

I could argue with her. I could say that she has plenty of opportunities, if she'll just work for them. I could say that maybe nanotech won't be completely banned, maybe she could work within the system. But the choice I'm forcing on her is bad enough without defending it with such stupid, self-serving lies.

"And you think it's worth it," I say instead. "Kill a few more kids, win this political debate, become famous? That's your plan?"

"You don't understand —"

"Will you help or not? You'll get out of here if you disable the nanocloud and name the Auntie who coordinated this. The rest is yours to choose."

Her lips twist like the red scarf she ripped in two. She stares at its pieces for a moment and then hands them back to me. "Some choice," she says.

"Make it, Lucia."

"Get your person to fix it," she says, nodding at the scarf. "It was my grandmother's. She wouldn't like the idea of nanotech either."

When I realize what she means, my knees almost buckle. Emotion comes rushing back at me like a wave. I hadn't known how afraid I was until this moment.

"Auntie Maria," she says.

She shakes her head a little and turns back toward the window, toward the bustling, pulsating, flashing heart of the city.

When I walk back outside, my cheeks sting with the sudden smack of a few unwary camera bots. Lights flash, casters shout questions, the few passersby stop and stare.

"Were you offering your support?"

"Have you seen the new stencils?"

"What do you think of Auntie Maria's new proposal to stop all immigration to Palmares Três?"

They talk and talk. I take a deep breath, and they pause for a moment. I have to say something. There's no getting past them, otherwise.

So I look down at the jagged seams of the ancient red headscarf in my hands. "I know someone who can fix this," I say. "And she'll use nothing but a needle and a thread."

"So you've converted?" It's Sebastião, a sheen of sweat on his face, but otherwise perfectly composed and somehow at the front of the crowd. "Is June Costa an isolationist?"

I smile at him. "It means . . . there's more than one way to fix a tear, that's all."

I push my way through them. Slowly, at first, until Sebastião helps clear a path. Eventually I'm alone again, on a pod shuttling up and up to the rarefied atmosphere of Tier Eight.

"City?" I say. "Can you take me to the northwest corner? Near Gil's?" I need to give Lucia's scarf to his mamãe.

"Of course, June," she says. Smooth and perfect.

"City?" I say.

"Yes, June?"

"I love you too."

Funny thing, though: Despite the effort Oreste expended to get a name, as far as I can tell, she does nothing with it. Fall makes friendly gestures to winter, parliamentary hearings drone on with Ueda-sama occasionally taken out of the strict seclusion of high security to give testimony, and still Auntie Maria sits serenely in the back of the hall. She gives public updates on the "state of security" in the city. She even personally attests to the destruction of the war-tech cloud, once Lucia's work has finished. In public, she and Oreste and Auntie Isa are as cordial with one another as ever. When I try asking Auntie Yaha, she just shakes her head and changes the subject conspicuously.

"But, Mother," I say tentatively, after another evening in which we find ourselves eating dinner alone with each other. "She practically murdered two people. She invited *war tech* into our city and she's the head of security. How can they just ignore it? Why bother to get her name in the first place?"

Mother twirls the wineglass in her fingers, looking somewhere between me and the ruby liquid spiraling up the inside of the crystal. "When I was at the university, before I became president, there used to be these . . . wars, I guess you could call them, between the various departments. Antiquities and Environmental Studies in particular hated each other. Getting Administration on your side was always a coup. At its worst, it seemed as if everyone was some kind of spy. It tanked careers, those wars. I remember the mind-set: Assume that everyone else wants what you have, or that they'll use you to get something better. Trust no one, except to the extent that you have something on them."

She trails off, still engrossed in that empty space between us. She takes a long sip of wine. I take a large, burning mouthful of my own. Mother hasn't talked about her old work since she married Auntie Yaha. Maybe not even since Papai died. I don't know what to make of this. She's so uncharacteristically loquacious. She reminds me . . . but I can't bear to think of who this mamãe reminds me of.

"So sometimes we'd find out that there was a spy in the department. Some new secretary we hired, some visiting adjunct professor. You'd think we'd just fire them, right? Report the spying to the Administration?"

"Doesn't that make sense? That way you get rid of the spy and make yourselves look like the good guys."

"But we didn't. At least, not immediately. We'd wait, June. For months sometimes. Years, once. We would wait and watch. We'd feed her false information and see what happened with it. We'd set traps and hope she'd fall into them. We made her life a living hell, and *then,* when we'd used her up, we pretended that we'd just found her and reported her to Administration. Best of both worlds. Sometimes, in a war, your best friend is your known enemy."

I understand her now. The cold calculation of the strategy takes my breath away. "But there aren't any wars in Palmares Três."

"There's politics. And that's what your stepmother fights in every day."

I pour myself the last of the bottle of wine. It's unusual for the two of us to finish a whole bottle on our own, but then, it's been an unusual night. "So you think they're watching Auntie Maria to see what else she plans to do? Isn't what she's already done enough?"

"Maybe they're watching her to see who else she's planning to do it with."

I consider this. It makes sense, but still something about it makes me stupidly, childishly upset. "Did Auntie Yaha tell you all this?"

She shakes her head. "She won't tell me any more than you."

But it's the only explanation that makes any sense. Unless Oreste and all the Aunties are in on the plot, and that I refuse to believe.

"I wish . . . is it so hard to just be *honest?* To just say, no, this is wrong, and stand up for that, and not think about advantage and placement and promotion and all that other Auntie bullshit for just one second? Is that all you grandes are? Is anything real?"

I slam my glass on the table; the wine spills warm and wet on my hand. I expect Mother to yell back at me about irresponsible wakas and accepting the world the way it is and not the way I want it to be, but instead she just puts her head in her hands. As if it's grown so heavy it might just droop off.

"Why do you think I left, filha? Too hard, without your papai around to keep me sane. João would always say to me, *But what is right, Valencia?* So that at least I'd remember, even if I went the other way."

It's the first time she's mentioned my papai since he died. At least, the first time that feels like a real *remembrance*, and not just a way of wounding me or blaming herself. The first time she's said his name, and I realize he was a man we both loved.

"What is right, Valencia?" I repeat very softly.

She sighs. "I don't know, June. I'm not an Auntie. I'm not even a university president anymore. I'm just a housewife, as you never tire of informing me."

If I blush, I blame it on the wine. "And Auntie Yaha?" I ask.

"She tries, June. You know that."

I know that. But . . .

"Why should the Aunties get to make such an important decision? What about Regina's and Wanadi's parents? What about the people who might get killed if another one of these clouds gets loose in the city? What about —"

"I know, June."

"What about everyone else?"

I'm crying. Oh, God save me, I'm crying. In front of my *mother.* I press my knuckles to my hot, throbbing cheeks. I try to force myself to stop, but it isn't working.

And then I feel her hands, cool as a rivet in winter, slip around my own. I hear her voice as I remember it: soft and comforting.

"Querida," she says, "this will be okay."

I want to believe her. But I remember that the same Aunties who won't bring Auntie Maria to justice plan to kill Enki at the end of winter. For the first time, I begin to think that I don't want this Queen's Award. Would Papai be happy to see me win like this, or would he shake his head: *But what is right, June?*

"I hate them," I say.

"It's a terrible system," says my mamãe, "but it's the best we have."

And I think, that's why she's a grande and I'm still a waka. Because she can accept that.

I won't.

*   *   *

Gil and I huddle together for warmth on a bench in Founders Park, the fragmented, muddled strains of some new bloco echoing from the bandstand on the other side of the green. Gil said he wanted to go out and dance like we used to do, to feel normal for once, but the casters and camera bots chased us away. We hid in a pod and then snuck back here.

Though I can't see him very well in the distant glow from transport tunnels far above us, I feel his sadness like a coating on my skin. But he tries to smile when he turns to me.

"Last night Ricarda said you, Octavio, and Bebel are the frontrunners for the Queen's Award."

I know he means this to cheer me up, but my chest tightens with confusion and a shameful rush of hope. "Enki thinks I'm stupid to care anymore."

Gil rests his head on my shoulder. "Think of everything you could do with it, menina," he says. "I understand." And I know he does. It would have taken his mamãe years longer to become a successful designer without that contest.

"I'm letting them win, if I give it up. Even if I hate Oreste." But I think of the weeks of silence surrounding Auntie Maria, and my justification sits uncomfortably.

Gil surprises me when he says very quietly, "I want you to win, and no one could hate her more than me."

"*You?*" I laugh. "Gil, you've never hated anyone in your life."

"No one's ever tried to kill someone I love before."

I pull away from him, astonished. He's crying silently, and for a strange, suspended moment, I remember my verde night and the way Enki looked when he realized that someone had stabbed him.

Panicked, I wipe at his face with the edge of my jacket sleeve, but it's hopeless. Gil looks broken down with grief, and for a moment, I hate Enki for doing this to him.

"Gil, Oreste is horrible but *she's* not killing Enki. He knew what he was doing when he declared."

Gil's hands imprison my own. He looks very fierce, though he still hasn't stopped crying. "And what if he changes his mind? They'll kill him anyway."

"He hasn't changed his mind." I suppose that some other summer kings must have regretted their decision, but Enki never would.

Gil denies this truth with a furious shake of his head. "Do you want him to die, June? Do you think it's okay that they kill the best of us at the end of winter?"

My mouth opens, but I can't think of anything to say. *Do* I think it's okay? I know Gil thought so back in the spring, when we were both so excited to vote for Enki to become summer king. Clearly, he's changed his mind. But the ritual of our summer king is as central to the identity of Palmares Três as the pyramid itself. Still, when faced with the question, I realize that one thing is true.

I don't want Enki to die.

"We can't do anything to stop it, Gil."

He looks at me very sadly, but at least his tears have stopped. "I wish we could at least *try*."

But I know better than anyone how dangerous trying can be, and how destructive. Maybe it's better to let bad things happen than tear yourself apart trying to stop the inevitable.

Couldn't that be art, June? whispers a voice like Enki's.

I ignore him.

His blood sanctifies his choice — I've heard the catechism all my life, though I didn't understand it until my papai took me to the park to watch Fidel die. It's barbaric and cruel, our ritual sacrifice of a king every five years, but it's all in the service of his choice. Every young Palmarina is taught the story of Alonso and Odete — our first king and Queen, who in the midst of the chaos and death of the dislocation, chose a different path.

The kings die so that their choice of the next Queen can be irrevocable, unassailable, and unprejudiced.

After all, there's no time for corruption when your throat is being cut.

They tell us the idea came to Alonso in a dream, sent to him by Ogum, the orixá of politics and prophecy. They say he realized that the new citizens would be willing to make sacrifices for the sake of their new home, if the leaders were willing to make a sacrifice for the city. The Founding Mothers reluctantly agreed with his reasoning, and when his year was over, he named Odete first Queen and he died. Even with the changed tradition of the moon years, our system seems to have worked pretty well for the last four centuries. It's true — a man about to die can make some surprising choices.

But it isn't much of a waka who doesn't wonder — *especially* during a moon year — if we couldn't find a better way. After all, the dislocation and its horrors are four hundred years past and would it really hurt anyone to let the summer kings live after their year-long reign?

Not long after Papai brought me to the park, I asked Mamãe why we didn't kill the Queens when they were done too.

"Kings are men," Mamãe said, "and they can't be trusted to give up power once they have it."

I believed her at the time. Now I think: Auntie Isa has been sub-queen for fifty years.

Now I think: Why else have moon years?

We have exams today. I've actually studied for a change, though I'm so restless it doesn't feel like it. I dig my sandals into the floor and attempt to peer above the shoulder-height walls of my carrel without making it obvious. Gil is in the front of the room, shoulders hunched, forehead screwed in concentration. It's news to me that he even knows what his subjects are this year, let alone that he learned them well enough to answer the questions scrolling across the examination arrays. Bebel sits two rows behind him, with better posture but even greater intensity. Her operatic hand gestures are only contained by the walls on either side. I can almost see her points accumulate in the air above her. She has a much better average this year than I do, and she's obviously planning to keep her streak. I wouldn't expect any less: My best rival wouldn't let something paltry like exam scores get in the way of her chances for the Queen's Award. I look back at the test questions, but they might as well be in English. At this rate, Bebel will stay at the top of the class rankings, and I won't have any chance of catching up.

At first, a familiar panic grips me: I haven't studied enough, I don't know the subjects, I'm going to fail and my mamãe will find out and my papai will be so disappointed. Bebel will win and lord it over me for days.

And then I remember: My papai is dead, Bebel is my friend, and I don't know how I feel about the Queen's Award these days.

I sigh and look back down at my own exam. The questions are history, and they seem to come to me from another planet.

Discuss the immediate effects of nuclear cooling and relate that to the failure of the Pan-American Treaty Agreement.

"Grandes are stupid?" I mutter, but I do my best to scrawl out some approximation of an intelligent answer. The next question is more of the same and the next and the next until I throw my own hands up in the air and let out a groan loud enough to make the two students on either side of me pause and look up. The teacher reading at the front of the room raises her eyebrows in mild reproach. Reflexively, I duck my head back down, try to make myself work.

Answering the questions feels like beating my skull against the wall of my carrel, but I keep going until someone taps my shoulder. I sit bolt upright and nearly fall from my chair.

It's Ieyascu, giant as ever, with that expression that used to chill my blood. Now I only feel exasperated.

She crooks her finger and gestures with her head at the door. She wants to speak to me outside. In the middle of exams? I'm frightened despite myself when I stand up, attempting to ignore the curious stares of my classmates.

She leads me down the hall and into an unused classroom. The door slides shut with a barely audible click that raises goose bumps on my arms.

"I hope this won't count against my exam time," I say, just to break the silence. Ieyascu looks much too intimidating, towering over me with her red turban and crossed arms.

"I'm doing this against my better judgment," she says.

"Making me miss my exams?"

She shakes her head. "Giving you this."

She hands me a sheet of paper. This surprises me so much that at first I'm afraid she's somehow found my stacks of paper drawings, that one of the more indiscreet ones is getting me in trouble. I had planned to selectively edit what I released to the public for the award.

But this paper is smaller, lighter. It has real writing on it, in some kind of ink.

"What is this?" I ask.

Ieyascu takes a few steps away and turns so all I can see is her broad, straight back. "Surely you can still read?"

I sigh and look back down at the paper. Handwriting is a pain to read, though we all had to learn it back in primary school. I struggle through the first few sentences, but my heart starts to pound once I understand what they mean.

June,
Renata will have just pulled you from your quarter final exams.

I look up. "Renata?"

Ieyascu turns around just enough for me to see the corner of a thin, tight smile crease her cheek. "The Queen and I have known each other since we were quite young."

"The Queen?" I say, even as my eyes scan to the end of the letter and see, of course, her name and an old, looping signature of the kind I've only otherwise encountered in history class.

Ieyascu resumes her pacing. "Lord above, June," she says, in time to the faint swish of her skirt. "*Read*, why don't you?"

I take a deep breath.

She has been monitoring your performance, and I have instructed her to stop you from testing if she did not believe you would finish within range of Bebel. As you are probably aware, Bebel is one of your main contenders for the Queen's Award. As the rankings currently stand, I would probably be forced to declare her the winner. You might wonder why I simply can't give the award to whomever I wish. The reality, of course, is politics. The dispensation of the Queen's Award must have every appearance of impartiality. Your school scores will be available to any government official who asks, June, and there would be scandal if I were seen to be giving this award to a subpar student.

My pulse starts to gallop. If I wasn't sure about the Queen's Award before, I am now. Even if everything else slips away from me, this is something I can hold.

It will probably come as a surprise to you, but I would very much like you to win. I admit that when Yaha first put your name to me in the spring, I felt mostly indifferent about your candidacy. Your selection was not quite a favor to your stepmother, but not very far from it. But over the course of this year, my respect for your independence and courage has grown, as well as my estimation of your talent.

However, as I said, politics interferes. Consider this letter my method of fighting back. Renata will provide you with instructions. Trust that she does this with my blessing. She will destroy this letter — and thus any record of my actions — as soon as you are finished reading it.

I still cannot guarantee you will win, June. Your final project must be stunning, whatever it is. But just trust that whatever my public demeanor, I am on your side.

Oreste

I drop the paper as I read the last line. Ieyascu stands by the window, the farthest point away from me in the room. Her erect carriage and upturned chin radiate distaste.

"You have . . . instructions?" I say.

"You won't always be the golden child, you know," she says to the window. "Eventually, the privileged ones like you run up against the limits of their talent. It's sad, really."

Ieyascu's contempt surprises me. I'd always assumed that she treated most students with that brusque distrust. But it seems she's always thought of me as an Auntie's brat.

"There's no way she'd do this all for Auntie Yaha."

Ieyascu smiles that tight smile. "At least you have some sense."

"She says she respects my —"

"June."

I take a few steps toward her. At least I'm angry. I try to keep hold of that.

"Bebel is no better than me," I say.

Ieyascu doesn't turn. "Debatable. But in any case, she's a better student. Oreste was more or less honest about the political situation surrounding her choice for the Queen's Award. What she left out is that there is much more riding on this year's selection, given the fiasco with Lucia. I daresay this is the first time a candidate has been caught committing treason."

"But why would she bother doing this? What does it benefit her to make me win?"

"What makes you so sure she wants you to win?"

"She said —"

"After all this, you still imagine Oreste ever fully means what she says?"

Ieyascu takes a few ground-eating strides and plucks the paper off the table. She smells sweet, of orange blossoms and the heavy starch ironed into her headscarf.

"She's leading me on?"

"Perhaps." She rips the paper clean down the middle — an efficient, brutal gesture. "And perhaps she merely admires your talent and determination. I'm just a school principal, after all. What do I know of politics?"

She stares at the two halves for a moment, then takes a long cylinder out of her pocket. It clicks and a flame erupts from one end. I watch, nearly shaking with the need to say something and having nothing to say, as she lets a flame incinerate the precious paper to a dusting of ash on the floor.

"There," she says.

"I *am* good," I say. "You might hate me, but you can't deny it."

Her lips pucker, like she took a drink of sour milk. "Your entitlement is truly a wonder to behold."

"Entitlement?" Everything has gone very still inside me. Ieyascu looks bright and flat, heavy strokes on an invisible canvas.

"What," she says, "makes you think you *should* win, June? For all your scheming, for all your attempts to hijack the summer king to raise your popularity, for every other thing you try, June, what makes you think you deserve this? With so many other brilliant wakas in the running, why are you always so endlessly sure that *you* should win?"

Her voice barely rises in pitch. Her hands hardly move, but her words have dealt me a blow. *Why?* is the thrust, endlessly repeated.

And then, a parry.

"But that's just art."

"I don't like your kind of art."

I meet her towering gaze, and perhaps I don't feel as small as I should. She sighs, looks away. Not a victory, I'm not stupid enough to assume that, but a relief nonetheless.

"That should be enough time," she says. "You can go back to your exam now, June."

"Back?"

"I can't very well help you if you won't at least go through the motions. Go back. Finish your test. If anyone asks, you had a family emergency. When the scores are posted, you'll score a few points above Bebel."

"But she hasn't even finished yet."

Ieyascu raises her eyebrows. "It's your decision, but make it quickly."

Panic makes me forget to breathe. How can I decide without taking the time to think about it? Without asking Gil for advice?

"Can't I tell you tomorrow?"

"The Queen's generosity isn't boundless. You have an offer. Accept it or go away."

"But couldn't you fix the results just as well tomorrow morning?"

Ieyascu laughs as if she would rather skewer me. "I could. The Queen chose not to exercise that option, and I am her humble servant."

She dares me to contradict her; I decline. One thing is true enough: Ieyascu might hate me, but she's not the one who's caught me in her web. Oreste is trying to manipulate me into accepting, but why? Because she thinks I deserve the Queen's Award? But that's too flattering and too simplistic. Because allowing me to win the award might help shore up her political position after the deaths at Royal Plaza?

Entirely possible.

And will I accept this manipulation? Will I hurt my best rival in the world with an exam score I don't deserve? *How much of yourself will you give them in exchange?* Enki asked, back when I couldn't have dreamed of a price this high.

"Yes," I say, fast, before I can change my mind.

Ieyascu's contempt is like a snake, coiling around her mouth and eyes. "Enjoy the Queen's favor, June."

She touches the door. It slides open with a smooth release of air that makes the bile rise high in my throat.

I won't be hurting Bebel, I reason. She'll still do as well as she was always going to. I'll just keep myself in the running, which is what I deserve to begin with.

Why? asks that voice. Maybe it's Ieyascu's, maybe it's mine.

Because I should win, I think.

I thank Ieyascu before I walk back into the exam room. I take my seat. I finish an exam I know doesn't matter because the Queen herself is cheating for me.

I do not care.

I will not care.

I don't normally copy other people's art, but this seems a worthy exception.

The isolationists have found a way to fight back. There's a new stencil in the city. It looks familiar to anyone who's seen the now-ubiquitous silhouette of Enki and me. But the two figures are Wanadi and Regina, upside down in clouds. Wanadi smiles, Regina frowns. Wanadi has a perfect bullet hole through the middle of his forehead. Regina holds a candle behind her back, the stark white of the flames engulfing her hands.

It's very good. I only wish I had something to do with it. So I do the next closest thing, and study a holo of the new stencil. Messy stacks of paper litter my bedroom floor, a fortune of wood pulp and graphite and ink. As the weeks have gone by, I've found my style changing, or at least growing, turning so deeply abstract that sometimes even I hardly know what I'm drawing. Most of these are faces: Enki and Gil. Auntie Yaha and Mother. Even a few of Papai, though his face is so deconstructed I doubt anyone but me would recognize him.

I keep meaning to show the sketches publicly and start building support for my award bid, but every time I start to scan them in I have a vision of Ieyascu's contemptuous face and I put them down. *Later,* I always think. *When I have more.*

Copying the isolationist art relaxes me, as though I'm meditating with the sure strokes of my pencil. In the two weeks since I cheated on that test, I've been nervous, jumpy, reclusive. I haven't been able to confess to Gil. He asks me what's wrong and I say I'm busy. He knows I'm lying; he knows I know he knows. We haven't spoken to each other much.

I haven't seen Enki at all.

These days, I mostly speak to Mother and Auntie Yaha. They both congratulated me sincerely on my test score. Whatever game Oreste is playing with me, it's not about Auntie Yaha. It's probably about Enki, but that's always where my thoughts stick. I don't know how or why she thinks she can use *me* to get to him. I think Enki has always been untouchable, but these days anyone can see it.

I haven't been able to look Bebel in the eye. I haven't been able to sit through a full day at school without feeling sick to my stomach. I shouldn't have said yes. I am a fool and a coward and I try not to think about it. If I win the Queen's Award, the self-loathing will bury me, but I don't know how to climb out of the hole I've dug for myself.

I'm barely conscious of my scribbling right hand, though the drawing unfolds steadily beneath it. But when I start to draw that artfully stark bullet hole, I stop.

For some reason, my thoughts have Enki's voice: "It looks too clean, right? Death isn't so pretty."

I look closer at the holo and then I understand: The bullet goes in, but nothing comes out.

"It isn't, is it?" I mutter as my pencil flies across the paper. I crack the graphite tip and grunt with frustration at the time to stop and sharpen it.

Instead of hair, I give Wanadi an exit wound. And instead of that mixture of brains and bone and blood I'll never forget, I give him flowers and vines. The plant life curls around Regina, merges with the stylized ribbons of flame into something that resembles mechanical circuits. A strange, inverted amalgam of life and destruction. Is it technophile or isolationist, this new version I've created? Is it both?

I want to show it to Gil, but I know that if I reach out to him, he'll demand to know what happened outside the exam room. I can't lie, and I can't bear to tell him. Not yet.

I cut the image from the holo, leaving only the floating graphic of our pyramid city, shining its light calmly in the bay.

"City," I say, activating the holo's com link.

"Yes, June?" says that voice I've grown so fond of.

"Could you tell Enki I miss him?"

"I'll try, June," she says, and I know I'm not imagining the sadness and confusion in her voice.

"What has he done now?" I whisper. She doesn't answer.

I wait an hour, alternating my attention between my rain-streaked window and the idealized city floating in the air above my bed. I love Palmares Três, but how I have begun to hate the Aunties who run her.

Finally, I shut off the holo, toss the drawing on a nearby stack, and open the door to my bedroom. Mother is alone, as usual, and watching the rain from the screened-in porch.

"Have you eaten?" I ask.

She shakes her head, but she's nursing a glass of wine; there's a bottle nearby. I take a glass and join her.

"Is Auntie Yaha coming back tonight?"

"She said not to wait up."

Maybe it's the rain, maybe it's the wine, but Mother looks as lonely and vulnerable as I've ever seen her. I almost touch her fingers but at the last minute pick up the bottle instead. I don't know if the bridge we're building is steady enough for that, yet.

"Is something big happening?" I ask.

"Tomorrow, Oreste is going to announce a full-session inquiry into the Pernambuco affair."

That's what the news casters have taken to calling the disaster with Ueda-sama and the technophile mob: *the Pernambuco affair.* As though everything about the mess that killed Wanadi and Regina wasn't entirely Palmarina, no matter who sold them the weapons. But still, if they're doing an inquiry . . .

"She's *finally* going to indict Auntie Maria?" I feel relief like a plunge into the bay, cold and shocking and exhilarating.

"Maybe," Mother says, and drains her glass. "They're only doing this much because of public pressure. Those stencils are doing more work than a hundred lobbyists."

Mother turns abruptly, gives me a long look. I blush, though I don't know why. I imagine Mother learning about my agreement with Oreste, and the blush deepens.

"You know I didn't do those stencils, right?"

She smiles a little. "I didn't think so, filha."

"You didn't?"

"They didn't look like you."

I wonder what she'd make of my latest drawing.

Mother stands, surprisingly steady given the half bottle of wine she just consumed, and walks into the kitchen. "There's some moqueca left," she says. "Should I heat it for you?"

The moqueca is Auntie Yaha's and reliably delicious. I remember that I haven't eaten since breakfast.

"That would be —"

I get a ping. Anonymous, of course. *Open your door,* it reads.

"I have to go," I say as I stand up and race to my room. "I'll be back later. Something for the Queen's Award."

"You sure you don't want to eat?" she asks.

"Sorry, Mamãe," I say. "Don't wait up."

Enki is across the street, standing in the rain. It pours in a steady shower, punctuated by an occasional flash of lightning. His back is to me; he watches the bay. No one else is near him, which ought to surprise me, but doesn't. If Enki wants to be alone, he manages. Even in the middle of a public street. I look up, reflexively, for the dozen or so camera bots that usually hover at the edge of the anti-bot zone surrounding the house. But the air is clear, save for the rain, and for the first time in months, I feel unobserved when I walk outside. Enki is soaked. I brought an umbrella, but I don't unfurl it.

"I missed you too," he says when I'm a few feet away. He still hasn't turned around.

"Have you been busy?" I ask.

"Oreste is having a big show trial starting tomorrow. She wants me to star."

The rain runs down my back, so cold my skin tightens like the top of a pandeiro. Enki wears short sleeves with a rip at the collar. If I squint, I can see a faint, hazy layer of steam rising from his exposed skin. I stand beside him and take his hand. He lets me, but he doesn't move to do anything else. Just touching him makes me feel warm and happy, but I wish I knew how he feels.

"Are you going to?"

He shrugs. "Maybe. I'll see what she has planned."

I almost grin at that, imagining the Auntie consternation when Enki yet again confounds their expectations. But then I remember the more pressing worry.

"And Auntie Maria?"

"Oh, June." His hand tightens around mine. When he turns, his wet dreadlocks splash my face. He doesn't smile.

"What?"

"You really thought they would do something about that?"

I don't know. I remember Mother's story about the wars in her department and the way everyone would manipulate everyone else. "But she killed two people!"

He smiles now, bitter and tender at once. "She's over a hundred years old, and she's been an Auntie for at least fifty of them. She has dirt on every official in Royal Tower, and they all know it. June, probably at least a few other Aunties helped her plan the whole thing. They can't indict her without putting the whole system on trial."

"So they sent me like a fetching dog to get the name out of Lucia, just so they could play games with her."

"Play *politics.*"

I open my mouth — to scream, I think, or maybe just to cry — but he puts a careful finger on my lips. I breathe a little of his steam, and it warms me all the way through.

"It is horrible and wrong," he says, almost a whisper. "A twisted-up grande thing. But you could always change that."

"How? Become an Auntie? I *never* want to be one of them."

He wags his finger gently before my face. "Of course not. You really haven't thought of this yet? Who else knows what Lucia confessed?"

A sudden crack of thunder startles me into a yelp. I jump away from Enki and nearly fall on the slick ground. He gives me one of his calm, searching looks; he knows perfectly well I've thought of it.

"They'd hang me from Royal Tower," I say.

He shrugs. "They'd exile you, at worst."

At worst. The very thought makes my teeth chatter. I huddle against the railing, avoiding his clear look, the bay's flashing beauty.

"Enki, I have a future to plan for. And you won't live to see spring." I regret the words immediately, but then, I don't take them back. I would blame it on the wind and the icy rain. On the lightning that's always made me nervous. But I'm a coward; why else would I argue in the first place?

His grin looks like a monkey's: a feral baring of teeth. "Do you think I really need reminding?"

"Why don't *you* tell the casters, if you think it's so important? You know too."

"Only because you told me. And the moment I accuse Maria, the Aunties will blame you anyway. So you'll still lose your precious Queen's Award and the Aunties will find a way to claim I'm lying. *I* wasn't the one who spoke to Lucia. You were, and everyone knows that."

I don't know what to say, so I don't say anything.

He shakes his head. "What did you miss, June? Me? Or your summer project? I'm sure it was exciting to play at being radical, but there's a time for fun and a time for reality, is that it? It's strange. I never really believed you would pick the Queen's Award, when it came down to it. But you have."

The steam wafting off his body gets thicker, heavier. He smiles again, but it's a little sad and a lot angry and entirely human. He turns his back to me. He starts to walk away.

"Enki, I didn't want —"

"Didn't you?"

I want to make this better. I want to feel good again, like a person I can admire. I don't want to admit what I'm terrified is true: The Queen's Award matters more to me than justice for two dead wakas. After all, I let the Queen *cheat* for me. I'm in too deep, too close to just give it up.

"I meant it," I say finally. "All of our art."

"Not enough." And then, with the faintest hint of a smile in his voice, "There's a song."

Because there's always a song.

I would ask him what, but he's gone too far away. I could watch him forever, and he vanishes before I can blink.

The second day of the hearings, I get a curious message.

Would you like to accompany me to this afternoon's session? — Toshio

It's from Ueda-sama. I haven't heard a word from him since our dinner more than a month ago, and I gasp from my seat in the back of the classroom. The teacher doesn't pause, but Gil turns his head and cocks an eyebrow at me.

"Ueda," I mouth, and he frowns. Maybe he harbors some lingering resentment over Enki's involvement with the ambassador, but I think it more likely that he worries what I'm up to. I glance back at my fono: one hour until the afternoon session starts. Should I run back home and change, maybe into something that shows off my light-tree? But no, too revealing if something happens at the trial that upsets me. Enki says he can see half my thoughts in those lights.

At least, he would if he were still talking to me.

The school's fields don't allow for much fono communication, but I figure if Ueda was able to get a message to me, then I should be able to respond. I tell him yes and he says to wait in the public entrance to the parliamentary hall. I wonder what Enki will think if he sees me there. That I've changed my mind about Auntie Maria? Will he stop hating me?

I grit my teeth. Forget him. He's too far down the path of his own death to see what it's like for a waka with centuries ahead of her. He thinks I can just sacrifice everything I might have in the world for the sake of some abstract justice, but it isn't that simple, as Auntie Yaha would say. As Mother would say.

What is right, Valencia? my papai says in my mamãe's voice.

Shut up, João, I think, because I could never have said it if he were still alive. I'll win the Queen's Award, I'll become a famous artist, and *then* I'll do good — when I have a position and influence and a life to do it with. If I make this one futile gesture, then what? I never get to see my home again? I get to stay, but I never have any professional success because I've been blacklisted?

"No."

I didn't mean to say this out loud. The teacher looks up from the English text he was reading to the class.

"You have such a strong objection to Atwood, June?"

Bebel, a few rows ahead, turns to look at me. "You okay?" she whispers.

My stomach lurches. God, I wish I could still hate Bebel. It was so much simpler.

"I need to leave," I say, and now the whole class stares at me.

He sighs. "Another unexplained absence? Do what you will, June."

He returns to the text. I pick up my things and head for the door. I have to watch this hearing. I have to prove to Enki that I'm fine with my decision. And maybe prove it to myself.

"*He's* the one who's being judgmental," I mutter as I stalk through the deserted hallway. "The one who doesn't have any empathy."

But the words feel absurd as soon as I speak them. For all our summer king's faults, he certainly doesn't lack empathy. I'm nearly at the outside doors when I hear the echo of canvas shoes running through the hallway.

"June," Gil says, "wait!"

I wait for him with resignation and relief. I've missed him so much. And soon he will hate me as much as Enki does.

"You're doing something with Ueda-sama?" he says when he's caught up with me. He almost touches my elbow but then pulls his hand back, stuffs it inside his pocket.

"He invited me to the hearings."

"Oh."

We stare at each other. Gil shuffles his feet, an awkward samba, but somehow still achingly graceful. My lights strobe hot and cold. Gil is my brother, my best friend. Why are we acting like strangers to each other?

"Gil —"

"June, I'm sorry —"

"I did something . . . I shouldn't have, when Ieyascu pulled me out of the exam. I was too ashamed to tell you."

He smiles suddenly. "I've been so wrapped up lately, I just didn't know what to say to you. It seems so silly . . ."

"Wrapped up?"

The smile fades a little, and I see that face, the one I'd mistaken for derision. It's that deep sadness that I glimpsed weeks ago in the park.

"I can't stop hoping," he whispers.

"About . . . saving Enki?" The phrase sounds nonsensical. You can't save a summer king any more than you can save a mayfly.

Maybe he sees my disbelief, because he sighs and changes the subject. "What happened to you?"

In the end, it's a relief to tell him. "I let the Aunties help me cheat on my exams to stay in the running with Bebel."

He freezes and stares. "Oh, June."

"I'm sorry." My eyes are hot, but I can't cry here.

"Will you tell Bebel?"

"But if I do —" I cut myself off, ashamed to even finish the sentence.

"You won't win," Gil finishes, and he touches my elbow. His disappointment is like a flashing sign above his head, but he doesn't let go. That's enough for now.

We look at each other for another moment, then he pulls me forward, very gently, and kisses me on the forehead.

"If you think of a way to save him, June, do you promise to tell me? Do you promise to let me help?"

I don't understand how someone as smart as Gil can't see this is a fantasy. "Enki made his choice. There's nothing we can do now."

He turns away and I'm overwhelmed with an echo, with the sense that the words in my mouth aren't my own. But of course they are. Gil is being foolish, and someone had to tell him so.

Just like your mamãe told you, when Papai died?

I gasp. "I'll try," I hear myself saying, before he can walk away.

It's all the reward in the world when he turns around and smiles.

Ueda-sama has a secretary meet me at the public entrance and escort me to our seats at the front of the giant parliamentary hall. No one important enough to be at these hearings would ever conspicuously snub him, and yet he stands as though alone in the sea of Auntie turbans and colorful dresses. He wears simple trousers and a shirt — perhaps the bird design around the collar subtly evokes his home, but perhaps not. He looks older than the last time we met. Exhausted in a way that goes beyond the dark rings under his eyes.

He smiles at me after I push my way through the milling crowd to find my seat next to him.

"I'm so glad you could come, June," he says. I'm here just in time — a second later, Auntie Isa calls the meeting to order.

Enki doesn't invoke the proceedings with a prayer this afternoon. He just sits quietly with the head Aunties and Oreste. He acts as he has for the last two days: like a model summer king from a moon year, beautiful and obedient. I try to catch his eye, but he looks straight ahead. Maybe he doesn't know I'm here, or maybe he's just ignoring me. Just looking at him makes me short of breath, makes me want to cry, makes me want to rage and scream. How dare he hold me in such contempt for having the temerity to control my own life?

There's some hubbub on the floor as the remaining two Aunties and one Uncle take their seats on the committee. In the audience, murmurs swell into a chorus, cloth rustles. Ueda-sama bends his head toward me and whispers, "Are you all right, my dear?"

I nod and take a deep breath. "Yes, of course," I say. "Thank you again for inviting me."

He shrugs. "I just had a sudden thought that you would like to see this. Perhaps almost as much as I do."

I wonder how much Ueda saw from his cage that day. I wonder if, amid the teeming confusion of the protesters and the nanocloud and the security bots, he saw those bullets tear through Wanadi and Regina. What would that look like to someone from Tokyo 10, whose citizens have forsaken death altogether?

"Do you think this will . . ." But I realize that he doesn't know about Auntie Maria, and I don't dare tell him in this space.

But still, he seems to understand. "We'll see, June," he says.

"The special investigative body is now in session," says Auntie Isa. The sudden silence is like an intake of breath. I look at Enki again. His smile would look smug if I didn't notice the sadness at the corners. In his stillness, he nonetheless conveys volatility, as though he must either sit still or explode.

"The goal of today's inquiry," says Auntie Isa, "is to continue investigation into ethical breaches that may have allowed the infiltration of war tech into our city."

And killed two people, I think, but of course the Aunties want nothing so grisly as fact to intrude on their sanitized hearings.

But, "Also," says Enki, leaning forward a few gentle centimeters, "resulting in the deaths of Wanadi Dias and Regina Silva."

For a second, Auntie Isa breaks her infamous calm — she glances at Enki, startled, before serenity returns to her ageless face and she nods once in solemn acknowledgment.

"Of course, as the king says, resulting in the tragic deaths of two of our citizens. And for our first testimony, we call Auntie Maria before the committee."

Auntie Maria makes her way from her seat in the front row of the audience to the solitary chair facing the committee, who sit in a half circle around her. It looks horribly intimidating to me, but Auntie Maria wears an expression of calm determination I'm sure she practiced in front of the mirror. My pulse speeds — no Aunties would give confirmation of who they would call for testimony today. I hadn't dared hope I might actually get to see Auntie Maria accused of her own crimes. I start to grin, but then stop when I catch curious glances from some of the people seated nearby.

I sometimes forget that I'm no longer the anonymous student I used to be.

"Good afternoon, Maria," says Auntie Isa in a convivial tone that sets my teeth on edge. "I trust you understand your presence here."

Auntie Maria doesn't move, except perhaps to straighten her already perfect posture. "There was an egregious breach of security, and I have been entrusted with our city's safekeeping. I would have volunteered myself had you not called me here."

"Then perhaps," says Auntie Nara, from the far end of the table, "you could begin by explaining to us, in your own words, how such dangerous tech not only got into our city, but into the hands of technophile extremists?"

Auntie Maria nods at Auntie Nara, grave seriousness tempered with just the right dash of self-recrimination. She looks just like a holo, even in real life.

Enki flashes that delightful mocking smile, but just for a moment. Then he's back to staid, perfect King Enki. What game he's playing I don't know, but he still hasn't noticed me.

"The trouble," says Auntie Maria, "is that I trusted the wakas too much. Lucia in particular, I'm afraid, and the others who were so enamored of new technology. I would never in my wildest dreams have imagined them capable of trading with guerrillas for such abominations."

Auntie Nara nods. "I understand, Auntie, but the question still remains: With all the myriad ways at your disposal to watch over this city, when these technophile terrorists chose to go outside the city for tech, how could you have missed it?"

Another Auntie whose name I've forgotten clears her throat. "I second the Auntie's question. This was a security breach of flabbergasting proportions. Indeed, I find it hard to believe that you had no inkling of the technophiles' plans beforehand."

I think I gasp — at least, my mouth hangs open — but any sound I might make is drowned by the noise of the audience. A few people rise from their chairs and shout in disapproval, while others clap. Auntie Isa purses her lips.

"Quiet, please!" she says, her voice booming through the acoustically calibrated chamber. "Auntie Cleusa, I hope you don't mean to imply any collusion on the part of our head of security?"

I watch Oreste, seated between Auntie Isa and Enki, hoping for the slightest twitch of emotion on that iconically impassive face. But her hands remain in her lap, her head turns slightly to the side, more like a beautiful robot than a human. Is there a mod for that, I wonder, and then choke back a laugh. At least that's one I can be sure Enki would never use.

The Auntie who asked the question clears her throat. "I think," she says, far more tentatively this time, "that the question should at least be raised. The time line the distinguished Auntie has provided us with has many confusing gaps. There are many errors in judgment that —"

Auntie Maria leans forward slightly, as though physically pained. "I am the first to admit my lapses, honored Auntie Cleusa. But I have served this greatest city, our light on the bay, I have been a true Palmarina for over one hundred and twenty years and an Auntie for fifty of them. Surely even a *political* opponent such as yourself wouldn't accuse me of betrayal?"

Shouts of support momentarily drown out even the carefully amplified members of the committee. I glance up at Ueda-sama, shocked. I would never have imagined Auntie Maria to have such support, even among the crowd that can attend parliamentary hearings.

"You make many friends in a long life," Ueda-sama whispers, close in my ear. I remember that he is more than three hundred years old, a technological Methuselah, and think, *Well, wouldn't he know?*

"So she'll get away with it," I say softly, and Ueda-sama gives me a sharp glance.

"Could you explain," says Enki in a voice that booms through the hall, "how it is that a group of loosely affiliated technophile wakas came to travel hundreds of miles outside this city over dangerous terrain to make agreements with guerrillas who would just as soon shoot them as give them nanotech?"

Oreste turns to Enki and raises one chilly eyebrow. He grins at her. "Honored Auntie," he adds, a perfect grace note of withering disrespect.

Some cheers, some boos, many confused murmurs. I barely hear it; my eyes have locked on Enki, and God save me but I love him, I love him, he can never be mine, and I want him more than art.

"Young king," says Auntie Maria, attempting to match his contempt but failing in a way that makes me hope she is finally afraid, "for all your accomplishments, you don't know much about the workings of the world. Perhaps a representative of the Pernambuco militia undertook the trek herself, after a remote communication. Why, perhaps they even had assistance from certain free agents in our own society with access to many mods. You would know about that better than I, my king."

Enki has more admirers than I'd imagined, here in this bastion of the Aunties. My angry shout is hardly alone.

Auntie Maria shrugs it off. She scored her point. "All I can say to you, my king, and to all my people is that I'm exceedingly sorry for my lapse in judgment. I assure you that all waka gatherings will be monitored with special vigilance, particularly those with demonstrated interests in antigovernment activity, protest, and illegal technology. So long as I remain at my post — pending the findings of the honored committee, of course — I promise you all that I will never let a tragedy like the Pernambuco affair happen again."

"Thank you, Auntie Maria," says Auntie Isa when the noise has quieted. "I believe we have all we need for now."

Auntie Maria inclines her head gravely to the committee and walks back to her seat. Everyone in the room watches her.

Almost everyone. My lights ripple and my stomach clenches even before I look up to find Enki staring straight at me.

"June," he mouths. Just my name, so gently, and I wish I knew what it meant. I wish I could take back this burst of *I love you*, so fierce and overpowering I feel as though I've been modded.

Auntie Isa looks up from her personal array. "For our next testimony, the committee would like to call —"

"Honored Auntie Isa, if I may intrude?"

Auntie Isa is not so good at controlling her expressions as Queen Oreste. Or perhaps she simply doesn't care as much. "Yes, Enki," she snaps, and even I recoil at the rudeness of using only his given name in this setting.

But my summer king, my beautiful boy, he merely widens his eyes. "I thought perhaps I could bring up my own witness."

"The king has that prerogative," she says, though grudgingly.

That feral smile. I shiver. "What's he doing?" I whisper.

"Who knows," says Ueda-sama.

"In that case," says Enki, "I call June Costa to the stand."

"Lucia gave you a name," Enki says.

The lights shine brighter here. Sweat drips down my back, slides past my ears. I should have known. I should have seen it in his steady gaze, in the way he mouthed my name. He was glad I had come. Not to see me, but because of the knowledge I refuse to confess.

"King," says Auntie Isa, "what —"

"Someone high up in the administration," he continues, oblivious. "Perhaps even an Auntie? We all know someone had to have helped the technophiles get the war tech."

This rouses Oreste to speech. "We all know nothing of the kind, Enki," she says in her mild, withering way.

Maybe Enki thinks he's alone. He leans forward. He looks at me like he did that time on the boat, just before our grand show, just before he kissed me. Time moves sticky and slow, just like then. For a moment, I have a flash of him in the rain: steam rising from his skin, water spraying from his hair. That surprised disappointment.

I am not as good as he thinks I am. I am not as good as I thought I was.

I am June Costa, a regular waka in Palmares Três.

"She gave you a name, didn't she?" he asks.

Oreste grips the sides of her chair. "Enki, this isn't —"

"Yes," I say. I shouldn't have answered him. I wouldn't have, even five minutes ago. But under these bright lights, I realize I've made a choice. There's movement in my peripheral vision, background noise that seems to hem me in, but Enki binds me like he has from the first moment I saw him, with smiles and dance and eyes that see clearly.

"What's her name, June?" We might as well be alone, arguing on the rock of O Quilombola, jumping and plunging and *Happy Christmas, June* and —

I stand. People move around me, they try to touch, but they can't stick. Two, three, four steps and I'm less than a meter away.

"June?" Enki says. I kneel. A subject to her king. I take his hand. His grip is firm and warm and dry; he smells of hibiscus and sea salt.

I never really believed you would pick the Queen's Award, he said. And he was right, in the end.

"The person —"

Enki puts his hand over my mouth. He looks scared. Has something else happened to the city?

"Quiet." His lips barely move.

"This meeting of parliament is over. As Queen, I declare a hiatus period effective immediately during which we will review our findings and pursue the possibility of reconvening another committee."

Oreste's voice. I can't see her or the crowd still shouting behind me, but the authority in it chills me. What did she do to make Enki so afraid? Threaten him? A moment later, someone drags me up by my elbow. I look for Ueda-sama, but he's vanished into the crowd. All I can do is keep hold of Enki's hand as we're pushed through the special Auntie entrance in back and down through a silent, carpeted hallway. I look at Enki, my face wild with questions, but he just shakes his head and I let them settle inside me.

The security officials lead us to a small room and tell us to wait. They close the door behind them.

"It won't be locked," Enki says.

I test it anyway.

"Should we leave?" I say.

"Where would we go, bem-querer?" He leans forward so his forehead touches mine. "What else is there?"

Tokyo 10, or one of the Parises or even Salvador might not be as bad as they say . . . but then I realize what I'm thinking, I realize what it would mean and he's right: Our whole world is Palmares Três. That unlocked door is a symbol. If we leave, they'll only bring us back.

A moment later, Oreste herself walks through, followed by Auntie Maria. The door closes behind them and part of me wishes we'd left when we had the chance.

"Well," Oreste says, visibly angry now that we're away from the cameras, "what a show, Enki, even for you."

"It seemed to me," Enki says, "that you might actually let her get away with murdering two people."

"I murdered no one, you stupid little boy," Auntie Maria says. She crosses her arms angrily; her turban slowly unravels in the back. "I made sure they had what they wanted and I let it happen. You have Lucia and her faulty programming to thank for Wanadi and Regina. The way you wakas overrate technology . . ."

I gape at her. "If you don't want tech, then why would you . . ."

Oreste and Maria share a wry look, the sort I've noticed among grandes before. It's a peculiarly deep friendship you would develop, I suppose, over the course of half a century.

"Since you are so curious, June," says Auntie Maria, sweet like burnt sugar. "I have no use for new technology other than certain interesting advances in security mechanisms. But I knew that, provided with war tech, technophile agitators could be counted upon to create an incident that would give more than enough cover for a thorough crackdown on imported tech. Given the spider-bot disaster this summer, we needed something like this more than ever, and it certainly worked."

I had told mother that I hated grande schemes, but I'd never dreamed of something this cold-hearted.

"Enki, of course, decided to play games," Oreste says. "And people wonder why we only have kings for a year. I'm surprised you told him, June. I'd have thought the Queen's Award would be more than enough."

Enki snakes his arm around my waist, and I don't know if it's an embrace or a restraint. My skin tingles, not entirely from anger or fear.

"You knew," I say in a voice flatter than paper. "You sent me to Lucia, but you already knew."

Auntie Maria sighs. "You'd think someone who causes so much trouble would have a little more aptitude at politics."

"I think that's precisely why," says Oreste, as if we were not in the room.

"She needed to know how much Lucia knew," Enki says softly, in my ear. "Lucia was protecting something. She needed to know if it was simply Auntie Maria's name, or something more incriminating to Royal Tower."

Oreste nods in almost businesslike appreciation. "More or less correct. The Queen's Award is yours, June, so long as you don't speak a word of this. And if you think to say something after you win, I will immediately release the evidence I have of your academic cheating."

The threat doesn't go far enough, especially after everything they've revealed in this room. I wonder how venal I must seem to her. Does she think nothing will break my ambition for public approval? But then, look at how much it did take.

I realize that she's lying, that the consequences of my breaking this pact will be far more onerous than just the public reveal of my cheating. But if so, why not just tell me?

Because she wants to see if I'm gullible enough. She wants to know if she even needs to provide me with greater consequences, because that will tell her how much of a threat I am.

And there is Enki behind me, afraid of something that he can't say, so uncharacteristically silent that he must be walking his own political tightrope in this room, hoping to help me without revealing himself to the two most powerful women in Palmares Três.

Oh, June, I hear, just like my papai would always say, *what mess are you in now?*

I am afraid, so I let it show on my face. I let my weight fall, very gently, against Enki. I say, "Yes, okay, yes. It's a deal. I promise."

Oreste stares at me for a very long time. Long enough to make me squirm, and I do that too. *Don't go too far,* I remind myself. *Don't let her see through it.*

And then she nods. "Good. You are talented, June. You could make something of yourself, one day. Come to me in ten years, and maybe we'll see what Royal Tower can do for you."

They leave without another word, though Auntie Maria gives us a long, enigmatic glance before following Oreste out.

I stare after them, too shocked to form a sentence. There passed my last illusions. Those are the women who will slice Enki's throat with a ceremonial blade at the end of winter. Those are the women who will proclaim his sacrifice to reinstate Oreste as the Queen for another five-year term.

Enki turns me gently toward him. "June, I —"

"Let's throw a party," I say desperately, touching his collarbone, his shoulders, his chin, and his lips. "Let's dance."

He cups the back of my head. "Whatever you want."

I wonder who they threatened him with. Whose life they said they would ruin if he didn't stop me from speaking. No other reason for that look of terror on his face. I can't ask him here, but I guess I don't need to.

"Gil will come," I say, and his relief is instant and the love follows soon after.

We throw the party in Royal Tower, in that grand banquet hall where Enki first met Gil. We invite the world, and they all come.

Bebel and Pasqual and everyone from my cohort at school. Casters, agitators, grandes and wakas, technophiles and isolationists. Enki went on Sebastião's feed to let the city know: If you think you should be here, then come. You have an open invitation.

The Aunties aren't happy — maybe they're only truly happy when they're scheming — but better to let us bring the rabble to Royal Tower than endure the fallout of trying to stop it. Enki is the most popular summer king in a century. Better to wait him out than fight that power.

Enki and I spent a day programming and rigging holos throughout the room. Gil wanted to help, but he had class and I haven't bothered to go back to school in the week since the parliament incident. For once, Mother hasn't hassled me. She says it's okay to go back when I'm ready.

I wonder if I'll ever be ready. I didn't realize how much my ambition for the Queen's Award was holding me together until I lost it. Now I feel as helpless as Gil as we stare down the end of winter.

The three of us wait at the very back of the glass bubble with its plunging view straight into the bay. We wear matching outfits of stark white that Gil's mamãe designed. The white suit and hat makes Enki look like the old, dapper statues of Exu, the trickster orixá. Gil has a genius for a mamãe. When the first guest arrives, I turn to Enki and whisper, "Now."

The holos turn on, revealing three monstrous projections at three ends of the room. One is the stencil of me and Enki, the second of Wanadi and Regina. And in between them, hovering over the bay is my changed version, the one that could be technophile or isolationist, that turns a bullet hole into ambiguity.

The rest of the holos project water, with floating seaweed and an occasional school of fish darting past.

Then music starts to blast throughout the room and Gil grins. "Even better than last time," he says.

"They'll always be better than last time," Enki says, running his fingers lightly up Gil's arm. "So long as we're throwing them."

I think, *That won't be much longer,* but Gil just leans in and kisses Enki hard on the lips.

I remember that first night, when Gil and I first saw Enki. When Enki and Gil first fell in love. I felt so alone and bereft and confused. I watch them now and wish for something even that simple.

They come to our party in twos and threes and then by the dozens. Gil dances like the old days, like he wants to tempt his own death. No matter how many people crowd in, he always has a space around him. Enki keeps pace for a while until I come up behind him, hook my fingers into his belt loop. He turns in a smooth pirouette and laughs at my frown.

"Come, bem-querer," he says, "don't you want to dance?"

"What if there are too many people?" I ask.

"Then they'll dance somewhere else." An eel slides past his face. He pokes his fingers through its insubstantial flesh and I start to laugh, though I don't know why.

"There," he says. He puts his hands, firm, on my hips.

"What —"

But he shakes his head. I'm silent when his muscles bunch and his hands tighten and I'm flying over his head, flying with my hands out and my head back. It burns my throat like strong wine. We're in the glass bubble over the city, surrounded by a thousand Palmarinas of all ages. I feel connected to the world, with Enki beneath me and the city glittering beneath us all.

Enki catches me under my armpits and sets me down lightly on the glass floor.

I mean to thank him, but instead, "When you called me in front of the committee . . ."

He cocks his head. "You wanted to kill me?"

"Never."

My stomach clenches at just the thought. Maybe he knows; he squeezes my hand in apology. "What, June?"

I take a deep breath. "I don't know if I would have said the name. I'm just not sure."

I'm still trying to gauge his silent, careful reaction when someone grabs me from behind, engulfs me in a messy embrace.

"June! I found you!" Bebel, apparently, has indulged in the wine. "Dance with me?" She plants her hands on my hips. I shrug and let her lead. I feel the hole of Enki's lost presence for a lot longer than I should, but at least Bebel's a happy drunk.

"Amazing party," she says, resting her head on the hollow between my neck and shoulder blade. In a fit of tenderness, I wrap my arm around her. She doesn't deserve what I've done to her. I've had a dozen chances to put it right, but instead I hide with Enki and Gil, hoping that this horrible thing I've done will just go away. But how can it, if the person responsible doesn't make herself change?

"Is this what it's like to swim?" she asks.

"You've never been?"

She shrugs. "My mamãe says it's dangerous."

"Mine made me learn as soon as I could walk."

I smile to remember this and Bebel smiles back. "I've been meaning to tell you, June. We're friends, I know we are, and I don't want you to worry about any of that bullshit with the class rankings and which of us will come out on top. You earned your place and I'm proud of you. And if you win the Queen's Award, I'll be even prouder. You deserve it."

I cough so hard I can hardly breathe. "But . . . Bebel, no, I don't . . ."

The knife in my gut: *I don't deserve anything I haven't worked for.*

But Bebel is Bebel, and she interprets my stuttering denial in the best possible light. "Doing so well even with all this extra pressure? I'm sure I wouldn't have managed half as well as you. I admire you, that's all."

She smiles at me without a trace of condescension. I can't bear to be near her any longer. I can't stand what that says about me.

"You'll win," I say very carefully.

She blinks. "June, I don't think —"

"I cheated. I let the Aunties help me cheat. They fixed my score on the exam."

I might as well have told her that Queen Odete never existed. She covers her mouth with her hands and gasps like she can't catch her breath.

"I'm so sorry," I say because I am, though I know it doesn't mean anything.

"I always . . . I thought the art mattered to you more than the prize. Didn't you want it to mean something?"

My heart feels like a shriveled fruit. "I forgot."

She stares at me for a long moment, as though she can discern in my face the tortured justifications and towering ambitions that brought us to this place, rivals separated by morality.

"You'll win," I say.

"With the Aunties on your side!"

"I'm going to disqualify myself and you'll win. Just remember I told you so."

I leave before she can respond. I leave before Enki can find me or Gil can pull me into his dance or any of the other hundred people who want my attention can get it. I push my way through the crowd, not bothering to dance, not bothering to smile. I don't even wipe the tears that have formed in the corners of my eyes. Nothing I do is right anymore. I'm not worth anything at all, and I can't believe that I once thought I was worth the love of a king and a city.

I hide myself in the control room, lit only by the ambient light from a few activated arrays. I make sure not to touch anything: I wouldn't want to ruin our undersea holo show outside.

I just sit on the floor, bury my head between my knees, and cry.

Enki finds me. He says, "I told them to leave."

"Everyone?"

He kneels beside me, but doesn't touch. My face feels stiff with dried salt, as if it will crack when I move. "Sure," he says. "We had a few hours."

The party should have gone until dawn, until the Aunties and their secretaries glared at us while we stumbled home. When I could have slipped away, unnoticed.

"Where's Gil?" I ask.

"Everyone," Enki says again. "I told him it was my mods."

His hair is still damp with sweat. He leans against the wall, so close that the cloth of his shirt brushes my bare arm. His breath hitches a little, but then, mine does too.

"Is it?" I ask.

He shrugs. "It's always the mods, these days."

His eyes roll back in his head; his breathing slows. "The Aunties are trying to get in." His voice is gentle over the speakers.

"Do they know they can't?"

His voice laughs, but his face remains slack. "I haven't told them yet."

"Enki," I say, "Enki, come out, look at me." I rub at my cheeks and move so I'm facing him, sitting on my ankles. His shoulders jerk and his irises roll back to their proper position — a process that would terrify me if I hadn't seen it so many times before. He shivers and gasps. Without thinking, I reach out to stroke his arms.

"What did you want?" I ask.

"Let me show you something."

He stands a little unsteadily and then reaches down to pull me up. I think we might look nice together, June and Enki in matching whites, if anyone could see us. The auditorium is deserted, though the holos still run. I like it this way: Even in fake water, Enki has an elemental beauty. I think, *We'll have to do that again next summer.* And then I remember.

He takes me to the far edge of the bubble and presses his nose into the glass. If I don't look behind me, it's as if Enki and I are floating.

"I shouldn't have called you to testify," he says. "You have a right to your own life. Like you said, you're the one who will get to live it."

I squeeze my hands so tight my nails dig hard half-moons into my palms. How I wish I had never said that. "But what's the price of a life?"

He takes my left fist and gently pries it open. "I've made compromises. I won't tell anyone what I know either."

"Only because they threatened Gil."

His eyes widen, but he smiles. "You know about that?"

"I know *you*."

He starts on my other hand, pulls the fingers up one by one. His touch is like eating a Scotch bonnet.

"Oreste picked Gil. She didn't think to pick you."

"What do I have to do with anything?"

"June, June," he says, like I'm the lyrics to a song. He has a beautiful voice, I don't know why I ever thought otherwise. "How many times do I have to tell you?"

"Tell me?"

That's what I say, when I know he means to kiss me.

This time Enki's lips are soft, his breath sweet like ginger. His eyes burn light and dark, constellations in a night sky.

"I love you," he says through the speakers.

"You love the world," I say, the words muffled in lips and tongues and hands.

"Not as much," says the city/Enki.

I fall to my knees on the glass. It rattles my teeth, but I don't feel it. I'm hungry; I grab his shirt and yank him down, so desperate for this thing that I hardly understand.

His lips trail down my neck; they find my tree. He unbuttons my shirt, kisses down the lights. They're bright enough to light up the blood in his lips. I can hardly believe the noises coming from my throat, but he's quiet. I'm cradled in city lights; I'm floating.

"I thought you wouldn't." I gasp as I climb over him. "I thought you didn't want me." *I thought you didn't love me.*

"I'm being selfish," he says in his own voice.

I don't know what he means, but I can't ask. I'm half naked against the glass. My words have broken down, my thoughts smear from my mouth like shapes, formless sounds expressing only emotion.

I remember how it was with Gil: tentative, awkward, fun. I hardly recognize this as the same act. The holo flickers and then gives out entirely. Enki's hands start to shake. Is it the mods? But he knows exactly what he's doing when he unbuttons my pants, slips them down my hips and to my ankles.

He's followed my tree.

I lose track. My hands tangle in his hair. A voice that must be mine cries out. I am myself looking upon myself.

June has wanted this so much.

He will burn her up. She doesn't care.

He smiles at me; the white of his teeth catches the white of the city lights. I squint, but I won't close my eyes. I can't. I want to see him, forever, until I never see him again.

Lights flicker, a firefly calling to mate. At first, I think it's the lights in the room, but no, here in the bubble there's only the city sliding to water beneath us.

Enki holds me very tight. Our sweat slicks the glass, smears the flickering white.

"What," I try to say. "Why?"

But maybe Enki has lost his words too. Even the ones he can make with the city. He just cradles my head, kisses me as if we have a thousand years ahead of us, and moves *inside*. . . .

How does that feel, June?

It feels —

*   *   *

The lights are out in Palmares Três.

In the dark, I seem to stretch. Without a body to witness, I grow and grow with my pleasure. I feel like a constellation, a concept hung on a scattering of stars.

But the moon is nearly full, and eventually my eyes adjust. We watch each other in the dark, dark night. We watch each other until we explode, until nerves force my eyes shut and his face crumples and our cries turn to gasps and long, shuddering sighs.

We lie, shaking in the dark for a long time. Then I slide off, curling into Enki's side. I feel his ribs, tracing each bump until they end. I rest my hand by his collarbone, so my index finger jumps a little with each labored heartbeat.

"You would have," he says, apropos of nothing. His voice is rough.

"Would have what?"

"Given Auntie Maria's name. Maybe you aren't sure, but I am."

I contemplate this. I can't say that he's right, really, but how happy I am that he thinks so. His mention of Auntie Maria reminds me of the scheming and the politics and the frenzy surely brewing in the unnaturally dark city below.

"Shouldn't you turn those back on?" I kiss him.

He kisses back. "Soon," he says. "They threatened Gil's mamãe too."

"Oh. Oh, Enki . . ."

He hardly moves when I hug him. I lower my lips to his ear. I mean to kiss it or whisper something kind, but instead I hear: "Run away with me." Maybe Mother couldn't save Papai. But I can do that most dangerous thing. I can *try*.

Enki's only reaction is an uncanny stillness. "Where?"

"I don't know. Anywhere. Tokyo 10. Accra. Salvador."

He says, "I've never seen Salvador."

I know that. He's never seen anywhere but here. Just like me. But somehow it seems important not to say so. His mother is from Salvador, I remember.

"Then Salvador," I say. "We can walk there, at least. That's what they say."

"Okay, June."

"Okay?"

"I'll run away with you."

From somewhere down below, a generator starts to buzz. The lights flicker and then burst back to life. Enki hugs me tight and plants a kiss on the crown of my head.

"We should leave," he says. "The Aunties are on their way."

He's crying, a little. I wipe his eyes before we stand.

Have you ever gone rivet surfing?

I know, you haven't. I like asking questions when I know the answer already. Have you ever gone rivet surfing? I ask, and then I imagine your voice, saying something like, "I was never dumb enough, Enki."

And now I wish I could know what you'll actually say, whether you'll frown or laugh or —

Here's how to go rivet surfing. You need a maglev board. Your nanogrip shoes would work great, but most surfers use mag shoes also. You find yourself a nice internal rivet. The kind with giant, gleaming metal that goes on forever. Pipelines are good, which is why you're almost always surfing into the verde.

Get a good thirty feet above the metal. Make sure you have some space to run. Then step, step, step, shout, and fall, all the while scrambling to get the maglev turned on, the board beneath you, your shoes to grip. You have about five seconds, and if you screw up, well, you're lucky to live.

But you might catch. You might get your legs beneath you and start to sail faster than a pod down and down that smooth expanse of metal.

You might win and you might lose.

It might be the best experience of your life, and you might never do it again. That's the trouble with —

Connecting the city's external weather sensors to her municipal energy production unit, that's where I put my love for you. It's probably still there, if you ever want to find it.

I spend the week before my birthday collecting presents, wishing that these could be for a celebration, and not for the most dangerous project I've ever attempted.

We might die out there. I'm willing to take that chance, and of course Enki is. When Gil asked me if there was a way to save him, I thought he was asking for a fairy tale.

But this isn't a fairy tale. With every self-heating blanket and fire starter and water purifier that I carefully stash away, I'm one step closer to abandoning everything I have ever loved in my life.

Everything except one.

Enki spends the time with Gil. I think he wants to say good-bye, since we've agreed we can't tell him of the plan. To protect Gil and his mamãe, we've arranged for the city to release sensitive information if anything happens to either of them. But Gil is famous; if something happened to him, the whole city would know. The Aunties might not take our threat seriously enough if his mother remained here, alone.

Two days before my birthday, Enki and I meet Ueda-sama in the ambassador's apartments. It was Enki's idea, but Ueda-sama seems relieved to see us, and surprisingly willing when we make our proposal.

"A distraction?" he says. "Of what nature?"

"Something that would make the Aunties pay attention for, oh, at least five hours," I say. "If you can manage it."

Ueda-sama nods thoughtfully, as though our request for him to further destabilize his relationship with the government is perfectly reasonable, only a question of logistics.

"Are you planning another art project?" he asks us.

Enki smiles. I shrug uncomfortably. "Something like that."

Ueda-sama doesn't press the issue. He just leans back in his chair and looks out the tall window of his apartment, where mist obscures all but the barest hint of the bay. I think again of how tired he looks, how old, despite the formal agelessness of his face. When he was born, there were people alive who had seen New York City and Rio before the blasts. When he was born, men still died of the Y Plague.

I wonder how it feels to bear that much history. I wonder what a man fifteen times our age sees when he looks at us.

"Yours is a strange city, Enki," he says, still staring at the mist.

Has he forgotten our request? I glance at Enki, but he doesn't seem concerned. "She's the most beautiful in the world."

"My Tokyo was beautiful once," Ueda-sama says quietly. "She lost it long ago, but oh, some mornings, to wake to the sight of our mountain skirted in mist and snow, the smell of my wife's jasmine incense for the *butsudan*, the call of a crane from the garden . . . they tell me there are ancient worlds in the data cloud, full re-creations of past Japan."

But Ueda-sama can't upload himself. "Do you wish you could go there?" I ask.

"They think they've gone to heaven," he says. "They don't realize that means they're dead."

Enki leans across the table and rests his hand on Ueda-sama's shoulder. "Will you help us, Toshio?"

The ambassador sighs, rubs his temples. "It would be an honor, Summer King," he says.

The day before my birthday, I find the last item on my list: a detector for the land mines I've heard are still scattered beneath the earth in the fields surrounding Salvador. This sort of tech is highly monitored and hard to come by, but I impersonated Auntie Yaha and strongly implied its necessity for some secret political mission. It worked, astonishingly. Hopefully she won't be in too much trouble when we leave.

I really like Auntie Yaha, as it turns out. I think of that angry, grieving fifteen-year-old she met when she first married Mother, and I can only shake my head. I'm lucky, I suppose, that she's treated me with kindness all these years. Yemanjá knows I haven't deserved it. I try to put all of that into the hug I give her when she leaves for work that morning.

"What's this, June?" she says, laughing. I'm not usually up early enough for her these days — Royal Tower has been busier than ever since my disastrous turn at testifying.

I hand her a piece of paper. I recopied the drawing I made of her at the wedding, adding a few details and a light color wash. She takes it, but she doesn't smile.

"It's a present," I say.

She hugs me, very tight. "For your own birthday? I'll see you tonight," she says. "I'll come home early."

"Mother would like that."

"I know," she says, and gives my drawing a look I never would have understood a year ago. She leaves. I spend the next few hours readying other things. A purchase of berth aboard a trading vessel bound for Paris, leaving tomorrow night. I use decoy names — enough, hopefully, to convince them that I don't mean to be discovered. I have maps of Paris beneath my mattress and some discarded plans for the Iberian countryside. With any luck, they'll assume we're on our way to Europe. I don't have any illusions that this will fool Auntie Maria forever, but hopefully for long enough.

That takes a while. Or maybe I'm just delaying going outside, talking to Mother, pretending that everything is normal — or, at least, as normal as anything has ever been for the two of us these past two years.

God, I miss her so much. Is that strange? To miss the woman sitting in the parlor a few meters away? I tie my shoes and heft my pack. A little much, sure, but I'm known enough for my art in the city that no one will remark on it.

Mother looks out at the water from her rocking chair.

We sprinkled Papai's ashes on the bay, didn't we? I wonder why I never think of that.

"There's eggs," she says without turning around. "And papaya, if you want some. The first crop from the hothouses this year."

I think I'll vomit if I eat anything. "I have something for you," I say, kneeling beside her chair.

I hand her a stack of paper, thick as my hand. "I don't know what to do with them," I say. "But I thought you might."

"June," she says, flipping through the first few papers. "I had no idea . . . I thought you stopped drawing when João died."

"But you still bought me the paper."

She shrugs and smiles a little. "I hoped, maybe." She always believed in my art, more than Papai ever did, though it stabs me to admit it.

I sit beside her and watch the water while she looks through the drawings. I remember how nervous I used to be when I would show Papai my art. But Mamãe gave all the approval he withheld, and I never bothered to believe her.

Eventually she stacks the sheets neatly together and puts them down on the table.

"They're wonderful. Are you sure you want to give them to me? It's enough that I got to see them. They'd work well for the Queen's Award. If you're still interested in it."

"I made them for you," I say. "Don't worry about the Queen's Award."

And, for a wonder, she doesn't. "I'm so proud of you, June."

"I'm proud of you too, Mamãe." I stand. "I'll . . . be back late, tonight. Don't wait up."

She looks up at me, like she's hoping for something, but then she shakes her head and subsides back into her chair. She misses him. I wonder how I never saw that before. I wish she'd tried harder to save him, but I understand her in a way I never could before. Too late.

Now, we only have time for good-byes.

*   *   *

When evening falls, I'm where I've spent the happiest moments of my life: in Gil's garden, listening to the latest from the King Zumbi bloco and talking. I have my pack with me, but I tell Gil it's for an art project and he's the last person to ever think that strange.

"Do you remember," he says, lifting the bottle of wine from beneath the blanket we're sharing, "that time we were ten and snuck away to Gria Plaza at night?"

I start to giggle, though I've barely tasted the wine. "We were so small we could hardly see anything. I remember thinking we'd get trampled when the music started."

He takes a swig. "But I felt so proud when we came back, even when Mamãe made me stay home for a month."

"Papai didn't speak to me for a week," I say. "Mamãe had to talk him out of it."

We fall silent. Gil leans more heavily against me and passes the bottle. I pretend to drink, but then he swigs enough for both of us. It's unlike Gil to drink so much, but I understand why.

"Have you thought of anything?" he asks, much quieter this time. "Some way to save him?"

My heart races so fast I feel sure he must hear it. "Gil, he's the summer king. What can I possibly do when the whole city is waiting to watch him die in a few months?"

It's harsh, but I meant it to be. Gil's bottom lip quivers. "June, I don't know if I can stand it. Not just to lose him, but to *watch* him die?"

"You've watched other years," I say, as if I don't know exactly how he feels.

He sits up straighter. "Enki is different. You know that."

"Maybe he is," I say. "But he isn't different to the Aunties. He's the summer king, and he dies at the end of winter. I wish I could change that, Gil, I do, but there's nothing. . . ."

The hypocrisy chokes me before I can quite get out the rest of the argument. Gil hears it anyway.

"Oh, I know," he says. "I just let myself dream, I guess."

"Gil," I say, hugging him, "it's okay to dream. It's why I love you. One of the reasons, anyway."

He takes a long pull of the wine. "Oh, yeah?" he says in a reasonable approximation of cheer. "What others?"

"Well," I say, "you *can* dance." I glance at my fono. I've stayed too long. I don't want this to be my last time in Gil's garden. I have to see Gil again, but not for months at least, and probably years. That's if I succeed.

If I fail? Well, this always had to be good-bye.

"I've got to go," I say, standing. "See you soon."

Gil lifts my chin. "Everything okay, June?"

I shrug. "Not really. Take care, Gil. I love you, you know that?"

"Of course," he says. "I —" He breaks off and looks down at his wrist fono.

"Something is happening," he says. "Breaking news ping. Something on Tier Ten, it looks like. Aunties, maybe?"

Ueda-sama. "Maybe," I say. "Look, I've got to leave."

He hugs me good-bye, but he's distracted, already calling to his mamãe to turn on the holo while I leave through the back gate.

There are no tears in my eyes when I race to Harassi Plaza, the transport node for Tier Eight. I'm nothing but forward momentum and a curse. Ueda-sama promised to give us our cover. Have I spent so long with Gil that I wasted the opportunity? I pay no attention to the buzzing of the crowds as I catch the first transport pod out. I use nothing but public lines, but at the end of the workday, they're efficient and anonymous. I make it to the verde about twenty minutes late, but hopefully it won't matter. Enki is waiting for me at the center of the spider's web.

"Sorry I'm late," I say. "We have to hurry. I think Ueda-sama —"

Enki's eyes are bleak. "Kiri," he says. "He cut his own throat."

My run slows, then stops. "Oh."

"We need to leave. Ueda — Toshio killed himself for this. Let's use his distraction."

I could choke on the bitterness of the way Enki says *distraction*. But he's right — no sense in waiting here, shell-shocked. Enki shoulders his pack and takes me to a part of the spiderweb I've never been before. There's a tunnel large enough for a small, self-powered vehicle.

"This leads through the cliff," he says. "I'd guess this is the fourth way they'll look for us to have left."

He starts into the dark. I hurry after him. "Enki, I'm —"

"It's my fault," he says. "It was my idea to ask him for help."

I reach out and find his hand on the third try. "Listen," I say, hauling him to a stop. "He was more than three hundred years old. Let's give him this much credit: He must have known what he wanted."

Maybe the bleakness clears Enki's face a little. Hard to tell in the dark. "And I know what I want too," he says.

It takes nearly forty minutes to walk through the steeply sloping tunnel to the cliffside surface. The city seems surprisingly far away, the expanse of untrammeled winter-dead grass surprisingly empty. The fresh air makes me clammy and afraid, but I don't even think of turning back.

It's Enki who pauses to look.

"Will you miss it?" I ask.

"I'm its king," he says simply.

And then, the king and I, we run.

WINTER

*W*e took the road to Salvador like pilgrims and like fugitives; every step I took with the silence of the city heavy inside me felt like a prayer — to the orixás, to Christ, to my mother.

I prayed so hard I heard her voice. She said, "Enki, what have you done to yourself?" and "Enki, you should have worn some better shoes."

I agreed with her about the shoes. You spent every real you owned on this fancy thermal pair and all I wanted was my sandals. When I tried to take them off, you said, "But it's winter, Enki," and I put them back on.

I realized this, on the road to Salvador: Mods don't go quiet just because they can't connect to a city.

And the things they speak to? The things they speak of?

You thought I talked in my sleep, and you never mentioned it. You thought I still held the city in my head, until you saw the hole she left inside me. Some mornings I thought I saw your worry frost our blankets, hang in the air with your cloudy breath.

But all the time we walked, you never looked back.

The first time I see the ocean, I stop breathing for a few seconds. I've spent my life near water, but I've never seen anything so raw, huge, and frightening. I didn't know water could do that. Eventually, my brain finds a place for that monstrous, beautiful, roaring seascape. I turn back to the map and follow the path.

We've been walking for a month, and over that time, the weather has only gotten colder and the landscape more desolate. I decided to follow the coastline even though I suspect that will make it easier for the Aunties to find us. The roads are all farther inland, gray arteries cutting through the endless red irradiated dust. Four hundred years after the dislocation, and almost none of this land is fit to live on. Near the ocean, the air breathes a bit clearer and we're less likely to need the warning buzz of our land-mine detector.

I've wrapped a headscarf over my face, both as a last-ditch effort to protect us from discovery and to guard against the dust. Every few miles, I have to stop and spit. Enki doesn't seem very bothered by any of it, though I made him wrap a scarf around his face anyway. It's funny that I can recognize Enki's eyes though cloth covers his nose and mouth. Even while walking through this contaminated husk of land there's a lightness to them, an awareness and a joy.

I'm glad we ran away. I'm glad, no matter what happens, because those eyes don't deserve to die the way the Aunties would have it. I've never met anyone more alive than Enki, and it would kill something inside me to watch them spill his blood on that sacrificial altar.

I start to shiver and Enki reaches for my hand. His warmth eases me, though I no longer find it reassuring. I don't know enough about the mods, I never will, but it can't be good for him to run such a high temperature for so long.

He hardly sleeps at night. Some mornings, I find him prone and wide-eyed, frozen in some state where he can hardly speak or move. We have to wait, for hours sometimes, until it passes. He doesn't tell me why.

He doesn't tell me anything, really, though we've talked more in the past four weeks than in the whole almost-year I've known him.

He doesn't tell me anything, but then, have I asked?

Enki straightens his shoulders against the driving wind. He says, mischievous, "Auntie you'd most like to see cleaning the algae vats with a toothbrush."

I consider. "All of them?"

"Against the rules. You only get one shot, so who deserves it the most? — Isa? Maria?" He pauses and gives me a sidelong glance. "Yaha, even?"

I shake my head — an abrupt, almost involuntary gesture. "Not Yaha."

"Ah. You should tell Gil when . . . someday. He always wished you would stop hating your family."

As always, the thought of Gil is an ache somewhere deep in my chest, the back of my throat. I don't regret leaving him behind, and sometimes that makes it worse.

"I know," I say.

"So, who? Your ideal toothbrush wielder."

"Oreste."

He purses his lips. "She's not quite an Auntie —"

"She's a super-Auntie. An Auntie's Auntie. We'll give her a toothbrush of ivory and gold, befitting her station."

Enki giggles, as I hoped he might. "She would curse your bones, June."

"So long as she scrubs —"

"And smiles for the camera bots."

We turn to each other in mutual, transient glee. Opaque cloth covers our faces, and still I feel his grin as my own.

"What would you do if you were Queen?" he says. Waves crash behind me. His eyes go wide, pupils dilated.

"I'd never be Queen," I say, shivering.

"But if you were?"

I try to laugh, to dispel the strange intensity that hazes the air. "I'd move all of Royal Tower to the verde. I'd make the Aunties learn to draw and get the best grafiteiros to paint the ceiling of parliament. I'd have a summer king all five years and I wouldn't kill him at the end."

Enki doesn't move at all, except to say, "Then he wouldn't be a summer king, June. Just a king."

"What's wrong with that?"

"You'd let men rule in your city of women?"

"But," I say, "you already rule. You're already king. And men can be Uncles. It's not as if anyone is stopping them from holding power."

He releases my hands. "Isn't it?"

I don't know what to say. He doesn't seem resentful, exactly, or even accusatory, and yet I feel myself on the defensive. I want to say, *We're walking through the mess men made of the world.* I want to say that the summer kings have real power — though only one year out of ten, and only then, mostly, to pick the next Queen. I want to say that maybe boys don't have as much representation, but they have plenty of freedom.

And everything I want to say makes me sound more and more like an Auntie. Like the Queen I could never be.

"I'm sorry," I say, though I know this means almost nothing.

He takes a few long strides toward the white sand beach. I follow him. "I love our city, June."

This should be in the past tense. It's not ours to love anymore. We've left it.

But Enki is always the one who looks back.

The closer we get to Salvador, the more life we see. The dead zone we passed through just north of Palmares Três finally gives way to flats of switchgrass, cracked and brown with winter's frost. Green bamboo grows in stands at irregular intervals — I make sure we sleep near them each night for cover. Aside from the occasional whir of what might be helicopters at night, we've had no indication of the Aunties' pursuit. I try not to let myself relax, but sometimes all my thoughts drift between Enki and the shore — our sex is a little death each time he touches me, much longed-for.

A few homesteads dot the landscape, but we give them a wide berth. No way to know who here has contacts with the Aunties.

Anyone could turn us in. I know that most of our trade comes from closer to Salvador, but the Aunties I've come to know in the past year wouldn't leave any place so close to their city free of a few tendrils of influence.

Some nights we sleep close enough to these lone outposts to smell their actual gas fires and the food they cook on them. I'm sick of the nutrient-rich reconstituted gruel that's all we've eaten for more than a month. Enki doesn't complain, but he turns his head to the unmistakable smells of real food as unerringly as I do.

And then one night the lights ahead of us are too bright for one house. From more than a kilometer away, we can see our first town as a torch on the barren plain.

We approach the lights slowly, but we approach. We should find a place to sleep for the night, but I think neither of us can resist the thought of a real town, a group of people, after so long with only each other's company.

"Fences," Enki says, his first word after hours of silence.

"What?"

We kneel in the tall grass and he points. I see, to the east of the lights, a bare smudge. "What are they for?"

"Cattle, probably," he says. "Some kind of farming."

The breeze picks up, bringing both the stench of the cows and the delicious aroma of cooking food. For a mad moment, I wonder if we could sneak in and eat.

But, no. This is the first town we've seen since leaving Palmares Três, and the Aunties will certainly look for us here.

I tug on Enki's sleeve. "We should leave."

He doesn't move. I'm not even sure he heard me. He's looking at the sky, though there's nothing in it but night and enough stars to hurt my eyes. Not far from us, a cruiser engine rumbles. The growling sound gets louder as we listen.

"Enki," I say, loud as I dare. "Get *up*. We have to go."

Is he having another one of those fits? How long will it take him to move this time? But those have only ever happened in the morning. Is he getting worse?

But then he pats my hand — absently, as if I'm an anxious dog. "Shh," he says.

I almost yell at him, but the cruiser is getting closer. The grass around us grows high enough to conceal us from casual observation, but that won't mean anything if they run us over.

I grip his arm and pull, but I might as well try moving a boulder. Just a few meters away, jouncing beams of light illuminate the swaying grass. The sound of the motor gets quieter, the beams steady. Have they seen us? Why aren't they going back to town?

I stop trying to move Enki. Either we'll be lucky enough to escape notice, or we won't. Nothing I can do about it now. I mentally curse him, but there's not much venom to it: My summer king will always be himself.

The engine coughs a little as it shuts down no more than ten meters away. A man gets out, his hands on his hips as if he's forgotten something.

"What is it, querido?" a woman calls from inside the cruiser. "The engine again?"

He shakes his head. "I just thought I . . ."

"Heard something," whispers Enki, very softly. I glare at him. He ignores me. The man freezes, takes a few nerve-jarring steps in our direction. I pray that he won't find us. That we'll stay safe.

And then Enki takes my chin and tilts it up.

A flier hovers over the town — only in this absolute stillness can I hear the whirring propellers and engines that keep it aloft.

On its black belly, I can just make out a stark illustration in glowing white paint: a pyramid.

The woman gets out of the cruiser. "Oh, crap. What's that? I thought we paid off the 'bucos already."

"Palmares," the man says very shortly. "At least they won't want a bribe."

"Who do those women think —"

"Torqada Township," booms the voice of our city. I want to cover my ears, and not just because of the volume. "As you have undoubtedly heard, our fair city has lost its king. We have reason to believe he and his kidnapper might be hiding somewhere in these pastoral lands. If you give us any information that leads to their capture, we offer a reward of one million reals, payable immediately. Please take this as evidence of our sincerity."

Against the lights of the town, I can just barely see a black silhouette, quickly streaking to earth. The thud it makes when it lands is audible from even this distance. I don't close my eyes; I don't breathe.

"Victor," says the woman, "is that . . ."

She sounds scared. I don't understand until the man puts his arm over her shoulders. "Not a mine," he says. "They wouldn't do that when they want something from us. It's probably money."

She relaxes a little and turns back to the cruiser. "Then let's see what it is."

Victor shrugs and walks back to the driver's side. And thank all the orixás, I think we might actually make it out of this alive.

He stops. His shoulders shake, just a little, like an animal tossing a flea. "Emil," he says, gesturing sharply at the cruiser. "Shut the lights."

"What? Vic —"

But he waves again and she turns off the lights.

In the dark, I am blind. I reach for Enki and grip his arm, so warm against this cold that mists my breath. I want to leap up and run or just curse everything that has brought us to this place, but I wait. Enki rests his fingers lightly on my thigh — even now, he isn't worried or scared.

Even now, he looks straight ahead.

"There's something in the grass," the man says softly. "Some . . . animal, maybe."

I don't think Enki even blinks. Just watches with those modded eyes, reflecting light in the way no human's should. Glowing in
the dark.

"Victor, let's go back. There's always a few rats around —"

"Not a rat." His voice is slow, distracted. He walks forward until
he's not even three meters away from us. My eyes have adjusted
enough to see the caked mud on his boots. They smell like clay and
shit and just a faint undertone of something antiseptic.

My hand vibrates with every thudding heartbeat. I will vomit all
over those quaint workman's boots. I will vomit over both of us.

And then Enki, calmly as a king, lifts his head just slightly above
the grass line.

Victor had been looking to our left. Now, his head snaps around.
He doesn't make a noise — not even a grunt of surprise — though his
hands tighten around some sort of stick in his arms.

He's younger than I'd have thought from his voice. Not anyone I
could call a waka, though I wonder if he's even ten years older than
me. Maybe the landscape ages you out here; maybe life does. All I
know is that this Victor, this farmer with shit on his boots and a stick
in his hands, will determine the course of the rest of my life.

One million reals.

He knows who we are. Even if he'd never seen a holo, how could
anyone mistake the *what* of Enki, the way he's not quite anything and
too much of everything?

And then Enki inclines his head.

The man smiles — not happily, but with some irony. He nods, brief
and sharp.

"A rat," he says, taking long strides back to the cruiser. "Right, of
course, querida. Let's see what bribe those women left us to find their
sacrificial chicken."

I stay in the grass for long minutes after they drive away. I
shouldn't. I should make us leave, make us walk through the night just
to get far away from this place. Instead, there's ice in my ears and

earth in my nose and stars in my eyes. There's a band of white across the sky. When I was eight or nine, Ieyascu told me that was an arm of our whole galaxy.

"One million reals," I say.

Enki lays his head on my chest. I know he does it to comfort me.

"He won't tell."

"How can you know that?"

"I can't."

I choke. *Just make it to spring,* I say to myself, my same mantra for the past two months, but now it has no power to comfort me.

"Enki, what —"

"We'll get to Salvador, June," he says. "I promise."

And I know he can't promise that either, and I believe him anyway.

Palmares Três has always loved its royalty. In the rest of old-Brazil, my mamãe told me, people think we're delusional — a city so sure of our own superiority that we actually crown our rulers. They think we're greedy and vain and utterly unaware of how we appear to others.

And we are, of course. Who would know that better than you?

(If you say that I would, you shouldn't. I'm dead, June, you can't forget that.)

But we still know something they don't. Have you ever heard of the divine right of kings? Royalty is an act of God, give thanks to our orixás.

That's why the Queen can't be elected.

That's why the king must be.

The king is legitimized by the people and sanctified by the gods. His choice is ultimate, and unquestioned, because he embodies a whole people. On the sacred altar, beneath the sacred blade, his blood has the power to turn a woman into a Queen.

This might seem unfair to you. Perhaps it is.

But I think our Founding Mothers meant it differently. No system of checks and balances has ever been stronger than the summer kings and their Queens.

Because we kings have power, and we must always give it up.

*   *   *

When we arrive, Salvador greets us at sunset with a body.

It's a man — a grande, but not by much — wearing just a pair of ragged jeans. I think someone has stolen his shirt and shoes. He has a bullet hole, neat as a painting, through the middle of his forehead.

It's messier in the back. Just like Wanadi. Enki turns him over with his foot, grimaces, and lets the body flop back onto the sand.

He looks at me, and then up at the city.

We can barely make out the buildings of High City from here — crumbling stone edifices nearly a thousand years old, and perhaps the only thing Salvadorenses have made a point of preserving. The whitewash of an old Portuguese colonial bell tower seems to glow orange in the sinking sunlight.

Closer by, in Low City where we've entered, rolling hills of piled rubble give way to hints of closely stacked shanties and market stalls.

The world has gone still around us, or maybe we entered a different dimension at some point during our long walk up the beach. We are in one of the biggest cities of old-Brazil, and the only people I see are Enki and a dead man. Waves crash, seagulls cry out overhead.

"Where is everyone?" I ask.

Enki acknowledges my question with a frown. His fingers twitch, trying to access the city, except Salvador doesn't have anything like a unified AI.

"A curfew, I think," he says finally.

"Did your mamãe tell you?"

He smiles a little and takes my hand. "Mamãe left here too long ago. It's gotten worse since then. I loaded my memory with everything Palmares Três knew about Salvador before we left."

I swallow. "I hope you were careful." If someone noticed his information grab, they could use it to track us.

"We should leave," he says. "Whoever killed him might come back."

He starts to climb the nearest rubble pile. I follow him, though I don't know where we're going, or if it's safe. Enki knows a hundred times more about Salvador than I do. And not, apparently, because of his mamãe.

Because he loaded the information into his brain.

Even here, I can't escape the implications of his mods. I guess I'd hoped I might. That he might turn miraculously human again, away from the influence of the city and its tech.

Over the second pile of barrier rubble, we find the first streets. Bright signs painted on tin shacks, advertising food and cloth and herbs and contraband tech. Doors are shut, curtains pulled closed, lights dimmed. If I listen, low-voiced whispers combine with shuffling feet and quiet humming into its own noise: the music of a sleeping city. Salvador doesn't sound much like Palmares Três, but I recognize something in it all the same. The streets have been carved into a warren of rubble. Remains of cobblestones line roads too narrow for anything but a bicycle. The streets twist and wind with no direction I can find, and even Enki seems confused. We pass by tiny, dirt-paved alleyways that must be shortcuts to other parts of the warren, but we don't go in them. Not enough room to fight, Enki says, and we still wouldn't know where we are.

He moves very fast. I stumble to keep up, making enough noise that I occasionally see faces peering through windows and cracked doors — wondering, probably, who would walk these streets after curfew.

"We need to get to High City," Enki says, pausing at an intersection. "It's safer there. Gangs control this part of town. People caught after curfew tend to end up dead."

"The man on the beach?"

Enki rubs his thumb along my knuckles. "Probably."

I start to shiver, make myself stop. Why did we come here? I wanted to save Enki's life, not kill us both.

But I know why. Because more than anything, he wanted to see his mamãe's Salvador. Even now, racing through the cracked shanty-town streets of a city more dangerous than anything I've ever seen on a holo, he looks around with endless fascination. Not happiness — something more.

The sun has vanished by now, and the shacks on either side of the narrow street cast inky shadows. Somewhere to our left, though how far away I can't tell, a sharp crack cuts through the eerie quiet of the nighttime city. A second later, colored fire arcs through the sky. Purples and greens and iridescent white shoot up and float down like strange, dying fireflies.

"What —"

"Fireworks," Enki says very softly. "I think it's a signal —"

Footsteps and gunshots and sudden giddy male hollers cut the night more sharply than the lights. It sounds like they're all around us, like they'll find us and shoot us like the poor man on the beach.

"This way," Enki whispers, and we take off down the right-hand path. Enki doesn't know where he's going — even the best map of Salvador couldn't possibly have these half streets and alleyways — but I trust him anyway. *Get to High City*, he said. Those beautiful, well-kept ruins on the ridge above the shanties.

Go up.

I think we must be, because my thighs burn and I keep tripping on the cracked cobblestones. But perhaps we're just running too fast and I am so tired from walking more than two months across barren fields and lonely beaches, tired of walking and hiding and walking. All to get to Salvador, a city that wants to kill us.

Enki stops. I run into him. I would speak, but he reaches back and puts his fingers on my lips. My breath stops in my chest. But I have gotten very good, these last months, at holding my fear.

A few feet ahead of us, two wakas argue in low voices. The girl holds a light that fades a few centimeters past Enki's thermal shoes, but she's too busy whispering something fast and furious to notice.

The boy does, though.

"Oh, shit," he says. His voice is so loud I wince.

The girl stops midsentence — something about her mother's house — and follows the boy's gaze.

"Heads or Hearts?" she asks, as if she's reading funeral rites.

"We're armed," the boy says. He gestures toward his pocket but doesn't reach inside.

Enki holds up his hands. I can't figure out why until I recall a pre-dislocation movie we watched in class once. A bunch of men ran around with guns in a desert and shot at one another for two hours. Raising your hands meant that you *didn't* want to kill someone. That no one had to get hurt.

"That's an orange," Enki says, his voice quiet.

"What?" the girl says. Her hand with the light trembles. She's still afraid of whoever she thinks we are.

"In his pocket." Enki keeps his hands raised, but his tone is conversational, with a touch of humor perhaps only I can hear. "Unless you Pernambucos have weaponized fruit?"

The girl shoots a glare at the boy, which tells me Enki is right. I almost laugh.

She squints at us. "We're not —"

The boy elbows her. "Zanita, shut up! Listen, whoever you are, you can't be sure what I'm packing. Is it worth your lives, eh? Let's just take a step back and go our separate ways. Before the Death Heads find us."

"And we're not Pernambucos," she adds. "I mean, you're not dead yet, right?"

"That's what it's really like?" I say before I can stop myself. "Nothing but gangs and killing?" No wonder Enki's mamãe wanted to leave.

Enki puts down his hands. The girl takes a step closer. Her hand has stopped shaking. She's dark, like Auntie Yaha said the flatlanders could be, though not as dark as Enki. She has bombril hair that reminds me of my own, plaited close to her head and fastened with colorful barrettes.

"You're . . . who are you guys, anyway?"

The boy gives up the pretense of hovering near his weapon. He grabs the girl's elbow. "Who cares, eh? You want the Death Heads to dump your body on the beach? We'll go to your mother's house, fine, let's just get out of here."

"Would you take us with you?"

We all stare at Enki. I know he's completely serious. He has that smile — lidded eyes, all lips, no teeth — that would mean he was talking to the city if we were back home.

The boy shakes his head. "What the hell? I was just about to blow your head off and now you want to tag along to my aunt's house? Are you crazy?"

"Yes," Enki says, "but it was an orange."

The girl — Zanita — starts to giggle. I think that maybe our summer king has done it again, even in this place where Palmarina traditions have almost no meaning.

"I like you," she says.

"Zanita —"

"Oh, shut up, Tomas. Look at them — they're just like us. Probably from someplace country."

"Those look like country clothes? His shoes? That's high tech. Maybe they thought we were 'bucos because they've been spending a bit too much time with them?"

Zanita was ready to take us with her, but she hesitates at Tomas's words. She raises the light and gives Enki a long look, head to toe. I know what she sees. A beautiful boy in clothes far too fine for anyone in this city without gang connections.

"Crap," she says.

In the distance, another series of cracks and pops cuts the stillness. The four of us look up in time to see the splash of colored fire against the dark winter sky. More fireworks? I'd enjoy them if it weren't for the sudden hollers — closer, now — and a rattle that sounds like a pandeiro but might be a weapon. I look around for a nanotech cloud, but at least the sky is clear.

"Burning Hearts," Tomas says, deep fear in his voice.

"It must be a bloom line," Zanita says. "They don't bring drums if they mean to kill."

"Drums?" I say, feeling relieved. "So it's safe —"

"*Nothing* with the Heads or Hearts is safe," Zanita says. "Bloom lines are still fights, people still die. Especially people who get in the way."

More colored fire, not far enough distant. Piercing shouts.

"We can't leave them here —"

"Christ, Zanita!"

"What if they die?"

"What if they bring the 'bucos down on us?"

Her head swings to Enki, but then back to me. "Where are you from? What are you doing here? And don't lie. God, Jesus, don't lie, because I don't want you to die. Okay?"

Enki meets my eyes. I must look wild, because he puts his hand on my shoulder, leans in, and touches my cheek with his own. "Say whatever you want," he whispers. "It'll be fine, I promise."

My summer king loves to make promises he can't possibly keep.

I love to believe them.

"Palmares Três," I say, low and fast. Tomas freezes. Zanita whistles.

"Jesus," she says, because she knows who we are. "Let's go."

Tomas stops arguing.

We go up. I might be grateful for that if it didn't seem we were heading closer to all the noise and the shouting. The streets smell of sulfur and smoke, but we only see our own shadows bobbing with Zanita's light. We cut through alleys that stink of shit, so narrow I have to turn to the side just to make it through.

I wonder where we're going, but have no breath to ask. Any precarious sense of the city I might have had is lost on that mad run. All

I can see in this run-past darkness are flashes of corrugated tin and concrete rubble. The streets get wider.

There's a light up ahead. Zanita snaps hers off, and now I can't tell if her hands are shaking, if she's as afraid as I am.

"We should turn around," Tomas whispers.

"And go where?" Zanita says.

My eyes have adjusted to the dark enough to see him turn away, cross his arms over his chest. The new light moves closer; it bobs like a firefly, graceful and hypnotic.

Enki touches my hand. He doesn't say anything — none of us do — but I imagine there are words beneath his burning fingertips. Words like, *You won't die, I promise.*

You can't promise that, I think.

Enki laughs, very softly. For an irrational moment, I wonder if he heard me.

There's a skull above the light.

A death's head with big white lips and frosted kinky hair. One by one, other skulls appear beside it. They each hold what I had thought was a light, but is something stranger: a large white carnation, inexplicably glowing.

Zanita starts to pray, solid Catholic prayers like you rarely hear in Palmares Três. Enki looks at her — with more recognition than I can explain — and gently pulls her back into the doorway of the only building on the street. Tomas and I crouch beside them. I wonder why we don't go back, find someplace else to hide from the deathless army, but a moment later, the ecclesiastical silence is broken by a sharp trill. The other Death Heads answer it. Their carnation lights get brighter, illuminating the rest of their clothes: skeletons painted over skintight black suits.

And then, back the way we came, an answer: bursting colored lights, wild and raucous laughter. The Burning Hearts, Tomas called them.

"Ready for us, esqueletos?" someone from the newest group calls.

The first of the skeletons stretches his painted lips wide. "Too easy," he says.

A moment later, one of each gang detaches himself from the others and walks to the middle of the street — almost directly across from us. I stop breathing. If it wasn't for his comforting, unnatural heat against my thigh and arm, I'd think that Enki was a statue.

But the two wakas don't see us. One is skeleton white and the other full of wildness and color, but they both have drums strapped around their necks, and the quiet look they share has a strange mixture of camaraderie and wariness.

"Bloom line rules," the first skeleton man says. "No knives, no guns, we stop at the first soldier down." He pauses and stretches his phosphorescent lips into a grin that terrifies me. "Or if you run."

"No one's running," the leader of the Hearts says without a smile. "Winner keeps the streets between Matatu and Tororó. Bound?"

"Bound."

I expect more words and posturing, but instead I get drums, hard and furious and fast. And then laughter in a blur of color and white. For a moment, I think that I must have been mistaken, that this isn't battle at all but some kind of strange Salvadorense *dance*.

Then the first flower explodes. A blizzard of white petal shrapnel flies everywhere — one of them slices my cheek before embedding itself into the rotting wood of the door behind me. I reach back to touch it, but it turns to ash as I watch, a slightly sticky black smudge.

"Nanotech," Zanita says in response to my blank expression. "Probably get it from the 'bucos."

Like the cloud that killed the wakas back home? But I had no idea that nanotech weapons could be so . . . beautiful.

The gangs are so busy fighting each other that they haven't noticed us. The din created by the drums and the explosions and the shouts is more than enough to cover any sound that we might make. Despite myself, I start to relax a little.

"So what exactly is a bloom line?" I ask.

"Young gang way of dividing territory," Zanita says. "They fight like this until one person goes down. Sometimes dead, sometimes not. At least they're not as bad as the 'bucos. If we can just get past the Heads, we're only a few blocks from High City."

"And how are we going to do that?" Tomas says, furious. "Ask them politely? In the middle of a goddamn bloom line?"

"I feel like dancing," Enki says.

We all stare at him. Zanita tilts her head. "You feel like . . ."

Enki grins at her, taps his foot to that mad, driving rhythm. It's something like the wilder releases from the blocos back home, but then, nothing like it at all. If I weren't afraid we were all about to die, I might want to dance too.

"Dancing," Enki says.

"Are you crazy?" Tomas says.

Enki shrugs. He looks at me and holds out his hand. For some reason, I take it.

"He's a summer king," I say.

"How about it, June?" he asks.

Just a few feet away from us, something explodes. The ball of flame lights the ends of a few of Enki's locks. He doesn't notice, so I put them out.

I have a sudden flash of the two of us in that bubble over the city, the lights shutting off beneath us. I don't think that even Gil really trusts Enki, much as he loves him.

But I do.

"Sure," I say.

Are Zanita and Tomas saying something? Probably a protest. I am in Enki's eyes, the flash of his teeth; it's hard to hear them. "You should follow us," I say. "We're going to get out."

I know they don't believe me.

Enki stands up and walks a few feet into the street. I follow him. Shrapnel petals fly past; a few nick my skin. This is a fight, but it's acrobatic, showy. This violence takes its time and the drums keep its pulse. I follow Enki's lead, letting adrenaline make my feet move faster than they ever have before. We dance with death, Enki and I.

I don't know how the gangs first notice us. Perhaps it's the way Enki moves so deliberately into the center of their melee. Maybe because the two of us are so provocatively unarmed. But the torches stop blasting, the flowers stop exploding.

The drums keep beating.

One of the Death Heads takes a step forward. He raises his flower, but his eyes are curious behind the glowing white paint. He keeps it in his hand. His feet shuffle lightly, keeping time. On the other side, the Burning Hearts with their bloodred feathers and beads don't need much encouragement. One of them tosses a ball in the air. It explodes in a shower of fireworks. I put out my hand to catch the ash. Perhaps there was a moment when this could have gone badly, but it's passed by the time the fireworks fade. Someone trills time on a whistle, someone else starts a chant. Everyone dances. Enki laughs and kisses me. Someone catcalls and I swear I blush to my bones.

Zanita catches up with us. She looks around like the dancing men might shoot her at any moment, and she clasps my hand like she might drown without it, but she dances.

"Where's Tomas?" I whisper.

She shrugs. "It looks to me like your king made a truce day come early. Tomas doesn't trust it."

I want to wave to him to come on, but if I draw any more attention to our hiding place, they'll know we've left one behind. All we can do now is keep going.

The Hearts and Heads have mixed in their dancing, fiercely competitive even without violence. The smell of hard booze mixes with the smoke and the blood. Sweat drips into cuts I didn't know I had, and I wince at the sting. Enki dances like he cares for nothing else in the world, but we move steadily closer to the far edge of the group. Toward the north side of the street and High City. I surreptitiously look back at the door, but Tomas still hasn't shown. Zanita just shrugs helplessly.

When we get to the far edge, the skeletons on that side stop dancing and look at us. They carry guns, not flowers. Enki stops and looks back.

"That was brave," one says, almost diffidently. "We can finish the line after you go." He lowers his gun. The other stares at Enki, shrugs, and turns back to the crowd. Enki walks through.

Zanita and I follow behind, looking for all the world like the king's stately retinue. My shoulders tense, expecting a bullet at any moment, but Enki only moves even more gracefully than normal. It's the only way I can tell that he's aware of the danger.

We're nearly to the bend in the road when we hear his voice behind us.

Funny that I notice the shout, given the roars from the gangs, evidence the dance is edging back to something deadly.

"Wait!" Tomas calls.

"Oh, God," says Zanita, both a prayer and an expletive. I don't know why he didn't just stay hidden.

Maybe I never will.

Enki starts running for him, but it's too late. Tomas breaks through the far edge of the crowd, elbowing aside one of the gunners who let us pass. The man steadies himself, frowns and raises his weapon.

I hear the blast like a drumbeat; Tomas falls to the ground.

Zanita takes us herself to the old neighborhood, though she doesn't say much. She told us that morning that she needed to get out of the house, and I couldn't blame her.

You'd have thought Tomas was already dead, from the prayers and the candles and the muffled tears.

Then again, he's not far from it, and I don't know how he'll recover without access to the one good hospital near São Roque. The prohibitively expensive good hospital near São Roque.

Zanita asked us if perhaps, since Enki is, well, royalty, did we perhaps have enough money . . .

I couldn't even speak. I had to shake my head. Enki looked her straight in the eye and apologized, and that was the last we've heard of it.

We're both glad to be outside, I think, and finally so close to finding his mamãe's old house. She lived in High City, but far to the west, near the university. It had been one of the safer neighborhoods, Zanita says, eighteen or so years ago. Until the Pernambucos bombed it in some protracted turf war with a militia so thoroughly decimated it no longer exists.

"A lot of those places are rotting now," Zanita says as we walk. "No one really moved back in. Happens like that sometimes. I don't know how much you're going to find."

"It doesn't matter," Enki says. I can't tell if he means it.

Enki doesn't have an address, he has a tree. An ancient soursop tree — one of the few that survived the encroaching cold — grew in her garden. They aren't very common, but it still seems like too little to go on.

So close to our goal, I allow myself to fantasize about the future. I've decided that we can't stay in South America if we want to have any peace from the Aunties. We'll find a merchant liner leaving from the docks here and take it to its next port of call, no matter where. We can do that for months if necessary, throwing off the scent. Eventually, we'll make it across the Atlantic, to Port Harcourt or Lisbon. We'll find another city, a place just as beautiful and strange as Palmares Três, and we'll make a home there. And eventually, when it's safe, we'll call Gil and tell him to find us and . . .

And what? We'll be a big, happy family?

I try to imagine it. I close my eyes and force the images to come: Gil and me laughing, Enki learning to live with his mods, decades of music and dance and art and love. But the images seem flat and washed out in the screen of my mind, something I can picture, but not really believe. When I open my eyes, Zanita has stopped and looks at me with that birdlike curiosity.

"Everything all right? You look like your mother just died," she says.

"My father," I say.

Zanita purses her lips and rubs my shoulder before pressing on. She doesn't say she's sorry, and I like her better for it.

Enki walks up ahead, his eyes scouring the boarded-up buildings with the avidity of an artist.

I don't know what's going to happen. I'm so scared of the future even my imagination is failing me. Every morning I wake up, faintly surprised we're both still alive. But I can't tell either of them that, and so I straighten my spine and I walk on.

Enki swears that the soursop tree survived the bombing, but the closer we get to the old neighborhood, the more I wonder. This part of town is deserted compared to the warren of Low City where we first came in. The rotting, crumbling buildings we pass are occasionally inhabited, but most often they've been raided for useful supplies and left for the grafiteiros. The street art here can't compare to even the worst of the offerings in the verde. Mostly I see names in blocky, stylized letters and an occasional white carnation. I ask Zanita about it, and she just snorts.

"These are just practice lanes. The real grafiteiros won't let these guys near the good spaces down by the old buildings. So they come up here."

Our destination, it turns out, is nearly an hour's walk from Zanita's mother's place in High City. Maybe there used to be transport pods in Salvador, but now the options are either foot or cruiser. Enki knows when we find the street, because he made sure to download every map of this neighborhood in the Palmares Três library before we left. I've glossed over the details with Zanita, though I think she suspects something unnatural about his knowledge of the city.

"There," he says, pointing to a tiny house a few feet ahead. The roof has caved in and the door is missing. I don't know how Enki can sound so sure until I catch up with him. The gap-toothed doorway shows a clear path to the backyard scattered with rotting tin, concrete rubble, and scraggly patches of grass turned brown by the cold winter.

And a tree, taller than I imagined it, right behind where the kitchen would have been.

"Are you sure?" Zanita asks. She sounds too quiet, worried. I wonder if she's thinking about Tomas.

Enki walks up the crumbling front steps and fingers what remains of the wooden lintel above the doorway.

"She carved her name here when she was small," he says. "See?"

My breath catches a little. I've never heard that kind of grief in Enki's voice before. It reminds me of my own. On my tiptoes, I can just barely make out the remains of childishly malformed letters: *Sintia*.

"I never knew her name," I say.

He shrugs. "I never told you."

We walk over the threshold together. From behind us, Zanita calls out, "Are you sure that's safe?" We ignore her. Rubble from the caved-in roof blocks a lot of the small house, but there's just enough clear space for us to get through to the garden. My hands and face are covered in sweat and grit, and I smile. This reminds me of when Enki and I first started working together, the satisfaction of dirty, hard, physically demanding art. Only, we don't seem to be making art anymore.

In the open space of the garden, I wipe my hands on my pants and look up. I've seen soursop trees in the hothouses of Palmares Três, but this doesn't look much like them. The leaves clump in brown, withered bunches. A few balls of desiccated fruit sway in a passing breeze. At least the tree hasn't fallen yet. It probably just died — this has been an unusually cold winter, even as far north as Salvador.

"Enki, I . . ."

I don't think he's heard me. He runs his fingers along the thick trunk. Then he just backs away and looks at it.

Behind me, Zanita has overcome her fear of the collapsing house and clambers into the garden.

"That's what he came for?" she asks. I can't tell if she sounds incredulous or sad.

"You have the shovel, June?" he calls.

I'm surprised, but it doesn't seem like a good time to question him. I shrug off my pack and rifle through until I find our tool kit. Two knives, a shovel, a brazier, and tent all folded into a box about as big as my hand. This cost most of what reals I had left over after the thermal clothes, but it's been invaluable over the last month. I take out the shovel, press the button, and watch it unfold itself on the ground.

"Jesus," Zanita says. "Is that nanotech?"

"Nah. The Aunties aren't such big fans."

She laughs a little. "Yeah, I'd heard that."

I take the assembled shovel and offer it to Enki. He kneels in front of the tree.

"I'm sorry," I manage.

He looks up at me, takes the shovel. "What for?" he says. "It's just a tree."

He frowns at the ground, and then makes a slow circuit around the tree trunk. He stops at the point closest to what must have once been a kitchen window.

Then he starts digging.

Zanita and I look at each other, but there's not much else we can do, so we sit on the ground and watch. Enki digs maybe a foot or so deep then stops. As far as I can tell, he's hit nothing but dirt and stones.

"Find any treasure?" I ask.

"Not yet," he says, and starts another hole a bit to the right.

He finds something on his third try. He digs a little deeper before he stops and tosses the shovel aside. He kneels beside the hole and scrabbles with his hands until he pulls a piece of dirty, rotting fabric out of the ground. He holds it up to the sun with a smile that makes me want to hug him.

"What the hell is that?" Zanita asks.

I shrug and walk over. It's a rag doll. Or it used to be. It has a simple hand-stitched face and a thick body wearing the tattered remains of a formal white dress.

"She looks like an Auntie," I say.

"Doesn't she?"

He stares at the doll with a bemused half smile. I sit down beside him so my back is against the dead tree trunk and my sleeve brushes against his.

"Just once, Mamãe told me she buried this here. I think she thought I was too young to remember."

"What is it?"

When he looks at me now I'm struck by how gentle he seems, how restful, even at peace. I have never seen Enki so relaxed.

"Oh, bem-querer," he says, whispering for no reason I can tell. "Sometimes you don't know me at all, sometimes you read me so clearly."

"Which is it today, Enki?"

He hands me the doll. "You should take this."

The once-white cloth of her dress stains my hands with red soil. She smells a bit like the catinga and suddenly, I'm so homesick I could throw up.

"But it's your mamãe's," I say. A little girl named Sintia had loved this. A young woman named Sintia, pregnant with the future summer king, had buried this in her garden. But why?

"Do you remember what I told you about her? About how she convinced the Aunties to let her into the city?"

"The library?" I say, and then I remember: She made two copies of the classified information before the university had been bombed to rubble. One, she brought with her to Palmares Três. The other . . .

I look down at the doll.

"Oh," I say, and remember Zanita.

She's studiously ignoring us, leaning against the crumbling wall and whittling a fallen branch with a penknife. I mostly trust her, but if I'm really holding the one remaining copy of Salvador's university library, it seems prudent to keep that to myself.

"Hey," I say. She looks up.

"You guys done? Mind if we wait a bit? This wood is really good to work with."

I lean over so I can get a better view. She's working on the tail of what looks like some four-legged animal — a cow, maybe, or a horse. She's taking her time with it, putting in detail that I can't help but admire.

"That's pretty good," I say.

She shrugs. "Just something I tinker with. Tomas says it's a waste of time."

"Art is never a waste of time."

Zanita flashes me the first genuine smile I've seen from her all day, but it's soon drowned by something else. I shift uncomfortably, remembering Tomas's shallow breathing in the second-floor bed, the hushed whispers as his family discussed their options.

Her cousin might die today, but Zanita is sitting here with us. People handle grief differently. I ought to know that.

Enki stands, breaks a wrist-thick branch from the dead tree and ambles over to her.

"Can you show me how?" he asks with surprising diffidence.

Zanita stares at him blankly for a moment, then shrugs and tosses the half-finished figurine to the grass. "Sure, why not?" she says. "We still have time."

I haven't done much sculpture before, let alone wood carving (it's a crime to cut trees in Palmares Três). I can no more resist a new kind of art than Enki can. I hover nearby, riveted when she hefts her small knife and demonstrates how to strip the bark.

"Always remember to go with the natural grain of the wood. Work with it, not against it, eh?"

Enki holds the knife with a sure, steady grip, as if he's been using one all his life. But then, growing up in the verde, maybe he did. His cuts are crude and unsteady at first, but he doesn't seem to notice. Zanita gives him tips, occasionally demonstrating with her own figurine. Enki watches with eyes that could swallow her, and then he tries again.

She touches his hand and then flinches away. "Are you . . . do you feel okay?"

Enki looks at me. *Well, should we tell her?* his eyes seem to say.

Saliva pools in my mouth; I have to remember to swallow. "The heat's just a thing the Aunties did," I say, though that's such a twisting of the truth it's almost a lie.

Zanita scowls. "Yeah, well, maybe that's the price for living in paradise."

Paradise? I love my city, but I would never call it that. Zanita looks angry and closed off. Enki shuts his eyes and rolls onto his back. The sunlight hits his face through the dead branches of the tree so that he hardly looks human. His breathing has turned shallow and irregular, but he's done that enough lately that I don't think much of it. Everything will be better when we get to Lisbon or Paris or wherever.

But for now, I find myself pulling out the two knives from my pack and unfolding them.

"I have an idea," I say.

"What, Princess?" Her voice holds more bitterness than her expression. I know she partly blames us for what happened to Tomas, and maybe she isn't wrong.

Enki opens his eyes. His pupils are dilated near-black; his mouth moves almost imperceptibly. Whoever he's listening to, it isn't me.

"Why don't we carve the tree? We can each take a third."

"That's . . . strange," Zanita says.

"It's art," I say.

She picks up her knife and flips it in the air. "You're kind of hung up on that, aren't you?"

I laugh. "My name is June," I say.

"And she's the best artist in Palmares Três."

I didn't think he could hear us; I didn't know he remembered that. He levers himself into a sitting position. Zanita shakes her head as though she can't believe she's listening to us, but she follows me when I walk over to the tree.

"What should I make?" she asks.

"Anything you like."

She frowns, but it's more from concentration than disapproval. A moment later, she starts in on the wood. Enki works on my other side. I take my knife. The trunk is firm but not too dense — perfect for carving, just as Zanita said. I'm not sure what to make, and I have no skill at this anyway, but that familiar stillness, that intense and sharp focus bears upon me like a tide. It's been so long since I've been able to simply create, to feel the joy of art in the absence of its politics or its consequences.

The afternoon sun sinks, warm on my back. In the street, kids shriek and scuffle. I imagine a game of football, like what Gil and I used to do on boring summer evenings before everything changed. I kick off my shoes and dig my toes into the sun-warmed dirt. I breathe earthworms and rust and fresh-cut wood. I don't look at Enki but I can feel him carving his mother's tree, as clearly as if he were an extension of myself. The dark of the backs of his hands, the light of his palms, the almost religious fervor with which he cuts, they are mine because they are his.

I think, *You are my heart*, and I know he hears because his hand reaches for mine. For once, I am sure inside Enki's love. The mods don't matter anymore. He can love the world, and I won't begrudge it.

I lose track of time. I didn't really know what I would carve until I started, but now I focus on it with all my intensity and limited skill. Maybe an hour passes — at least, the sun has burned down to an ember and I find myself squinting to see the detail in my work.

There's a noise in the street outside. More kids playing ball, I think, and keep carving. Zanita steps away from the tree.

"I had to," she says.

I ignore her. Just a few more minutes, and I should be finished. It's been so *long* and I don't know when I'll have another chance once Enki and I continue our journey.

Powerful lights illuminate the house, glancing off the tree enough to help me work. I don't bother to turn around; I've spent all my life in a city of lights, after all.

But this is Salvador, and its militias and gangs have never gone in for much illumination.

Enki puts his hands around my waist, rests his head in the hollow of my neck.

"June," he says. "Bem-querer."

"June Costa." I'd recognize Auntie Maria's voice anywhere. "Put down your weapon and step away from the king."

"Tomas will die otherwise," Zanita says, and I want to tell her to *shut up* and crawl back through the house with her million reais and save Tomas's life because she's just ruined mine.

But we have so little time, too little to waste on something as useless as anger.

"Run," I say, leaning into him, letting his body fill all the space between us. He smells like wood, like grass, like his mamãe's doll forgotten on the rubble. Like the earth, burning.

"I'm going to die anyway," he says. His tongue flecks my ear. I shudder. "It's the mods. From the very first one they gave me, in the ceremony after I won. No matter what, June, they always make sure we'll die in a year."

My mind feels clear as a pond. I understand him perfectly. "So why come here?"

"For this. For you."

He lifts my chin and I'm forced to see. Our tree has turned into something too beautiful to mark something so ugly. Zanita has made a carnival, a Death Head's skeleton jumbled with feathers and fire. It's the battle that nearly killed Tomas, death and life dancing in the ruins of a city. And Enki? He's made an altar, the kind in the main city shrine. A crude, rough-hewn figure lies beneath a blade.

"You knew they were coming?"

"I heard her. The city. She helps pilot their aircraft."

"We could have gotten away."

"I'm still dying."

"But why should they have you!"

My voice is loud and broken. Auntie Maria asks again for me to step aside and Enki doesn't move.

"It's time to go home, June," he says. "We need to go home."

For some reason, I look back up at the tree. The middle carving is cruder than the other two. I'm not any good, after all. But it's my papai who looks at me from the dead tree. My dead papai who smiles and plays music and *lives*.

He lost the music, and maybe that's why he could never find my art. I've had to find it for myself.

"Summer King," says Auntie Maria, "we should leave now."

Enki kisses my ear. He turns my head until I taste just the corner of his mouth. I am crystal clear, I am a pond, I am a light.

I am nothing at all.

He lets me go. "There's a song," he says. He takes a step back.

"There's always a song," I say.

Auntie Maria hovers right behind him. Two security officers take my arms, but they don't move.

"Forgive me if I dare to confess," he sings, badly. *"I will always love you."*

"Are you sure that's right?" I say, though of course it is.

He smiles. *"Oh, my God, how sad, the uncertainty of love."*

"We're leaving, Enki," Auntie Maria says. Enki doesn't seem to hear her.

"Wait for me," he says. "I'll be dead, but wait for me."

He turns. He walks away. Unthinking, I call out. I try to follow him and the security guards pull me back. One of them lifts my sleeve, the other pricks my arm.

Enki walks away with an Auntie who will kill him in two weeks.

His dreadlocks in the light from their cruisers. The shoes he hates walking through the ruins of his mamãe's house. The clothes that are dirty from the garden. The hands that just touched my own.

Does he look back? I sink to the ground. My head lolls against my shoulder.

Does he look back?

I burn where he last touched me.

I stare at the space where he has been until everything fades.

My papai died in July, which I think he meant as a kindness.

He was unfailingly *kind* in those last months, which always made it worse. Mother and I tried to reason with him at first. We sent him to priests and mães de santo and doctors. We tried to be understanding, but in the end, the only thing we needed to understand was that he was done with life.

"I've lost the music," he said, and so I tried to sing it for him. But we both knew I had never understood music the way he did, and he would merely smile and turn away. He gave away his collection to one of his colleagues at the university. I bought more and tried to play it for him. He gave away his clothes and his books. He registered with medical services to donate his useful parts before cremation. He attended the required therapy sessions, wrote the required explanations, waited out the required holding period. And throughout it all, he never wavered, never once seemed to question his decision.

The kiri board approved his request. Mother had ten days to register a formal family protest — it would have given us a reprieve of another six months in which to reason with Papai before the kiri board could review his case again.

She refused. "João wants to do this. I just have to respect his decision. I can't drag him through another six months."

But I knew what she meant: *She* couldn't bear another six months of watching her husband of forty years patiently, gently, *kindly* longing to die.

"You're killing him!" I remember screaming. I think I yelled worse. That's when it started, of course. Not after, when she introduced me to Auntie Yaha, or at their wedding. Of course not. I stopped loving my mamãe when she decided to let my papai go.

I didn't understand much about letting go, back then. I suppose I didn't know very much about love.

I tried to file the protest myself. The registrar handed me a tissue and waited for me to stop sobbing before she explained that you had to turn thirty before you could petition to delay the kiri of a relative. I said that he was *my father*. She said that it was a shame, but you just couldn't trust wakas to know when it was a grande's time to go.

Gil never said much back then, but he would listen. In a world of grandes who talked, his silence kept me sane. Gil has always been great at understanding. And not just me — my mamãe and my papai too. He understood the whole sorry mess and could see no better way out of it than the rest of us.

Papai's request passed the formal review process. He scheduled a date: July 3, because at least then I wouldn't always associate my papai's death with my name.

I didn't want to associate my papai's death with anything, I said, but Mamãe just stroked my hair and told me to be strong.

He gave me his copies of *The Zahir* and *True Palmarina*, two paper books that he brought with him during his long merchant ship journey around the world. I'd loved to touch them when I was little but I hadn't thought of them for years.

I refused to take them. When he insisted, I tossed them into the bay.

I cried more that day than a week later, when he actually died. He seemed so blank, so sad and uncomprehending. And now, with over three years of his absence behind me, I could punch that girl I was; I would kill her if I could. What right did she have to do that? To squander the last moments with her father? To destroy the piece of himself that he had meant to leave behind?

Papai wore a white shift and no shoes. In the vestibule, he seemed distracted, but happier than I had seen him in months.

He kissed mamãe and whispered something in her ear. She nodded and her eyes stayed dry.

To me, he offered an embrace. I refused him.

"I hope you have a happy life, June," he said. "I believe you'll be great."

That was the last time we saw him alive. They delivered the urn a few hours later.

"He passed peacefully," the intake nurse told us.

We scattered his ashes in the bay, into a frigid wind on a boat where we could watch the sun set behind the city.

Neither of us cried.

They've removed my tree. I laugh when I first realize it, staring at my naked body in the single half mirror. They did a good job, at least. The faint pale marks where the lights used to glow will fade eventually. Then I'll look just like everyone else again. My laughter hurts.

It seems petty — as though they imagine that by removing my signature body art, they could remove the spirit of transformation that has gripped this city.

I don't remember much of how I got here. Just snatches from a long overland trip in a cruiser: a rotting ship, just off a sandbar. A pile of wood, bleached like whalebones. Rivulets of brackish water cutting channels to the ocean.

I try to remember the ocean, because I don't know if I will ever see it again.

I don't know if I will ever see anything but this small room. It's much like the congenial prison where they kept Lucia: bare floors, a single hard bed, a desk without even the most basic fono array, and a bathroom. Unlike Lucia, I don't merit a window. They have given me nothing to write with, nothing to draw with, nothing to communicate with. If not for the meals periodically deposited by security bots, I'd have no sense of the passage of time. A few of my own clothes are in the closet, so at least Mamãe must know what has happened. I wonder if they will let me speak with her. I ask the bots questions when they enter: What day is it? What time is it? Where is Enki? Where is Gil? Where's my mamãe? The bots say nothing, but I know they record my questions. Maybe if I beg enough the Aunties will relent, but it seems a frail hope.

Of all my questions, the first is the most important: *What day is it?* I remember learning that carnival used to be in February, at the end of summer — winter in the northern hemisphere. We kept it that way down here in the south for centuries, but the first Palmarinas decided to change it. I suppose if you're sacrificing a king to the gods in a rite of spring, it doesn't make any sense to do it at the end of summer.

They caught us at the start of September. Two weeks away from the sacrifice and affirmation of the Queen's position. Two weeks away from his death. Enki would ask why it matters, but I can't bear the thought that he might die without my even knowing.

That he might already be dead.

A week or so in sedation, making that steady, painfully slow land journey back to the city. I wonder if Auntie Maria herself planned that particularly cruel bit of torture. And then? Two days in solitude here, praying to any orixás that will listen to spare Enki's life, or at least let me see him one last time.

That leaves two or three days until the ceremony. He'd be in seclusion by now, preparing himself for that final communion, for his most sacred duty. He wanted this. I never understood before, but I do now. Enki might not respect the Aunties, but for some reason he wants to play their game to the end. Our detour to Salvador was just his final chance to say good-bye to his mamãe.

Maybe even to say good-bye to me?

I left his doll on the ground in his mother's house. The one thing he had been so desperate to find, and I dropped it like a worthless toy, like it wasn't the last piece of him I would ever have. I cry thinking of his happiness when he pulled it from the ground. I cry so I don't have to scream.

Eight meals and three sleeps into my confinement, I get my first visitor.

Oreste carries my food tray herself. I let her put it on the desk, though courtesy demands I take it from her. If this petty rudeness annoys her, she doesn't let it show.

"How have you been, June?" she asks.

"What day is it?"

"September fourteenth."

Two more days. My teeth start to chatter. "Can't I at least get a fono?"

Oreste's regretful smile holds just a hint of triumph. "We don't think that would be very wise, June, given the circumstances."

"What the hell could I do with just a fono?"

Oreste gives a delicate, regal shrug. "You've proven yourself very adaptable with technology. And very resistant to the natural sacrifice of this particular summer king. Consider it a compliment."

I stare up at her. She has refused to sit in my presence and I don't trust myself to stand. "You won't even let me watch."

Now the triumph is unmistakable. "You caused us quite a bit of difficulty, June. You actually kidnapped the summer king. The government of the next five years was being called into question. We nearly had a revolution on our hands. Did you really think I'd reward that by letting you witness the sacred ceremony?"

"Is it really the fourteenth?" My voice is barely a whisper. I cough.

"Of course," says the Queen. "When the boy dies, you'll know."

"Tell me, who's his second? Who did he pick?"

Oreste snorts. "Gil, of course. The whole city can't get enough of their epic love story. I could hardly refuse."

I try not to let my relief show. At least he'll have Gil with him at the end. I ache for them both, but at least he won't be alone.

"Could I see Gil? And my mamãe?"

She goes very still for a moment, then turns just her head, like a hawk stalking prey. "Why on earth should I let you?"

I remember the last conversation I had with this formidable, terrifying woman. I remember my shock at the dirtiness of her politics and the scope of her ambitions.

I think of how to play her game.

"You remember the message we left with the city?"

Oreste frowns, which tells me she hasn't found a way to disable our insurance policy. "I recall your note telling me of its existence, yes. But you aren't in much of a position to trigger it, now are you?"

I understand the rigid technological isolation a little better now. It makes me feel stronger. I'm finally a threat. "I can't," I say. "But Enki can."

Her eyes widen almost imperceptibly. She waves her hand in swift negation. "Ridiculous. He's in seclusion more rigorous than yours. He can't access anything but his own brain at this point."

"You don't seem very sure," I say. I think I'm lying, but then I realize it's true. "You don't know what kind of mods he has anymore. You don't know what he can do. Do you want to risk everything? Gil wants to see me, and Gil has access to Enki even you can't cut off."

"And you don't think he'll be afraid of who else we can hurt?"

"Is it fear that makes you vicious?"

"Is it stupidity that makes you so stubborn?"

We stare at each other, blades drawn in our eyes. Her breath is labored. Finally she lets out a shaky laugh. "Easier to let them come. Take care, June. Perhaps you haven't noticed, but you're still very much in my power."

She sweeps out of the room. I wait for the door to shut before I curl on the bed and cry.

Gil comes the next day; he brings Bebel.

"She begged me," he says after we've hugged for at least five minutes. I had thought he might hate me — I cry a little with relief when I realize that he doesn't.

"I'm so sorry," I say. "I should have told you."

"Do you know what I felt when I found out what you'd done? Joy. I asked you to save him, and you did."

"But I failed, Gil."

He shakes his head and pushes me back so I can look at his face. "At least you tried."

Bebel sits quietly beside the door, tactfully averting her gaze. I can't imagine why she came, but it's strangely good to see her.

"Still in the lead for the Queen's Award?" I ask.

She smiles, but only for a moment. "So they say. I'm going to do something."

Gil and I exchange a glance. "Do something? Like try to win it?"

"No. Maybe. Do something you would do. Like —"

I take a step toward her and shake my head softly. She stops. I can't be so obvious as to look around the room, but the Aunties are almost certainly listening in. Bebel can be so trusting.

"Like sing," she says after a moment.

"Well, that's a good idea."

"Would . . . would you like to hear it? The song I'm going to try?"

I nod. She clears her throat, stands up. Like anyone growing up in Palmares Três — like anyone growing up in old-Brazil, probably — I've heard "Manhã de Carnaval" at least ten thousand times. Those classic notes might as well be the beeping of transport pod doors for all the attention I pay to them. But Bebel sings them like a knife to the gut, like a knockout punch before you've even registered the blow. Am I crying? Gil is too. That lingering saudade, that swelling of bittersweet, how had I never noticed before? How had I never felt that sadness at the start of carnival, especially in those years when it's ushered in with blood?

It might be our municipal anthem, but in Bebel's voice, it sounds faintly blasphemous.

And then I start to understand what she might be planning.

"Jesus," I say very loudly. "I'm so sick of that song."

Bebel opens her mouth in protest — she always knows when she's been good — but then closes it. "Yeah," she says after a moment. "I thought it might be boring. Anyway, thanks for letting me try it out on you. It's not the same without you in school, June. Good luck with everything."

She lets herself out. Gil and I share a small smile. I think, *If Bebel can contemplate rebellion, anything can happen.*

"How is he?" I ask.

Gil shrugs. "Quiet. Last night, we danced for five or six hours. I've never felt anything like it before. I swear, June, he was burning up."

"He wants to do it," I say.

"I know."

This doesn't seem to comfort him any more than it does me.

"He told me to give this to you." I hope for a letter, some piece of art. Instead Gil pulls out a white cloth.

No, I see, when he unfolds it: a simple shift.

"He wants me to take vows?" I ask, though this is even simpler than the white outfits used by initiates in the orthodox Candomblé terreiros.

"How would I know?" He sounds bitter, which frightens me more than almost anything in the last two weeks. Gil has always understood.

"I'm sorry," I say.

"Not your fault."

He gives me one last hug and stands up. "I should go."

And now it's my turn to understand. Enki will be dead in less than twenty-four hours. I should let them have their last day together.

"Gil, do you ever wish we didn't go to that party? That we didn't dance above the city?"

"Sometimes," he says.

When he leaves, I realize that I never have.

My fourth visitor comes late that night — at least, I'm almost sure, because it's hours after the security bot brought me dinner and I'm yawning with exhaustion I won't let myself feel. She knocks on the door politely, and I tell her to come in.

When I see my mamãe, I nearly fall off the bed. I have spent three years entombed in resentment, but now I can't believe how much I've missed her.

"I asked to see you as soon as they brought you in," she says. "Yaha has tried for days, but no one listened."

"I threatened Oreste," I say. I almost want to stick out my tongue, in case she's watching.

Mamãe just stares at me and then decides, very prudently, to leave well enough alone.

"We're trying to get you out of here," she says. "At least to get you a trial or a charge for something."

I look around the stark room and then back at my mother. She seems older than I remember, with gray in her hair and lines around her eyes that she hasn't bothered to treat. She looks like she's been up for days.

"I'm guilty of a hundred crimes, Mamãe. I kidnapped the summer king. I don't think the Queen will be letting me out anytime soon."

"Yaha mentioned a possibility."

"What?"

"Would you recant? Maybe work publicly for the government? She thinks she could convince them to cut a deal. You've become a bit of an icon since you left."

I consider this, taking into account my mother's penchant for under-statement. It occurs to me, for the first time, that my own notoriety might have gone far past stencils of me and Enki as technophiles.

"Oreste said there was almost a revolution?"

Mamãe laughs. "I don't think it went that far, though the Aunties certainly reacted to it that way. I don't know, June. It's been very unsettled lately. Yaha thinks that if you help smooth things over, you might be able to get out."

"And if I don't?"

The question hangs in the air between us. I might never see the sun again. I might never see the verde or the light on the bay or any-thing except this one bed in a technologically dead room.

"I'll think about it, Mamãe," I say, just to make her feel better.

She smiles. "Oh, June, I'm so glad. Auntie Yaha will talk to you soon. After . . ."

"After."

When she's almost at the door, I call her back. "Mamãe," I say. "Three years ago, when we all said good-bye to Papai, he whispered something in your ear. I've always wondered what."

Her eyes go wide with shock. Her throat quivers, but she gets the words out. "He asked me to believe in you, June. He said your art was the most important thing in the world to you, and I should trust it. But I didn't, did I?"

"Papai said that?" My skin burns with the ghost of lights. "Papai never liked my art."

"Oh, June. He loved you. And music isn't the only kind of art. He understood that, eventually. Didn't he say you'd be great?"

He did. But I'd never allowed myself to believe that's what he meant. He left us alone, and so I had failed.

But I was always going to fail. No art could have saved him. Just like Enki.

"Thank you, Mamãe."

I meet her eyes from across the room, her straight-ahead April eyes. She nods. "I'll see you soon."

"What time is it?" I ask.

"About midnight."

Seven in the morning. That's when our summer kings die.

Ten years ago, my papai woke me at dawn to watch Fidel choose Serafina. Now, I can only count the hours in circuits around the room, in marks scraped into the walls with my fingernails. They've turned bloody and cracked, but I don't care.

At what I think might be six thirty, I bang on the door. "Please, someone, just let me watch. I'll do anything, please!"

Not even a security bot. Not even an Auntie come to gloat.

A half hour later, I fall to my knees. I clasp my hands. It feels like prayer, but I can't bear to pray.

"At least Gil is with him," I say, just to ease the tension in my head. I wonder if it's happened yet. Shouldn't I feel something? Some jolt through my body, some recoil of the severed connection? When we carved that tree in Salvador I felt as though he were part of my body. Now I don't even know if he's still breathing.

I remember what else he said in Salvador: *I'll be dead, but wait for me.*

"What the hell did you mean, Enki?" I ask, but he can't answer.

The white shift Gil brought me lies on the bed. When I look at it now, I feel a resonance, a memory of the Enki of a year ago, dancing barefoot before the Queen in slave clothes. I strip my pants and shirt in a second and unfold the simple dress. It's heavier than I expected. My hands linger on a strange, stiff fabric that's been sewn around the middle. Shiny and thick, it reflects the light, refracting a rainbow if I bend it. I feel a tickle of familiarity, but desperation and terror have emptied my thoughts. I lift the shift over my head and everything else slips away. After a moment, I remove my shoes.

Naked but for a scratchy, barely tailored sack of cloth, I feel armored. Like whatever the Aunties might try can't get past the simplicity of this gesture.

Love is its own power, Enki says, a voice close in my ear.

I close my eyes. Is he trying to speak to me? Is he dead?

Of course I am, bem-querer. Haven't I already told you?

I knuckle my eyes, but tears escape them anyway.

He's dead.

I know it like I knew my tree, like I knew his lips, like I knew my papai. It is minutes past seven, and his soul has greeted the dawn.

My door opens.

I freeze, but no one comes through. "Hello?" I say.

There's no one in the hall. The door opened on its own. I step outside. I think to get my shoes but something makes me stop. Maybe it's the voice I hear, getting stronger as I walk down the hall. Every door is closed but one abutting a staircase. I go up.

"Manhã tão bonita manhã," sings a voice like a knife-edge.

I thought I would cry. I thought I would break down and give up, but instead that strength bunches inside me. It vibrates. My bare feet slap the metal stairs as Bebel's voice gets louder. I have never been more alone in my life, and I have never been less afraid. The stairs go up and up until I reach another open door, and a rooftop. The building overlooks a smaller plaza on Tier Two that I've seen maybe a handful of times in my life. It's filled with thousands of people, all so unnaturally quiet that I can hear my feet crunching on bird droppings. *He is dead,* say my feet. *Your lover is dead,* says the strength inside me. I look down. The people stare at me.

No, they stare at a holo on the roof. I have walked inside it like a ghost. The wood of the altar steps goes through my feet. Flies buzz in my ears — but no, those are camera bots.

Oreste stands beside the altar. She is glowing with sweat; her face is savage and confused. There is blood on her dress and a knife on the floor and Enki, so close I could touch his insubstantial projection — Enki is dead.

He is twisting away from her, as far as the ropes will allow. He has died with his outstretched hand covered in his own blood. He reaches toward me. Toward where the path to the roof has led.

From where I stand, it looks as though he is touching me.

Something vibrates on my stomach. The strange cloth heats and hums with its own energy. I look down. For a second, for a flash, I think I see words there, upside down so I can read them. *I love you.* But they disappear before I can focus and I look up, half blinded by words half seen.

Oreste stares at me. At *me*, though I'm on a prison roof on Tier Two and she's in the sacred shrine on Tier Ten. I recall the buzzing of camera bots above: My image must be projecting into the shrine.

"You!" she says.

A whisper has started in the crowd below. I don't understand it at first, but then I do: "In blood." An echo of the words from the sacrificial ceremony: *You will mark your choice of the woman to be Queen, in gesture or blood.*

"You're not a legitimate choice," Oreste says.

It occurs to me to look down. If the words were there, they have vanished forever. In their place, a mark more indelible — a bloody handprint across my belly. In a decade, no one has forgotten how Fidel marked Serafina. No one can mistake this for anything else.

I finally recognize the cloth. It's old tech, more than a century, nothing the Aunties would have worried about. But Gil's mamãe sometimes uses it in her designs because of its uniquely changeable surface. It's not really cloth, but a kind of array. A flexible, programmable screen.

It shows the red bright enough, fresh enough that I feel as if he has punched me. I imagine I can smell his blood.

Like Oreste can.

How did it feel to cut his throat? I want to ask. *To watch him die on the altar once he'd made you Queen?*

But did he?

"In blood!" the whisper grows bolder now.

"He picked me," I say.

"This violates a dozen rules. The courts won't support it. You should give up while you can."

"He picked me."

My voice is pure, flat, and uninflected. But perhaps people other than Oreste can hear me, because the crowd below has gotten boisterous.

"Our summer king picked June," they shout.

I stand there, barefoot and alone above a sea of people. Oreste glares at me. I turn from her and the body of my beloved. I walk away.

"I'll fight this, June!" Oreste shouts behind me.

"You've already lost," I say, not turning around. "Don't you know it?"

"I will —"

"No," I say, sharp enough to cut her off. "His blood sanctifies his choice, Oreste."

The crowd roars.

I don't want to be Queen any more than she wants me to, but Enki is dead, and Enki has chosen.

You know this doesn't end, right? You'll die one day — kiri like your father, or claw your way into your third century by the skin of your reconstructed teeth, your story won't last forever. But for now, it's yours, a lot longer than mine, and if you think I could use my life as a canvas?

The summer king has nothing on the Queen.

Don't ever forget the art.

Take care of Gil. He won't believe I'm dead, but I know you will.

* * *

They've given me an apartment reserved for special dignitaries on Tier Ten. Oreste has reluctantly agreed to abdicate her throne based on Enki's surprise selection. She didn't have much choice, in the end.

It turns out the city takes the institution of its divine summer king far more seriously than its own Queen does. It might be the first time in a century that a Queen has lost her position in a moon year, but the king's word is his death, and both are final.

I haven't managed to watch the footage of Enki's final ceremony. I think about other things: the light show and our plunge from the rock, the wild parties and the way he would dance with Gil. I remember his happiness to finally find his mother's house in Salvador.

The doll I never thought I'd see again arrived yesterday in an anonymous package. The letter said: "Tomas comes back home tomorrow. I think you left this behind. I'm not sorry."

No, I thought, *I never imagined you would be*. I got Lucia to dig out the memory chip. The files haven't degraded — miraculously, given their long burial. Sintia had flagged an audio file of first Queen Odete on her deathbed. When I heard it, I understood why.

"I promised Alonso we would only use the sacrifice for the next two cycles," she says, her voice brittle with age though she was only a hundred years old. "It was his idea because they all hated him for those leaks about his work with the CIA. He was dying anyway, he said, use the sacrifice to build their confidence. But I promised him it wouldn't be for long, and now it's been, oh, fifty years? I backed down, Sara . . ."

First Queen Odete didn't mean for the summer king ritual to be permanent, and the mother of our last summer king kept this information buried in a doll in her garden. No wonder they let her inside. I wonder if Enki had some idea of what was in those files — perhaps he wanted me to have them as much as he wanted to see his mother's garden.

I've released public copies of all the files into the main library. We'll see how people react.

Some people are calling me the waka Queen, but it seems like a contradiction in terms. I might only be eighteen, but I feel like a grande. When I stand in front of my window and look out at the bay, my responsibility for this city sits like a weight on my chest. I remember telling Enki that I would never want to be Queen.

Knowing Enki, that's probably where he got the idea.

Gil hasn't left his garden since the ceremony. I've visited a few times, but he can hardly bear to speak. I just sit and try to be there for him the same way he's always been there for me. Even if he can't speak, I can still listen.

I think of Enki as an earthquake who left us with his wreckage. But then, who's foolish enough to fall in love with an earthquake?

I walk back to my window and press my face against the glass. The bay at night never fails to calm me. It makes me remember love, and that's not something I can bring myself to regret.

"June," says the city, over my emergency speakers. I jump and then close my eyes. Not another crisis, not so soon.

"Yes?"

"I'm supposed to deliver a message."

I stare at my reflection in the glass: tattered pants, a bloco shirt Gil and I scored from the verde almost six years ago, bare feet. Waka clothes, but grande eyes.

"What is it, City?"

"He says, *Sorry about the Queen business. I hope you'll get used to it.*"

It's his voice. "What —"

"*I'm dead, June,*" says his voice.

"You think I don't know that?"

"*But the city kept pieces of me.*"

My head snaps up. I look around, half convinced he's going to step out of the shadows of my room, crawl over the balcony in his hunting outfit, and laugh at me.

But I'm alone.

"I'll be dead, but wait for me," I whisper. Finally, I'm beginning to understand.

"*Bem-querer,*" says the ghost of my beloved, "*I'll tell you a story.*"

And that's the third time the lights go out in Palmares Três.

AUTHOR'S NOTE

Palmares Três is a dream city, a future vision rooted in the Brazil of today, but fermented in my imagination. The bay of Palmares Três does not (currently) exist on the coast of south Bahia. Its particular Afro-Brazilian culture with hints of Japan, North America, and West Africa reflects the multicultural mix of modern Brazil through an authorial looking glass. The syncretism of Catholicism and Candomblé is very much alive today, but these traditions have changed in unexpected and unlikely ways in my imagined future.

Any errors of interpretation or extrapolation are my own.

ACKNOWLEDGMENTS

This book owes a debt to the coffee shops of Vancouver, where I completed the first chunk, and to a certain magical apartment on Second Avenue, loaned to me during a difficult time, where I finished the rest. For the good knives and the state-of-the-art stove, you know who you are, and you are awesome.

The work of turning my undigested hunk of prose into a readable novel is based on the advice of a number of generous, talented, and wise people. I would like to thank the attendees of Sycamore Hill 2010 for taking on this novel as a partial. My fellow members of Altered Fluid (in particular David Rivera, Kristine Dikeman, Eugene Myers, Tom Crosshill, Paul Berger, and Devin Poore) took this book apart in the best way possible; you guys are some of my favorite people in the world.

Justine Larbalestier and Tamar Bihari deserve huge thanks for reading a draft so rough I could hardly get through it and seeing the value of this project. I could never have gotten here without your advice and support.

Jill Grinberg understood and believed in this book from the moment she read it; I couldn't have dreamed of a better advocate, or a better team than everyone at Grinberg Literary. Arthur Levine and Emily Clement devoted incredible time and energy and insight to June's story, teasing out facets even I didn't see. You guys make me look smarter than I am.

My family, as always, is a huge source of influence and support. My sister Lauren inspired me with tales of her travels in Brazil, my cousin Alexis encouraged me to develop the first kernel of the idea that became *The Summer Prince*, and my father's love of bossa nova sparked my own passion for the music of Brazil.

Cristina Lasaitis, Fábio Fernandes, and Christopher Kastensmidt went above and beyond to help me with my Portuguese and to answer cultural questions. The generosity of my fellow writers never ceases to amaze me.

Finally, Eddie Schneider has talked me down from so many ledges he might as well have a helicopter. Thanks for listening, for keeping me sane, and for being such a marvelous human being. You make me happy every day.

Muito obrigada, my friends. You're all invited to the party.